Monet & Oscar

The Essence of Light

Joe Byrd

Giverny Books

ISBN: 979-8-9914969-0-2

Contents

To my wife, Linda, who spent
thirty years on this journey with me.

Chapter 1 – Monet Meets Oscar

Oscar Bonhomme's palms sweated as he crept from the warm kitchen filled with the spice-laden aroma of frying sausage mixed with the smell of aromatic, dark coffee into Monet's yellow dining room.

He'd used what little money he had to purchase new work clothes for his first day on the job. He twisted his still-stiff brown woolen cap between his sweating fingers as he glanced at his reflection in the picture glass to see if his pale skin betrayed his stay in the military hospital. Did his slight frame and frail stature look well enough for rigorous gardening work? No one would believe he was once tanned, muscular, and robust. Did his prematurely graying hair and the red circles around his eyes reveal the trials he had endured at the front? Although thirty-four, he felt and looked much older.

Oscar summoned his courage, pulled from somewhere deep inside himself as he did when climbing out of the trenches and facing the enemy. "*Bonjour, Monsieur* Monet."

No movement. The newspaper Monet held did not lower. The first salvo had fallen short.

He fired off another. "*Bonjour, Monsieur* Monet."

Still no response. Second salvo, off-target.

Perhaps Monet was hard of hearing. Oscar added more powder and fired the third shot as he shouted, "*Bonjour, Monsieur* Monet."

The paper lowered to reveal piercing black eyes and a long white beard stained yellow with nicotine. Monet resembled the newspaper photos Oscar had seen of him—short, stocky, and with an intense gaze that seemed to miss nothing around him. His hands, with translucent skin and heavily veined, looked muscular and tanned, befitting a painter who mainly worked outdoors.

Monet stared at Oscar as if trying to remember who was this invader of his dining room and disturber of his early morning coffee. He wore an English herringbone wool suit buttoned at the neck, with just an inch of white ruffled shirt cuffs showing at the sleeves.

At last, he spoke. "Who are you?"

He sounded irritated.

Oscar drew in his breath and squared his shoulders to make himself look the part before responding with, "I'm your new gardener, *Monsieur*."

Monet frowned. "I don't remember you. Who hired you? Why should I hire a gardener in the middle of the winter?"

Oscar stammered as he gathered enough breath to reply. "You... You did, *Monsieur*. Yesterday. At least, that's what I was told."

He gripped his newspaper tighter, shook his head, and frowned. "So, what are you doing in here? This isn't the garden."

"*Madame* Blanche asked me to meet you here before dawn to carry your paintings for you."

"Humph!"

And with that, Monet raised the paper again. Oscar remained standing in the doorway, unsure whether to stay or go.

Oscar stood twisting and untwisting his cap and wondering if Monet would dismiss him, fall asleep, or begin their first day together. Could this cranky old man be his father? Probably not. But he might know who is.

Since it was his first day on this new job, he remained to see what would happen next.

He looked around the room after one, two, three, four, five minutes with no response. Yellow was the theme color. Even the chairs and light fixtures were Provence yellow, as his mother called it. Monet seemed obsessed with the color yellow and eating, by the looks of the dining room with its multiple sets of dishes and an abundance of silverware.

The odd prints that hung on the walls perplexed him. They were most unusual and not yellow. He saw dozens of them depicting an assortment of Japanese people in native costumes through scenes of Japan. They reminded him of photos his Japanese friends in San Francisco had shown him. The prints featured plants and animals that he didn't recognize.

Oscar scratched his head and thought, why would one of the world's most famous Impressionist painters have these Japanese prints on his walls instead of his art or that of his colleagues?

Lying in the hospital, he had dreamed of what he would do when he was released. He never imagined he would work in one of the most famous gardens in France. This job was the start of his new life; he was excited and frightened to be here.

Curiosity was getting the better of him as he walked around the long table, examining the prints. Each one seemed more colorful and stranger than the one before, and someone had labeled every one with the artist's name. He made a note to ask *Monsieur* Monet about the prints. They must have been significant to him if they were hanging in his dining room. Undoubtedly, he would have dictated the decoration of this space, the essential room for entertaining.

Finally, Monet's hand emerged to crush out his cigarette in his overflowing ashtray. He lowered his paper, rose from his chair, and shuffled to the door.

"Are you coming?" he threw over his shoulder.

Caught off-guard while still staring at the prints, Oscar felt he was a puppy following its master and hurried through the door after him, down the steps, across the garden, past the cart, and into the massive darkened studio.

"Put these in the cart and follow me."

The paintings looked to be in various completion stages, and Oscar assembled them back-to-back so as not to smudge the fresh paint. Later, he'd need to add wooden partitions between them to keep them safe. Equal measures of fright and honor washed over him as he quickly managed this chore and set off behind Monet in the pre-dawn.

Once outside, his inquiry about where they were going received no response—Monet lived up to his storied reputation as a reluctant speaker. Oscar acknowledged his role was to obey commands and keep silent.

After some minutes struggling with the loaded cart down the garden pathway, up a hill, across the railroad tracks that divided the two pieces of Monet's property, down an embankment, and across a bridge, he stopped beside Monet at the edge of the water lily pond. Oscar was sweating and exhausted.

Monet chose the first canvas of the day. It proved to be large and awkward to place on the easel that Oscar set up under the umbrella used to shield Monet from the sun or rain. He settled on his stool and prepared his palette with paints, squeezing first one tube, then another. Monet allowed no distractions. Speaking was a distraction.

Oscar's lungs burned from the exertion, his breath short and choppy. His arms and legs hadn't worked so hard since he'd left the front. It would take a lot of gardening to get his body back into the shape it was in when he worked for his mom at Golden Gate Park.

He stepped back to take in the scene Monet was painting. The pond covered several acres, encompassed by trees, flowers, and shrubs. They'd crossed over a Japanese-style bridge covered with bare wisteria branches. It was still winter, and the famed water lilies were waiting for the season when they would again cover the water's pea-green surface.

But that was not what Monet was painting. Instead, he captured the fractured light on the water's surface and the rays filtering into the depths beneath them. No ground, no sky—just the water and the willows interwoven in patterns of colors and shapes. He looked to be painting the essence of the light that moved on the surface of the pond.

It was not the typical garden scene Oscar had studied in landscape design classes at college. The lily pond represented a living canvas upon which the sun painted a constantly developing picture, just, he supposed, as Monet had designed it. His Japanese gardener friends would say it felt reminiscent of a Japanese garden, but this one held far more prolific planting. Monet had covered every inch with stocks and petals of exotic and familiar domestic plants.

As the sun changed positions, so did the subtleties of light on the water. When the light changed, so did the colors. And so did Monet, who switched to another painting location.

"Let's move down the path. Follow me."

"*Oui, Monsieur.*" Caught up in the scene, he had nearly missed Monet's command to move on. "I'll pack up and be right there."

He carefully removed the canvas from the easel so as not to smudge the wet paint, placed it back in the cart, and secured it for the brief journey around the pond with the easel, stool, and umbrella. Once he'd arrived at the new spot, he repeated the set-up routine, and Monet was once again ready to continue with a different canvas.

This time, Oscar watched the creation process more closely, so he didn't miss the time to change locations. He observed every detail of the painting to understand how light affected the scene Monet was painting.

He set ten canvases up in ten different locations over the morning. After several tedious hours, it was time to pack up for the journey back to the studio. The light at noon proved too harsh for the effects Monet desired. After unpacking the cart, the time came for him to begin the job he believed Monet had hired him to do.

Monet led him into the *Grande Allée* of trellises, down to the bottom of the garden. The trellises supported pink roses intertwined in their metal arches. He explained how he wanted the rose canes trimmed. Oscar shook his head in annoyance, if not disbelief—as if he hadn't done such a menial task before. Then he realized Monet had no idea what his new gardener knew or didn't know. He was used to working for a perfectionist, his mother, after all. Monet couldn't be any more exacting than she was.

Clearing the trellises of dead rose blossoms, diseased leaves, and dead canes took all afternoon, and he did not finish. Usually, he didn't trim climbing rose canes, but Monet knew best how he wanted things done. Oscar was ready to head back to the room he'd booked in a local boarding house. His arrangement with Madame Blanche, Monet's daughter-in-law, was he would work ten to twelve hours a day but have evenings and weekends free to do as he pleased. This would give him time to research the Impressionist painters his mother had met in the south of France. According to her, one of them was his father. That's the most she would tell him.

But first, he took some lathing and rigged a frame that would hold ten paintings so they wouldn't touch when he next hauled them over the hill to the lily pond. He hoped his boss would appreciate his ingenuity.

Oscar was exhausted from the hours of work as he passed by the large studio door. He heard a voice calling to him from inside.

"Hey, boy. Come here."

Oscar was exhausted and ready to go back to his room but he felt trapped. What did Monet want now? The man had barely spoken to him all day. Had he done something wrong? He reluctantly followed the sound of Monet's voice into his cavernous studio as his hands began to sweat again.

The view inside the newly built studio was stunning. Two-story windows flooded the space with soft northern light. The size of the 6'x14' canvases mounted on rollers before the artist dwarfed the 4'x3' paintings Oscar had carted around all day. Being in the master's presence was like reporting to the principal or his company's commander.

"The paintings I did today were studies for these." Monet stretched out his arms to encompass the most enormous paintings Oscar had ever seen. "Come sit on the couch, so I can get to know you."

Monsieur Monet, who'd barely spoken a dozen words to him all day, now wanted to get to know him. He shook his head, hoping this wouldn't become a habit—just another chapter in a strange, scary day. With luck, he might learn something about his employer. Perhaps his father was someone Monet knew.

"Boy, tell me your full name and where you're from," Monet said as he handed Oscar what he explained was a glass of *Calvados*, the local apple brandy.

Oscar, embarrassed by his appearance, brushed the dirt from his hands on his pants, accepted the glass, and took a sip before answering. The color was deep amber, the taste a cross between rotten apples and kerosene. He could barely speak as the liquid fire burned a path down his throat. "My... my name is Oscar Bonhomme. I was born in Antibes and raised in California. My mother's family is from Lyon."

Monet paused, raised his eyelids, and then glanced at him sideways as he asked about his father.

"Not a part of my life. He left my mother before I was born," was all Oscar could bring himself to utter.

Monet lit a cigarette and watched the smoke curl up toward the disappearing ceiling before commenting. "Oscar is a good name. It's my first name. I used it growing up before switching to my middle name, Claude, when I began painting. Tell me about your life growing up in California."

Oscar couldn't believe that the most famous painter in the world, Monet, who hadn't so much as acknowledged his existence all day, wanted to know about his life. The incredulity made him blink a few times.

"There's not much to tell. My mother raised me on her own with help from her friends since we had no family around. She was a landscape designer and gardener for some mansions in and around San Francisco. I followed her into that field. We worked together with Japanese gardeners creating the Golden Gate Park. I learned more from them than from many of my college professors."

"I don't like Americans," Monet responded dismissively.

Oscar smiled. "I can't say I blame you, *Monsieur*. Americans can be pushy." Monet responded with another sideways glance and took a long sip of his *Calvados*.

The artist then launched into a brief history of his garden and lily pond, how he had bought the house in 1886 and added the land for the lily pond in 1890. He had designed the garden as his canvas, featuring colors and designs that would blend well in his paintings. He selected colors to match his palette and enjoyed mixing white flowers with colored ones to achieve a shimmer in the scenes as he painted.

As someone who loved beautiful gardens, Oscar was deeply touched by Monet's description. He saw how much his garden meant to him.

"I've heard so much about your garden. That made it intriguing and first inspired me to experience it for myself," he explained. "I want to learn how to adapt such an approach for my future clients." He felt privileged to be able to work in the master's living canvas.

Monet stared at him with a frown darkening his face. "So, you wish to copy my garden designs so you can use them in California, do you?"

Oscar gulped. He'd overstepped his bounds. "Not right away. I have a lot to learn before I can even consider that. Would you mind telling me how you got started in painting?"

He hoped he'd handled that challenge well enough.

"Not now. Maybe later."

With that, Monet drained his glass, crushed out his cigarette, and slowly rose from the couch, giving Oscar his cue to leave.

Oscar was being dismissed, and he tried to end the conversation on a friendly note. "I'd like to return and study the paintings in your dining room sometime."

"They're not paintings. They're Japanese woodblock prints. Perhaps."

It seemed that would be the only commitment his employer would make. But Oscar didn't mind—he would accept it for the time being. It was not a good ending for his first day at his new job. He knew that, somehow, the Japanese prints had a role to play in his quest. It was too early for him to tell what that role would be.

On the way back to his room with its bed, one chair, and a dresser, he wondered if Monet would ever speak about his family and his struggles to become a successful painter. He felt compelled to learn more about Monet's life and career since he was the painter his mother admired the most.

Oscar lay down on his bed, exhausted from the first hard day's work he had done since entering the hospital months ago. Compared to Monet, he was having difficulty catching his breath as he pushed the cart of paintings up the hill and over the tracks to the lily pond. Monet seemed in great shape for a man of around eighty years old. He had survived the first workday despite offending his boss. He fell asleep as soon as his head hit his pillow.

Mom, I can't believe I'm here working for one of the greatest artists and gardeners in the world. If only you could see me now. All those times you talked about returning to France and showing me the grand gardens.

They had been planning the trip together before the war began. Oscar traveled to France to fight for their home country and was wounded in battle. His mother died alone before he could return to her.

I miss you so much...

Chapter 2 – Bing's Maison l'Art Nouveau

To say it was a relief to be on the train to Paris after a trying week with Monet would be an understatement. Each day had been the same. The only exception had been the drink, which had only occurred once on the first day. Oscar looked forward to more opportunities to speak with Monet about his life and art and, most importantly, his Impressionist friends. Monet limited their conversations to giving directions on doing the gardening work that followed the painting sessions. The exception had been the brief conversation they'd had the previous night.

"Oscar, Blanche tells me you're going to Paris to learn about Japanese woodblock prints. You must pay attention to the effect of this art on Impressionism," Monet instructed him. "It was the unifying factor for our group. We were just a bunch of young artists rebelling against the Salon establishment when we discovered these prints. They changed our artistic outlook and unified us around a common style."

That was it. Monet gave no further explanation. Oscar grew irritated with this kind of treatment, Monet lecturing him like a professor from his college days. But then, the old man sent him off to learn about Japanese woodblock prints. It was exactly what he had in mind to do. Perhaps this would lead to his understanding of the relationship between painting and landscape design or the role gardens played as the subject of his artwork in Monet's case. He hoped it would give him a way to get closer to Monet through a shared interest. What made him think that Monet was interested in him? Perhaps this was just wishful thinking as he continued his search for the father he never knew.

He thought back to when he'd interviewed for the job. He'd told Monet he would be his gardener as part of his research on landscape design for his work in California. He hadn't mentioned his other, more personal research project. Because of the massive number of French men killed in the Great War, laborers were in short supply, and Monet had taken a chance on a wounded American soldier. He'd said he'd hired him at the suggestion of his friend. Monet called the friend Tiger. This man had befriended Oscar in the military hospital. He didn't care how he got the job so long as it allowed him to stay in France and become acquainted with the Impressionist artists.

Oscar arrived in Paris at the Gare Saint-Lazare train station. Monet claimed in a newspaper article that he'd bribed officials to stop all train traffic one morning to enable him to paint the station without disturbance. Monet painted the billowing smoke, the clouds of steam, and the shadowy figures on the platform that Oscar saw while departing the train. The station felt appropriate for his arrival in Paris since he was on a mission from Monet. Oscar asked the porter for directions to 22, Rue de Provence.

Bing's Maison Art Nouveau shop was a fifteen-minute walk from the station. The gallery he stood staring at seemed more of a cathedral than a shop, with its massive front windows and broad entrance. The identical Japanese prints he'd seen in Monet's dining room hung on the walls.

He had worn his used French Army uniform for the train ride to Paris and felt underdressed when entering such a grand establishment. He stammered when addressing the distinguished man standing beside the carved Asian desk just inside the door. The gentleman, dressed in a black suit, white shirt, and gray tie, had a thin, well-trimmed mustache, and he looked Oscar up and down with disdain, sneered as he stood with his cap in his hands.

"M-My name is Oscar Bonhomme, and I have come at the request of *Monsieur* Claude Monet."

The gentleman raised his eyebrows upon hearing that name and then scrutinized him more.

"*Oui, Monsieur* Monet, one of our favorite clients. Does he wish to purchase more of the Japanese prints?" The man had become much more deferential when he heard Monet's name.

"*Non, Monsieur* Monet sent me to learn more about the Japanese prints and how they came to be important to the Impressionist painters," Oscar said.

"Is that so?" he said with a smirk. Oscar was not of the class of clientele who frequented his establishment. "Let me introduce you to my manager, Madame Kuroki, who enjoys educating clients on Japanese art and culture. She helps our clients become more knowledgeable collectors. Please follow me."

The gentleman hurried through the store to the back office as Oscar looked left and right, trying to take in all the lovely Japanese prints, and tripped over a display cabinet of samurai swords. The many types of Japanese porcelain he saw fascinated him. He had visited the homes of Japanese friends in San Francisco but had seen nothing this elegant.

"Atsuko-san. This is *Monsieur* Claude Monet's associate, Oscar Bonhomme."

Madame Kuroki bowed deeply and inquired politely, "How is *Monsieur* Monet in these troubling times?"

Oscar returned her bow as he had learned from his Japanese friends. "He's doing well. *Merci* for asking. He sent me here to learn about the woodblock prints. I asked about them when I visited his dining room. He said if I wanted to know about them, I should learn from you. They seem so important to him, and I wonder why. Can you help me understand?"

"With pleasure, but first, would you like to have some tea?"

"I'd be honored to join you in the tea ceremony," he said as he had learned of the ritual of tea ceremony in San Francisco's Japantown.

Atsuko Kuroki, a lovely, petite, dark-haired middle-aged woman wearing a traditional silk kimono embroidered with a floral design, led him into her office, which looked like a Japanese tea room, not a typical office. The furnishings included a small lacquered table, cushions for Westerners who weren't used to kneeling for a long time, and tatami mats covering the floors instead of rugs.

She invited him to sit on the cushions and began the tea ceremony. She selected two drinking bowls from her collection with simple, measured movements and put a water kettle on the charcoal brazier. Oscar watched her scoop green tea powder from an ornate container and place one measure into each bowl. Next, she used a bamboo whisk to froth the tea powder as she poured the hot water.

She picked up one bowl and turned it around in her pale, delicate hands, seeming to admire its unique glaze and color. When she'd finished, she handed Oscar the bowl. He followed her lead, admired his bowl, and waited to drink the tea until she did.

This entire process took many minutes as he waited to learn more about the prints, not realizing at first that the tea ceremony was part of the story Atsuko wished to tell him. He looked around the room and noticed nothing on the walls—just a simple altar with a flower arrangement and a scroll behind it.

As they drank, Atsuko asked Oscar about himself.

"Where are you from, *Monsieur* Bonhomme?"

"San Francisco, California."

"Wonderful. I've never been there, but I have family there. They say it's beautiful.

"I hope you enjoyed this simple tea ceremony. I find it helps to set the mood and sharpen your focus on what I'm about to discuss. Japanese culture is different from Western customs in so many ways. Let me now discuss a brief history of our woodblock prints and what makes them important to *Monsieur* Monet and his fellow artists."

Atsuko spent the next hour detailing the history of woodblock prints and how they changed since they were first introduced to Japan from China in the sixteenth century. They developed from simple one- and two-color religious posters to multi-colored representations of famous actors of the Kabuki theater and explicit views of the prostitutes of the "floating world." Some included national landscape treasures' views and were designed to be keepsakes that ordinary citizens could afford and enjoy hanging in their homes.

She shifted her position on her knees and began her discussion of the prints Monet collected. "I suspect that, since *Monsieur* Monet sent you, the landscape prints are of most interest to you."

"It is all fascinating to me," Oscar replied. "The subject matter of lovemaking confuses me. I understand our two cultures are very different on that issue." He could feel his face turn red, realizing he had stepped over the line of propriety. "I don't mean that making love confuses me." He paused, realizing that he was confusing Atsuko. "What I mean to say is why are the artists painting the subject?"

Atsuko placed her hand over her mouth to hide her laughter. "Our cultures are not so much different as you might think. Lovemaking is as much an art as any other. Many of the woodblock prints in the 'pillow books' are meant to be instruction manuals.

"Now, I want to tell you about one artist, Utagawa Hiroshige, who has created over eight thousand prints, some of which *Monsieur* Monet has collected. His life parallels *Monsieur* Monet's in ways that will help you understand more about this art form and why it's important to him."

Oscar spent the next few hours listening as Atsuko explained how Hiroshige's career intertwined with Monet's career. They spent much of their earlier careers painting famous scenes like Mt. Fuji for Hiroshige and the Rouen Cathedral for Monet. Much of their later work included garden scenes. Each man was too stubborn to give up their art for the safer conventional lives of their parents.

He was so fascinated that he lost track of time and stayed later than he'd planned to. "Atsuko-san, I fear I have taken up too much of your time, and now I must leave."

"It has been my pleasure. I trust you will return, so we can discuss this further. Please accept this small token of appreciation for your kind attention to my story." Atsuko handed him a small package artistically wrapped in Japanese paper with a dried flower attached with a silk ribbon.

As they both bowed deeply, the calm and eloquence of Atsuko, who'd told him so much thought-provoking information, moved Oscar to bow once again out of respect.

From there, he raced to the station so he could catch the next train. He couldn't wait to tell Monet about his adventure learning about Japanese woodblock and Impressionist art.

Chapter 3 – The Girl on the Train

Oscar stopped in the boulangerie/patisserie next to the station and grabbed a baguette sandwich. So many mouthwatering choices were artfully laid out in the glass display case—tarts, croissants, and cakes—but a simple baguette with cheese and ham was all he could afford. He entered the station at a trot with his chest heaving as he tried to catch his breath. Dammed mustard gas! If he caught the next train, he could return for a sunset stroll along the Seine from Vernon to Giverny if it wasn't too cold.

He didn't enjoy waiting for the local train from Vernon to Giverny, even though it would get him to Monet's house sooner. His boss would have to wait 'til Monday to hear of his adventures. The walk along the Seine would help to build up his shredded lungs.

He settled back in his seat on the train and munched on his baguette as he opened the package from Atsuko, being careful not to tear the decorative paper. In the trenches, he was told that the best baguettes were pain à l'Ancienne, baked in Paris with their crisp crust and soft, tasty center.

Atsuko's gift was a book of Japanese woodblock prints. As he paged through it, he couldn't read the Japanese text but loved the colorful images, some like the ones he'd seen in Monet's dining room.

"What a wonderful gift," a young lady standing in the aisle proclaimed.

"What? Who are you?"

"*Bonjour*. My name is Isabelle. It is delightful." The butter-soft American voice belonged to a young woman with short auburn hair and green eyes who just dropped into the seat facing his. "You must be an extraordinary person to receive such a beautiful gift. Is it from a lady friend?"

"I … ah. Yes, it is." His eyes surveyed every part of her, from hair to face to dress and shoes.

When she stood back up to shove some of her packages into the overhead rack, Oscar's eyes couldn't help but notice her short red silk skirt creep up above her knees and along her thighs. He gripped his seat rests tightly to keep his hands from caressing her. Every pore in his skin began to heat and pulsate. If the dress rose one inch higher, he…

At last she sat down, and he was nearly able to compose himself.

"Hello, I'm Oscar. Yes, the book is from a kind lady who was generous with her time. I'm not so sure about the receiver," was all he could think to say.

"Generous with her time? Sounds intriguing. Those are Japanese woodblock prints, aren't they? Some are very erotic, I understand," she added with a knowing smile. "I find them fascinating."

"What?" He was surprised that she knew about them and even more shocked that she knew them by name. "Yes. How did you know? About the prints, I mean. About the landscape prints. Not the other ones." He felt himself stammering, trying not to dig himself deeper into a hole.

She laughed. "I studied art at the Sorbonne. We learned about them in class. I'm fascinated by how they influenced the Impressionists."

"What do you mean?" His head was spinning. It seemed too much of a coincidence that this goddess would have interests like his. Perhaps he was dreaming? He stomped on his foot to make sure he was awake.

"Do you know that one of the best Impressionist artists, Monet, lives just up the road from Vernon in Giverny?"

Oscar wanted to tell her he worked for Monet, but he felt he would disapprove. One of the other gardeners told him the boss was leery of young artists showing up and wanting something from him.

Was this why she had sat beside him? He was a small, serious man whom women rarely approached. There were many other seats on the train. She must have sat here for a reason.

"Ah, I've heard of him." He felt he should distract her by diverting her attention. "What influence did these Japanese prints have on the Impressionists? I don't quite understand the connection."

Isabelle explained that Monet and many other Impressionists had created some of their early paintings based on how the Japanese artists used large blocks of color. The Impressionists had debated what there was to learn from Japanese artists, and some had copied their techniques.

"Monet even created his lily pond and his bridge based upon the famous Japanese gardens represented in these prints," she added.

"Ah, yes, the Japanese bridge over the lily pond," he said.

"That's it. You've seen it, then?"

"No. I … uh … I've heard of it," he stammered, uncomfortable about lying to her. However, Isabelle, with her art education, might be helpful with his research into Impressionist artists. But he couldn't go in forcefully—such a bright person would see through his game and ask pointed questions he wasn't ready to answer. So he changed the topic. "I visited Bing's today."

"That's where you met the lady who gave you this book?"

"Yes. I met Atsuko, the manager, who told me about the prints and even performed a Japanese tea ceremony for me."

"I've heard of Bing's and have heard you must be wealthy to shop there."

"She helped me with my research. She was very kind."

Isabelle looked confused.

"Excuse me for saying this, but why would a store like Bing's take the time to help someone who doesn't look like he could afford to shop there?" Her intense stare pierced him to his soul. "I noticed your uniform. Were you at the front?"

"Yes. I just left the hospital last week." His mind flashed back to the shells bursting all around him as he ran from crater to crater toward the enemy bunker. His heart raced, and his breath came in short gasps. The smell of smoke and death filled his lungs. He felt lost.

She squinted as she stared at him. "Are you alright? Which hospital were you in? You look familiar."

He shook his head. "Yes, but I don't wish to discuss the war. Please tell me about yourself."

She had a strange look of recognition on her face. It was like she knew Oscar from another place and time but wasn't quite sure. She chattered on about herself, but he could see her watching his reactions closely.

"I am an *au pair* to a nice family in Vernon. The children are two and seven. I'm teaching them English, and they're helping me with my French."

Oscar nodded. "I'm a gardener for a large house in Giverny. The garden is full of interesting plants. I'm studying its design and hope to use what I learn in my landscape career in San Francisco at some point."

"Who are you working for?" she asked.

Out of the corner of his eye, he saw his stop approaching. To avoid any further conversation and another need to lie to her, he jumped up. "Oh, goodness, this is my stop."

Isabelle got up to follow him off the train. "Vernon is my stop, too. Do you live here?"

"Thanks for the chat," he said as he dashed into the station, ignoring her question pointedly.

"*À bientôt,*" Isabelle shouted after him as he hurried away.

He was too busy catching his breath from his memories of the front and the encounter with Isabelle to reply.

He hurried from the station and headed for Giverny. Once he was out of sight of Isabelle, he slowed down and strolled along the Seine in the late afternoon sun. It felt good to be out in the cold, fresh air and away from her difficult questions. His heart gradually recovered after soaring to the sky after meeting Isabelle and crashing to the ground when he surmised that she was an artist interested in meeting Monet.

The birds played hide-and-seek in the wheat field. The grain stalks were months from bowing their heavy heads with the weight of golden grains of harvest time. The swallows were soaring and diving to capture as many bugs as their mouths could hold to fatten themselves for winter. The air was sharp and cutting, but Isabelle's fragrance was all he could think of.

This must indeed be paradise—how fortunate he was to have stumbled upon this goddess. He had seen his fair share of beautiful women in the States and France, yet he'd never known such beauty as Isabelle.

Isabelle. Isabelle. Isabelle. He loved this time of day and any season of the year that had her in it. All he could think of was Isabelle. Her short hair and skirt, her almond-shaped green eyes, and her creamy white skin. Would he see her again? He could only hope to see her in his dreams. He longed to be near her once more.

By the time he reached his boarding house, it was almost dark. He had trouble reading the note tacked to his door. "Would you like to take a ride in our automobile and have a picnic with us tomorrow morning?" Signed, Blanche Hoschedé-Monet. Monet's stepdaughter, who had then also become his daughter-in-law when she married Monet's oldest son, Jean. Oscar met her when he'd interviewed for the job. She had been kind to invite him to the kitchen to warm up that first morning.

He could tell she ran the house from that first encounter. She must also manage social engagements. The invitation was exciting as he looked forward to reporting to Monet on his visit to Bing's while on the outing. It would be fun relaying every detail, except the part about meeting Isabelle.

Early the following day, Oscar and Monet's family, including Blanche, her sister Marthe, and brother Jean-Pierre, piled the picnic baskets into the back of the Panhard automobile with the help of Sylvain, the chauffeur. Blanche looked to be in her mid-fifties and was stout like Monet, with blue eyes and her graying hair wound up on top of her head. Marthe, dressed less conservatively but with the same hairstyle, seemed younger than Blanche. In his early forties and the youngest of Alice Hoschedé's children was Jean-Pierre. He wore flashy clothes and still acted like an older version of the bratty younger brother he must have been with his sisters. All were much friendlier than their stepfather, Monet, who married their mother, Alice, after their father died.

They were off to visit the Tatin sisters, two old spinsters who ran an apple orchard and a hotel that sold baked apple tarts and distilled apple cider and *Calvados.* Hours later, they arrived, spread tablecloths in the apple barn the sisters provided for their outing, and began discussing what they had brought for lunch.

The meal began with stuffed eggs, and scones with Monet's stepdaughter Marguerite's famous brandied cherries, salt cod croquettes, chicken in aspic, and finished with their hosts' celebrated apple *Tarte Tatin* smothered in fresh cream. They washed all this down with apple cider.

Blanche knew how to feed her family well. Smiles and laughter were shared. The guests offered toasts and compliments on the food. Even Monet's face lit up as he told stories of the trip he and their mother, Alice, his second wife, had taken to Venice. Oscar was ready to nod off after so much food and drink when Monet invited him for a walk through the orchard. Monet struggled to get up but wouldn't let anyone help him. Strong for his age, he refused to use a cane, so they strolled carefully through the trees.

Oscar opened the conversation as they started walking. "It was a wonderful lunch. Thank you for inviting me."

"It was Blanche's idea. She handles such things for me. I've never been much good with organizing groups of people. I gave up trying after raising funds to purchase Manet's *Olympia* painting. Signing up contributors was like herding sheep."

Oscar thought of Blanche as an ally in his efforts to get along with Monet, but he wasn't sure he understood why she would be. "I'm pleased she thought of me. She's very kind."

They stopped and turned back to view the scene of the picnic. The bare tree limbs cast shadows on the ground, and the sunlight belied the cold they experienced. Looking inside the barn, they could see that each group member was striking a different pose, speaking to one another, or lounging by themselves in the sun.

"This reminds me of the first large painting that I tried to enter in the Salon competition. I painted it using four life-size panels. I didn't finish it after the judges refused it, but I never lost interest in creating large paintings. Now I'm painting even larger decorations to donate to France."

He lit a cigarette, looked at Oscar out of the corner of his eye, and said, with a hint of suspicion, "Blanche seems to see something familiar in you. She's an excellent judge of character that I rely on. I'm not one for inviting strangers into our family gatherings. Somehow, you seem like someone whom I can trust, and I'm glad she invited you."

Oscar enjoyed the warm glow of acceptance into Monet's family. "I feel very comfortable with her, too. She makes me feel like I'm at home with my mother," Oscar said with a sense of accomplishment. When he found his father, he hoped he could join a family as warm and accepting as Monet's.

They continued to walk and paused along the way to observe the patterns of sunlight and shadow on the trees and pathway. When a breeze came up, the snow cascaded from the trees and covered them, including Monet's beard. Any lull in the conversation could have served as an opening to further discuss Japanese woodblock prints and the questions Oscar had after visiting Bing's. Still, he decided against bringing up the topic. It might interfere with the closeness of their time together.

The two continued their walk, Monet smoking, and Oscar discussing whatever Monet wanted. Topics ranged among the devastating effects of the war on the surrounding countryside, the recent cold weather that made his painting so much more difficult, and the current political climate, which influenced the gift of his giant lily pond paintings to France, which he hadn't divulged yet.

The conversation then came around to one of Monet's everyday irritations: young artists, mostly Americans, who had invaded Giverny to learn how to paint in his style using the light and location that he had discovered.

"These intruders need to develop their style and struggle like we all did to find their venues. They need to discover their inspiration," Monet grumbled. He huffed and puffed and continued. "They want me to teach them Impressionism, but why should I train my future competitors? I'd rather spend my time painting. They need to sacrifice to develop their own style like I did."

He scowled as he spoke, and his expression seemed to reflect his low opinion of these upstarts.

Oscar then remembered Atsuko's words from yesterday. "Isn't that how it's done in France and Japan, where a teacher instructs apprentices in how to paint in their style until they can go out on their own?"

Monet gave a disgusted snort. "That may work for others but not for me. These intruders fill Giverny and clutter the boarding houses and cafés while trying to become a new version of my friends and me."

Oscar knew that they even came to his house trying to meet Monet or see what he was painting. He didn't comment, but his heart sank. He hadn't told anyone about the young artist he'd met on the train. She'd seemed so nice and friendly, almost as if she had met him before. Could she have been using him to get closer to Monet, like the others he had heard about? He'd need to be more careful about who he trusted.

The two walked on in the brief afternoon sun, enjoying the orchard and their conversation. Oscar appreciated Monet's company. By the time they returned from their walk, the picnic remains had been placed in their containers, packed in hampers, and loaded back in the automobile. Their purchases of apples and cider were safely stowed in the back.

Blanche and her sisters were chatting with the Tatin sisters. Monet paid his respects to their hosts and thanked them for their hospitality. They gave him a bottle of their famous *Calvados* and lots of kisses on his cheeks in exchange.

With fond farewells said and the kisses shared, the guests got back into the vehicle and set off home. This time, Oscar was in the front next to the driver instead of in the back with Monet. The ladies in the back seat were bundled against the chill and chatting about the lunch. They had enjoyed the day, and as they drove through Vernon, they discussed the menu for their next outing, whenever that might be.

As they left Vernon, Oscar spotted Isabelle wearing a red winter coat and walking what looked to be her young charges down the street. When she saw him sitting in the vehicle's front seat, she smiled. Isabelle must have suddenly remembered him and raised her arm to wave excitedly. The young children with her cheered for her new friend she must have told them about. Then her mouth fell open as she must have recognized Monet seated in the back—Monet, the man every artist in the area wanted to meet, was wrapped in a blanket with only his famous hat and beard exposed. This was enough for her to identify France's most recognizable painter.

Fearing she would try to use him to meet Monet, Oscar frowned and struggled to turn his gaze away. Perhaps the painter who captured every nuance of light and color in any scene had not noticed Isabelle. Not likely. She was quite a beautiful young woman.

He rode the rest of the way in silence. He descended from the vehicle at his boarding house and dashed inside after a brief *Merci* to his hosts. No one discussed what had happened in Vernon, so he put off the confrontation until tomorrow.

Chapter 4 – Visiting Rouen

Oscar lay awake most of the night worrying about Monet's reaction to the scene in Vernon. He realized that perhaps he was making too much of this event, but he had heard that other gardeners had been fired for less. Monet's privacy was sacrosanct and any violation was punished severely. Each time he closed his eyes, he could see the look on Isabelle's face when she had recognized the artist.

Her beautiful, exuberant smile was just too lovely to resist. For now, Oscar couldn't risk thinking about her and what she might do with this information. Why had he ever spoken with her? Someone that attractive always meant trouble for him.

After little sleep, he dragged himself out of bed and dressed warmly for work. He was not looking forward to the questioning by his boss as soon as he arrived. Monet's valued privacy was bothered by young artists approaching him to critique their work and give creative suggestions. He wouldn't fire him over this ... or would he?

Monet was in his studio, smoking and waiting for Oscar to load the cart with the day's paintings. As Oscar placed the canvases into the cart, he spoke.

"We're also working late this afternoon to catch the afternoon light. I love to paint this time of year when the days are short, and the light turns pale yellow just before sunset."

Oscar kept his head down, expecting Monet to mention the girl. But when he said no more and left the studio, Oscar couldn't believe that Monet had not lectured him about what had happened with Isabelle the day before. His apology no longer seemed necessary. Perhaps Monet would fire him on Friday, when he had completed the week's work and Blanche had found a replacement. He followed Monet up and over the hill to the pond with the cart. At least the climb was more manageable as he gained strength in his legs and lungs.

After completing his morning work, he turned to gardening, which wasn't going well. The leaves on two of the new plants that had arrived had turned from green to yellow. It could have been the shock of shipping during the cold weather and transplanting into the cold frame, but he always worried when new plants didn't thrive. This time was more serious. Would Monet count it as another strike against him?

Then it happened! He was distracted while pruning the roses and cut a vital cane by mistake. He'd ruined half of one of the trellises for painting this year. How much more would go wrong in one day?

Late in the afternoon, he loaded a different set of canvases on the cart. Still not a word about Isabelle. Monet had not spoken all day, which was not unusual. When the cart was ready, he just stared at him with his piercing, all-seeing eyes, lit a cigarette, and shuffled off toward the pond.

The sky's reflection on the water went from a crisp blue to soft yellow, and clouds changed from white to pink and then to mauve as the sun set. Long yellow rays of the pale afternoon sun softened the colors and the surroundings in general. All except Oscar's somber mood were affected. He couldn't even bring himself to smile at the natural beauty that enveloped him.

The next day and the rest of the week were the same. More work and less talk than during previous days. Even a beautiful pond couldn't overcome his somber mood.

Monet spoke at the end of the day. "Come. Let's talk."

Oscar thought the worst. He hesitated and was not looking forward to what he was sure was going to happen next. He longed to befriend his boss and family but felt he had failed them.

"*Calvados?*" Monet asked as he strode across the studio to the sideboard.

"*Oui. Merci.*"

After Monet had filled two glasses, he led Oscar across the room to the worn couch, sat down, and handed him a drink. He took his time lighting a cigarette, then offered a toast. "*Santé.*"

Oscar responded. His palms were so wet, he felt the glass slipping through his fingers.

Monet scowled. "This is not my idea, but Blanche wants you and that girl we saw last Sunday to come to lunch this Sunday."

Oscar was so stunned that he spilled his drink on his sweaty work shirt. He tried to repair the mess by dabbing at it with his handkerchief and gave up. Maybe a kick in the throat from *Calvados* was what was needed. He took a long drink of the remaining *Calvados* and gagged. It was much stronger than he remembered. What had he just heard? He couldn't believe he wasn't being fired. If Monet fired him, he feared he'd never learn the identity of his father.

"Me? Her? Why?" was all he could mutter.

"It's a complicated story. The girl's name is Isabelle Brescher. Her father is Dr. Antoine Brescher of Chicago. It turns out that my agent, Paul Durand-Ruel, met him and sold him several of my paintings during his first show in New York. The doctor is also on the Board of Directors for the Art Institute of Chicago. They have almost a dozen of my paintings in their museum and are looking to purchase more."

Oscar just stared. "I can't believe it. How did you find out all of this so quickly?"

Monet smiled. "Blanche found out. I told you she's good in such matters. She asked after her in Vernon. That girl has an excellent reputation, if somewhat daring."

Exhausted from worrying about his job all week, Oscar took some time to collect himself before responding to the request. His heartbeat settled down to a calmer rhythm, his lungs no longer constricted. He had to admit the *Calvados* also helped. He summoned all available courage and took a deep breath. "If she has such an important father, why is she working as an *au pair* in Vernon? Besides, I thought you didn't like American artists invading your privacy."

Monet brushed ash from his beard and lit another cigarette. "I suppose she's trying to improve her French. Her family is from Alsace-Lorraine. I like to support my customers, and her father is a significant customer."

Oscar shook his head in disbelief and took another large swallow of *Calvados*, which blazed down his throat and fueled the small fire of courage in his stomach to help him dare speak up next. "I don't even know where she lives or how to invite her. I'm not even sure she'll come."

Monet waved off his objection with a smile. "Blanche will handle all of that. What are you doing tomorrow?"

Oscar thought for a moment. Sunday lunch was settled despite his objections. Was Saturday going to be another work assignment? He needed some rest after the week of extra work and worry he'd been through. "I have nothing planned."

Monet went over to the sideboard and returned with the bottle to refresh their drinks. "I'm taking the automobile on a trip to Rouen. Would you like to come?"

Oscar was surprised and gripped the glass so as not to spill his drink again. "I'd love to. Why are you going there?"

"I want to revisit it. The cathedral at Reine was bombed during the war, and I want to make sure Rouen didn't suffer the same fate. I spent a great deal of time painting there some years ago and grew rather fond of the cathedral, the people, and the town." Oscar knew that the fighting was heavy in that region, and Monet was right to be worried. He seemed concerned at the fate of the subject of his series of paintings. "Now, it's getting late, and I'm tired."

Both men rose to their feet, drained their glasses, and headed home for their evening meals. Oscar trudged back to his boarding house, trying to make sense of the events of the past hour. Not only had he *not* lost his job, but he'd also been invited to Sunday lunch again. He was to see Isabelle once more and was accompanying Monet on a drive to Rouen. Spending all week with Monet and now both Saturday and Sunday were too much for him. He needed time on his own to sort out what he was feeling about Monet and his family, as well as Isabelle. But refusing was not an option. Not if he wanted to become closer to his boss.

The following day, the two climbed into the leather rear seat of the vehicle behind Sylvain and sped off to Rouen. Oscar had had a good night's sleep dreaming about Isabelle and was over the evening's surprising revelations before but was still reserved. He desperately wanted to see Isabelle again, but he didn't want her to cost him his job.

He calmed himself by watching out the window as the winter farm landscape rolled by. Just a hint of snow graced the hills, and a fringe of ice clung to the edges of the ponds. "Our troop transport train passed through Rouen on the way to the front. I could see the cathedral towers sticking up above the buildings in the town below the tracks. They didn't seem damaged from the train. It's such a striking cathedral. But why did you paint it?"

Monet lit a cigarette and used it to gesture in the air as he described his work. "I was intrigued by the play of sunlight and fog on the stone surface of the building. Sunlight passed from the left to right across the face of the church, casting shadows on the blue stones. The light changed with the weather and time of day to reveal different colors and facets of the stone surface."

Again, silence overtook them. Monet had spoken more than he usually did, and when he was done, that would be it. Oscar sat back and enjoyed the ride, trying not to think about Sunday lunch and Isabelle. And not about the war.

When they arrived in Rouen, Sylvain parked the automobile next to the train station and helped Monet climb out of the car. He and Oscar walked down the hill on the slick cobblestone street, through the town to the cathedral. Oscar's head was like on a swivel as they passed by centuries-old half-timbered buildings. He loved how the half-dozen Gothic church spires soared into the sky high above the other buildings. Oscar slowed his pace as Monet seemed less steady on his feet than usual.

They arrived at the massive stone building with its ornate carved stone decorations that flowed from the top of the towers to the ground and encircled the twelfth-century Gothic structure. Monet alternated, with a cigarette in hand, looking first at the cathedral and then at the surrounding buildings. He seemed to be searching for something.

He walked up to the church, turned his back to it, and stared at the buildings from that angle. "I painted the cathedral from over there somewhere? If I study the town with my back to the cathedral, I think I can find where I stayed."

"There it is," he said and crossed to two half-timbered storefronts with rooms above facing the cathedral.

"I can't believe it's still here after the war."

"I painted the cathedral from windows in rooms on the second floor of these two buildings. The first shop where I painted in 1892 belonged to a lingerie and fashion milliner named Levy. The ladies used the area where I worked as a dressing room, so they had to screen where I was sitting next to the windows. When I returned in 1893, that room was no longer available, so I found a vacant apartment above a shop owned by a man named Louvet." He paused for a moment to think and then said, "Yes, Louvet."

He smiled as he seemed to enjoy the memories of his time there.

"Louvet's shop had fewer distractions than the dressing room, but I missed the ladies changing clothes," he said with a wink. "I also painted outside when weather permitted." He turned to Oscar after a moment of reflection. "Let's get something to eat. I know a little hotel where I used to dine when I was working here. Let's see if they're still open."

Oscar could almost see Monet sitting and painting in the windows day after day. He envied such dedication to his art. Famished since he'd missed breakfast, he quickly crossed the plaza to the three-story hotel with a half-timbered design that housed a restaurant on the street level.

The hotel was still standing after all of the shelling in the area during the war. Oscar hurried to open the door for Monet, and a wave of tantalizing cooking smells assaulted his senses. He felt his stomach growling and his mouth salivating in anticipation of lunch.

The somber old waiter escorted them to a table overlooking the plaza in front of the cathedral. Dark wood paneling covered the walls, and the tables had white cloths and napkins. This was the finest restaurant he had been in since he'd arrived in France or perhaps ever. It was the only nice restaurant he'd eaten in. Lunch alone with Monet. What could be better? And he wasn't being fired. His breathing came easier as he relaxed in Monet's company for the first time.

An older gentleman, dressed in a well-worn but neat and clean suit, carried a bottle of wine as he approached the table. "*Monsieur* Monet, I haven't seen you in such a long time. I'm pleased you're with us again."

Monet rose and introduced Oscar to Guy Bernard, owner of the Hotel Bernard. "Won't you sit with us, Guy?"

"Only if you accept this bottle of our best Bordeaux as my gift to an old friend."

The waiter seemed more attentive when he returned to the table with three glasses.

Monet and Bernard exchanged pleasantries as the man poured the wine, and then Monet asked, "How did the war treat you and the cathedral?"

"As you know, Rouen was the British Army supply center for the western front. But you may not know that we were also the hospital for the wounded soldiers. My hotel was the command center with officers living in my rooms upstairs. What I lost in room rent, I made up for in wine sales," Bernard said with a smile. "Do you like the wine I've chosen for you?"

"*C'est très bon*. And the cathedral?" Monet asked with concern in his voice.

"The bombs didn't damage the cathedral because it was turned into a hospital ward treating both Allied and German soldiers. Your cathedral was safe ... this time." Bernard got up to leave and motioned for the waiter to return with the menus.

"I was in a hospital housed in a church," Oscar mentioned as he reviewed the menu. "I remember little as I was unconscious and wore eye patches much of the time."

Monet looked sad. "I'm sorry to hear that. We lost so many young men in the war. How are you feeling now?"

"I'm feeling better each day. The doctors said my lungs would heal." He cursed the mustard gas attack under his breath. "The bombs and bullets were bad enough, but the gas did the real, lasting damage."

After this, they made no further mention of the war, as if a truce had been reached, and Bernard retreated to his kitchen.

Oscar and Monet ate a delicious lunch in quiet conversation about the time Monet had spent in Rouen. Monet had the rabbit in a cider sauce while Oscar had the duckling *à la rouennaise*. He savored every morsel as politely as he could manage.

It was during Monet's time in Rouen that he had purchased the land for his pond. He'd also had one of his first successful showings and married Alice. Oscar realized he was learning about Monet's life by listening to what the old man wanted to say when he was willing to talk. He acquired so much more information about him than if he had asked questions and felt he was being treated like a friend, not just an employee.

At the end of the meal, Bernard returned to their table.

Monet smiled. "*Merci* for the wonderful wine. It is nice to see your hotel has not suffered from the war. I hope to return for another visit soon."

In Bernard's eyes, Oscar could see that he didn't believe this would ever happen as each of them was coming to the end of their life's journey. A tear rolled down Bernard's cheek as he bid farewell to his dear friend.

"I will never forget the many long nights we spent dining and talking together during the two years you painted the cathedral. It was one of the high points of my time managing this hotel."

Monet and Bernard embraced and kissed each other's cheeks. Oscar was seeing another side of the man who could be so gruff most of the time. He was quite loyal to his friends and sentimental about their well-being.

Oscar and Monet made their way up the hill through the streets overhung by buildings with shops on bottom floors and apartments above, leading to the train station and their waiting vehicle. Halfway up through the town, Monet stumbled and grabbed Oscar's arm for support. They held on to each other until they reached the automobile, where Sylvain helped Monet into his seat. Oscar just settled down into the plush seat and felt embraced by the day's adventure and Monet's trust. He and Monet seemed to be drawing closer than employer and employee. They were getting to know each other. He hoped that when he found his father, he would be a man like Monet.

Just then, Monet turned to him. "What are we going to do about that girl tomorrow?"

What could he mean? Oscar started worrying all over again. He dreaded the thought of Isabelle embarrassing him in front of Monet and his family. He feared and longed for the next day to begin and end. "I'm not sure what you mean," Oscar blurted out.

Chapter 5 – Sunday Lunch

Oscar arrived before the appointed hour for the Sunday lunch. Standing on the porch in the doorway to the kitchen, he hesitated to enter Blanche's domain. The morning sunlight streamed into the room to illuminate the flurry of culinary activity. The aroma from bubbling pots and the warmth of the oven flooded his mind with thoughts of his mother preparing Sunday lunch for her friends when he was young.

He'd loved helping her in the kitchen. She placed him in charge of cleaning and chopping the vegetables and meat while she prepared the sauces and managed the stove. She called him her sous-chef. He was also responsible for the fire in the stove, from starting it with kindling to feeding in the larger pieces of dried oak at the right time to keep the oven at a constant temperature. They were a good team, with the results praised by all who'd shared their meals.

Blanche stood by the windows next to the massive cast-iron, wood-burning stove, directing the cook and her assistant in the preparation of the lunch. One of the copper pots started boiling over, dripping soup on the stovetop and down its side onto the floor. As the liquid splashed onto the terracotta tiles, the harassed cook grabbed the pot from the stove while her assistant rushed to mop up the spill.

"You must watch the pots closer," the cook scolded her assistant, who continued to clean up the mess in silence.

Blanche beckoned Oscar inside to hear the menu. Based on the cooking smells, it would be a sumptuous lunch. He salivated just envisioning the feast, which reminded him of his mother's recipes handed down from her family in Lyon. It would start with baked field mushrooms and stuffed artichoke hearts followed by herb soup. That was the pot that had boiled over. The main courses were chicken with crayfish butter and cold beef à la mode.

"We use Christine's recipe," Blanche said. "The side dishes include baked kidney beans, glazed carrots, and poached truffles. Monet's favorite green cake with pistachio cream filling will be our dessert. We will dine on the porch."

Blanche turned from the menu to issue serving instructions like a military commander. The staff stood at attention and nodded in agreement as Oscar wondered who this Christine was.

She then turned back to Oscar. "For casual meals, *Monsieur* likes to dine less formally by using the yellow dishes with the blue rims, the plain silverware, and the crystal drinking glasses, not the wine goblets. Lunch will be in two hours. Make sure everything is ready for *Monsieur's* review in one hour. Do you understand?" She nodded toward the cook.

"Yes, *Madame* Blanche," the cook responded. "All will be ready for his inspection."

Her assistant, using a towel, began cleaning food splashes on the blue and white tiled walls.

Oscar was about to leave when Blanche spoke.

"*Merci* for traveling with Monet on your day off yesterday. The trip meant a lot to him, and I was too busy with lunch to accompany him."

"It was nothing. I enjoyed spending time with him and visiting Rouen. Uh... There was one thing that happened. I hate to mention it, but he stumbled on the way back to the automobile." Oscar was not sure it was his place to mention this.

Blanche sighed and said with concern in her voice, "That's been happening more often lately. I'm so glad you were there to help him. I'm afraid his eyesight is failing so he stumbles over unseen objects in his path."

"My pleasure," Oscar said with a slight nod.

The doorbell rang, and Blanche hurried off to answer it. Oscar retreated to the porch to inspect the view of the garden. Anything out of place would be an issue for Monet.

That must be Isabelle. Right on time. I'm sure Monet will like her punctuality. I wonder how she's dressed today. I hope not too provocatively. Blanche won't like it if she is, but Monet will.

Blanche hurried through the dining room door onto the porch with Isabelle trailing behind.

"There you are!" she exclaimed. "I'm sure you remember Isabelle."

Isabelle's appearance stunned Oscar. A green ribbon shone in her auburn hair, matching her short green silk dress and an embroidered cape draped over her shoulders. She was even lovelier than he remembered. How could he forget her? He'd worn his army uniform again since he had no other clothes appropriate for such an event. It was clean and pressed and would have to do for the occasion.

"Nice to be with you again." A rush of heat made him flush and his heart race.

"I hope so," Isabelle said with a cheeky tone. She flashed him a mischievous smile from ruby lips he wanted to kiss, despite himself. "You didn't seem so happy with me last Sunday when you were riding through Vernon."

Her words rooted him to the spot.

"I ... I ... I'm happy you're here this afternoon," Oscar stammered.

"Oscar, please take Isabelle on a tour of the garden," Blanche said. "I'll send for you when lunch is ready. Monet is working on his correspondence and will be down later for lunch. I'm needed in the kitchen to make sure all goes well."

She rushed off to the kitchen as she called out that Monet would be there in forty minutes.

Oscar's blush gave way to a tingling sensation in his legs and arms. He was caught between grabbing and kissing her, and running to the river and throwing himself in. He loved and feared his new assignment. During the week, a gardener and painter's assistant. Now a tour guide. Yesterday, he'd been a traveling companion. He held a variety of roles and strived to do them all well.

He was at a loss for words regarding his latest assignment until he identified his best option was to focus on being an expert tour guide. "Isabelle, I'd enjoy showing you the garden and lily pond, if you like."

"I can't think of anything I would enjoy more at this moment." She smiled and took his arm as they descended the stairs.

His heart surged faster as he led the way to the lower garden. They strolled down the *Grande Allée* of rose trellises. To keep his mind on the tour and off Isabelle's body so close that he could feel the heat from her hand through his sleeve, he identified which plants were in each of the beds as they passed by even though she couldn't appreciate them in winter. He pointed out the border of aubrietias, snowdrops, jonquils, pansies, irises, and more, explaining how Monet used flower combinations like yellow daisies with black centers and white forget-me-nots to add contrast and shimmer to floral scenes he intended to paint.

"Oscar, I know you're a gardener. You don't have to impress me with the names of all the plants," Isabelle said with another chiding laugh. "I'm much more interested in how Monet has selected and blended color combinations to create a palette he wishes to paint. He seems to have an excellent command of color theory."

Oscar, offended that she had accused him of being pompous, stood with his mouth agape. She saw the garden differently than he did. He had not thought that could be possible. She focused on the blending of colors and he focused on the blending of flowers to create a floral design. "If he sees attractive plants in nature, he tries to reproduce the same colors in his garden using local or imported plants," he said. "How do you know what he's done with color?"

"Simple. It's the color theory that I learned in school. I'm surprised you didn't learn that as a gardener." She smiled, and her dress swished as she released his arm and walked away from him down the path.

He stood watching as she flounced away, his forearm suddenly ice-cold under his sleeve where her touch no longer provided warmth. She made his heart itch. It wanted what it wanted—to love and be loved in return. His head fought a brave but losing battle for control.

At the bottom of the garden, they turned back to admire the scene before climbing the hill to the lily pond. Her comment still had him miffed, and he tried to show that he, too, understood something about color. "The long pink house with its green trim is the jewel in the crown of colorful flowers surrounding it. Monet has complemented the color of the house with the flower colors. He had red bricks ground up to make that particular color for the house."

He embarrassed himself as he tried to win her admiration.

"I agree. You catch on fast," Isabelle said as she reached up and kissed him hard on the lips.

His gasp strangled in his throat as his hands clenched into fists, a reflex to keep him from grabbing her shoulders and pulling her to him. No, that wouldn't do—he was a gentleman. Yet, the warmth of her lips on his set fire to his mind and body. His head continued to lose the battle.

This was the surprise he had feared. Something in him had known he should be wary around her—Isabelle was unpredictable. He could simply lose his way and forget his purpose because his heart traveled in one direction and his head in another. His heart wanted more—oh, how it wanted more!—but already, he feared it would go too far.

This splashed cold reason onto the embers of his lust, and he stumbled a step back. He had to get a grip, for goodness' sake. "What was that for?"

"Didn't you like it?" she said with smiling eyes and pouting lips.

Oscar was both annoyed and flattered once he'd caught his breath and regained some of his composure. He had always been uncomfortable around young women, especially bewitching women. There was only one girl at college he had felt at ease with.

"That's not the point," he gasped. "What if someone saw you do that? I work here. They could get the wrong idea. I'm not a fellow who kisses young ladies when they first meet them."

Isabelle dared him by sticking her soft, warm, pink tongue out and licking her lips slowly from right to left. "Have you forgotten we met already on the train and perhaps before that? Shut up and kiss me!"

This woman … This goddess! He shook his head, abandoning all reason in the process, and did as he was told. This—she—was inevitable. He no longer cared that his head was spinning, that his knees buckled. He pulled her close to him and tried to kiss the breath out of her.

But then she went limp, and his whole body became rigid. Had he gone too far? He backed away from her and tried to clear his head, to regain control. What had he done? Why would he surrender himself to this tease? He should know better.

Isabelle laughed as she recovered her footing and ran up the hill toward the lily pond. Was she trying to get away or to get him to chase her? Either way, she was teasing him, and this upset him. Oscar had only known one woman like Isabelle: his mother. He didn't care to know another.

But today, she was his guest, so he had no choice but to follow her. Her scent of warm roses and the taste of honeysuckle nectar lips still lingered, though, driving him mad. He liked it, but she scared him to death. After his injuries in the war, he felt so indecisive. But not her. What would she do next?

He tried to stop shaking and forced his legs to carry him up the hill after her. She stopped short when she topped the rise and spread her arms wide to embrace the majesty of the lily pond. Her skirt caught the wind and rose so high that he gasped again and looked away a moment too late. She caught him. After being brought up by a consummate flirt, he'd promised himself to never fall for one like her. Now, look at him!

The pond shimmered in the noonday sun. The pinks, purples, and yellows of the plants that should have been around the water were absent, but the blue sky with white clouds reflected on the surface made up for them. Oscar came up close behind her but not too close. He was keeping his distance, staying away from her electric touch, tantalizing lips, and overall seductive presence.

They descended the hill and onto the Japanese bridge. The fragrance from her perfume enveloped him, making his head turn, so he leaned against the railing to steady himself. Isabelle pressed herself against him. He grew so dizzy from her touch and intense heat that they both almost fell into the water. All Oscar saw was her ruby lips, less red from kissing him but still heightened by the reflected glow of the sun. Her perfume—the latest from Paris, he learned later—imprinted itself on his brain and his clothes.

He steadied himself for another kiss, but she was off across the bridge and down the path next to the water, shouting, "This pond is glorious!"

Oscar tried to regain control of himself when he caught up to her. A cold shower was not available, so he grabbed the nearest weapon at hand: facts! Perhaps telling her the history of the pond would distract him from wanting to seize and kiss her again. And again.

"Monet purchased the land in 1892 while he was painting the Rouen Cathedral and began building the pond after battling with the town for months over the water rights to the River Epte. A wealthy and influential businessman from Vétheuil, where Monet lived prior to Giverny, persuaded the Giverny town council to grant Monet permission to build his pond."

He summoned more facts while trying to help his head overcome his heart.

She turned and looked into his eyes as she placed her hands on his chest.

Head zero. Heart one hundred forty over ninety.

"How interesting. Tell me more," Isabelle whispered.

She threw him this lifeline that he almost missed. Perhaps the facts were helping calm down the situation. He babbled on with more points since they seemed to support his head in sorting out this situation.

"Over the years, he added a wide variety of plants to the garden surrounding the pond and in it. Many of the lilies were shipped to him by his friends in Japan since they weren't available in Europe."

She adjusted her dress and, in the process, revealed more of her legs for a long, agonizing instant. "Amazing."

He thought it impressed her until she slowly licked her lips again with that soft, pink tongue.

"He, ah, he chose plants that responded to the faintest breeze for planting around the pond. As they moved, the reflection on the surface of the pond shimmered, making it more lovely to paint."

"Do you mean like this?" She spun around, making her dress shimmer and rise higher and higher. "Do you like what you see?"

Oscar gulped and felt his face glowing as he tried to regain control of himself. Isabelle smiled as she seemed to pay attention to what he was saying. She suddenly ceased her flirtation and was most interested when he described how Monet painted around the pond, moving from scene to scene, using fresh canvases as the sunlight shifted.

"I've not heard of a painter paying such close attention to the changing effects of light," she said. "He must see tiny changes in color and shades that the light creates as the sun moves across the sky. No wonder Cezanne called him 'the eye.' He sees all."

They rounded the pond and started on their way back to the house when they saw the assistant cook coming toward them. It was time for lunch and for Isabelle to meet Monet. Oscar was intoxicated and sobered that she'd taken his hand when he offered to help her down the hill. The tingling of her touch proved so disconcerting that he suppressed a gasp. She kept holding it as they returned up the *Grande Allée*. Worried what Monet might think of him, he pulled it back as they neared the steps leading to the porch. She shot him a disapproving glance.

"*Monsieur* Monet, I'd like you to meet *Mademoiselle* Isabelle Brescher. Isabelle, may I present *Monsieur* Claude Monet."

"My pleasure, my dear. Welcome to my home and garden." Monet bowed as he took her hand. Isabelle did her best curtsey and tittered as she lost her balance and almost fell into Oscar. Monet chuckled. "I'm not used to lovely young ladies falling at my feet."

Isabelle tossed her short hair and smiled. "The pleasure is all mine, *Monsieur.*"

Monet seated her next to him, and they began a chat that lasted through most of the meal. They forgot Oscar for the moment, and he turned to help Blanche into a seat beside him.

"I know a flirt when I see one," he muttered under his breath.

Blanche nodded in agreement, then her brow furrowed. "I hope for your sake she's more than just a flirt. Perhaps you'll discover more than that when you get to know her better. I can tell you're taken with her."

He gave a faint smile, embarrassed that his feelings for Isabelle were so obvious. He decided to focus on the other guests to keep his mind off Isabelle and conceal his feelings.

Blanche looked the opposite of Isabelle. She piled her long, graying brown hair on top of her head in an old-fashioned style, whereas Isabelle's was cut short and curled around her face. Isabelle's short dress was quite a contrast to Blanche's attire, which was long and white with puffy sleeves, and the hem stopped a few inches above the floor.

She and her two sisters, Marthe and Germaine, discussed the new Paris fashion wave that Isabelle represented. Overhearing them, Oscar observed that they were tactful in their comments for his sake but critical of Isabelle. Germaine was the middle sister, younger than Blanche and older than Marthe. She dressed more in Paris's current fashion with a dress of peach color with straight sleeves that rose above her ankle. She was more cutting in her criticism of Isabelle than her sisters.

"I saw that style of short dress and cropped hair when I was in Paris last week. I never thought it would reach here so soon," she said with a disparaging sniff.

"According to my friends in Vernon, Isabelle graduated from the Sorbonne," Blanche said. "She's intelligent and accomplished in her artistic studies."

"That explains it. Those Sorbonne girls are all fast and loose," Germaine added with an edge of contempt in her voice.

"Also, you can tell she's American." Blanche rolled her eyes in disapproval, and her sisters followed suit.

"Humph. Americans!" Germaine harrumphed. "What do you expect?"

Marthe commented from a mother's viewpoint to a daughter, Lily, a few years older than Isabelle. "I watch Lily going through changes in dress and attitudes because of these changing times. She's not gone as far as Isabelle, but she's a lot different from us when we were her age. Mother had some of the same thoughts about us when we insisted on all dressing alike. Don't you remember?"

Blanche and Germaine nodded in remembrance, if not total agreement.

Oscar focused on the long table, which had a white tablecloth embroidered in yellow with napkins to match. Two wine glasses, one for a Cabernet Franc from the Loire Valley and another for a white Chinon Blanc. The masses of gleaming silverware overwhelmed him. He was sure it must be appropriate for all the items on the menu, including dessert, but which piece to use for what course proved a quandary.

He shifted his attention again, stared at the Japanese woodblock prints, and tried to identify any that might be in the book he was given.

After the guests passed, sniffed, complimented, and consumed the dishes laden with delicious-smelling food, they leaned back in their seats with glasses of wine and slices of goat cheese to listen to Monet.

"Isabelle, I understand you studied to be a painter, but why are you working as an *au pair*?" Monet awaited her response as he settled back in his chair, lifted his glass of red wine to admire its color, and savored the taste. He looked keen to hear her explanation. She was a young woman with alluring green eyes and big dreams, not to mention her long legs.

Isabelle smiled and straightened her shoulders before engaging the world's greatest living painter in a conversation about her future. "*Monsieur*, I'm trying to understand my young charges, so I might paint children better. I've none of my own to study. However, I've studied medicine, so I also understand something about their anatomy."

"That's wonderful," Monet said with a warm smile. "I've always thought it is important for a portrait painter to understand what is going on beneath the skin. Have you practiced medicine?"

"*Oui*. I was a part-time nurse at the front while I was at the Sorbonne. That's where I met your friend, Prime Minister Georges Clémenceau."

"Oh, *oui*. I remember now. Georges mentioned your father, Dr. Brescher." Monet smiled at the mention of his friend Georges. "Since you're focused on women and children, you are following in the footsteps of my Impressionist friend Berthe Morisot."

"As best I can, *Monsieur*. However, I'm more interested in painting pregnant women and newborn babies," Isabelle replied.

Germaine gasped and choked on her wine. "One does not speak of such delicate subjects in mixed company," was all she could utter as everyone stared at her when she spilled wine on the tablecloth.

As soon as her coughing had subsided, Monet continued the discussion, chuckling at Germaine's display. "Those are topics that are controversial, as you can see, and few artists have painted them."

He seemed pleased with this direction the discussion had taken as he turned to Isabelle for her response.

"They should. Each of us experiences the birth process at least once. It's such a wonderful part of life that artists have painted in classical and religious contexts, but not realistically." She had a defiant look in her eyes.

"I applaud your courage, my dear," Blanche said. Marthe nodded in agreement. Germaine just shook her head in disgust as she used her napkin as a tool to recover her dignity. First she blotted wine from her lips, then her dress and the tablecloth.

"Leave it," Blanche said. "It won't be the first tablecloth you've stained. I joined the Salon and painted landscapes like Monet. Landscapes, too, were controversial when he started. I can understand your fascination with your chosen subjects. I'm sure our departed friend, Berthe, would approve." She looked sad as she mentioned Berthe's name.

"*Oui,* I remember all too well when I started as a painter," Monet concurred. He sat up straighter in his chair, lit a cigarette, and began telling about his life as a young artist. "I wanted to paint seascapes and landscapes instead of the classical subjects and portraits of the wealthy that most accepted painters chose."

He related his struggle with his father and aunt when he'd wanted to move to Paris and learn to paint. "They insisted that I study at a studio acceptable to the art establishment, the Salon. Those Salon judges decided who exhibits in their annual painting exhibition."

"Are you saying anyone who wanted to succeed had to exhibit at the Salon?" Isabelle asked.

"*Oui.* Instead, I chose the Académie Suisse, where there were no restrictions on what I could paint and which medium I chose. It was a very free place to learn and experiment. Later, I changed to the Académie Gleyre, where I made friends with other students like Bazille and Renoir. Together with the others, we formed the group later called the Impressionists."

When the conversation waned, Blanche called for Monet's favorite green cake that he'd named *vert-vert.* The yellow-green fondant frosting covering the entire cake shimmered and glowed in the afternoon light. The very sight of it got the whole table talking again. Each guest had at least one piece, and then, one by one, pushed back from the table with a sigh of contentment and a cup of coffee.

"Before we leave the table, I'd like to invite you all on an adventure," Monet said. The guests snapped to attention. "I'd like to take you all to Le Havre, so I can show you where I grew up and began painting. It will be in a few weeks, as soon as Blanche can arrange it. Are you interested?"

Oscar watched as the faces of the guests turned from surprise to interest to joy. He looked at Isabelle, who returned his steady gaze with a smile. What did she have in mind now? He shivered with anticipation and fear as a drop of sweat slid down the back of his neck.

Monet stood up to say, "Now let's take a turn around the garden and let this delicious lunch settle. Isabelle, after you, my dear."

Oscar took Blanche's arm. "Might I have a word when the others have gone?"

Blanche descended the porch stairs and led him to the planting beds on the right and away from the others as they strolled with Monet down the *Grande Allée*. She looked concerned as she asked, "What do you want, my dear?"

Oscar felt ashamed as he shuffled from foot to foot. "I can't accompany you on the trip you're planning to Le Havre."

"Why not? I'm counting on you to be Monet's traveling companion, as we agreed when you were hired, and help him navigate some rigorous parts of the journey," Blanche replied with narrow eyes and an edge to her voice.

He was surprised, not expecting her to become annoyed. "I'm not comfortable being that close to Isabelle for several days."

Blanche placed her hands on her ample hips. "Oscar, what has gotten into you? Are you afraid of a little harmless flirting?"

He struggled to put his fears into words. How could anyone understand what it was to be with a constant flirt unless raised by one?

"I'm embarrassed to say that if you only knew what she did, you'd understand. She's just too forward. She's trouble, at least for me."

"I could see what went on. I saw you two kissing at the bottom of the *Grande Allée*," Blanche said with a knowing smile, perhaps thinking of her youth with Monet's son, who was her youthful companion and first husband.

Oscar's eyes widened. "*Mon Dieu*, I knew you'd see that and think less of me."

"Not in the least. Like you, I know a flirt when I see one. What's the problem?"

"Let me tell you a story," he offered with a sigh. "There was a young artist, very much like Isabelle, a beautiful flirt. She met a rather famous artist in Antibes and, well … one thing led to another, and she got pregnant."

"Not all that unusual in the world of artists," Blanche said with a grim look. "That's why my mother would not let Monet paint models."

"As you might imagine, the artist loved someone else and was not prepared to marry the young woman. They separated, and she never heard from him again."

A light went on in Blanche's eyes as she guessed the connection. "Let me guess. You're the result of that affair."

Oscar leaned over to inspect the bedding plants to regain his composure. "*Oui*. The young woman, my mother, remained in France until I was born and then traveled to California. She raised me without a father. She was a wonderful, loving mother, but she could not make up for what I missed: a father. From time to time when I was young, there were men I called 'uncle,' but none of them was around very long."

"Didn't your mother ever tell you about your father?"

He shrugged. "She wrote me a letter on her deathbed, telling me that my father was a famous artist who never knew about me. I would have liked to ask her more, but I was in the military recovering from bullet wounds and a mustard gas attack. I didn't receive the letter until months after she'd died."

Blanche looked quizzical and frowned. "Why didn't you ask her before you left home?"

He could only lower his head in shame and mumble, "I tried."

She took his arm. "Do I understand that you don't want to be around Isabelle because she's a tease?"

"No, I'm all right with her being a tease. I want to be around her too much. I'm afraid of what I might do if I'm around her too much. Do you understand? I don't want anyone to suffer the consequences. Accidents do happen."

Blanche took a moment to think about this and then said with confidence, "Lily. I'll get my niece, Lily, to help. She's close to Isabelle's age and can convince her not to play flirting games with you. She can say that you are in no shape to defend yourself since you lost your mother while you were recovering in the military hospital."

Oscar dropped his head in embarrassment. "*Merci* for your help and Lily's, but I feel I must speak to her myself and explain my situation."

Blanche shook her head. "That'll never work. She'll take winning you over as a challenge. She'll not give up unless she knows the challenge is hopeless. Let me see if Lily can help. I could ask Monet to talk with her. "

Oscar bit his tongue. He had told Blanche much more than he had intended, and now she would get Lily involved. He needed to leave. "No, no. Don't get Monet involved. I must go now. Please offer my grateful appreciation to our host. I'll be at work in the morning. *Merci* for your kind attention and offers of help. I doubt it'll work out, but I appreciate your concern."

He couldn't keep from running back around the house and onto the road toward his boarding house. How could he have let himself get into this mess? But instead of going there, he turned and ran

across the fields toward the River Seine. When he reached the water's edge, he dropped into the grass along the bank, rolled over, and
cried out in frustration. Isabelle's behavior and losing his mother
tore at him. He hoped that only the insects heard him. He was sure
they would keep his secret.

Chapter 6 – The Journey to Le Havre

Oscar reluctantly returned to work on Monday. He was not ready for a week of shame over his performance with Isabelle the previous day. His discussion with Blanche after lunch could have cost him his job or, at the very least, cost him the respect of her and Monet. Perhaps he would hear their reactions today.

"*Bonjour,* Oscar," Monet said with a smile. "I enjoyed meeting your young lady friend yesterday. She seems interested in Impressionism and my garden."

Monet's reaction surprised Oscar. He searched for some way to continue with this discussion of Isabelle. "She spoke to me about her vision of the garden in a way that was new to me. She saw it in an entirely different way than I did."

Monet cocked his head. "How so?"

Oscar was relieved that he'd avoided being fired over his conduct with Isabelle. He tried to keep the conversation going in a positive direction. "She focused on the color combinations you have chosen. She mentioned how you used the complementary colors of the color wheel in designing the garden. Fascinating."

Monet nodded. "She is a very perceptive young artist. I'm sure you'll enjoy our visit to Le Havre. I'm looking forward to showing you where I grew up."

After selecting the canvases for the day, Monet smiled again and walked off toward the lily pond, whistling to himself. Something he never did.

Very unusual behavior for Monet. Looks like Isabelle has charmed him, too.

Oscar was concerned that the affair with Isabelle was his fault, and now the Monet family was becoming involved. He was about to follow Monet to the pond when Blanche called to him from the porch.

"Come and find me when you're ready to leave this evening."

"*Oui, Madame.*" He suspected that the pressure for him to join the Le Havre adventure was starting earlier than expected. This left him more than a little agitated.

Oscar trod up and over the hill along the path leading to the pond, pushing the cart full of paintings. The day was long and torturous as the bridge and several spots around the pond reminded him of his intimate moments with Isabelle. After having such an exciting afternoon, he was about to drive her away. Was he making a mistake? What was wrong with him?

Blanche was waiting on the porch for him, holding something in one hand and inspecting it. She stood beneath the pear trees where Isabelle had first taken his arm as he helped her descend the steps.

"Oscar, please come up here."

He climbed the stairs, expecting nagging about going on the trip.

Blanche handed him the garment she'd been inspecting with a broad smile on her face. "Monet wants you to have this, so you can wear something nice on our trip. He wore it seldom back when he was much thinner."

Well, he had certainly not been expecting this! He took the brown tweed suit, made of fine quality wool. What else could he expect from a man rumored to have always dressed in the best clothes even when his family was going hungry? He'd never had such a suit even when he'd gone off to college. The buttons were bone, even three on the pant cuff. The style was out-of-date, but who was he to complain?

Would Isabelle approve?

But why should he care? There were more important matters to address.

"I can't accept such a generous gift," he said as he tried to return it to Blanche. "Besides, I doubt that it will fit me."

Blanche didn't stop smiling. She was not one to give up easily. "You can't continue to wear your army uniform. This will look very nice on you when it's altered. Take it to the address on this card. My seamstress, Cosette, will alter it to fit you. She'll also make a few shirts for you."

A rush of heat burned up his chest to his ears. "*Merci*, but I can't afford to have it altered nor extra shirts. It's out of the question."

"It's all arranged," she said with a dismissive wave. "She'll put it on my account. Be sure to get there today, so she can deliver it back here next Friday with my new travel dress. Oh, I almost forgot the shoes." Blanche reached behind her on the table and brought out a pair of dusty brown shoes. "Take these to the cobbler and have them polished."

No point fighting the inevitable, it would seem. Oscar had learned when to bow before feminine determination, thanks to his formidable mother.

"I learned to clean and shine my shoes as a soldier," he said.

This time, she laughed out loud. She had triumphed once again. "I bet you did. I can't wait to see how good you look on our trip."

At this, he bristled. "Trip. I thought we'd settled that yesterday."

He knew full well they hadn't, but he needed to stand up for himself, at least a little.

"I talked it over with Marthe and Lily. We'll all ride in the same automobile as Isabelle. Which will allow us to speak to her. She'll no longer be a problem for you. You and Monet can ride with Jean-Pierre."

Once again, Blanche was in control of the situation. Oscar needed to go along for the ride. He suspected that Isabelle would be more of a challenge for her than she was for him.

Too flustered to say any more, he waved goodbye with the shoes in his hand as he descended the stairs. Off he went to see Cosette with the suit in one hand and shoes in the other. He'd been right. It was a most embarrassing day, but not how he'd expected.

The Friday before the trip came much too soon for him. Work went well, and the conversation with Monet was once again at a minimum. Isabelle haunted his thoughts. Now he was back at the porch steps, where Blanche stood with the suit in hand. It looked the same as before. Hopefully, smaller.

"Here you are. One lovely suit sized to fit you." Then she reached on the table behind and pulled out three white shirts. "I had them made without the ruffled cuffs that Monet wears. I thought you'd like that better."

Oscar overcame his embarrassment to force a smile. "*Madame*, I can't thank you enough. I have never had such a fine suit of clothes. You're correct about the shirts. I cherish these wonderful gifts."

"Don't thank me. Monet was the one who insisted I do this for you. He wants you to feel comfortable when we visit Le Havre tomorrow. We leave at eight. See you then."

"*Merci*, I won't be late." He bowed his head and left.

Dear God, I wish I could be late and miss this trip altogether, he thought as he walked home with his arms full of packages.

Saturday morning arrived, and Oscar was early, as usual, waiting by the open-air automobiles in the lane behind Monet's house. His small canvas bag held two new white shirts and clean socks and underwear. He was self-conscious wearing the remaining gifts as he felt he looked like a young Monet.

Soon the Monets filed out, first Blanche, followed by Germaine, Jean-Pierre, Lily, and Marthe taking up the rear. They were all decked out in new finery fresh from Cosette. Monet and Sylvain were smoking cigarettes on the opposite side of the lead vehicle, Jean-Pierre's new Hotchkiss touring automobile. Blanche took a long look at Oscar and gave a nod of approval and a warm smile.

The men got into the lead auto with Jean-Pierre driving. The ladies climbed into the second vehicle, the Panhard-Levassor, helped by their driver, Sylvain. The first stop was Vernon to pick up Isabelle.

The autos were parked in front of the house where she lived. Moments later, she flounced out, full of enthusiasm and vivacity. Until she discovered Blanche beckoning her to ride with the ladies, including the challenging Germaine, not with Oscar and Monet. Her expression turned from sunny to cloudy in an instant.

Oscar tore his gaze from her face to take in the rest of her. She wore an English horse-riding costume, the riding breeches so tight across her bottom that his eyes bulged out of his head. The matching tight white blouse and long black boots topped off the image of a young huntress. Was he the prey? If so, he would surrender without a fight.

Was he insane to pass up on this gorgeous young goddess? He sank back into his seat just as Jean-Pierre smirked and said, "I'd love to hear the conversation going on in that vehicle."

"Knowing your sisters as I do, I wouldn't even want to guess what's being said," Monet said with a grin. "Too much drama for me."

Oscar burrowed even deeper into the leather seats as his business was being discussed in not one but both vehicles. He felt his face flush and his throat tighten. It had been a humiliating two weeks from beginning to end. First the fear of being fired, then the donated clothes, and now the entire family discussing his affair, which he didn't have. Not yet.

"Poor Isabelle. The conversations must be hard, but I'm sure she can hold her own."

Monet and Jean-Pierre turned to look at him as he spoke. He was sure he looked more worried than he'd meant to. Perhaps these two knew what the sisters were discussing, but no one said.

The vehicles sped along the road following the Seine, through fields of emerging green winter wheat stalks, bumping along closer and closer to the sea. The breeze wafting through the open carriage smelled of salt air and coastal heather. Seagulls soared overhead. They were nearing Le Havre and the end to this bumpy ride over dusty roads with his raw nerves. Oscar could only imagine the poisonous look Isabelle would give him as they dismounted at the journey's end.

He was the first to jump from the lead vehicle as he tried to sneak off to explore the dockside location alone. He planned to walk to the seafood restaurant Monet had chosen for lunch, but he couldn't keep from watching Isabelle dismount.

He tried to turn away before she saw him, but she caught his eye and gave him a warm smile. In shock, his knees buckled, and he nearly slipped into the water beside the dock before regaining what remained of his composure. He tried to find a hiding place to wait for the others. Despite his efforts, she sauntered directly to him. What was she up to now?

He couldn't resist staring at the shape of her body that was all but revealed by her outfit. She flounced up to him and gave his face a re-sounding slap.

"That's for telling the three sisters that I am a dangerous flirt."

She then leaned into him, took his face in her hands, and delivered a resounding kiss on his quivering lips. She pulled back the instant before he ran out of breath.

"That's for falling in love with me. Nice suit, by the way."

She spun around on her boot heel and strode off down the dock. Heads turned, and mouths fell open as she passed the fishermen and dock laborers.

Oscar turned to see if the others in the party had noticed what had transpired. They had. Monet and Jean-Pierre were laughing so hard that tears were streaming down their cheeks. Blanche scowled and helped Marthe support Germaine, who had swooned. Lily smiled and fanned her aunt's face. Sylvain ignored the scene, got his lunch from the vehicle, and walked off to find a shady spot to eat and rest. Oscar slumped back on a nearby bench and abandoned all hope of resisting her, at least for today.

Blanche gathered the party like a mother hen shooing a flock of baby chicks and headed them down the dock, searching for *Saveurs Ile Maurice*, the restaurant Monet had chosen. She said it was large enough to accommodate their party and was next to where the ships docked. She stopped next to Oscar long enough to apologize for failing in her mission to keep Isabelle under control. Oscar couldn't respond.

When they arrived, Isabelle was standing out front, chatting with the *maître d' hôtel* and pointing at a sailing ship gliding away from the dock nearby. The group assembled and were escorted inside to their table. Isabelle clung to Oscar's arm so he could neither fall nor get away. The heat of her body and her captivating scent made him lose his focus again.

Monet ordered white wine from the Loire Valley, and Blanche went to the kitchen to assure herself that the menu she'd chosen was being suitably prepared. She'd selected shrimp to start, the main course of baked sole with spring vegetables, followed by assorted cheeses, and then crème brûlée for dessert. Oscar struggled to think of something, anything else but Isabelle, to no avail.

Monet lit a cigarette and held forth on his childhood in Le Havre. "My father managed my uncle's maritime grocery business just down the dock from where we are now. He wanted me to follow him into the business of supplying ships for long voyages."

Jean-Pierre spoke up with a hint of sarcasm in his voice. "Does that mean that you could have had a nice prosperous life as a grocer instead of a starving artist?"

"I would have hated the restrictions and the boredom of business. I left school before graduating so I could devote myself full time to drawing caricatures of prominent citizens." He drew some quick strokes with a pen and created a caricature of the *maître d'* on his napkin that he handed to the waiter after his guests had seen it. The *maître d'* came to the table and thanked Monet.

"Was there any money in that?" Jean-Pierre asked.

"I sold them in a local framing shop. In a year, I saved enough money to fund my first visit to Paris."

Isabelle looked straight into his eyes. "Why did you stop doing something you enjoyed that was so successful?"

"It was all Eugene Boudin's fault." Monet smiled. "He saw my caricatures and said I could do much better painting seascapes. He taught me what painting could be. I never returned to caricature drawings after that."

Isabelle perked up at hearing this. "Do you mean you started by painting, not by pencil drawing as they taught us at the Sorbonne?"

"*Oui*, he taught me to use pastels and oils from the beginning." Before Monet crushed out his first cigarette, he used it to start the next one. All three of his stepdaughters waved their hands to fan the smoke away from their faces. "That first summer, I exhibited in a show at Honfleur, the town we'll visit after lunch. My father didn't think Boudin was a suitable teacher for me, but I didn't care. I was learning so much at the age of seventeen."

"That's young to be in a show," Isabelle said, looking surprised.

"I was ambitious. Soon after, I was off to Paris to visit the Salon exhibition," Monet said as he gestured to the waiter for more wine.

"Didn't you just love the art of France on display there?" Isabelle asked.

"No. I didn't find much that I cared for at the Salon. It was all too much of the same uninspired classical nonsense," Monet said with a scowl.

Isabelle looked shocked at Monet's reaction to the revered painters of the Salon.

Marthe tried to be positive by asking, "Didn't you find anything you liked?" She sounded hopeful.

"I admired the work of Constant Troyon, so I took two of my paintings to his studio to show him." Monet seemed proud of this bold action.

"That's forward, even for someone like me," Isabelle said.

"I loved his studio. It had great northern exposure and smelled of oil paints. It made me want to move to Paris, so I could have a studio to paint in." A look of nostalgia crossed his face.

Germaine spilled a drop of wine on her new dress. "I'm sure your mother said you were much too young to be on your own in Paris. Isn't that right, Lily?"

She started dabbing at the spot with her napkin, dipped it into her glass of water to aid in her attempt.

Lily just shook her head at her aunt. Oscar could tell that this was an ongoing family argument that she didn't care to engage in.

"My mother died when I was quite young, so no, we did not discuss such things," Isabelle snapped at Germaine.

"Did Troyon give you any advice?" Isabelle asked Monet.

"No. Troyon recommended that I study figure drawing and enter an established studio to spend my time copying paintings at the Louvre. The same advice I heard from an artist uncle of mine."

"That's how I learned. Is this how you were taught painting?" Isabelle asked.

"No. That wasn't for me," Monet snapped. "I couldn't follow the rules of painting any more than I could follow the rules of the school or the grocery business."

"Sounds like you were stubborn even then," Germaine said, still blotting the wine spot, which was growing more prominent the more water she added.

"Only around you, my daughter with the big wine spot. After lunch, we'll travel to some of the areas on the coast where I painted."

Germaine fumed in silence.

"How exciting." Isabelle jumped up from the table.

"I said after lunch." Monet looked irritated. "We haven't had our coffee yet. Please sit down."

Germaine looked up from her wine spot repair, and Blanche shook her head in resignation. Oscar tried not to notice or at least be seen to have heard.

When lunch was over, the group took a stroll along the dockside and then assembled back by the vehicles. This time, Isabelle grabbed Oscar's arm and wouldn't let go.

Monet looked peeved that Isabelle was taking charge. He joined his daughters in the other vehicle, leaving the couple to travel with Jean-Pierre and Lily.

They left Le Havre and traveled south along the coast on their way to Honfleur, through fishing villages with nets drying in the waning sun. When they stopped at one of the beaches where Monet had painted in his youth, Oscar tried to impress Isabelle.

"This cliff and the rocky shore remind me of the Pacific coast south of San Francisco. The meeting of the sea and the rocks is re-markable."

To his chagrin, she ignored his effort.

"I agree. The beauty and power are staggering," Monet replied. "I remember one time when I was so intent on painting the waves washing against the rocks, I forgot to watch the rise of the tides."

"Did you get wet?" Isabelle asked with a voice of concern.

"Soaked! I almost lost my paintings, brushes, and paints, not to mention my life. I never made that mistake again." Monet chuckled at his foolishness.

"The cliffs are fascinating," Oscar said as the group looked up to see the rocks covered with colorful moss and lichen.

"I'm sorry we can't go up there today. The wildflowers are so lovely against the background of the long green grasses in the spring, and the clouds are in constant motion, creating a scene that I loved painting. I painted quite a few scenes there with my favorite model, your sister, Suzanne," Monet said.

Blanche and her sisters brushed back tears as Marthe said, "It's tragic that we lost her so early."

No one mentioned how she'd died.

"I'm sure you must have painted those lovely flowers and blos-soming trees," Isabelle said as she stared up at the cliff just as a wave came up to the ankle of her right boot. Oscar tried but failed to rescue her. She just laughed.

"I did. One time, I was painting a beautiful bare tree in a small val-ley, which I could not complete in one day. I came back a few days later to finish, and the tree had come into full leaf," Monet said as he waved his arms in exasperation.

"Whatever did you do?" Isabelle asked while drying off her boot with Oscar's handkerchief.

"The only thing I could do. I hired two farmers to strip all the new leaves from the tree. I finished it before I left it again."

"Next stop, *Le Cheval Blanc* in Honfleur," Blanche announced to the group. "We will spend the night there. They serve an excellent dinner."

The vehicles shuddered and started.

"It must be the moisture from the sea air that makes them hard to start," Oscar said. Jean-Pierre nodded.

They were off to their destination for dinner and a good night's rest.

He needed both.

Upon arrival, Blanche began directing the porters where to take which bags—Monet's to one suite, Blanche's and her two sisters' to the other suite. Oscar learned he was to share a room with Jean-Pierre. Lily smiled at Isabelle as they were assigned to share another. Germaine looked triumphant.

Oscar was relieved to be sharing a room with someone.

Isabelle did not seem pleased.

Everyone headed off to their rooms to dress for dinner once Blanche had checked them in and given them their keys.

Oscar returned to the lobby first as he only had one suit. No significant change was required. He had washed up and put on a clean shirt and arrived early so he could be in a splendid position to watch as the others came down. After surveying the lobby with its leather sofas and wingback chairs, he chose one positioned so he could enjoy seeing the others descending the grand curved staircase into the white and gray marble of the lobby. The crystal, gas-light chandelier cast a warm glow over all beneath it. This would be a highly complementary light for the ladies' dresses and sun-kissed complexions. His mother had taught him to appreciate the beauty of building interiors and how people interacted with them.

Monet and Jean-Pierre were the first to descend as they chatted on their way down. Blanche arrived next in her new pink linen dress with embroidered white silk flowers that he'd seen at Cosette's shop. She looked lovely and apprehensive as she hurried off to the kitchen to check on the dinner preparations.

The next ones to arrive were Germaine and Marthe, with Lily a few steps behind. They also wore lovely gowns of pastel shades of pink and yellow. Lily had on a blue silk dress shorter than her mother's but not as brief as Isabelle's outfit had been several days before. Blanche emerged from the kitchen, followed by two waiters, one with aperitifs and the other with *hors d'oeuvres*.

Oscar was about to rise from his chair and join the group when Germaine let out a massive gasp as she swooned on a nearby couch. All eyes turned toward her and then to the staircase where she pointed. Isabelle posed in a very, very short dress of red sequins.

Oscar overheard Germaine ask Lily, who was fanning her, to describe Isabelle's outfit since she was too faint to take it in.

"Aunt, the dress has a body-skimming fit down to her thighs, with a scoop neck and shoulder straps," Lily said in a low voice. "The tiered fringe reaches her knees. She's wearing black net stockings and matching red sequined shoes and a hairband. I don't believe she is wearing any...."

She whispered in her ear, and he couldn't hear the rest, but his imagination filled in the blank. Germaine sighed and continued to ask Lily to fan her. Blanche and Marthe grimaced and turned away from Germaine to see what Isabelle would do next. Monet smiled and picked a prime position to enjoy her fashion show.

Oscar was relieved he hadn't gotten up from his chair or taken a glass of wine. He could not have remained standing with a drink in his hand without spilling it on his new shirt. He barely remembered to breathe as Isabelle made her way toward him. After giving him a long, up-close view complete with a twirl, she pulled him to his feet and against her body for a passionate kiss. All he could do was hold on for the ride and try to remember to breathe.

The call to dinner came too soon after her entrance. Isabelle grabbed Monet's arm with her left hand and Oscar's with her right as she breezed into dinner escorted by her two conquests. He could hear Germaine fuming to Marthe behind him. Jean-Pierre and Lily were whispering about Isabelle's dress. Blanche had disappeared into the dining room ahead of them, saying, "I want to rearrange the seating cards to allow Isabelle and Oscar to sit on either side of Monet. They will sit there anyway; I might as well make it official. They want to monopolize Monet's attention."

When everyone had found their seats, Monet rose with his glass for a toast. "Please raise your glasses in a toast to my lovely daughter, Blanche. When my beloved Alice died, I was lost. It took me two years to recover and begin painting once again. If it weren't for Blanche, I don't know if I would ever have picked up a brush again. My passion for painting had drained from my body, and Blanche brought me back. Through her kind ministrations, I rejoined the living and painted once more. Now she's doing so much for our entire family and me. She organized this outing so I could revisit my favorite places one last time. Please join me in celebrating our dear Blanche. *Santé.*"

A chorus of *Santé* rang out from those around the table. Smiles of appreciation and a few tears came from all. Blanche looked embarrassed at the compliments and seemed relieved when the first course arrived.

Oscar looked around at the venue and its table decorations as the others chatted about the dinner and their journey. Anything to keep from staring at Isabelle. They'd hung the small banquet room with another large crystal chandelier matching the one in the lobby. The walls were paneled in polished dark-red mahogany. The floor was also of smooth white and gray marble with a large red and blue Persian rug under the round table. The etched-glass crystal and polished silverware complemented the china, likely from Limoges. Nothing but the best here. At least that's what Oscar overheard Blanche saying. It was a perfect *Belle Époque* era setting for the guests dressed in the same style. All except Isabelle.

He noticed the painting over the fireplace behind Monet.

"*Monsieur.* Is that painting above the fireplace one of yours?" he asked.

Monet slid his chair back from the table, lit a cigarette, and took a sip of wine before replying. "*Oui.* I got an idea to paint popular tourist locations from the Japanese artist Hiroshige, so I came here to paint some seascapes visited by tourists from Paris. I thought they would sell well."

"I remember that time," Marthe said. "We had moved from our beautiful country estate to a house you'd rented for your wife Camille and the boys. Father had lost everything, including all of our mother's fortune. We had no money and little food. You took us in and fed us."

Blanche and Germaine nodded in agreement. Both looked sad and angry.

"It was a tough time for all of us. Your father, who collected many of my paintings, had to auction them off. Camille was ill from childbirth. We had no money, and my paintings were not selling for much money on the rare occasions when someone bought one," Monet said as if this had opened an old wound.

"I don't know how we survived," Blanche said. "You had eight extra mouths to feed, and two of them, Jean and Jean-Pierre, were infants."

"Your mother took care of the boys and Camille. I went off to paint scenes that would sell and bring in some money. That brings me to this painting. I had no money to pay for room and board while I was here painting, so I traded this painting for it."

"So you were you staying in this fine hotel while we were starving?" Germaine asked.

Monet frowned at her accusation. "No. I stayed at a small, cheap boarding house. They must have sold the painting to this hotel."

Blanche smiled. "That's one reason I chose this hotel. I wanted you to see his work in a most charming setting."

Isabelle spoke up. "Did your plan work?"

"*Oui.* I met Gustave Geffroy while here."

Her face lit up. "Wasn't Gustave the first critic to support your work? At the Sorbonne, we learned that he started praising the seascapes just after meeting you by chance on this coast. Didn't you meet at dinner?"

"*Oui* and *oui.*" Monet grinned. "So now the Sorbonne is teaching about me. I can't believe it after all these years of ignoring my work. *Très bien.*"

Oscar noticed that Monet's children, except Germaine, and grandchild, Lily, smiled at him as the man who'd helped them conquer such troubling times.

"Most of the time that I painted here, I endured icy winds and rain or the sea spray, sometimes both at once. In those days, the weather didn't matter to me. I could paint for hours and not even notice the cold and dampness. I was young and so dedicated to my work and providing for the family."

Isabelle, as usual, was the one to engage him in this discussion. The others listened to the discourse. Most seemed to have heard the stories before. However, Lily was on the edge of her seat, enthralled at hearing the stories. It was clear from her face that she loved her grandfather despite his gruff nature.

"How could you not mind the weather?" Isabelle asked with an involuntary shiver.

"The weather was not important to me. All that mattered was the light. The clouds, winds, rains, waves, and the sun were all part of how the light affected the scene. When the light changed, I moved on.

Years later, I hired a local man, Pauley, who helped me move my canvases and pointed out local spots with scenes I might like to paint. He was such a help that I painted his portrait to immortalize his service."

"Did you give him the painting?" Jean-Pierre asked.

"No. Why should I? I paid him for his work, and the painting was too good. I sold it much later. It fetched a good price."

"*Très bien.* I'm sure we could have used the money," Jean-Pierre said with a hint of bitterness.

Oscar was upset to think that Jean-Pierre showed more interest in money than art or kindness. Perhaps he'd been hardened by the times of poverty experienced at an early age. Oscar thought back to the times when they had little food and no money. He wished there'd been a father then to provide for their family.

Their group conversation went on for what seemed like hours. Oscar didn't know what the rest of the night would bring. He felt fortunate to have Jean-Pierre as his roommate to protect him. Isabelle was a force he couldn't resist, and he doubted he could summon the energy to try.

Riding in the open vehicle, strolling along the sea, and sitting close to Isabelle brought a rosy glow to his cheeks. His chest was tight from inhaling Monet's cigarette smoke and her scent for hours. Monet and Isabelle seemed to enjoy each other, so he slipped away to his room. As he climbed the stairs, he didn't like the mix of emotions he was experiencing. He wasn't sure if he was jealous of Monet or Isabelle or both.

Chapter 7 – Honfleur Rumors

Oscar was sitting in the wingback chair by the window in his darkened hotel room, watching the boats bobbing in the shallow waves by the dock and waiting for Jean-Pierre to return. With its woven wool fabric, the chair brought warmth and comfort to his body, like snuggling in an old blanket. The drive and the constant interaction with the 'family' had sapped all his energy. He was used to a quiet life working for Monet. Dealing with Isabelle had been a challenge that had proven way too much for him. The day wasn't over yet. He knew it but couldn't resist the opportunity to spend more time with her. She brought a lovely warmth to his body and heart. He waited for the unknown, but not for long.

His mind was swirling with a myriad of questions. Why was he here? Why did he put up with a grouchy old man and his family? Would he even want to be part of this group? Perhaps he should return to San Francisco and forget all about the quest to find his father. It would be so much easier for him to forget about this adventure and return to his life surrounded by flowers, not family. It would be much less complicated.

The door burst open, and Jean-Pierre bounced in, followed by Isabelle and Lily, all a little tipsy and talking at once about the evening ahead.

"Get up. You're coming with us," Jean-Pierre announced.

Oscar gritted his teeth. "What? Where to? I'm too tired to go out. Jean-Pierre, why don't you go without me? You'll have more fun."

"I'm taking us out dancing. There's a new jazz club that just opened. It's the latest music from America. Perhaps you've heard of jazz before."

"I don't dance," he said, unmoving. "Besides, I don't like that kind of music."

"You will tonight," Isabelle insisted as she pulled him to his feet. "I need a dancing partner, and you're it. Come on, let's go."

He felt helpless as he took his time putting on his shoes and, rising from the chair, resigned to his fate. And what luck, going dancing with two lovely ladies. Come to your senses, he thought to himself. This was every soldier's dream, going out drinking and dancing with a beautiful girl. At least, that's what they'd fantasized about in the trenches. He felt lucky to have survived the war in one piece, even though the gas attack, explosions, and bullets had left him shell-shocked and with weakened lungs. Now he must have fun for those who didn't get the chance.

He joined the trio as they strolled down the street to Jazzmatazz, the best late-night entertainment Honfleur had to offer for Parisian visitors. They entered the door, and Isabelle grabbed his hand and pulled him onto the dance floor. The loud music and close, smoky quarters made his head swim and his chest hurt.

Instead of one of those new flapper dances, the band changed to a slow number he could handle. She pressed her body so tightly against his that he almost fell into a Germaine-like swoon. He'd never danced so well nor so close to his partner. His body had never felt so warm, from his ears to his toes and some private parts in between.

He was surrendering himself to the pleasure of her body pressed against his when the song ended. The band broke into what Isabelle called the Charleston. He delivered his companion to Lily, who seemed to know the same dance steps as Isabelle, and joined Jean-Pierre at their table. They both drank brandy and watched the ladies entertain themselves and the crowd.

As he listened to the music, he tapped his foot to the rhythm. It reached inside him and brought out a feeling he hadn't experienced in years. Was this some of the *joie de vivre* he thought he'd lost on the battlefield of the Meuse-Argonne? Was he coming back to life thanks to the music, or was Isabelle doing this to him? For him?

Jean-Pierre leaned closer to see more of his face. "Oscar, are you well? You look a little pale."

He held his hands over his face, shutting out all light. This was a trick he'd taught himself while at the front to help him shut out the world and concentrate. "Isabelle has that effect on me. I can't get enough air when I am around her. When I do breathe, I inhale her scent, and it makes me lightheaded."

Jean-Pierre laughed so hard, he turned away to keep from spitting his drink in Oscar's face. "You must be in love or lust. Neither one is fatal, but it could make you feel ill. Enjoy yourself."

He slapped Oscar's back, and, in the moment's exhilaration, Oscar felt the comradeship with Jean-Pierre that he'd left behind in the trenches.

He couldn't resist dancing the following few slow dances with Isabelle despite Lily's efforts to keep them apart. He danced her around the dingy room with its well-worn wooden dance floor that had lived another, rougher life. The hall was not large, and with its low ceilings and well-used and abused tables and chairs, it reminded him of some of the juke joints he visited in San Francisco's Filmore district. The band, clustered together on the small stage, seemed adept at their instruments. Two of them were Black musicians from America. The cloud of cigarette smoke drifted lower and lower over the dancers. As soon as Isabelle and Lily hit the floor for a foxtrot, he escaped the smoky haze through the French doors onto the terrace.

He found a quiet table next to the railing within sight of the dancers. Sitting with his glass of brandy and watching Isabelle on the dance floor was a great alternative to the crowded room. The harbor ships were rhythmically rocking into each other, as were the loving couples out for a stroll.

Just as he tilted his head back to look at the stars in the clear night sky, Isabelle's face popped into view above him, her heavenly ruby lips coming in for a kiss and her firm breasts caressing his head. He first thought to keep the chair from tipping over backward, but he no longer cared. A kiss from those lips would be worth it.

She kissed him and then let him right himself up and admonished him. "Again, why did you tell Blanche and her sisters I'm a dangerous flirt?"

He panicked. "I ... I only told Blanche. She must have told the others."

"What did you tell her about me?" Her face flushed, her nostrils flared as she placed her hands on her hips. She looked like an avenging Valkyrie.

"It wasn't about you," he said in protest, defending his actions. "It was about my mother. She was a flirt. Men flocked to her but never seemed to stay for long. Neither did my father. He never married her." He was gasping for breath after the smoke, her kiss, and the verbal assault. "There were a few 'uncles' from time to time, but no one permanent. I wouldn't wish that life on any child. Besides, what would Monet think of me if I had an affair with you?"

Now Isabelle looked offended. She flung herself into a chair. "First, I'm not offering to have an affair with you. Second, even if I am a flirt, it doesn't mean I'll have a child and subject it to what you lived through. Third, you don't know what Monet would think after what he's done."

"What do you mean by 'what he's done'?" Intrigued, Oscar jumped at the chance to change the subject away from himself.

"I heard rumors about him while I attended the Sorbonne that you probably haven't heard," she said with a look of triumph.

"What are you talking about?" Her superiority irritated him.

"Never mind. I heard vicious rumors from some students," she said as she retreated from the topic.

"Not so quick. You insinuated something about this great man, and you need to either apologize or explain yourself."

"He got his model, Camille, pregnant." She turned away to signal an end to the discussion. "There! Now you have it. Now let's not discuss this anymore. Get me a drink."

"I'm sure there is something more that you aren't telling me. Out with it."

"She had his child, but his father refused to support him if he married her. He left her to care for the baby with no support from him while he went to London to paint and avoid the draft. He didn't marry her until a few years later. Now, about that drink. I'm thirsty. Make it white wine." From her expression, he could tell she was tired of this discussion.

"At least he married her," Oscar said. "That's not so bad. It's more than my father did."

Although Isabelle was reluctant, she continued with her story. "He brought Alice Hoschedé and her passel of kids to live with them. All the while, Camille was recovering from the birth of their second child."

"That was a kind thing to do," he said in defense of Monet.

"Let's leave it at that," she pleaded. "I'm thirsty!"

"Are you saying that's the end of the story?" He took a sip of his drink. "None of that is so bad. It would still disappoint him if I had an affair with you."

She grabbed his glass and drained it. "Get it through your thick skull that I'm not having an affair with you. Not if you were the last man on earth." Tears of frustration rolled down her face as she turned to face the ships in the harbor.

Her tears melted his anger. He wanted to hold her in his arms and kiss them away. "I'm so sorry," he apologized. "I didn't mean to upset you and don't think Monet deserves these ugly rumors being told about him. He's a great and decent man."

"You're right. Monet is a wonderful person and an artistic genius. But that doesn't mean that he can't also be human and perhaps make mistakes. Or do things that people think are wrong but are right for him and the other parties involved. You're so provincial."

He was incensed at being classified as a rube. "I may be provincial, but I can't believe he would do anything worthy of such rumors. I can't believe he'd father a child and leave the mother to raise it on her own as my father did."

"Perhaps, but there was more to this situation. I've heard rumors that Monet may have been the father of Alice's last child, Jean-Pierre, while she was still living with her husband. Later, Alice left her husband and moved in with Monet. Alice even took care of Camille while she lay dying, and Monet was gone painting in London most of the time. He married Alice three years after Camille died and a year after her husband, Ernst, died."

"No. No. No. I don't believe it. I won't believe these cruel rumors." He felt his face getting flushed and his heart pounding as he gasped for breath. He kept shaking his head from side to side in disbelief. "He can't have done what mine did to me—father a child with a woman he didn't marry. Why would a decent man do that to his son?"

Isabelle took his head in her hands and drew him to her breast. "I didn't mean to upset you. I wanted you to understand that our involvement wouldn't upset him. How could it? What we're doing or thinking of doing would be acceptable in his eyes. After all, it is what he did when Camile got pregnant with Jean. It took Monet two years to marry her."

She combed his hair with her fingers, the way his mother did when he was upset.

"You don't understand. How could you understand what this means to me?" He turned away so she wouldn't see his tears of frustration and disappointment. His hands trembled as he reached up to brush them away. How could he love and hate a father he never knew? His fantasy of a loving, trustworthy father came crashing down on him. He desperately needed time to sort this out.

"What's with you two?" Jean-Pierre interrupted their whispered conversation. "Are you ready to head back to the hotel? Lily has worn me out."

"We're just having a deep discussion about how much Oscar loves me," Isabelle blurted.

"It's no wonder with the outfit you're wearing. Be gentle with this poor man. He was a war hero, you know." Jean-Pierre stepped back, weaved from side to side, and saluted.

Oscar turned back to face them and felt his face getting hot.

Isabelle looked at him as if confirming her suspicions. "Oscar, why didn't you tell me?"

Their previous conversation seemed forgotten for now, by her at least.

Jean-Pierre came to his defense. "A genuine hero doesn't brag about such things."

Isabelle smiled and turned to look at him in awe. "What made you a hero?"

"Nothing. I don't want to talk about it," Oscar said.

"See what I mean?" said Jean-Pierre.

He got up and left the others standing there on the terrace, bewildered by this sudden reaction. The last thing he could hear was Lily urging them to go back to the hotel. Hurrying away, he arrived at the hotel before the others and headed straight to his bed. Jean-Pierre opened the door and fell into the room sometime later. Oscar pretended to be asleep.

He did eventually fall asleep for a few hours.

He rose before dawn and went down to the dock to watch the fishermen prepare their boats and nets. He sat a long time in the cool sea air, watching the sky turn from pale yellow to the soft pink of a winter sunrise. He was mulling over the events of the previous night and the shocking rumors Isabelle had told him. His wool suit jacket kept him somewhat warm, but his eyes still watered from the cold and his disappointment of the night before.

It was a mistake coming on this trip and an even greater error coming to work for Monet. The family has been very kind and generous to me, but I don't belong here. I certainly don't deserve to be involved with a beautiful woman like Isabelle. She is above my class. Now Jean-Pierre has told her about my time at the front. I don't want to talk about it. I never should have let that old mustached bastard talk me into coming to work for Monet. I should have gone straight back to San Francisco. I don't belong here.

He sat by the sea, lost in thought, and missed breakfast on purpose. The crisp sea air did wonders to help him clear his mind. Blanche sent a search party out, Lily said when she found him. She looked lovely, dressed in a simple, pink dress with a dark wool sweater pulled tight against the morning chill.

"I'm glad you came to fetch me," he said. "I've been watching the fishermen and lost all track of time."

He didn't feel good about starting the day off hiding his feelings about the night before.

Lily ignored the apparent lie. "We're ready to load up the vehicles for our return trip. Aunt Blanche thought it best for you to ride with us. Isabelle will ride with Jean-Pierre and Monet."

"Fine. If Blanche feels that's best," he said with resignation.

Lily put her arm in his and guided him to the vehicles. He felt so much better in her care. His heart warmed with her caring for him and holding his arm.

The group started getting into the vehicles once they saw that he'd been found. Jean-Pierre carried Oscar's bag and his own. Even Isabelle wore a short but not too short dress, a floral print caught up at the waist with a large white bow under a wool sweater. Blanche and her sisters wore beautiful pastel dresses, but not as impressive as on the day before. The group was subdued after the late dinner and an evening of drinking and dancing for some.

Oscar relaxed in the vehicle's front seat with the ladies following Jean-Pierre, in the lead, out of town down the same road back along the Seine. The sun felt good on his face as he leaned into the wind. The trees and fields looked lonely with bare branches and expanses of untilled fields along the roadside. Blanche and her sisters were discussing the dinner of the previous evening, its ingredients, and its preparation.

"The sauce on the poached salmon was divine," she said.

"I think the spring vegetables were prepared to perfection in the pastry shell," Marthe offered.

"Our dessert must have contained a dozen eggs and a pound of butter for each serving," Germaine complained.

"Speaking of food, I almost forgot. Oscar, here is a croissant I brought for breakfast since you didn't join us," Blanche added.

He nodded. "*Merci.*"

When he'd finished eating, he spoke. "If you don't mind my asking, were conditions during those early years as difficult as *Monsieur* portrayed last evening? I didn't realize it."

"*Oui*, we've come a long way in the past twenty years," Marthe said with a smile as she recounted some of the trials they'd been through. "Monet worked so hard to keep us fed and clothed. He fought the men who controlled the Salon to have his art accepted by the critics and sold to patrons."

"Our deadbeat father lost all of his family's money, and our mother's," Germaine said.

She sighed and looked at Oscar as if all men should bear the sins of her father. "It was such an elegant estate with an enormous stone house and vast gardens where we played as children. Guests came from all over to attend our parties. Artists stayed for weeks painting portraits and landscapes."

"Monet even used our tame turkeys as models for one of his paintings," Marthe added. "If he'd not taken us in, I'm not sure what would have become of us."

"We lived in several rental houses in villages like Vetheuil, Argenteuil, and Poissy," Blanche added. "Each one along the Seine had a lovely garden, which Monet painted with us as his models. They were very trying times, but happy ones."

"I remember the first time we saw our house in Giverny, *Le Pres-*

soir," Marthe said. "The gardens were so lovely. Little did I know then that we would spend the next years hand-watering all those flowers and the many more that he planted!"

Oscar turned in his seat. "Did *Monsieur* do a lot of traveling like to Le Havre to paint different settings? I'm sure his trips would have been hard on the family."

"*Mon Dieu*. Did he ever," Blanche answered. "He painted in England, Holland, Norway, and Italy outside of France. He painted in many different places in France, from Normandy to Antibes in the south, to Paris, Fontainebleau, and villages all along the Seine. Our Monet was quite the traveler and would be away painting for weeks and months at a time."

"Antibes?" Oscar asked. "That's where I was born."

"*Oui*. He went there to paint with Renoir and then returned to paint on his own for more than a month. He said Renoir distracted him from his work," Marthe said with a quizzical look. "That was odd since he and Renoir had painted side-by-side ever since they'd met as young men at a studio in Paris."

Oscar remembered his mother gardening in and around Antibes as a young woman. She'd moved from her home in Lyon to work in that glorious southern climate of the gardens along the coast. She mentioned that the Impressionists worked there to take advantage of the light. "Do you remember when he painted in Antibes?"

"It must have been the summer of 1888. I remember it was around the time our mother was battling with Father," Marthe said. "I remember she was so angry with Monet for being away so long in Antibes. She was worried that he couldn't make up his mind to marry her or not. Not an easy time for us."

Oscar turned to sit forward in the front seat and fell into musing about his mother as he watched the fields flow by his window in a haze.

What would it have been like for me if he'd married my mother instead of theirs? I might have been raised in France instead of San

Francisco. Would life have been more comfortable for me to live with a father and a mother? Would I get along with my two half-brothers? Times would have still been hard for us and doubly hard for Alice and her passel of kids.

The lead vehicle stopped in front of Isabelle's house in the late morning. Isabelle said her goodbyes to Monet and Jean-Pierre and then moved back to the second vehicle and thanked Blanche for inviting her on this journey. She said *à bientôt* to the sisters and Lily, then moved to the vehicle's front door to bid farewell to him.

Oscar opened the door and joined her on the street. "I'll walk home from here. *Merci beaucoup* for inviting me on this interesting visit to the coast. I'll see you tomorrow."

He closed the door and took his bag from Sylvain.

Isabelle took his left hand that held the bag as he waved farewell with his right. She brought her bag into the house and returned to sit beside him on the front porch swing to talk.

"I feel I must apologize for upsetting you last evening," she said with a pouty look.

Oscar pushed the swing with his feet as he planned a response. "That isn't necessary. I'm sure you believe what you told me was the truth as far as you know. The other upsetting part was that you asked me about my role in the Great War. I'm not ready to talk about that part of my life just now. Perhaps later. But not now."

"I spent enough time as a nurse to men from the front to understand what you mean. I won't pry."

They sat in silence for a few minutes before he picked up his worn brown leather bag and rose to leave.

"There is one other thing that is upsetting me. On the ride back, I learned that Monet and Renoir were painting together in Antibes the year before I was born. Perhaps Renoir met my mother and knows who my father is. I must ask him about that time. Now I must go."

"Wait. Don't go," Isabelle pleaded. "I want to make sure you're not upset. I do care about you, despite what I said last night. Can you for-give me for that, at least?"

"I'm not sure I want to," he said with a smile. "I'm not used to having beautiful women play with my emotions. If you want to have an honest relationship, let's start with honesty. If you just want to flirt with someone, please move on to someone else." He was proud that he could be so honest but terrified that she would turn away from him.

Isabelle closed her eyes and lowered her head. Then she raised her chin to stare straight into his eyes. "If that is how it is, then let's have an honest relationship. If we are to be friends, I must be honest. You need to know that intimacy will be part of our relationship. There's nothing wrong with Monet's relationships. It's part of his life and loves. The same goes for you and me. That's what I've been try-ing to explain to you. The rumors are vile because they invade his privacy. Not because he was wrong to be doing what he did."

"But there are consequences to such relationships. People can get hurt. Careless affairs can ruin lives," he said with all the sincerity he could muster. "Look at what happened to me. I was raised without knowing my father. That's a consequence that I wouldn't wish on an-yone."

"You're right. People are hurt, but not so much by the affair as the lack of honesty that ruins lives. Not love."

Oscar felt both relieved and upset at her words. "Let's start with friendship and then see where that goes. I need a good friend just now more than anything."

He leaned over to kiss her on the cheek as a friend, but she stood up and turned her face to kiss him full on the lips like a lover. Rather than withdrawing, this time, he leaned in and kissed her back. So much for having a simple friendship. He was not getting what he asked for, but what he really wanted and needed.

With that, he tore himself from her arms, retreated down the front steps, and only turned back when he had reached the front gate. As he raised his hand to wave, she blew him a kiss and added a look of longing for good measure. Her pink tongue caressed her lips. He gripped the gate tightly to keep himself from returning to kiss those lips.

"Yes, a force to be reckoned with," he mumbled to himself on his walk back to Giverny.

The sun was shining, the birds were singing, and he whistled a tune for the first time in years.

Chapter 8 – Pierre-Auguste Renoir

Oscar strolled to work at a slower than usual pace on Monday following the journey. He had something on his mind, besides Isabelle, that he needed to talk over with Blanche. He asked her in the kitchen if he could speak to her at the end of the day.

Since he had arrived in Giverny, Monet had complained about his eyesight and his difficulty painting the way he saw his subjects in the colors reflected by the light. The light was everything, and the colors were not what he thought they should be. He moved from place to place as he always had because the light changed, but now, he could no longer trust his diminishing eyesight.

"Oscar, let's move on to the next location. I can't seem to get the colors right. My eyesight is still acting up. It's like I see through fog with the colors distorted."

Oscar felt that soon Monet's eyes needed to be addressed. It would be impossible for a man who depended on his eyes to create his art.

As he approached the porch at the end of the day, he noticed the pear trees needed to be trimmed before they started to leaf out. But even the lovely trees couldn't overcome his depression over Monet's health.

"*Madame*, is there anything that we can do for *Monsieur* Monet's eyesight? It seems to be hindering his work. Even with that, he seemed to smile more today."

"We are working on the eyes. Not the smiling," Blanche said with a chuckle. "The eyes have been a troublesome issue for some time.

Thanks for asking, but don't concern yourself about it just now. Please inform me if you notice anything unusual occurring regarding his sight. He is resisting the surgery he needs. As for the smiling, you'd better ask Isabelle about that."

Blanche said, "I need to request a great favor of you. I realize this is a lot to ask, but we need your help."

"Anything, *Madame*. Just name it."

"Monet would like you to visit his friend Renoir, who lives in the south near Nice. It's a long way and will take several days' journey by train."

Oscar was overwhelmed with the opportunity to meet Renoir, one of the painters that his mother had mentioned meeting in the south. Perhaps he would know something of his father. "I'd love to go, *Madame*. But I have my work here to do."

"Monet and I have discussed the issue, and I'll return to helping him with his paintings until you are back. I'm afraid this is an emergency." Her voice trembled as she, too, gripped the railing. "Our dear friend is dying," she said as tears ran down her cheeks. "Monet doesn't have the strength to make the arduous journey to the south. We need you to take him something very personal that can't be sent by the *Poste*. Can you do this for us?"

"*Oui*," Oscar replied as he bowed his head in sadness and respect. "I promise, I'll do anything for you and the *Monsieur*. You have treated me so well, and I'm most happy to do anything to assist you."

He couldn't be more honored than to have Monet trust him with such a critical mission to his friend Renoir.

"Oscar, there is one other thing. Monet told his plan to Isabelle on the ride home yesterday. She insists on accompanying you on the trip," she said with a touch of irritation in her voice. "I'm sure you understand that it would be a great honor for a young artist like her to meet such a master. We realize it's an unusual request since there would be no chaperone. If it's too much of a burden for you, I'll tell her she can't accompany you."

This news knocked him back again. It irritated him that Isabelle was intruding on his urgent mission and caused his heart to race at the thought of staring at those long, beautiful legs for days on such a journey. Who knows what dress she'd wear? He turned away from Blanche, pretending to look over the garden as he spent a few moments gathering his thoughts. Traveling with Isabelle would be delightful, but it had so many complications. These could be more than he'd care to deal with. How could he pass up the opportunity to kiss those ruby-red lips and press her body against his? He gripped the handrail tighter.

"She can come along. But please ask her to behave. If not, I'll send her back," Oscar said with conviction, although doubting such a thing would be possible. He could always tease her with this threat if need be.

"*Très bien*. I'll make the arrangements for you to leave next week. Monet will write to Renoir tonight. *Merci. Merci beaucoup*. What did you wish to speak to me about?"

"It's nothing important," he said. "We can speak of it when I return."

"The seamstress is altering another of Monet's suits for you to take on your trip."

"That's too kind of you."

"It's the least we can do. The suit will be ready at the end of this week." She turned to the table and picked up a package. "Here are some shoes to go with the suit."

Oscar nodded to Blanche in appreciation. He couldn't believe what had just happened. Blanche had granted his wish beyond his wildest dreams without his having to ask. He would meet Renoir and ask about his mother, and Monet would pay for the trip. The only worrisome part was traveling alone with Isabelle. He had no idea what that would mean, but he could just imagine the exciting trouble it would invite!

It was such a cold winter evening, but he took a long way home to contemplate the journey. The birds were chirping as they competed with the bats for the flocks of bugs that came out in the sunset hours. He roamed down by the river to enjoy the quiet around him. His thoughts of traveling south with Isabelle were buzzing in his head like insects as they started his heart racing and his palms sweating.

It was departure time before he knew it. Cosette delivered his suit, altered to his exact measurements. It was of the fine British wool like the previous one, and she'd tailored it to fit him. Though he was uncertain if Isabelle would approve of the style, he was eager to show it to her. She might like the soft gray color.

As with the first such delivery, it included three additional shirts. Oscar purchased his wool cap to match the suit. His old one couldn't measure up to this luxurious journey. He didn't understand what the train accommodations would be, second class or sleeper car. Either way was sufficient for him, but Isabelle would be more demanding.

Monet met him in the studio, where they discussed Renoir over a glass of *Calvados* in the waning light of the late afternoon. He took a drag on his cigarette and a sip of his drink before rising from the sofa. He fetched a parcel from his cluttered desk in the corner.

"I want you to take this letter and package to Renoir," he said as he handed Oscar an envelope and a rolled package. "Please ask him to read the letter before opening the package, or you can read it to him if his eyesight isn't good. Then, and only then, give him the package. Come back and tell me what he says. Exactly, word for word."

"I'll do as you request and try to remember everything he says."

Monet squinted through the cigarette smoke. "And everything he does."

"*Oui, Monsieur.*"

"Give him my love, and let him know how sorry I am that I can't be there in person. He's been one of my closest friends for over sixty years."

"I understand," Oscar said.

"I don't think you do. How could you?" Monet said with a sigh.

"We're the last of the Impressionists. We developed this novel way of painting when we were beginners, and now we're the last survivors of our group. I fear soon I'll be the last one standing. *Très tragique.*"

After lighting another cigarette, Monet sat down on the couch and drained his glass before pouring another for them both. His beard and hair seemed grayer, and his eyes less focused. He looked older as his sight turned inward.

"I'm sure he'll be happy to read your letter and receive your gift," Oscar said, trying to overcome his *faux pas* of saying he understood what this relationship with Renoir meant to Monet. "It will be my honor to convey your heartfelt wishes." Then he raised his glass to propose a toast. "To Renoir."

Monet raised his glass but was still looking at something that only he could see.

"*Santé. Merci beaucoup*, Oscar, for doing this for me," he said as he refilled his glass. "I realize it's not your job, but it means a great deal to me. I look forward to your report upon your return. Take all the time you need on the trip. Oh, and give my love to Isabelle."

Oscar gulped.

"I'm certain that Renoir will enjoy meeting her. He always liked the young ladies and always had more success with them than I did." Monet managed a slight smile at this remembrance of his dear friend's charm.

After finishing their drinks, Monet embraced Oscar. This first physical contact between the two brought tears to Oscar's eyes and a lump to his throat. Despite Isabelle's stories of him, he still felt proud to be his friend and would be even prouder to call him 'Father' if that should be the result of his quest. If his father turned out to be Renoir or another of the Impressionists, he would still admire and love Monet and his family.

Blanche bade farewell to Oscar with a kiss on each cheek. She handed him an envelope containing his train tickets and instructions on where to stay at his destination station and how to meet Renoir's driver. She had included money for him to pay for the trip.

"*À bientôt, mon cher.* You're doing a kind deed for Monet and Renoir. I hope you enjoy yourselves. I have sent word to Isabelle to meet you at her house at nine tomorrow. And I warned her to act like a proper young lady. Sylvain will pick you up at your door at eight-thirty. Have a safe journey. Take your time. We won't expect you until we see you."

Oscar felt like his mother was sending him on an errand. He was proud, honored, and anxious to be taking his first lengthy holiday in years. His stomach was tied in knots over having to take Isabelle with him. He had no way to get out of his promise, so he hurried home to pack. His new suit and shirts would make an excellent addition to his meager travel bag. What trouble would Isabelle cause? Traveling with her excited and worried him so much that sleeping that night proved impossible.

Sylvain arrived early, but Oscar had been on his porch for an hour already, waiting for the journey to begin. Having to make all the train connections made him nervous. He was concerned and excited by what Isabelle would wear on the overnight portion of the trip.

Sylvain drew up in front of Isabelle's house at nine and whisked them both off to the train station. Next stop, Paris, then Lyon, and finally Nice, and then a brief ride to Cagnes-sur-Mer. When they arrived at the Vernon station, Oscar helped Isabelle out of the vehicle. He hadn't noticed her outfit until this moment. She wore a loose-fitting beige dress that had a low scooped neck, as Lily would describe it. It had beaded embroidery, an uneven hem, and layers of netting and satin. He had to step back and ask her to open her coat so he could take it all in. He'd have the most beautifully dressed woman on the train sitting next to him. The two large bags Sylvain hauled from the back of the vehicle must contain many more surprises like this.

"Not that I'm complaining, but how am I going to carry all of your bags? We have several train transfers to manage."

"That's what porters are for, silly," she said.

Oscar shook his head. "Come on. Let's hurry."

Isabelle took his hand and sashayed into the train station. "I can't wait to show you what I brought for tonight."

Then she winked.

He glanced at her sideways, unable to speak or breathe. A warm glow that started in his loins grew into a blaze when it reached his cheeks. He struggled to keep his mind on the train and off the passenger by his side. He ached to have her seated next to him and feared it at the same time.

The rest of the day was a blur for Oscar. He could only think of the night ahead and try to keep his eyes open. He focused out the window at the miles of leafless grape vines followed by budding wheat fields with quaint villages scattered in between. That her warm body was between him and the window didn't make this easy. Blanche had booked first-class seats for them that converted into sleeping berths for the trip's overnight portion. He fell asleep on her shoulder and was about to miss their stop in Lyon. She kissed him awake just in time to gather their bags and hustle off one train and onto another. If this was what it was like sleeping next to her, he wanted more of her. His heart demanded more warmth, love, and trust.

The evening turned into night, and the porter rang the dinner chimes for their car. Isabelle had been in the bathroom for thirty minutes already and made him wait for another ten before she returned to his side. She wore her evening outfit.

"Oh, my, what a change," he said as she stepped into view. "I can't believe that such a lovely woman is having dinner with me. How could I be so fortunate?"

Isabelle wore a short black dress covered with sequins and a matching black hairband. A fringe on the bottom of the dress ended in long strands of black beads. Her beaded shoes matched. This time, her twirl was quite a sight. He gulped for air, took her arm, and off they went to dinner. This meal would lighten his money envelope's weight, as it was a champagne and caviar evening.

After dinner, they took a stroll through the train and out onto the rear platform to enjoy the crisp night air. The sky was clear, and the stars bright. She slipped her hand inside his jacket and pulled his body against hers. He could feel the sequins on her dress through his shirt. His heart pounded against her chest, and he could feel her firm breasts against his chest. Before he could take a breath, Isabelle kissed him so hard, it crushed his lips against his teeth. He felt faint, and she jumped back into another couple who tried to exit the door and join them on the platform.

He breathed. She sighed. The other couple gasped. It was all over in an instant, leaving him in a daze that nearly cost him his life as he lost his footing and landed against the railing. Oscar and Isabelle headed back to their car to find their separate berths made up for the night. He offered to take the top bunk, but she would have none of it and scampered up the ladder.

He lay in his berth, not knowing what would happen next while remembering the men who visited his mother for long weekends with mixed feelings. Should he, or shouldn't he? What would his mother say or do? Perhaps he should do the opposite of her. He didn't understand what to do about Isabelle. He didn't even know if she would give him a choice other than to fall off the back of the train. He'd already been there.

A few long minutes later, she was back down the ladder and through the curtains into his berth. He could see the outline of her breasts through her sheer silk chemise in the dim light. They were even more full and firm than he had imagined.

Isabelle kissed his face, his ears, and then his chest, pausing at each of his nipples for a nibble. As her lips moved down to his feet, every one of his erogenous zones was awakened along the way. He was about to lose all control when she slid back up the berth to lie on top of him. She took him inside her and moved in ways he'd not known for years. He tried to utter a protest, and she pushed her breast against his lips. The heat of her caresses brought him back to life for the first time since the war. He felt a deep urgency to say that her love had touched his very soul. He knew that it was possible to put the war behind him and rejoin humanity for the first time. Then he lost all sense of place and time. There was just pure, tumultuous love.

"No talking. Don't spoil the mood."

At long last, he took command of his role in their relationship. He slid on top of Isabelle and fell into the rhythm of the rocking train, moving inside her this way and that for what seemed like miles until he exploded. It brought her to the point of ecstasy and beyond. No one heard her cry out because, at that moment, a train came rushing by in the opposite direction. Fortunately, it was a long, slow, noisy freight.

They fell asleep in each other's arms and didn't stir until the pre-breakfast chime sounded. Isabelle slipped out of the curtained heaven and scampered back up the ladder to her berth. He had one last glimpse at her creamy thighs as she ascended. He stretched out, remembering what had happened the night before, and beamed as he mumbled, "Why did I resist her for so long?"

No answer proved forthcoming.

She joined him for breakfast in the same outfit as the day before. "I apologize for not wearing different clothes, but I was rushed." She blushed then.

He grabbed her hands and kissed each palm. He felt at ease placing his heart and fate in her hands. He trusted her with his life that she had helped him rediscover.

After breakfast, she cleaned up and changed into a more conservative maroon dress with tiered chiffon ruffles that reached below her knees. Oscar was too busy with maps, directions, and lips to notice her outfit at first. She got up and twirled, so he would appreciate the effect she sought. He held her gaze as she sat back down and couldn't seem to let go until they reached the station in Nice where they changed trains for Cagnes-sur-Mer.

They stepped down from the train onto the tiny station's platform and spotted a man with Oscar's name on a sign. He waved as he walked to meet them. After fetching their bags, he guided them to his waiting vehicle.

The ride through the medieval town of Cagnes-sur-Mer past ancient lanes, steps, and passageways was delightful. The narrow cobblestone streets separated two rows of houses built hundreds of years ago and painted the gay colors of the south. They even painted the wrought-iron balconies' railings blue, not black, and made them curved, not straight. The atmosphere appeared relaxed, with people sitting outdoors at tables with colorful umbrellas.

"Renoir came here in the 1890s, hoping the dry heat would ease his arthritis," the driver said. "In 1907, he built this house, *Les Collettes*, and has spent his life here since. Everyone here loves him, including me. I've worked for him since he arrived."

"*Monsieur*, Renoir is expecting you," was the response when the two travelers knocked on the massive blue front door set back into the creamy stucco wall at the end of the camel-colored flagstone walkway lined with mature olive trees with silver leaves. Renoir liked colorful surroundings as much as Monet.

Oscar took time to observe the grand entrance hall, decorated with flowers, before being ushered into Renoir's presence. Thinking of his mother, he hesitated before entering the room to meet Renoir. He knew that this encounter could very well end his quest to identify his father.

Renoir and Monet were his mother's favorite painters. She loved their work and the intensity with which they followed their beliefs in the new genre of art they had pioneered. She had referred to both often as examples of what she had hoped to become, a landscape artist who developed a new approach to creating lovely gardens. Oscar had such reverence for Renoir from his mother that he wasn't sure he should meet the great man in person, but he'd met Monet, and that was going well enough.

Isabelle pushed him forward through the door. He gathered his courage and footing just in time.

"*Bonjour, Monsieur* Renoir. I'm Oscar Bonhomme, and this is Isabelle Brescher."

Renoir turned to face Isabelle, ignoring Oscar as he spoke. "Ah, you're Dr. Brescher's charming daughter that I have heard so much about from my dear friend Monet. Welcome to my humble chateau."

Renoir, in his wheelchair, gestured with his contorted, arthritic hand for them to sit down. His gray beard and hair could not diminish the youthful charm in his voice and smiling eyes as he chatted with Isabelle. He was a man who liked beautiful young ladies, and they liked him.

He had covered the yellow-painted walls with artwork by himself and his friends. The room contained a bed hung with curtains, two chairs set in front of Renoir's wheelchair, and a small desk next to the window. He also had easels of various sizes scattered about. He kept other furnishings to a minimum to enable him to maneuver the wheelchair, Oscar assumed.

"Come and sit before the window," Renoir said to Isabelle. "I want to see you in the morning light." After studying her for a few moments, he said, "I'd like to sketch you, *Mademoiselle*."

Oscar was amazed that the crippled old man who sat before them could still think of creating and flirting. Isabelle was flattered beyond words. She did as he requested. A servant put a pencil in Renoir's hand. Oscar brought one of the easels close to support his sketch pad, which he used while talking. The servant brought them pastries, fruits, and juice while Renoir drew and chatted about his time painting and arguing with Monet.

When Renoir took a break from sketching, Oscar brought out the envelope and package from Monet. Renoir took the offerings and tried to open the envelope. Oscar opened it and handed the letter for him to read, which he did with some difficulty. When he'd finished, he laid it in his lap and laughed so hard, he fell over in his wheelchair.

He recovered his seat, and Oscar retrieved his checkered lap blanket and the letter, then opened the package, which contained a rolled-up painting. After unrolling it for him, he held it up for Renoir to see. This inspired another fit of laughter.

"That old dog," Renoir said with a warm smile. "I never knew he had it in him. Monet bested me at last. I never suspected he'd returned to Antibes after we'd traveled north. Please roll up the painting. You can admire it later." He gestured to Oscar for his pencil and continued sketching Isabelle, who looked surprised by these events. "Calm yourself, young lady. This won't hurt a bit."

"Are you all right, *Monsieur*?" Oscar asked as he examined Renoir's physical condition.

"I'm fine," Renoir responded as he adjusted his pencil in his hand using his teeth.

"*Monsieur*, Monet asked me to convey his heartfelt wish that he could be here in person," Oscar said with a pang of sadness at seeing the condition of the aging painter. He had fulfilled his mission. Now Oscar understood why Monet had sent him on this errand instead of one of his children or grandchildren. Monet didn't want his family to know of his activities with Renoir while living with them and Alice.

"I bet he would have loved to see my reaction as I opened his letter and package. I'm sure he asked you to tell him every detail when you return."

"*Oui*," Oscar said.

"Would you like me to tell you the story behind this package and letter? Isabelle, please sit still, and try not to move those lips. I want to kiss them with my pencil on this canvas."

Isabelle blushed and did as he instructed her, but her expression showed she was unhappy about not being included in the conversation.

"Monet and I have been friends since we met as young men in

Paris. Over the years, we have painted together and often competed in selling paintings and bedding girls. He always won at selling paintings, and I always won with the ladies. But not this time. By the looks of this painting you have brought me, he won."

"I didn't realize he was so competitive," Oscar said.

"*Mais oui!*" Renoir said with a tone of defiance. "If he wasn't so determined to be the best at his painting, he'd never have survived against the forces of the Salon. They tried to keep him from being a successful painter. A lesser man would have given up long ago or changed his style."

Oscar was perplexed. "You're saying the painting establishment didn't want him to succeed?"

"Impressionism was at odds with the traditional style of painting. We developed a novel way of approaching art and choosing our subjects thanks, in part, to the Japanese woodblock prints. The art establishment was committed to the past, and we were its future. They were cowards who lacked talent and foresight."

Isabelle couldn't keep quiet any longer. She eased her way back into the conversation after making sure her lips were on the paper. "Why did the Salon refuse Monet's work and not yours?"

"I tried to work within the system more than he did. They also ostracized others like Pissarro, but Monet took the brunt of their wrath. He was so defiant in his actions and personality that they rejected him most times he applied." Renoir shook his head. "He was too stubborn to bend to their rules."

"How did he ever win them over?" Isabelle asked.

"He never did. If it wasn't for Americans like your father, he'd never have succeeded. Some patrons in France kept him from starving by buying his paintings and loaning him money, but the Americans and the Japanese were most responsible for his great artistic and financial success."

"My father loves his work and yours," Isabelle responded. "I remember him purchasing paintings from the Durand-Ruel Gallery when they first exhibited Impressionist paintings in New York. The paintings were so unique and exciting that he couldn't resist them."

"If it weren't for Durand-Ruel, we would all have starved, and Impressionism would have ended before it began. We all leaned on him for support while we battled for recognition. But enough about ancient history. I must rest now. Would you like to meet later for dinner?"

Isabelle seized upon the opportunity. "We would love to."

"Wonderful. I'll meet you at your hotel at nine, and we can dine on their beautiful patio. Have a wonderful afternoon enjoying our lovely village. My driver will be here shortly to take you to your hotel. In the meantime, enjoy my olive grove."

"*Merci, Monsieur. À bientôt.*" Oscar was excited to have dinner with Renoir and learn more about his time in Antibes. Despite his initial misgivings, he had felt at ease sitting and chatting with one of the greatest Impressionist masters. He had been treated with kindness and respect by a wonderful man who was generous with his time.

Isabelle kissed Renoir on each cheek as they were taking their leave. Their host beamed. It was clear he still enjoyed attention from the ladies. Isabelle remained the consummate flirt.

As they left the house, Oscar took her hand to help her down the steps into the garden and didn't let go. The green and silver leaves of the trees sheltered the small green olives thriving in the warm sunshine.

She turned and kissed him repeatedly on his lips and each cheek. He stopped her from going any further. "I can't believe we have spent so much time with a living icon who took the time to sketch me. My friends will be so envious. I can never thank you enough for bringing me to spend time with one of my heroes."

The driver took them back along the sea to the Hotel Le Grimaldi. Set back in a patio of umbrellaed tables, the centuries-old exposed-stone building overlooked the Mediterranean. Its situation in the heart of the medieval village beneath the historic Grimaldi family chateau made it the perfect location for tourists and lovers like them.

Oscar was checking into the two rooms that Blanche had booked for them when Isabelle spoke up. "We will only need one room with a grand bed for tonight and perhaps tomorrow night."

The desk clerk smiled, gave a sideways glance at Oscar, and did as he was told.

Oscar blushed at the thought of checking into a hotel, a rare occurrence in his life and the first with a beautiful woman who was not his wife. They followed the bellhop up the stairs to the large bedroom with a balcony overlooking the sea on the top floor. The room with its red walls, floral print drapes, beamed ceiling, and the *pièce de résistance*, a sizeable cream-colored stone fireplace, was just what Isabelle had in mind.

"Can we have a fire laid for us to enjoy at midnight?" she asked as the bellhop was departing.

"*Oui, Madame*, it will be cozy when you return," he said with a smile as he bowed and backed out the door.

Oscar caught up with him in the hallway and handed him a generous tip, and asked him to bring a bottle of champagne when he laid the fire.

"Oscar, I'm tired. We didn't get much sleep last night," she said with a twinkle in her eye.

"Let's take a walk down by the sea," he offered, knowing full well that what she had in mind was not the rest he needed.

"You go ahead. I'll get some rest for the night ahead of us," she said with a smile and a wink. That wink again meant trouble or ecstasy. Or both.

He smiled warmly, sighed at the thought of leaving her, and departed after she gave him a long kiss goodbye that almost convinced him to stay.

He climbed up through the town on the narrow cobblestone passageways and arrived at the *Chateau Grimaldi*. After staring up at the yellow stone edifice, he turned to look out over the village's red-tiled roofs to the sea. The water's brilliant blue was a lovely complement to the colorful village houses with their red and yellow walls and blue wrought-iron railings. He inhaled deeply to fill his lungs with the clean, fresh sea air, which renewed him. He had a glimmer of hope that his health would return to him after being ravaged by the gas attack. After all, Isabelle's love had restored his faith in the goodness and love of others. His mind shot back to that time and place where so many had lived and lost their lives.

He emerged from the transport with his comrades into the farm fields muddy from hundreds of troops and horses trampling the wheat fields. The war had scarred the once beautiful landscape with trenches, barbed wire, and shell craters. Shells continued landing out of sight, and men moaned from medical tents wedged into the trenches.

He was trying to get his bearings when the men in line behind him shoved him forward toward an empty trench in front of the barbed wire. All he could do was hold onto his rifle and pack and scurry down the ladder into the fetid water in the trench below. The water was black with mud, blood, and vomit from the men who had gone through the barbed wire before him and never returned. Now it was his turn. He tried to sleep standing until they ordered the men up the ladders, through the wire, and into the rain of bullets falling upon them in the hour before dawn.

He made it to the next line of trenches before his comrades, some of whom never made it, including his sergeant. Without a leader, they would indeed be lost. He had no choice but to take over command and lead his men to take out the machine-gun emplacement that aimed to kill them all.

With little idea of what happened next, surrounded by shouting, screaming, and gunfire, he crawled toward the enemy fire and threw his grenades until the machine gun stopped. The world around him grew quiet, and the men crawled into the shell craters, exhausted. They stayed the night to secure the position and wait for reinforcements.

When the mist was rolling in in the early hours of the following day, he smelled something like hot dogs at a summer picnic. The smell of mustard, garlic, and onions was becoming stronger and stronger. He dreamed of the hot dogs at the annual Fourth of July picnic. He woke and realized what the smell meant. It was not the mustard for eating but mustard gas for blistering skin and lungs. He stood up and screamed, "Gas! Gas! Put your masks on now!"

Perhaps if he had put his mask on instead of warning the others, he would have saved his lungs. As it was, he collapsed, and medics carried him from the field. Reinforcements arrived a few hours later. The rest of his time was a blur until he awoke in a field hospital in one of the trenches. He would recover because he had to. There was no one to take his place. He must return to the fighting.

He was angry at himself for letting these thoughts intrude upon the joyous occasion. He locked these memories back into their hiding place and wandered down the village streets, hung with baskets of flowers and colorful laundry, until he arrived back at the shore. The hotel provided tables set beside the water, where he sat and ordered a pitcher of rosé and a basket of *frites*. He put his feet up on a chair and settled in for a relaxing rest in the sun. The thoughts of war were waiting to return another day.

No sooner had he finished his first glass and was pouring a second than Isabelle sashayed up to his table.

"Look what I bought," she said as she spun around, modeling her new sun hat with a bright-red bow. "Do you think Renoir will like it?"

"He'll love it, but why would you wear a sun hat at night?" He lowered his legs, seeing that his short-lived rest was now over. "Perhaps he will paint you at the dinner table."

"He just might. I'm not wearing it at night, silly. Will you request another glass for me?"

"I've been thinking of taking a trip to visit my hometown tomorrow. Would you like to join me on a trip to Antibes?" he asked. "I'd love to see the town where I was born."

"Wonderful idea. I've heard it's a beautiful place. Perhaps Renoir's driver can take us."

Isabelle and Oscar spent the rest of the afternoon chatting in the shade. The red, gold, and purple sunset told them it was time to change for dinner. Neither wanted to leave their quiet spot. Oscar leaned over to embrace her before they returned to their room to prepare for the evening. He slipped his arm around her waist and felt relaxed for the first time in years. He enjoyed sitting on the bed, watching her change into her outfit for the evening. The entire experience exhilarated him for the night ahead. He couldn't wait for dinner to be over.

The two lovers sat beneath the umbrellas at the table reserved in Renoir's name. As Renoir rolled onto the patio, all the other patrons stood in silence and bowed as the great man entered.

"*Bonsoir, Monsieur* and *Mademoiselle*," Renoir said.

"*Bonsoir, Monsieur*," the two said in unison.

"It's a lovely evening and such a charming restaurant that you have selected for us," Isabelle added.

"I can take credit for the restaurant, but not the evening. The evening is provided by a higher power whom I hope to meet soon, but not too soon," Renoir said with a chuckle.

The waiter brought a bottle of *Château de la Galinière*, a *vin rosé* from the Côtes de Provence, for Renoir to taste. It was approved, glasses were filled, and a toast was raised by Renoir. "To my dear friend Monet, who inspires us all."

"*Santé*," said Oscar and Isabelle.

"If you don't mind, I'll order for you," their host said.

"*Oui, Monsieur*," Oscar said with a broad smile. "I'm sure you know what is best here."

The waiter returned.

"We will start with the local tapenade, followed by salade niçoise, and then beef daube and ratatouille."

"My mouth is watering just thinking about it," Oscar said. "Monet told me how much he loved the Provençal food."

"It sounds delicious," Isabelle said.

"*Mademoiselle*, you look delicious," the old flirt said. "Tell me about your art. I understand that you graduated from the Sorbonne."

"I appreciate your compliment. But I'd much rather hear about your art. I'm interested in painting women who are about to give birth. Do you have much experience with that genre?"

Renoir laughed. "Not my interest, I'm afraid. I've always been much more involved in the process leading to that eventuality."

"I see," Isabelle said, disappointed. "Can you tell me more about how you overcame the struggle to get your art accepted?"

"I had an easier time than Monet, but not by much. I was an Impressionist who focused on an acceptable subject, portraits of beautiful women. Monet chose common scenes and landscapes. This gave him an extra hurdle to overcome. The Salon didn't like familiar scenes in a world of art that focused on the historical and classical scenes."

Oscar was learning a great deal about the Impressionists' struggle against the Salon and specifically Renoir and Monet's trials. The fact that they were not successful at first seemed more to do with the actions of the rulers of the Salon than with their talent.

"Are you saying that I would have an easier time since I'm focusing on portraits of women?" Isabelle said as she leaned forward with anticipation.

"Perhaps, but you have to overcome the fact that most men do not find women with children attractive or acceptable."

"Then I shall paint pregnant women for women customers," she said with a defiant tone.

"Well, then you have limited your market to a small portion of the population that has money to spend on art. Perhaps you could do what I did. Make the Salon think you are playing their game. While at the same time, I also painted what I wanted but never showed it to them. By not submitting the work they don't want, you don't upset them." Renoir seemed pleased that he had been able to outwit the Salon judges in this way.

"I'm not sure I could do that," Isabelle said. "I would sell out my art."

"That's what Monet said. It took them a long time to accept him and his art."

Oscar's pride in Isabelle for standing up for herself and her art in her discussion with Renoir showed as he smiled at her, took her hand, and caressed it. She and Monet seemed to share self-confidence, dedication to their art, and a spirit of defiance against the art establishment.

Isabelle's face glowed then. "Now look at him. He's successful. And he's done it on his terms. That's the artist I want to be."

Oscar squeezed her hand to distract her and calm her down. He wanted to keep her from insulting their host further. She pulled back her hand to reject his interference. Then she thought better of her move and reached out to stroke his arm.

Renoir laughed. "Bless you, my child. This is the same conversation I had with Monet years ago. God, how I miss those nights in the cafés battling over our principles. I miss the friends, the laughter, the wine, and the women. Oh, the beautiful women."

They continued their conversation over dessert, cheese, and wine for hours into the evening. After three hours, Renoir called for his driver, who arrived carrying two packages. Renoir handed the small one to Isabelle. He gave her a kiss on both cheeks and added a third to express his admiration for her. "I hope you enjoy this humble gift. Perhaps you can return for more such conversations. I wish you all the best in your career.

"Oscar, this one is for you," Renoir said. "It's the painting that you brought to me from Monet. It is, by all rights, yours. I'm so pleased to meet you. I'm sure you are a great credit to your mother."

What an odd thing for him to say. "How well did you know my mother? Do you know who my father is?"

"We were friends before you were born, but she was much closer to Monet. By the looks of this painting, you should ask him those same questions."

He reached up to touch Oscar's face and looked deeply into his eyes and smiled. "My boy, I hope you're like her. She was a wonderful person."

He was then wheeled across the patio as the other guests stared after him with looks of admiration.

He said over his shoulder as he was being rolled out, "My driver is at your service tomorrow. Visit Antibes, where your mother lived, or anywhere you wish."

Isabelle and Oscar looked at each other with sad smiles as they waved to their gracious host. They both seemed to know that they were witnessing the passing of a legend.

She took his arm as they strolled along the seashore. "I feel a chill. Let's go back to our room and see if the fire is burning."

"My fire is burning," he whispered.

With that, their steps quickened toward their room and a night to remember. He put his arm around her shoulders and drew her closer as they hurried to the front desk for their key.

As they were leaving the front desk, Isabelle pushed him away.

Stunned, he stayed rooted to the spot. "What's wrong? What did I do?"

"Nothing, silly. Go into the bar and order a nice warm drink. I'll see you in thirty minutes." She turned, stuck out her rear, and he gave it a love pat.

"This could be the longest thirty minutes of my life," he said as he strolled up to the bar. "At least since that day going over the top."

The bartender turned and gave him a questioning look as he ordered a coffee and brandy.

Chapter 9 – Love in Lyon

Oscar followed Isabelle's instructions to wait thirty minutes before going to their room. He finished his coffee, picked up his glass of brandy, and wandered outside by the sea. His goal of calming his nerves before meeting her was a lofty one. The sound of the waves lapping against the shore should help soothe him. The brandy sent a warm glow down his throat and into his stomach. Focusing on the day spent with Renoir helped distract him from thinking of the night to come with Isabelle. His breathing, always his weakness after the war, proved the most challenging part to control. It came in short gasps.

He checked his watch for the fifth time and saw that twenty-five minutes had passed. After draining his glass, he straightened his clothes, dropped his glass on the bar, and headed through the lobby to the stairs. Through concentration and self-discipline, he took the first flight one step at a time. The second flight, he took two steps at a time. The third flight was a blur. He stood sweating before his door. Summoning up his remaining courage, he flung the panel open and looked in. The room was dark except for the soft orange glow of the fireplace.

Isabelle stood by the fire in a pale-blue satin nightgown that clung to every curve from her uplifted breasts to her firm hips. He wanted to stand in the doorway and admire her longer, but she interrupted him with, "Come in or go out." She teased him with a wink. "I charge by the hour, and *Monsieur*, you're wasting my time."

"I have money to burn," he said, reaching into his pocket as his heart pounded.

"Then bring it over to the fire, and we can burn it together."

He crossed the room, took her into his arms, pressed his throbbing body into hers, and delivered a kiss to her ruby lips that was deep and warm and never-ending. Her skin was hot to the touch due to the fire and her desire. He released her, let his hands caress each hill and valley of her body as he dropped to his knees. Her gown slid from her shoulders down her body like a soft wave, slowing at each curve before reaching the floor in front of the fire. His eyes and heart followed every inch of the descent. He couldn't stand having a barrier between his flesh and hers, so he ripped the clothes from his body and flung them in every direction.

"Make the most of your time," she said as she slid to the blanket and stretched out with a look of complete surrender.

He gripped her feet, crossed her ankles, and turned her onto her stomach. She let out a soft squeal of surprise and anticipation. He wanted to caress every inch of her as he brought her toes to his lips and kissed them one by one. When he'd finished, he rubbed them. He kissed and massaged his way up her back from her feet to her earlobes, missing no part along the way.

Her skin grew hotter, and her body began to pulsate under his touch. When he finished with her earlobes and scalp, he avoided her grasp. He returned to her feet, turned her onto her back, and began the same process on her front. He wanted to drive her wild with the same desire he felt each time he got close to her. No squeal this time. Just a moan. She was losing control. Every fiber of her being was his to do with as he wished. His one wish was to bring her to the zenith of desire.

She was writhing and moaning with pleasure as he took a long time on her middle before gliding to her breasts. Her skin became hot to touch and salty to taste. She was his to do with as he wished. Arriving at her mouth, he kissed her hungrily as he moved his body onto and into hers. He rolled over so she was on top of him. She became a wildcat, clawing and biting his neck and shoulders. When he felt her energy was spent, it was his turn to relish her ever so slowly to give them both the most pleasure. When he was finished, she collapsed on top of him with just enough strength to mumble three questions, "Where? When? Who?" which he left unanswered.

He rolled her off him and carried her to the bed. He was guided by the light of the moon streaming through the window. The fire had long since burned down to ashes, like him, with just a soft glow remaining.

In the morning, he found her with one leg over him, pinning him to the bed. He tried to wriggle out from beneath her, but she wouldn't budge, so he lay beside her in bed, tracing hearts on her breasts and thinking about the last time he'd felt this close to anyone. Oscar was happier than he'd been in a long time or ever. As he worried that something would come between them to spoil the mood, he felt suspended between utter joy and heartbreaking anticipation. Why was he suddenly so worried?

At last, she opened one eye and then the other. "What are you doing?"

"Practicing my art."

She grinned. "If last night is any example, your art doesn't need any practice."

He blushed and reached out for her, but she jumped back.

"You didn't answer my questions."

"What questions?"

"Where? When? Who?"

After thinking a minute, he remembered her moaning something before she fell asleep. "My girlfriend in college was a Japanese exchange student."

"I can't wait to meet her and offer my deepest gratitude," she teased.

"I'll tell her the next time I see her."

"You had better not be seeing her soon," she said as she punched his stomach. Then her face lit up. "Our gifts. We haven't opened our gifts."

"Gifts. What gifts?" He frowned, trying to understand what she was referring to.

She threw off the covers and pranced across the room with no clothes on. "The ones Renoir gave us, silly."

His heart leaped at the sight of her naked body, burned into his brain. He wanted to hold onto this moment and call upon it when needed. It would keep him warm at night, make him smile when he was hard at work, and comfort him when he was lonely.

She returned with the two wrapped bundles, opened her package, and squealed with delight. Renoir had given her the small sketch he'd made of her during their visit. He must have spent several hours before they'd met for dinner finishing this drawing. "It's a wonderful portrait that captures my *joie de vivre*."

"I'd like to capture your *joie de vivre*. Come closer." He reached for her, but she scooted away to get his gift.

"Now open yours," she demanded.

Oscar untied his package with dread as he remembered what Renoir had said as he gave him the painting he had brought from Monet along with the letter. As he looked closer at the face in the portrait, he could tell it was his mother when she was young. His chest grew tight, and he gulped for air as he started to rewrap the package.

"What's the matter?" Isabelle asked as she grabbed for the painting.

He yanked it back and continued rewrapping it.

"Oscar, what are you doing? I only want to look at the painting. You're so rude," she said as she drew the sheet around her and sat in the bed, pouting.

He had to change the subject. "I can't accept this. A painting by Monet is too great a gift. I must take it back."

He felt angry as his face grew hot, and he felt like shouting, not at her but at his mother. Monet and Renoir had no right to torture him this way.

"Now you're silly," she said, trying to tease him out of returning it.

"It's a gift. You can't return a gift. It'll insult Renoir. Besides, you saw his condition. It'll just be given to some worthless relative." She stood up as she raised her voice to match his.

His ruse had worked. "How could you say that? You don't even know his wishes or his worthless relatives."

He stuffed the package into his bag.

"I don't want to discuss it," Isabelle said as she flounced off to the bathroom with her satin nightgown in hand and the sheets wrapped around her. "You're so unreasonable that I don't want to be with you."

He had succeeded in destroying a most beautiful moment, the most beautiful moment in his life. "Stop! I don't want to talk about it, but I will tell you this much. That portrait is of my mother as a young woman."

"Your mother?"

"Yes. My mother seemed to have known these two men." He gulped for more air. "And that's all I can say for now."

"You can't talk to me about this after last night? That's all it meant to you? I thought we had grown closer and could share our intimate thoughts. Perhaps last night didn't mean the same to you as it did to me." Tears streamed down her red cheeks as she slammed the bathroom door.

They went down to breakfast together without speaking further about the gifts or anything else. The subject was far from closed but on hold for the time being. They ate in silence until Oscar said, "I'm so sorry. I didn't mean to upset you. Please forgive me."

"Well, maybe if you're sorry. And promise not to be so rude to me again." She had put on her best pouty expression.

He tried to look like someone she should forgive. "Renoir made a very great gesture, and I must accept his gift. Monet painted this picture of my mother, and that Renoir also knew her has upset me so much that I no longer wish to go to Antibes. I feel that I'd be returning to the scene of the crime. I'd like to take the train to Lyon and spend the night there. Do you mind?"

"Scene of the crime. I can't believe you'd call your conception and birth a 'crime.' You'd be lucky to have either of these men as your father. They're great and good men, and you should be honored rather than calling them 'criminals.'"

Oscar hung his head to hide the embarrassment he felt over his comments. His anger at his mother and father had gotten the better of him. He wasn't strong enough to accept it at this point, and going to Antibes would be more than he could deal with. "Okay. You're right. I just don't want to go there, if you don't mind."

Isabelle sat in silence for a few minutes before smiling. "I accept your apology. Fine. Let's go to Lyon. I'll ask the desk clerk to recommend a pleasant hotel for us. Please don't let this upset you further. It's only a painting."

"I suppose you're right." He felt relieved that their first argument was over and that the subject of the painting was closed.

"I am. I'm always right," Isabelle said as she stood, kissed his cheek, and hurried off to the front desk.

Oscar sat contemplating the entire exchange before calling for the check and heading back to their room. Was this going to be the nature of their relationship from now on? If they were going to have a relationship, would she be the one in charge? He'd apologized as expected, and she'd accepted. Was this what he could anticipate for his life with her? If there was to be a life with her, would it be in France, Chicago, or San Francisco? Perhaps her price was too high. Then again, last night was worth any price. He had so many questions, more questions than he'd started on the trip with.

The desk clerk provided a letter of introduction to a hotel in Lyon and booked transportation to the train station. Oscar had to admit that Isabelle knew how to handle arrangements for them. Once they were aboard the train with their luggage stored, they both curled up in their seats and fell asleep. Neither had gotten much sleep the night before.

They both awoke as they were nearing the Lyon Perrache station.

Refreshed but ravenous, they set out looking for lunch as soon as they'd checked into their hotel in the old section of the city, dropped off their luggage, and freshened up. They wandered through the Vieux Lyon, the town's old quarter, enjoying the fifteenth-century cobbled streets, past many restaurants with outdoor seating, to *Le Savanah*, situated in a small courtyard shaded by a large tree. They looked at each other and said in unison, "Perfect."

Their lunch started with a *Salade Lyonnaise*, a green salad with bacon strips, a poached egg, and mustard dressing. For their main course, they had sausage brioche and gratin potatoes. They chose different desserts—Isabelle selected the *tarte pralinée*, and Oscar chose his favorite, *tarte au citron*. After so much rich food, they sat back with a glass of crisp white wine and discussed a vigorous walk to settle their lunch.

"My mother told me that her father helped create an enormous park here in Lyon, the *Parc de la Tête d'Or*. I'd like to see it if you don't mind," he said.

Isabelle grabbed his hands across the table. "We must go. How do we get there?"

"We walk. Do you have walking shoes?"

She raised her skirt to show him her shoes and more.

"There will be none of that until we have had our exercise."

"This is also an excellent form of exercise," she said as she raised her skirt higher to reveal her thighs.

He could feel himself blush. "True, but we need to be out in the fresh air, too."

"That's a great idea. A roll in the hay in the sun," she said with a giggle.

He smiled, shook his head. "Let's go."

He got up and disappeared through the door next to their table. Isabelle opened the ancient wooded door and followed him down a dark passageway inside a fifteenth-century stone building. It was dark and cool and smelled very musty. She lost him in the shadows.

"Oscar, where are you?" she called with a slight note of panic in her voice.

Then he grabbed her out of the dark, drew her body to his, and kissed her.

"You frightened me. Where are we?"

"In one of the *Traboules*," he said. "Lyon has dozens of these old covered passageways between buildings. They allowed the silk weavers to carry their goods to the river boats without getting the fabric exposed to the rain or sun."

"I love it. Great place for couples like us to…."

He held her and kissed her again.

They emerged from the tunnel and crossed two bridges over two rivers, the Saone and the Rhone, then walked arm in arm along the Rhone River to the park's entrance.

"The entrance is grand," Isabelle said. "With its massive green iron gates trimmed in gold, it looks like the gates to a chateau."

"My grandfather worked here for over thirty years. He helped design some of the botanical buildings, greenhouses, and display gardens. His favorite was the boating lake. Let's tour around the grounds and then have a drink at the café by the lake that my mother told me about."

"Sure, let's get this exercise thing over with," she said as she grabbed his hand and scurried down the broad gravel path.

They discussed how the rose garden surrounded by white trellises would make a beautiful wedding venue. As they strolled past the large glass-and-iron greenhouses with tropical plant displays, they discussed how wonderful it would be to honeymoon in a tropical paradise and see the plants in their natural environment. They wandered through the zoo and debated how much a child would love to see such animals. They walked along the shore of the vast lake and envied the young lovers who were boating across its calm green surface.

After several hours and many miles of walking, they stopped at the lakeside café for the promised drink, a cool, fresh *Beaujolais*. They toasted Renoir, Monet, and each other as they held hands across the table.

"Do you like your grandfather's park?" Isabelle asked after taking a sip of her wine.

Oscar thought for a moment before responding. "Yes, I do. I heard so much about it from my mother that I had to see it for myself. It's lovely, but it's a bit too formal for my taste now that I have become used to Monet's gardening style. I dreamt about what it was like to be here after listening to my mother's stories. It's hard to say I'm disappointed, but my tastes have changed. What do you think about the park?"

She twirled the wine in her glass before replying. "It's hard to think of a garden in the same way after seeing Monet's."

"I miss Giverny," he said. "Don't you?"

"I hope we can spend more time there together after we return," she said, reaching out to touch his cheek.

He kissed her fingers. "I'm sure we will. Perhaps *Madame* Blanche will offer us a solution."

"I'm not all that sure she likes or trusts me."

"I'm sure she does. You just take a bit of getting used to."

"If you're done with this exercising, it's my turn to choose the next activity," she said as she closed her legs around his knee.

"Then we had better get started on our long walk back to the hotel."

Isabelle slipped her arm through his as they started the journey back. They stopped at the hotel desk to retrieve their room key, and the clerk handed them the key and a telegram.

"Isabelle, it's addressed to you, from *Madame* Blanche."

Isabelle frowned. "How could she have found us here? That woman is scary."

She ripped open the envelope, read the telegram, and her face turned pale. "It's about my father. He's had a heart attack, and I'm asked to return home as quickly as possible."

Oscar's mouth dropped open. "To Chicago?"

"Yes, by the next available ship."

"I'm so sorry. Then we must return on the next train. How can I help? I'm glad we're still packed. Let's get ready to go." He was anxious to take care of her in this crisis.

Isabelle seemed lost in confusion. "Yes, let's leave on the next ship, I mean train. Please find us a ride to the station."

Her usual command of any situation seemed absent.

"I'll take care of it," Oscar said, doing his best to calm her in this emergency.

"My poor father. I don't know when I'll get to see you again. I'm so mixed up. Please telegraph Blanche to book me on the first ship out of Le Havre for tomorrow. I need to stop in Vernon and pack for the trip." She looked at Oscar. "I'm sorry to leave you like this."

"Let's get you to the train."

Oscar realized that this was what he'd worried about in bed this morning as he saw the rest of their trip crumble in a heartbeat. He feared that his life with her was out of his control and always would be.

Chapter 10 – Passion to Compassion

They raced down the long halls of the station to the train with moments to spare. Their seats were in second class. First class was sold out, which meant sleeping, if possible, would be sitting up. Oscar made Isabelle as comfortable as he could in the noisy, sweaty car. He stroked her hair and massaged her neck until she closed her eyes. She slept with her head in his lap. Her face was moist, and she snored. She must have hated him seeing her like this—not in control.

He sat awake, thinking of their future together or perhaps the lack of one. After the past few days, he couldn't think of his life without her in it. She had inhabited his thoughts and put him in touch with his emotional needs and hunger for love. How his life had changed from loneliness to intimacy and back to loneliness again once she'd set sail. He couldn't bear to spend the rest of the night wallowing in self-pity. He'd known from the start about the dangers of getting involved with Isabelle. Still, he couldn't help falling in love with her. Passion had driven him, and now he had to adapt to compassion. This was a terrible time for her, and he wanted to support her in every way possible. Even if it meant losing her to life back in Chicago.

When they had sat by the sea in Cagnes-sur-Mer, she had told him she'd lost her mother to complications of childbirth. It was not only her mother who had died that night but also her sibling, who'd barely drawn a breath. The loss had cemented her relationship with her father. He was not only her father but also her caregiver, playmate, and best friend. His medical practice may have suffered, but Isabelle never had. They were constant companions, and she told him every-thing.

Her father, Antoine, had become so upset when she'd left for the Sorbonne that she'd considered canceling her trip. He was worried for her safety but more concerned that she would not return after school to their ancestral home in Chicago on Lake Michigan's shore. She had promised that she would write every day and tell him everything that happened to her. But like many young adults, she hadn't.

Oscar had thus found out that Antoine knew about him. She described her father as a short, balding doctor with gray hair and thick glasses. From her description, he could tell that Antoine was as devoted to his lovely daughter as he'd been to her beautiful mother. She had shown him a photo of her parents in front of their home in Chicago. They'd looked happy together. She said she loved him for what he was, a kind man to everyone he met. She said he brought out the best in people and they in him. He was her model for the type of man she wanted to marry.

Oscar understood her reasons for loving her father and wanting to be with him in this time of crisis. There was nothing he wouldn't do to help her get there by the fastest means possible. If she asked, he would leave France to be with her, but she didn't ask. Instead, his concentration was on making her trip as swift as possible. He checked the timetable for the change of trains in Paris to Vernon. He would telegraph Blanche from their stop in Paris to see if Sylvain could drive them to Le Havre to meet the ship. The train schedule was too tight to make the necessary stop in Vernon and still arrive by train at the dock in time to meet the evening sailing schedule.

He focused on planning the trip for her until he fell asleep. They slept through the two announcements of their arrival in the Gare de Lyon station in Paris. If the commotion made by the other passengers exiting the train hadn't awoken them, they would have been on their way elsewhere and missed the connection to Vernon.

As it was, they had to run to the next platform and race to the departing train to not have to wait another four hours for the next departure. They collapsed into their seats and looked at each other, and broke into laughter. They knew they must have been a hysterical sight, Isabelle running full speed with her dress rising above her knees and Oscar trying to keep up with his arms full of luggage.

"I thought you were watching over our schedules to get me to the next train on time," she said with mock disapproval.

"The train schedule was in my hand the entire time. Do you mind if I love the way you look in the morning? Your skin is so fresh and kissable."

"Don't start that. It won't excuse your lack of vigilance." Then she started tickling him.

"If you don't stop that, I'll wet my pants," he said. "Speaking of that, we didn't have time to eat, either. I'm off to find nourishment and take care of that other matter."

"Don't forget to come back. I have plans for you," Isabelle said.

He was pleased to have taken her mind off her father for a few minutes while they'd rushed for the train. Now he'd find them something to eat; next stop, Vernon. Thinking of Vernon reminded him that he'd failed to send a telegram asking for a ride. *Quel dommage.*

This time, they stayed awake and gathered their belongings as they neared the Vernon station. Oscar wasn't sure how he would get to Giverny and ask for Sylvain to drive them, but he would run the whole way if he had to.

Thanks to Blanche's foresight, Sylvain waited on the Vernon platform in his chauffeur's cap and took them to Isabelle's lodging. While Isabelle packed for the trip, Oscar found a café next to the train station that prepared lunch for their Le Havre journey.

As soon as Isabelle announced she was ready, Sylvain loaded the vehicle, and they were off to meet the ship. Not much time, but Sylvain said he'd make it. He was experienced at driving Monet at a breakneck speed.

Isabelle and Oscar nestled into the rear seat and discussed their previous trip down this road. So much had happened since then. They now knew each other intimately. She promised to write to him about her father's condition, and he said he would reply with news of Giverny. He held her, and she wrapped her arms around his waist as they talked about their time together. No plans for their future were discussed. Neither dared to plan beyond the moment the ship set sail. They wanted to reinforce memories of their moments together, for they had little else. He dared not kiss her for fear he couldn't stop.

Sylvain arrived at the dock with fifteen minutes to spare. He and Oscar raced to get Isabelle's mountain of luggage to the ship.

"How could she pack so much in the few minutes she was in her room?" Oscar asked Sylvain, who just smiled and shook his head in response.

She returned, kissed him, and ran up the boarding ramp, her short skirt lifting in the breeze. She waved and blew kisses to him from the deck rail and then disappeared. Oscar was disappointed she had not remained until the ship was out of sight, and he turned back toward Sylvain and the vehicle.

But then he heard Isabelle shouting, "Wait! Oscar, wait!"

He turned back to the ship. Isabelle flew into his arms and kissed him deeply, shoved a small package into his hand with her Chicago address on the outside. Then she kissed him again and whispered in his ear, "I love you to Chicago and back."

With that, she raced to the gangplank as it was being pulled up. Oscar's heart shattered, and tears rolled down his unshaven cheeks. Had he lost the love of his life without even telling her what she meant to him? And what was this gift she'd given him? He had given her nothing other than his heart and body.

"I hope your father gets better," he yelled as the tugboat towed the ship away from the dock and out of his life. "Please, please, please come back to me, soon," he cried as loud as his lungs would let him. "I love you to Chicago and back."

He had no way of knowing if she could hear him. She was gone, and he was alone. Again.

Chapter 11 – Facing the Tiger

Sylvain dropped Oscar off at his boarding house late in the afternoon. He had difficulty dragging his body and his luggage to his second-floor bedroom. The train trip, the drive to the ship, and Isabelle sailing for Chicago exhausted his body and broke his heart. He opened the heavy wooden door, dropped his bag on the floor with the gift from Isabelle in it, and fell across his sagging iron bed that moaned as he collapsed onto it. It was calming to be back to the relative quiet of his shabby room.

He closed his eyes, then sat up in bed, remembering Isabelle's gift. He dragged his bag closer to the bed with one foot and retrieved the package. After reading her address written on the outside, he tore it off and put it aside so he could write to her. As he opened the gift, he recognized what she'd given him—Renoir's sketch of her.

Before falling asleep on the bed, the last thought he had was that he would hang both gifts from Renoir on the wall above his dresser to hide the crack in the plaster. The two most precious women in his life together watching over him. Loneliness crept in while he was sleeping and covered him with a blanket of dread.

Waking late the following morning disoriented him. Twelve hours of fitful sleep and not much food for twenty-four hours didn't help his concentration. He was suffering a colossal loss. He jumped out of bed, startled by the worry that he'd be late to work, threw on his work clothes, and rushed out the door. He remembered to stop at the patisserie to pick up an egg and cheese croissant for breakfast and his usual ham and cheese baguette for lunch on the way to work. He was out of breath when he arrived just as Monet was entering his massive studio.

"I wasn't sure you were coming to work today," Monet said as he smiled and looked pleased to see him.

Oscar tried to catch his breath between words. "Sorry I'm late. It was a long day from Lyon to Le Havre and back here."

"Did Isabelle make her ship in time?" Monet asked as he lit a new cigarette with the one he was holding before crushing it out.

"*Oui*, with just a few minutes to spare. Thank you for loaning us Sylvain and the vehicle," Oscar said as his breath came more easily when he realized that he was not in trouble for being late. "Without that, she wouldn't have made the ship's departure."

Monet continued to pry. "Do you know when she's returning?"

"I'm not sure when or if she'll return," Oscar said, glancing down to avoid Monet's always piercing gaze.

Monet put his arm around Oscar's shoulders. "*Quel dommage.* She's such a lovely girl who seems to care for you very much."

Oscar was uncomfortable with Monet's interest in his private affairs. "*Oui, Monsieur*," he said as he looked away, blinking back tears.

This was the first time Monet had shown him any affection. He seemed to be comforting them both for their loss of Isabelle. She brought them closer in shared abandonment. They were like two lovers losing the same object of their affection.

"I'm so glad you made it back today. We need to prepare for a famous visitor. He'll be here for lunch," Monet said as he hurried to make his studio more presentable.

Happy to have the topic changed and the attention focused away from himself, Oscar straightened his back to rise to the occasion. "Who's coming? How can I help prepare?"

"My friend Georges Clémenceau is coming to inspect my progress on the water lily decorations I'm donating to France. He wants to check on my health, too, I suspect. Please make sure the gardens are ready for his visit."

"I will. I'm sure the gardens and pond are in fine shape."

"Just the same, please check on their condition and make improvements where you feel necessary. The others may have missed a few things while you were away."

A wave of pride washed over Oscar as he realized how much Monet relied on him to oversee the gardens' condition. He'd seen himself as just another of the gardeners, but suddenly he knew better. "I'm honored to help."

Now he must live up to that honor and the accompanying expectation and was pleased that this could help him avoid thinking of Isabelle every moment.

"Another thing. I want you to have lunch with us today."

Oscar looked down at his work clothes and shoes. "I'd love to, but I'm not suitably dressed to dine with you and your friend."

Cigarette in hand, Monet waved away the objection. "Nonsense. See Blanche. She has something for you to wear."

"*Merci. Merci beaucoup.* I can't impose upon your generosity any further. You've given me so much already." Oscar felt guilty that he'd already received two suits, two pairs of shoes, and quite a few shirts.

"I don't remember giving you a choice. Now off you go to inspect the grounds," Monet said as he lit up yet another cigarette and examined his massive *Grandes Décorations*.

Oscar made a minute inspection of the grounds and gave the five gardeners suggestions for a few significant improvements before returning to the house and climbing the stairs to the porch. Blanche was supervising the preparations for lunch that Monet wanted to be served as soon as his guest arrived. He knew his guest would be famished from his journey and in a better mood once he'd eaten one of their famous lunches.

Blanche looked up to see him as he reached the top step. She threw her arms up in joy and crossed the porch to welcome him back with a kiss on each cheek and a hug. "You look tired. Isabelle has worn you out. Did she arrive at the ship on time?"

Oscar grinned at her greeting. "*Oui. Merci* for making all the arrangements. It was a wonderful trip, if somewhat tiring."

"*Très bien.* I want to hear all about it after this day is over. Did Monet tell you about the visit from his friend Georges? There's a suit, shirt, and shoes ready for you in the drawing-room. You can dress there, and no one will disturb you. It's great to have you back. Monet has missed your help. Let's talk later," she said as she turned back to her work supervising the preparations for lunch.

Oscar went to the drawing-room and found another of Monet's clothing gifts waiting for him. This suit was a soft tan color with broad, darker brown stripes. Like the others, Cosette had tailored it to fit him perfectly. The shirt and shoes fit, too. At least now he was presentable.

He heard a vehicle chug to a stop on the street behind the house.

"Monet, our guest has arrived," Blanche called from the porch.

Monet was climbing the steps as Oscar reemerged onto the porch, looking dressed for a formal lunch that was important to him.

"*Très bien. Très bien*, Oscar. You look wonderful," Blanche said.

Monet smiled his approval. "You look much better than I did in that suit. It was styled for a younger man like you."

Oscar basked in the compliments and warmth from these two. Perhaps his journey had made them appreciate him more. Whatever the reason, he enjoyed the reception he was receiving.

There was a knock at the door, and Monet went to answer it himself. "*Mon ami*, Georges. It's been too long since you were here."

"Much too long," Georges replied. "I hope my visit finds you well."

After surviving a long battle with age and illness, the two embraced with kisses on both cheeks and hugged like two comrades in arms.

"Better than can be expected for a man of my age. And you?" Monet, without waiting for Georges to answer, turned toward the porch door. "Come outside. I have someone I want you to meet. Oscar, this is my dear friend Georges Clémenceau."

Oscar had been watching the two old friends greeting at the door without seeing the guest's face in the house's dim light. When he came out of the door into the sunlight, Oscar blurted out, "*Le Moustachu!*"

Georges was the heavyset man with the robust mustache who had visited him in the hospital. He was the man who was so kind when telling him about his mother and had informed him of the gardener position with Monet. The man with the mustache, called 'Tiger' by the other patients, had visited him several times as he recovered from his injuries.

He looked much like Monet in his dapper suit and rumpled hat. In the hospital, he'd dressed in a large overcoat with a dark fur collar. His face had deep lines from what he assumed was worry and stress, and his eyes seemed dark with sadness. He'd looked stooped over and short in the hospital, but now he stood straight and a few inches taller than Monet.

Oscar smiled and shook Georges' hand. "*Monsieur*, it is a pleasure to be formally introduced to you. I never knew your name, so I made up my own for you."

Georges' portly frame shook with laughter. "I've been called many names, including 'Tiger,' but never, in my many years, '*le Moustachu.*' I rather like it, although I can't for the life of me understand where you came up with that name for me." He laughed even more, with everyone joining him in his little joke.

"Let me correct that now," Monet said. "Georges is the prime minister of France, and he spends weekends visiting the hospitals and the front lines, meeting and encouraging the soldiers. You were one of the hundreds he visited in the hospitals."

"You were very special to me," Georges said to Oscar with twinkling eyes. "You were one of the few Americans who joined the French army to help us. I admire your heroism and sacrifice for our country in its hour of need. I look forward to having more time to speak with you, but right now, we must enjoy the delicious lunch the Blue Angel has prepared for us."

"Who is the Blue Angel?" Oscar asked in confusion as he looked around to see who responded to that name.

"*Monsieur* Clémenceau insists on calling me that because of my blue eyes," Blanche said to him with a smile of pride. She went to Georges and kissed his cheeks three times in a sign of affection. "Please sit."

"Blue is for her eyes. Angel is for her heart," Georges said with a wink.

Blue must also have been for the dress that Blanche no doubt wore in honor of their guest. Oscar was pleased to join this small group of Monet's family and their dear friend for lunch and honored to be asked to sit on one side of Monet with Georges to sit on the other. He was humbled to be sitting with these two great men. He had worried about what he would discuss with them and was relieved when the subject immediately turned to gardening. These two avid gardeners had many questions for him that drew upon his horticultural education and experience.

Lunch began with a leek and potato soup, followed by goat cheese and pear salad on greens. He guessed the pears came from Monet's pear tree last season. The main course was pike in a white butter sauce accompanied by a Chardonnay from Burgundy. For dessert, they had baked pears also from their trees. Monet liked to eat his homegrown fruits and vegetables when he could. He purchased a house and garden next door to have a vegetable garden nearby and hired a gardener to manage and harvest the produce.

Georges wiped his hands on his napkin and brushed crumbs from his waistcoat. "*Un repas délicieux.* Blue Angel, you have outdone yourself. This meal was the best I have had since I was here last."

Blanche accepted the compliment and smiled at Georges. "*Merci, mon ami.*"

Georges then turned to Oscar. "How are you feeling after your ordeal and stay in the hospital?"

"Much better," Oscar replied. "*Merci.* My work in these gardens has helped restore me to health and happiness. Your visits and the recommendation for this job contributed to my recuperation. That helped me through the long recovery period after my injuries and learning of my mother's death."

"I learned about your mother's passing a few days before you did. It was a terrible shock. She was so young and beautiful," Georges said. "I'm so thankful that the young American nurse found you for me."

"I don't remember an American nurse. I just remember an angel taking care of me, tending to my every need even if I couldn't see her."

"Trust me. This angel was a beautiful young woman. Too bad you missed seeing her. She was extremely devoted to you."

Oscar sighed and took a moment to remember his mother and the day when he'd been told of her passing while he lay in the hospital bed. Then something flickered in his mind, and when he focused again on what was being discussed, he asked, "*Monsieur* Clémenceau, how did you know my mother?"

"*Mon fils*, I met her while I was visiting San Francisco. She was the speaker at a dinner I attended. She discussed her work on the Golden Gate Park and the Japanese Tea Garden. I was interested to learn more about her gardening techniques, so I could share them with my friend Monet. We talked a long time after dinner about her work, Monet's garden, and my own. We were friends for a long time when she mentioned that you'd traveled to France to join our army to fight for her family's country."

"My country, too. I was born here," Oscar said.

"*Oui*, that's what she told me. She asked me to check on you since she hadn't heard from you in a long time. That was what I did as soon as I returned. I was unable to locate you until after I was told by friends that she had passed on. Thanks to that nurse, I found you in that hospital bed, and you know the rest," Georges said as he stroked his mustache.

He struggled to understand why he was sent to Monet of all people. Had his mother told him about his father? Did Monet know more than he was revealing? These questions were welling up inside him. "*Non*. I'm not sure why you sent me here for this job."

Georges shrugged. "You needed a job, and my friend Monet needed help. It was as simple as that."

Was it that simple? Why didn't he suggest Oscar return to San Francisco? He could have sent him to one of his contacts there for a job.

At that moment, Monet stood with his glass raised. "Please join me in a toast to France's greatest leader and my dearest friend, I give you Prime Minister Georges Clémenceau. *Santé.*"

"*Santé*," rang out from the assembled guests. Oscar responded to the toast with, "Good health to us all."

Georges stood to embrace Monet. "My dear friends. In the darkest days of the war, I remembered our lunches here with you when all around me was going to Hell. This gave me the strength to carry on. I want to thank my Blue Angel for bringing us together and preparing this wonderful meal. Please raise your glasses once more, this time to my Blue Angel."

New conversations broke out as the guests nibbled on the dessert and cheese courses. Monet and Georges rose once again, this time to take a tour of the garden. Monet asked Oscar to join them.

They strolled through the garden, and Monet pointed out new plantings that he claimed would improve its picturesque nature. He attributed many of the latest additions to Oscar. Georges commented on the flowers he had given Monet from his garden that were doing well. They discussed the flower shows they had visited together in the past and wished to attend again.

Oscar, uneasy with the unexpected praise he was receiving, slowed his walking and took time to inspect the plants. He wanted to give the old men time to talk alone, but he picked up his pace when he overheard Georges saying, "Monet, it's time to schedule your cataract surgery with our friend Dr. Coutela."

Monet squinted through his cigarette smoke at his friend. "Not yet. I can still see. I need to complete my *Grandes Décorations* first."

Georges pressed him. "At least come to Paris and meet with him. You can do that much for me."

"Perhaps," Monet replied and then changed the topic. "Isn't the garden lovely this time of year? It's going to be a good growing year. I owe much of its recent success to Oscar. *Merci* for sending him to me."

Oscar felt his face turning red in embarrassment. Was Monet pleased with him, or was this his way of changing the topic? Or both?

"Not only has he worked in the garden, but he also helps me move the paintings each day. I don't know what I'd do without him. Look how well everything is growing."

"Well done, young man," Georges said. "Monet, don't think I'll forget about your eye surgery. I'll be here to help you when you're ready for it. For now, we can get you examined and plan for the future."

Monet looked cross but accepted his friend's argument.

Georges stopped as he quoted, "In the words of your friend Octave Mirabeau, 'The dahlias tremble and twinkle atop fragile branching arms. The air is filled with so much glimmering and so much quivering.' Your garden makes me quiver."

Oscar tried to contribute to the conversation. "These flowers come from Mexico. They often grow over three meters high. We've planted many different species throughout. They lend color and a certain nobility to the garden."

He was doing his best to sound knowledgeable and relevant, even though he knew he wasn't.

Monet smiled at Oscar. "Georges, do you see what I mean about this young man? Let's make our way over to the studio. I have much to show you since your last visit."

Georges grinned. "Now let's see how you're coming along with your *Grandes Décorations*. The government is excited to hear more about this glorious gift."

"I'm still waiting to hear about their new home. Have you made any progress on that?" Monet shot back.

Georges waved his hands in the air. "Patience, my dear friend. Patience. The work at the *Musée de l'Orangerie* is coming along well."

They continued their stroll up through the garden to the large studio that Georges hadn't seen finished on his previous trips. He stood back to admire its size and design.

"It's large enough to hold your *Grandes Décorations*. Make that <u>our</u> *Grandes Décorations*," he said with a chuckle.

Monet entered his studio ahead of his guests and approached the large paintings. "Not yet ours, dear friend. We have a lot to discuss before I let France have them. Oscar, please help me line up the paintings so Georges can see them as they will be displayed."

The six-and-a-half by fourteen-foot canvases were on rollers, which allowed Oscar to move them around the massive studio. He brought each canvas forward for review and then lined it up in the latest order Monet required. Georges studied one after the other. He stood back, then approached each one and stroked his mustache. Monet stood to one side, smoking and studying his friend's reaction to each canvas.

After Georges had finished reviewing each of the paintings that might make up the *Grandes Décorations*, he summed up his opinion in one word. "*Magnifique.* The people of France and the world will honor these for all time."

"Don't get carried away," Monet said. "I still need to work on them. Besides, I'm not sure how many paintings there will be and which ones I'll donate."

Georges sat down on the sofa and pulled on his mustache in thought for some moments before responding. "Monet, you will be the death of me. I had less trouble defeating Kaiser Wilhelm than negotiating with you on this gift. Dealing with you has never been easy, but now you've become impossible."

Oscar's eyes widened at the former prime minister's reference to France's mortal enemy. The Kaiser had killed thousands of Frenchmen as he'd tried to defeat France. The devastation was everywhere.

Cities had been bombed, and farmlands ripped apart. How could these old men joke about such things?

Monet chuckled. "Tell me the size of the exhibition space, and I'll tell you which ones I'll donate." He walked over to the sideboard for the *Calvados*. "Oscar, bring us some glasses. We need to discuss this over drinks."

Monet retreated to the couch and lit a cigarette. He filled their glasses and proposed a toast. "To old friends."

"And new ones," Georges added.

Oscar's heart swelled with pride at being included in this select circle of friends, even though he knew he didn't belong.

The two comrades continued to argue for the rest of the afternoon. First Monet was to give twelve and then as many as twenty paintings. Neither one could agree. The *Calvados* seemed to help. At the end of the afternoon, neither could quite remember the number of canvases that had been decided upon. Both agreed to continue their discussions and arguments soon.

"Time for me to return to Paris," Georges said as he stood to leave. "I've tried to make sense of this chaotic situation."

"I apologize for being so difficult, *mon ami*," Monet said. "These paintings are my children, and I have a hard time letting go."

"I understand, old friend. We'll continue our discussions. Don't forget I've arranged your appointment for your eye examination with Dr. Coutela next Wednesday at eleven. He'll keep you there for two hours. Have Oscar accompany you on the train, as you won't be able to see well enough to return by yourself."

Now he was included in what was sure to be an uncomfortable day traveling with Monet to do something he didn't want to do.

"You seem certain that I will attend the examination," Monet said with an inebriated stubbornness.

Georges, who was equally inebriated and even more stubborn, said, "The Blue Angel and now Oscar are on my side. I'm confident that you'll be there. Oscar, you and I can adjourn to my apartment for a nice chat while Monet is examined. I've got some things to discuss with you about your mother."

My mother. What could he have to say about my mother? I thought his meeting with my mother was only casual. How could he know more about my mother? I hope she didn't have an affair with him, too.

Chapter 12 – To Chicago and Back

My Dearest Isabelle,

Your departure has left a hole in my heart. Our few days together were the most wonderful of my life. I can't begin to think of the many ways my life has improved thanks to you. For the first time in years, I have started to feel hope and love again. I'm counting the seconds until your return. I hope your father will regain his health quickly so that we can be together soon. I wish I were there with you tonight to feel your warmth against my heart.

I must tell you what's happening in Giverny. When I returned to work today, it was as if I were their long-lost son returning home. Monet put his arm around my shoulders to comfort me on your departure. He genuinely misses you. Blanche welcomed me back with kisses and hugs. I felt more loved by both than I could have hoped for. It was such a surprise that I'm curious as to its reason.

We had a visitor for lunch today from Paris, the Prime Minister, Georges Clémenceau. It turns out that he's an old friend of Monet's and the person responsible for his gift of the water lily paintings to the French government. I must tell you how I first met him.

I was lying in a hospital ward close to the front lines. It was in an old church with its towering ceilings and stained-glass windows. I couldn't help but feel as I lay on my cot that I was in a casket, witnessing my funeral, and I was lying there waiting for the service to begin. I was in and out of consciousness for days or weeks, I'm not sure. Finally, I managed to stay conscious for several days in a row. I'd been shot in the shoulder and leg and had breathed enough mustard gas to blister my throat and lungs severely for the second time. When it looked like I would survive, the hospital staff brought me a letter from a family friend that said my mother had died of lung cancer.

You can't imagine how destroyed I was at this point. I was not sure I wanted to go on. The agony in my body and heart were almost too much to bear. I spent most of my time in bed, asleep, to avoid the pain. I remember one nurse who occasionally came to comfort me. She was my personal angel, but my eyes were so burned by the gas that I couldn't see her. She was the only person to visit me until one day, I awoke to find a heavyset man dressed in a massive overcoat with a fur collar and a giant mustache. He was staring down at me. From what little I could see, he looked very kind, like an angel of death come to take me away. I was ready. I sat up to go with him and said, "Take me, I'm ready."

He laughed so hard that he shook all over. I felt so foolish that I tried to go back to sleep, hoping it was all a dream or a nightmare. When I opened my eyes again, he was still there, sitting next to my cot. He apologized for frightening me and asked if I knew about the death of my mother. I began to cry. All the pain and loss were too much for me, and I just broke down. He sat there for an hour trying to comfort me and then was called away.

A week later, Le Moustachu (he didn't tell me his name, nor did I ask) returned to ask how I was recovering. I felt less like giving up but not quite ready to commit to moving on with my life. I can't believe that I told this stranger my most innermost thoughts about survival, but that's what I did. He listened intently and then was called away again. He turned as he was leaving and asked if I would like a job. I had no idea what he was offering nor why and could not reply.

A week passed, and then another before Le Moustachu returned. In the meantime, the kind nurse came and went, but my vision was too hazy to see her clearly. This time, he said he recommended me for a job in Monet's garden in Giverny. Of course, I'd heard about this famous garden in my landscape classes at college. I'd no idea of where Giverny was nor what I would be hired to do there. Besides, how did he know I was a trained gardener?

Nevertheless, Le Moustachu insisted I give it a try. I agreed to visit the garden to see if it was suitable for me to work there. He handed me a letter of introduction and directions on how to get to Giverny when I was well enough. That's the last I saw of him until today.

Today, he told me that he met my mother in San Francisco during his visits to America. He even attended one of her lectures on garden design. They spoke afterward, and she mentioned that I had joined the French army to fight for our homeland. She asked him to look in on me if he had the opportunity. He visited me in the hospital on one of his weekly visits to the front. I feel she sent him to save me when I needed her the most.

Today he asked me to visit him in Paris, so we could discuss my mother further. I'm excited to go. I'll travel with Monet to the eye doctor next week and then visit Le Moustachu while I wait for him.

I'm sorry to rattle on this way, but it's silly to fill a letter with how much I miss you and how I want to hold you in my arms. I can barely catch my breath when I think of seeing you again like you were lying in front of the fire with your eyes glowing like two coals and your body shimmering in the light from the flames.

The good news is that I have that lovely Renoir sketch of you hung in front of my bed where I can see it the last thing at night before I go to sleep and the first thing in the morning when I awake.

Please write and tell me about your trip and the condition of your father. I hope all's well.

I love you to Chicago and back,

> *Oscar*
> *The luckiest man in the world*

Chapter 13 – Georges in Paris

"Bonjour, Monsieur. Are you ready for our trip to Paris?"

"Harrumph," was all that Monet said before reading his newspaper and continuing to crush out one cigarette as he lit another.

Oscar could see that Monet was still resisting his journey to the doctor in Paris. He told Georges that he feared losing his eyesight because of the operation as several of his friends had done. To him, a little blurry vision was better than none at all. Oscar empathized with Monet's position but disagreed with his belief that he would go completely blind. Georges had told him that Monet had little to no sight in one eye and only ten percent vision in the other. How could the master paint in this condition?

He climbed into the rear seat behind Sylvain and settled back, prepared for a very grumpy ride to catch the train in Vernon. He wore his gray suit, hoping it would be stylish enough for Paris. Monet wore his usual shirt with ruffled cuffs, crumpled hat, and a sour expression along with his three-piece suit.

Today would be a long one for them both. Blanche was so helpful in making all the arrangements, including train tickets and transportation from the Gare St. Lazare to Dr. Coutela's office and back. The driver would take him from the doctor's office to Georges' home and back to the train station. It would be an excellent opportunity for him to see more of the city—he mostly wanted to see the Tuileries Garden. They had been damaged during the war and were being brought back to life.

After dropping Monet at the doctor's office, Oscar left for Georges' home but took a detour to the *Jardins des Tuileries* and vowed to return so he could stroll through the gardens and study their layout. There had been a dedicated effort to restore these royal gardens after the war. By riding past these gardens on the Rue de Rivoli, he could tell that a great deal of renovation had been carried out, but more needed to be accomplished before it attained its former glory. He was determined to see *L'Orangerie,* where Monet's Water Lilies series would be on display. From what he could see at a distance, it looked like an abandoned building with no exterior work going on as they drove past. For now, he was more interested in what Georges had to say about his mother.

The driver turned up the hill away from the Seine and onto Rue Benjamin Franklin and stopped at number eight. It was a modest building that few would have noticed had it not been painted an eye-catching red. Its entrance was set back from the street. His driver pulled into the courtyard and let Oscar off. The driver would return to the doctor's office to wait for Monet and then come to pick up Oscar.

Oscar rang the bell. The bottom half of the double doors was painted black, and the top half was filled with multiple leaded-glass panes. It was an impressive house, but not what he expected for the prime minister of France. He straightened his jacket and brushed his trousers as he stood before the home of this famous man. He felt out of place and wished he hadn't agreed to the visit. He hoped no one would answer the door, and he could return to visit the *Tuileries* instead.

Just as he was about to leave, a slim, elderly woman answered the door. She had gray hair and wore a long gray dress with a white apron.

"You must be Oscar Bonhomme?" she said.

"*Oui.* Prime Minister Clémenceau invited me to visit."

"He's busy at present. Please follow me."

Oscar plucked up his courage and followed the woman. She

showed him to the entrance hall outside Clémenceau's office and asked him to wait.

"The prime minister will be out in a few minutes. Please make yourself comfortable."

As if he could do anything of the sort. Oscar turned first one way, then the other. Georges had decorated his entry hall with photographs and paintings, and he was looking for something to take his mind off where he was. Above the sizeable gold-framed mirror were two photos of Georges and Monet and two Japanese woodblock prints by Hiroshige. These could be pleasant topics of conversation should the need arise. An old sofa against one wall, next to the glass-paned doors leading to the garden, made the room feel inviting, helping him relax. A yellow couch with its blue stripes reminded him of the Provincial colors in Monet's dining room.

Oscar went into the garden to enjoy its plantings, and as he looked up, he gasped when he saw the *Tour Eiffel* between the trees. The irony of a view of Paris's icon from the garden of France's hero made him feel privileged to be here.

Georges had filled his small garden with a variety of shrubs bordering a circular walkway paved with pebbles. It was peaceful even though it lacked the combination of colors that flowers would provide. Oscar worked with so much color in Monet's gardens that he expected more of the same from Georges.

He sat on the stone bench, enjoying the serenity of the garden and the view of the *Tour Eiffel*, when Georges appeared in the doorway.

"I love this garden," he said. "Therefore, I didn't move to the Hôtel Matignon, the prime minister's residence. I need the tranquility that this garden offers to clear my head and keep my thoughts straight."

"*Bonjour, Monsieur. Merci* for inviting me to your home." Oscar smiled as he rose to greet his host.

Georges walked across the garden with a friendly smile and offered his famous vigorous handshake. "The pleasure is all mine. I'm pleased that you could accompany Monet to the doctor. He needs to have his eyes mended. You helped make that possible, and for that, I'm grateful."

"He wasn't happy about the trip," Oscar said. "I'm afraid I upset him when I sided with you on the need for this doctor visit. It's just that his eyes have been troubling him so much."

Georges gave him a reassuring look. "He's grumpy with anyone who takes him away from his beloved Giverny. He hates to leave for a doctor's examination or any other reason. Don't take it personally."

Oscar twisted his cap in his hands as he looked for a way to change the conversation to his mother, the primary reason for his visit. "I noticed that you have some Japanese woodblock prints hanging in the hallway. Do you collect them?"

Georges sighed.

"I did at one time. I had an extensive collection but had to sell most of it to support my political ambitions. You can't make money being an honest politician. I learned that the hard way." Georges looked sad at having to give up something he cherished. "However, I couldn't part with all of the prints. These last two were my favorites. The geishas look so charming in their kimonos, carrying paper umbrellas."

"Yes, I see their charm and eloquence. I hope you don't mind me asking, but is this charm and eloquence what you see in *Madame Blanche?*"

Georges' face lit up with a broad smile.

"It is. How perceptive of you. Blanche is the most elegant member of Monet's household, and I cherish her for that reason." He laughed. "That old man needs all the charm around him he can find."

Oscar smiled and cast about for another topic and noticed a gondola painting. "Is that painting of a gondola by Monet?"

"*Oui.* Monet painted that while on a visit to Venice with his wife Alice. He so loved the soft light and how it played upon the water of the canals." Georges pointed to these details in the painting. "Note the shimmer of the water. That is my favorite part of this painting. Alice was ill when he returned to Giverny after their trip to Venice and took to her bed. He promised himself to return to the south and continue painting this inspiring light, but alas, he never did."

Oscar had plucked a bud from a plant and was examining it as Georges spoke. He perked up his ears and dropped the bud at the mention of Alice. He was curious to know more about Monet's relationship with her and her children. "Why didn't he return to Venice if he loved it so much?"

Georges looked sad as he turned to stare at the *Tour Eiffel* in the distance. "Alice never regained her strength after that trip. He loved and depended upon her to keep his life on an even keel. She catered to the needs of his ten-person household. He stopped painting for two years after her death. His oldest son, Jean, died during the war around this same time. These deaths devastated him and made him a recluse who seldom ventures far from Giverny."

Oscar reflected on the difficulties Monet had suffered. "I guess you never know what trials even successful people go through. I didn't understand how much he depended upon her. It's so sad to lose your love."

Georges paused and pulled his mustache as if he was considering his dear friend's long, challenging life. He nodded in agreement with Oscar's assessment.

Georges again tugged at his mustache. "That's a complicated subject. Let's go to my office where we can talk in private. Do you like *foie gras*? I'll have a snack prepared for us to enjoy when Monet arrives."

He turned and led the way inside.

They entered Georges' large office with its red walls, matching the building's color. He'd lined the walls with bookshelves crowded with what looked like legal documents bound in simple paper covers. This looked more like a legal office than the study of a scholar. The center of the room was a carved, semicircular desk that surrounded Georges as he worked with his books and papers. He sat inside the semicircle with his back to the substantial white fireplace that dominated the room.

Oscar didn't quite know how to respond to Georges' question. "I've never tried foie gras. I've heard it's goose liver, but that's all I know."

"No matter. I'm sure you'll like it. You're French." He laughed and clapped Oscar on the back so hard that he felt he might pitch forward onto the desk.

Georges moved inside the enormous desk and sat in his red leather chair. Oscar chose the yellow chair beside the window. The midday light coming through the panes lit Georges' face so Oscar could see his expressions. He sat back, crossed his legs, and waited for the great man to begin.

"Oscar, I want to tell you a story that will provide you with some answers to questions I'm sure you have." He rose from his chair, turned to his left, and brought glasses and a decanter from the shelf. "I almost forgot. First, let's have a toast to your mother, a woman I admired."

Oscar hesitated as he took the glass of dark-brown liquid. Was this going to be another one of those fiery drinks like Monet's that burned his damaged throat?

"I don't know what questions you mean, but I'm curious to hear the story," he said. A mix of interest and apprehension stirred in him. "I've always had lots of questions about my mother's life."

"Here's to your mother. *Santé.*"

Oscar took a sip of the potent brandy and coughed as it burned down his throat to his stomach.

"You may know that I moved to New York City many years ago to escape the changing politics of France. There I met and married my first wife, an American. Over the years, we had two children, and I practiced medicine. However, as time wore on, my wife and I argued. I returned to my life in France to pursue politics and publishing, my two passions. After several years of this, divorce seemed to be the next step, and we were ready to take it." Georges frowned as he spoke of divorce. He took a long sip before refilling his glass. "It went against my Catholic upbringing to divorce her, but our lives were in different places."

Oscar nodded in acknowledgment and declined a refill. He hadn't consumed much of his first serving of the fiery amber liquid in his glass.

"It was during this troublesome time that I attended a lecture on flowers by a gardening expert in San Francisco. You may have noticed from my visit to Giverny that I share Monet's love of gardening. The lecture was fascinating, and the speaker was beautiful, smart, and French. I was so enthralled that I asked her to dinner after the lecture."

Georges seemed to enjoy the memories and telling his story. He smiled as he looked out the window at his garden and into his past.

Oscar dreaded what was coming next. Would this be another conquest by the ultimate flirt, his mother?

"We sat at dinner and talked about flowers, politics, and France. She was so charming. I didn't want the evening to end. She agreed to meet me in Golden Gate Park the next afternoon to continue our discussions and tour her garden design and plantings."

Again, Georges smiled. Oscar grew more impatient to hear what was to come.

"This was the first of several such meetings in the coming days as we grew closer together. After about a week, I was so captivated with your mother, I asked if she would like to take the relationship further. She looked at me with those lovely blue eyes and gracefully declined. When asked if there was someone else, she told me about the one true love of her life. She had met him in her youth and was not willing to consider another."

Georges' mood had turned to sadness at this point, and his smile faded. His face grew somber, and his mustache drooped further. The sadness changed to anger as he stood up abruptly and crossed the room to pick up the photo of Monet. He stood staring at it for several moments and then turned it over and slammed it down on the shelf with such force that the glass broke. He seemed resentful of his friend who captured a woman's heart and then ignored her. She was then unavailable to him or anyone else.

The noise startled Oscar, who jumped in his seat. The rapid mood change made him sit up and stare at Georges. What had brought on such a violent reaction?

"It turns out that my rival was my dear friend. She'd met him in Bordighera near Antibes, and they'd had an affair. He asked her to marry him. At that time, he was in a relationship with another woman, Alice, whom he also loved. There were many children involved. He and Alice were having a tough time since she refused to divorce her deadbeat husband who had abandoned his family years earlier."

Oscar became irritated at Georges for disrespecting Monet, whom he idolized. He was again torn by his mother's behavior, but most of all, he was excited to find out more about his father's identity. Was his father Monet?

Georges' face betrayed a fit of anger that Oscar hadn't expected, one of his mother's flirtation conquests to be jealous of her other friends. He felt sorry for him and was angry with his mother for leading him on when she had no intention of taking the relationship further. It was one more reason why he distrusted flirts.

"Also, your mother knew Monet dedicated his life to his art. Any woman who married him would have to give up her life to support his." The sadness returned to Georges' voice, and a tear rolled down his cheek. "One night, she left his bed and disappeared. He never saw or spoke to her again."

Georges' face was wet with tears. For his friend? For himself? Or for the tragedy? Oscar wondered.

Oscar could hardly breathe. He was finding out the possible identity of his father. But why didn't his mother marry him? This was a piece of the puzzle he had sought for so long, but the pain of it was almost more than he could comprehend. Why did she leave without saying anything? This was more complicated, and his mind flitted from fact to fact as Georges continued. She could have given him a father but had turned him down by fleeing the scene.

"She had left a note that said, 'I love you too much to stay and just enough to leave.'"

Oscar leaned so far forward to catch every word that he nearly fell out of his chair. He couldn't believe what he was hearing. All his life, his mother had had many close relationships like the one with Georges, but none had ever lasted. Now he knew why. She was still in love with Monet. If only she'd said "yes" to him, their lives would have been so different. He loved and hated his mother and father so much that a cry of anguish escaped from his lips.

"I don't understand," he said as tears ran down his cheeks. His thoughts continued to swim in search of the safety of reason. Georges was confirming what he'd learned from Renoir.

Georges seemed to realize the effect this was having on him. He came around the desk and put his hand on Oscar's shoulder and offered him a handkerchief. "My boy, I never meant for this to hurt you. I don't know how I could be so thoughtless. Please forgive me for my anger and self-pity."

Oscar dried his face and looked up into Georges' eyes. His kindness and sorrow were apparent and almost overwhelming. "Please go on with your story. I've waited so long and traveled so far to hear the truth. You mustn't stop now."

Georges returned to his seat and continued his story. "The young girl had discovered she was pregnant. That's why she left without telling Monet and moved to Antibes to find work and have her child far away from the pain this would cause her parents. She wanted to give you a fresh start in life without bringing shame on her family."

Oscar stood and thought of running into the garden. He needed to escape the anger and pain of these revelations. He wasn't sure how much more of the story he could endure. Georges' words felt like gunfire ripping into his heart. His mother had left because of him. His war wounds, the death of his mother, and now this revelation was too much for him. He rushed into the garden to get some fresh air.

He sat on the bench, trying to make sense of it all. His mind flitted from one subject to another, grasping comfort from none of them. He tried again to sort his thoughts into a logical order to make sense of them. All was chaos. He needed to get out of this place and think about everything. He just needed the strength to stand and make a getaway. If only his breath held out, he would run and not stop 'til he reached the Seine. Then he would be free to sort things out or throw himself in.

Before he could rise to his feet, Georges came out to the garden. He sat down on the bench beside him and put his hand on Oscar's shoulder so he could not escape.

"I understand that you're upset, but I need to tell you the rest of the story. Your mother and I continued to correspond over the years. She sent me flowers to plant in my garden and share with Monet, and I updated her on Monet's career and struggles. Before the war, I went to visit her in San Francisco. That's when she asked me to watch over you." He squeezed Oscar's shoulder to provide reassurance. "She was so ill that we were sure she would not survive to see you return from the battlefield."

The pain of this revelation flooded Oscar's whole being like the poison gas in his lungs. He'd not thought of her last days, and he was glad Georges had been there to comfort her. Why hadn't she told him? She had let him wonder who his father was all his life. Now that he'd discovered the truth, how could he face Monet again? Did Monet even know that he'd had a child by her? Had he forgotten his mother ever existed? He must have some memory of her. If not, Monet wouldn't have sent him to deliver the letter and painting to Renoir. God, these answers he'd been seeking brought up so many more questions. Was there no relief from all this anguish?

Oscar imagined his mother taking him in her arms and comforting him. Telling him all would work out for the best. But how could he trust her after she'd withheld the identity of his father? Why had she done this to him? His heart ached with disappointment and loss. He was alone and abandoned.

He didn't run out the door. He summoned the courage to return to Georges' office to face whatever was next like she'd taught him.

Georges continued his story. "When we talked at Giverny, I could sense that you had questions about why I arranged for you to work for Monet. You were right—there was more to my decision than I let on. I wanted you to get to know each other without the barrier of your past. I'd promised your mother to help you find your father, but on your terms and in your own time."

Oscar sank into his chair with the shame of not trusting his mother to look out for him. She had wanted him to find his father in his own way at his own time. He needed to first understand his father.

Georges walked over to the shelf and turned Monet's photo up again. He removed the broken glass piece by piece and threw it into a small wastebasket next to his desk. "Monet must never know that I broke his photo. He does not know of my desire for your mother."

Oscar's head was still spinning.

"What am I supposed to do with this information? I've been trying to find out the identity of my father. Now what? Do I stay? Do I leave?" He put his head in his hands. "Do I tell him? What will Blanche and the others in the family think of me? What has my mother done to me now? I miss her so much. If I could only talk to her for a few minutes, I'm sure she could help me determine what I'm to do next. Oh, I'd give anything for just a few minutes with her."

Georges reached out to put his arm around Oscar's shoulders.

At that moment, Monet burst into the room shouting, "Georges, you dog! What've you done? Nothing! Not one thing is going on at *l'Orangerie.* No one is working on getting the museum ready to receive my *Grandes Décorations.* Why should I bother finishing them?"

Chapter 14 – The Duel

"Monet, settle down. What are you talking about? How are your eyes?" Georges tried to get his friend under control by smiling and moving toward him, offering to shake his hand.

Oscar looked on with his mouth open. He couldn't believe what he was seeing. He'd never witnessed Monet in such a rage. His face was flame-red, his snowy white beard about to ignite. He was shocked and saddened by Monet's behavior.

Monet snarled through clenched jaws, "My eyes? My eyes? He gave me some drops so I could see better. Don't change the subject, you swine. My eyes are well enough to see your treachery. When were you going to tell me the *l'Orangerie* is not being prepared for my *Grandes Décorations*?"

Georges' face was turning as red as Monet's at the barrage of insults his friend hurtled at him. "It takes time to get such projects started. You know that. Besides, you're nowhere near ready to deliver the *Grandes Décorations* based on what I saw a few days ago."

Monet shouted louder. "I don't know how I got talked into trusting you to handle this for me."

"*Moi!* You're the one who keeps backing out of his commitment," Georges shouted even louder.

"My work is much further along than yours, you scoundrel!"

"Not by much! You're an old fraud!" Georges snapped back.

Oscar was worried that these two old men would hurt themselves if they kept at each other. He had to do something. "Please stop this arguing. You'll hurt yourselves."

Turning to glare at Oscar, they both shouted at once, "Stay out of this!"

"You'll give each other heart attacks if you keep this up." He was fearful for their lives and his own.

Oscar shook his head. Neither of the old bulls would listen to him. But what could he do? Perhaps he could introduce humor as he did in the trenches when two men were fighting. It was a dangerous move that carried certain personal risks.

He tried to stand between them, thought he could force them to retreat. Both old men shoved him aside. He stumbled backward over a chair and hit his head. The more they shouted, the closer they got. The two were belly-to-belly in the center of the room, each pushing against the other until vest buttons popped. Oscar ducked behind the desk to avoid being hit if one of these two behemoths fell or stumbled toward him.

Monet glared at Georges. "Fraud? Who's a fraud? You're a political hack!"

Georges sidestepped a powerful lunge from Monet, who fell against the bookshelves by the door. As Monet was recovering his footing, Georges moved to a cabinet by the window. He bent down, panting, opened the cabinet door, and lifted out a carved mahogany box. He carried it back to his desk and opened it to reveal a matched set of silver-plated dueling pistols nestled in green velvet.

"I've fought duels with men for less than you've called me this afternoon!" he announced.

Monet pulled himself up taller to match Georges' height.

"Bring them out to the garden, and let's see if they still work!" He shook his fist. "I'll cut you down to size, you coward."

Georges bristled at the insult. "Coward? Coward, did you say? Who are you calling a coward? You fled to France rather than fight the Germans back in seventy. You ran off to England again when you saw France was in danger."

Monet screamed and rushed at Georges.

"I ruined my eyesight serving France in North Africa." His hands were shaking. "Coward! Fight me, you coward!"

The housekeeper entered with a tray of food, saw the debacle, and retreated out the door.

Oscar sniggered. Both men turned to face him, and he laughed louder. The more surprised they looked, the more he laughed. After catching his breath, he gasped out, "One of you can't see well enough to hit the other with a cannon, let alone a pistol. The other would lose his medical license if he failed to treat his attacker. Much as I would like to see if these old pistols could fire, I suggest you keep your powder dry."

At that, he laughed even harder. The two old men looked at him and then at each other, shocked and then embarrassed. Each smiled, first Monet, then Georges. Both seemed to realize that they had no choice but to join in Oscar's guffaws. They were foolish, but not enough to hurt a dear friend.

When the laughter had subsided, Georges closed the box of pistols and returned it to the cabinet. He then called the housekeeper to bring back the snacks. Brandy flowed and flowed as each offered a toast. Oscar tried the foie gras and then consumed more than his fair share.

Monet raised his glass to offer a toast to Georges. He tried standing and then settled back into the leather chair by the door. "To my dear friend Georges, who came to my aid when my darling Alice died. I was ready to give up on painting and life. You saved me from ruin. I'll be forever grateful for that."

Oscar turned his head to face the garden and away from Monet. He hadn't realized how much Alice had meant to Monet's life. His father depended upon her as much or more than upon Blanche. He could see that his mother could never have fulfilled that role for Monet. Monet was right to marry Alice and not his mother. She must have known this when she decided to leave. Being in love was not always enough to forge a life together.

He turned to look around the room at the photos of the many good times these two old friends had shared. Perhaps he was intruding upon their private moment of friendship. With this realization, he rose to depart. However, the brandy kept flowing. The empty decanters were lining up on Georges' desk, and he realized that he had to stay to help Monet return home.

Georges attempted to deliver a toast, and he also struggled to stand before flopping back onto his desk chair. "I'll be forever grateful that you're giving France the magnificent gift of your *Grandes Décorations*. They will be a fitting tribute to the brave souls who fought and died in the Great War. France will forever be in your debt. That is, as soon as you allow me to tell them about the gift."

His words came out slurred, but the meaning was understandable. These two old men loved each other and had been saved from a terrible duel that could have destroyed them both. Emotions of the day—Monet's eye examination and Georges' lost love—ran so high that they had surrendered all reason in the heat of the moment.

Despite his better judgment, Oscar tried to enter the conversation. "What did the doctor tell you about your eyes?"

Monet placed his hands over his eyes. "He gave me some drops to try. They seem to work a little so far. He still urged me to submit to surgery for cataracts."

Georges leaned forward to take up the doctor's cause. "I hope you agreed to schedule the operations as soon as possible."

Monet held up his right hand as if to stop Georges from interfering. "Not now. I've seen the harm these surgeries can do. Too many others have been blinded. My work on the *Grandes Décorations* must be completed before my eyes get much worse."

The events of the day had exhausted Oscar. The weight of these two behemoths had fallen on his shoulders. He tried his best to help Monet, but his eye surgery was going nowhere. He felt personally defeated by this. Georges' efforts to persuade Monet to get surgery were also to no avail. This trip was a waste of time in that regard but he did gain a better understanding of his mother and his father's identity.

"We must go, or we'll miss our train." He rose and crossed the room to help Monet out of his chair. He was very heavy to lift to his feet, even though he didn't resist Oscar's help.

When the driver arrived in the room, both older men were so pickled in brandy that neither could have aimed a pistol or even held one steady. They stumbled into each other as they walked to the door.

Monet kissed Georges on both cheeks and was escorted to the vehicle by the driver.

As he was leaving, Oscar thanked Georges. "It was quite an afternoon. I enjoyed the *foie gras*."

"And I enjoyed getting to know you better. Please return soon. We have a lot more to discuss. *Merci* for making us laugh at ourselves."

"It was the only way I could think of to keep you from killing each other," Oscar said with a smile. "I learned that trick in the trenches from a sergeant whose father, it so happens, served with Monet in North Africa. Perhaps that's why he joined in the laughter so eagerly."

"Whatever the reason, I'm glad he did." Georges laughed. "I'm not the doctor I used to be."

The journey back to Giverny proved uneventful. Monet was quiet except for his loud snoring when he fell asleep on the train. Oscar didn't mind because he was lost in his thoughts about what he had learned from Georges.

He was still trying to sort things out when Sylvain dropped him off at his boarding house. He skipped dinner and dashed upstairs to his room, and pulled out paper and pen.

My Darling Isabelle,

I'd like to tell you about my day in Paris and hope that this letter makes sense. It has been a struggle sorting this out.

I traveled with Monet to visit his eye doctor. He can't see well enough to travel by himself. After dropping him at the doctor's, I went to visit Georges Clémenceau. Yes, the prime minister of France. He's a close friend to Monet and my mother. He delivered a message from my mother, who spoke with him in the weeks leading to her death.

I'm not sure how to write this, so I will just do it. I think Monet is my father. He and my mother had a brief affair in Antibes while he was painting there. He was between wives and fell in love with my mother. It turns out that she fell in love with him as well, so much so she refused to marry anyone else for the rest of her life. He was the one true love of her life.

She knew that he also loved Alice. He'd lived with her and her six children for years. My mother was not willing to tear that family apart, so she sacrificed her happiness and mine, too. Monet married Alice a few years after my mother left him and her husband died.

My mother left Monet when she learned she was pregnant. To avoid causing her parents the embarrassment of explaining her pregnancy to her family and friends, she stayed in Antibes to have me. She then emigrated to America to get a fresh start. I knew almost nothing about my father when I was growing up.

On one of the few occasions my mother even mentioned my father, I'd come home early from high school to find her sitting at the kitchen table crying. Momma, what's wrong? Why are you crying? I asked.

She told me that the man she saw made her so angry because he reminded her of my father. She said he only thought of himself. She said she couldn't be with a man like that.

I begged her to tell me more and asked if she'd left my father because he would put his interests above hers and that of her child. Then I asked her if I looked like him.

She said I have his eyes and told me he'd had a very piercing stare that would sweep a scene from side to side, taking it all in. Then I was told I did the same thing.

I went to my room, thinking about what she'd told me. Was I as selfish as my father had been? He doesn't seem like a very good man. What did my mother see in him?

Georges met my mother years later in San Francisco and fell in love with her. Remember I told you she was a great flirt. Men were always falling in love with her. She turned down his proposal of marriage, but they remained friends throughout the rest of her life. In the end, she asked him to watch over me during the war and tell me about my father when the time was right.

That's the straightforward part, but the hard part came next. I was looking for the identity of my father. Now that I have done that, I'm lost. I don't know what to do next. Shall I leave Giverny? Do I tell Monet what I think I have found out? And Blanche? Do I leave France to be with you in Chicago? Or should I stay in France and make a new life for myself?

Most of all, I need to decide about joining Monet's family or not. I've always wanted a father and brothers and sisters. Is this the family I have been searching for? Would they even accept me?

I wish you were here, so I could talk with you about this. When are you coming back? When are you going to answer my letters? Do you still care for me as much as I love you? So many questions. Is it any wonder that I feel lost? And alone?

I love you to Chicago and back,

Oscar

The following morning began like most any other. Oscar posted his letter to Isabelle after buying his baguette for lunch. It was cold out in the pre-dawn darkness. He pulled his jacket around him and rushed down the lane to Monet's house. He started preparing the cart for the day's work as usual and stood next to the studio, awaiting

Monet's instructions about which paintings he would work on that day. As he stood by the door, he was thinking about the events of the day before. Blanche called from the back porch.

"Oscar, please come here."

She looked warm and charming in her long white dress, yellow sweater, and smiling blue eyes. Oscar wished she would take his hand and tell him everything was going to be all right, the way his mother would have done.

As he approached, she said, "Monet will not be painting today." She smiled and added, "He's still under the weather from yesterday."

She had a pleasant way of putting it. He was tired but not under the weather. His decision to stop drinking way before the old men had been a sound one.

"Monet would like you to continue with your gardening chores and meet him in the large studio after lunch."

Oscar didn't understand him again. Now what was Monet up to? Had the way he'd handled the confrontation at Georges' apartment offended him? Did he know about his conversation with Georges concerning his mother? What could Monet want now?

Chapter 15 – The Promotion

Oscar finished his work and walked across the garden to the large studio. He stood at the door, calming himself before entering, brushed the garden soil from his clothes, and walked into the large room to respond to the summons from Monet. He always felt apprehensive being summoned into the master's presence, especially after his encounter the day before.

The room was empty except for Monet's *Grandes Décorations*. He'd visited the studio many times but had never taken time to observe its grandeur. The late afternoon sunlight gave a soft, golden glow to everything inside, including his host. The comfortable setting made Oscar want to curl up on the couch and read a good book. It wasn't a good idea, but it was a pleasant thought. Anything would be better than facing an angry old man.

Monet turned around and greeted him. "Come in, my son. Take a seat."

Did Monet know that Oscar was his son? How could he? It was a strange choice of words given the previous day's revelations.

"*Oui, Monsieur. Merci* for inviting me."

Monet, dressed in his usual suit jacket with just the top hole buttoned, lit a cigarette and moved to greet Oscar with a warm handshake. "My pleasure."

This was odd because he'd never greeted him in that way before. Oscar shook Monet's large, rough hand and took a seat on the couch.

"What were you working on today?" Monet asked.

"I added the orange dahlias and the yellow cosmos to the *Grande Allée* borders you mentioned last week."

Monet seemed pleased that Oscar had remembered the assignment and taken care of it.

"I'll finish the border tomorrow with the orange and yellow African marigolds and the blue salvia."

"Don't forget to include some impatiens to add shimmer."

Oscar laughed. "Of course. It's not a Monet garden without shimmer."

Monet's face lit up at the joke as he reached over to pat Oscar on the shoulder. "I didn't invite you here to talk about work. Well, not exactly about your work."

Oscar felt the conversation take a severe tone, and his chest tightened. He didn't seem angry with him over the events of yesterday. At least not yet. Still, he twisted his cap in his hands, waiting for the bad news.

Monet lit another cigarette from the one he was finishing and crushed out the spent one in the overflowing ashtray on the table in front of them. He cleared his throat before speaking. Oscar realized he was not the only one who was nervous.

"I want to apologize for my behavior of yesterday."

Oscar sat back in the deep seat of the soft couch, shocked by this confession. Monet was not a man to apologize.

He looked down at his paint-stained hands. "I shouldn't have become so upset and never should have shoved you. Now I can see that you were only trying to help."

Oscar cringed. This discussion was not one he felt comfortable with. He crossed and uncrossed his legs. "It was nothing. I knew you didn't want to hurt Georges."

Monet looked into Oscar's eyes. "If you hadn't made us laugh at ourselves, it's hard to say what we would have done. Nice trick. Where did you learn that?"

"The son of your Army buddy from North Africa taught it to me in the trenches."

Monet paused and looked away as if gazing back some sixty years.

"His name was Philippe, I think. Yes, that was it. I'd all but forgotten him. He helped me when the desert sun blinded me. He bandaged my eyes with cool compresses until the pain subsided."

"I guessed that if laughter worked in combat," Oscar chuckled, "it would work with you two old warriors."

"It did." Monet smiled but still seemed embarrassed by his behavior. "I'm glad you did that when you did. I was in danger of either popping all my buttons or getting shot." With that, he laughed so hard, he threatened to pop another button or two.

Oscar laughed until he couldn't breathe and began coughing. When he'd caught his breath, he asked for a drink of water and held up his hand to decline the offered *Calvados*. "I think I had enough to drink yesterday."

He finished his glass of water and sat back to relax, trying to get comfortable for what was still to come. He wasn't sure what it would be, but his boss was up to something. Oscar had known him long enough to understand when he wanted something.

Monet took a sip of *Calvados* before he began. "You know that we lost our head gardener to the war. Until you arrived, we tried to make do with a few inexperienced men who meant well, but they didn't have the knowledge you have, nor the dedication to the garden that you've shown. So, for the past year, we've gone without."

Oscar sat forward on the couch and stared at Monet's face to catch every subtlety of this discussion. He couldn't quite figure out where Monet was taking the conversation, but it didn't seem to be in a dangerous direction.

Monet took another sip before continuing. "You know, or I hope you know, that I value your leadership in managing the garden work. You seem to understand what I want to be done and how best to accomplish it. For this, I'm grateful."

He paused long enough to drain his glass of *Calvados*.

Oscar waited as calmly as he could. His chest felt tight, and his breath shallow with what he'd say next.

"Oscar, I want you to accept the position as head gardener, starting now."

The offer took him by surprise. He hadn't expected such an honor. He tried to assess the ramifications of accepting this offer.

"I'm raising your salary. Oh, and one other thing: I want you to move into our gardener's cottage. I'd like you to be close at hand so we can discuss the garden's progress in the evenings. Besides, it'll save you paying rent. Perhaps Blanche will feed you from time to time." Then he laughed again, tempting his buttons. "What do you say?"

Oscar leaned back in his seat. He'd thought Monet might reveal that he was his father. This had been uppermost in his mind. Monet was offering him a job, an important position, but not the relationship he'd dreamed of. A sense of relief mixed with disappointment washed over him with this unexpected news.

He exhaled. "I need a drink."

"I bet you do." Monet chuckled to himself as he headed to the sideboard to pour a glass of *Calvados* for each of them.

It wasn't so much that Oscar needed the drink as he needed the time to think. He needed to spend a few moments considering how to respond before Monet returned with the glass.

He received a larger-than-expected drink from Monet and sat up in his seat to not spill it. His voice cracked as he began, but he forced himself to carry on.

"I love working here. The garden has become my home, and your family, my adopted family. If it weren't for my work here, I'm not sure what would have become of me." He lowered his head and his voice at this admission and realization.

On the one hand, he wanted the job, and on the other, he needed Isabelle.

After a few moments composing himself, he continued. "The position you've offered me is more than I could ever have hoped for. There is nothing else I would rather do."

Monet lit another cigarette and fixed his gaze on Oscar's face as he waited to see what he would say next.

Oscar took another long sip of the brown liquid. As usual, it burned his throat, warmed his stomach, and stoked his courage. "I'm not sure your men will like my becoming the head gardener since I'm new here and an American."

"Oscar, it's hard to say if they like you, but I'm sure they respect you."

Oscar put down the drink, looked away, and thought for what seemed to him like a long time. "I understand your offer and appreciate your faith in me. The real reason for my hesitation is Isabelle. I don't know if she wants to stay here when she returns. She may want me to return with her to Chicago."

"Have you heard from her since she left?"

He shrugged. "No. But I expect to hear from Isabelle any day now. It's a long way to Chicago. She may not have arrived there yet."

Monet looked exasperated as he pressed forward with his offer. "Let me make sure I understand what you are saying. You're considering turning down my offer to be the head gardener of the best private garden in France, perhaps in all of Europe. You're thinking of rejecting this opportunity because of a woman, whom you've known for only a few weeks, and who has left you. She has traveled thousands of miles away and has not communicated with you since. You don't even know if she still cares for you or not. Do I have that right?"

Oscar lowered his head in embarrassment. "You're right. How can I be so stupid over a woman I recently met? I feel like an idiot."

Monet shrugged and sat for a few minutes as if considering what to tell him. "Love makes us stupid. I once was ready to give up Alice and her six children for a young woman I met while painting in the south. She was so beautiful and oh so smart. We had our love of flowers in common, and I was completely taken with her. I would have married her on the spot, but she left me."

This admission by Monet overwhelmed Oscar. It could be an opportunity to discuss his parentage. He leaned forward in his seat, could hardly wait to hear what he was going to tell him next.

"What happened?" he asked.

Monet took a large drink of *Calvados* and continued. "We were sleeping together one night, and she was gone in the morning. She left a note saying, 'I love you too much to stay and just enough to leave.' I never quite understood what she meant, but I always remember what she wrote."

"She must have loved you very much." Oscar's mind raced. Should he take this opportunity to tell Monet that this woman was his mother? That he was his son?

He was working up the courage to say something when Monet spoke again.

"Perhaps. But why wouldn't the young woman say goodbye?" Monet asked as a tear trickled down his cheek. "I never heard from her again. In looking back, I'm sure it was for the best. She would have distracted me from my painting. Perhaps she knew that."

Oscar and Monet looked at each other as if contemplating their lost loves. They toasted, "To lost loves." Then sat drinking in silence for a few minutes before Blanche walked in.

She smiled and looked from one face to the other. "Why the sad faces? I thought we had something to celebrate. I've baked a peach cobbler, and Lily has made ice cream."

Monet looked up and said with a regretful tone in his voice, "Oscar is about to turn down my offer. He's not sure if this is what Isabelle would want."

Blanche moved to Oscar's side. "Oscar, is this true? Have you heard from her? How is her father doing?"

Oscar rose to his feet and then took Blanche's hand to steady himself. He really should avoid drinking with Monet.

"I haven't heard from her," he said with eyes downcast. "I'm honored to take this position. But I don't want to take it and then have to leave to be with Isabelle."

Blanche held on to his hand and turned to face Monet. "Can't he take the position now and decide about leaving later? That way, he could help you with the garden while these things sort themselves out. What would it hurt?"

Monet rose to his feet.

"Blanche, once again you've come through with an excellent solution. This means that we can have our cobbler and eat it, too." Monet chuckled at his little joke. "What say you, Oscar?"

"If you don't mind, I'll let you know tomorrow," he said with slight hesitation. "I must apologize for leaving now, but I have a lot to think about tonight. *Merci beaucoup.* I appreciate this wonderful opportunity. I have some hard decisions to make. I'll give you my answer in the morning."

He couldn't make eye contact with Monet or his stepdaughter. Monet and Blanche looked stunned at his abrupt departure. He pivoted and hurried out of the studio and down the road to his boarding house.

His mind was as confused as it had been the day before in Paris. When he reached his boarding house, he skipped dinner, headed upstairs to his room, and closed the door. He threw his work clothes at the old wooden chair in his room and crawled onto the bed with pen and paper.

My Dearest Isabelle,

I can't believe I'm writing you another letter so soon. It's just that I have a tough decision to make, and I desperately need your advice. Since you are not here to help me, writing to you is the next best thing.

Monet offered to promote me to head gardener today. I would oversee the other men and manage the plantings. Perhaps I could even help with the design of the landscape. I would work under Monet's tight supervision. That would not be easy, but I could handle that and am doing well with him so far.

This is a great opportunity. After being a head gardener at one of the most famous private gardens in France and all of Europe, I could get a job anywhere. The opportunity is even more significant than Monet realizes.

Oscar laid his pen down and stretched out on the bed. He wasn't sure how to continue with the letter. *Dare he ask her the questions he wanted to ask? Would this make her shy away from ever coming back to him?* He didn't want to lose her or the job opportunity. Putting his hands under his head, he lay thinking for a long time about what he wanted to ask.

His other reason for considering Monet's offer was that working closely with him and living in the gardener's cottage would mean that he'd be, in some ways, joining the family. Being part of the family, with no one knowing that he was a part of the family, could provide benefits without the embarrassing revelation of his secret to anyone. He'd always wanted a father and brothers and sisters. This would be his chance. How could he give this up?

He's also providing me with free rent in the gardener's cottage next to the big studio overlooking the Grande Allée. I've been to the place. It's comfortable with lots of windows letting in glorious light for painting. Could you see yourself living in this beautiful garden? He's giving me a pay increase. I'm not sure how much, but I think it would be adequate to support the two of us.

Can you guess what I'm leading up to? Would you consider living here with me? I'd hate to take this job if you would rather live somewhere else. You wouldn't have to marry me if you didn't want to.

I'm sure I'm making a mess of this. Please write to me soon or come back to me. I miss you so much.

With all my love,
Oscar

He read and reread the letter before inserting it into an envelope for mailing. It worried him that he'd scare Isabelle away or make her uncomfortable by asking or not asking her to marry him. That question should be asked in person.

Most of his night was spent stewing over the situation. He got a few hours' sleep and awoke more confused than he'd been when he went to sleep.

Should he take the job or not?

Did Isabelle still care for him?

Did Monet still want him as a head gardener?

Chapter 16 – No Choice

Oscar lay in bed, staring at the white bead-board ceiling and counting the boards, hoping that would help him fall asleep. He was trying to decide whether to accept the promotion Monet offered or not. After wrestling with this all night, he still couldn't make up his mind. Oscar got up, ate breakfast, bought his usual lunch, mailed the letter to Isabelle, and dragged himself to work. He'd promised Monet an answer but had none. His lack of commitment made his walk feel colder, lonelier, and longer than usual. He hated being indecisive.

As soon as he rounded the corner of the house, Blanche called out.

"Oscar, please come here," said Blanche from the porch.

The tone in her voice jolted him out of his thoughts. She sounded more anxious than he'd ever heard her. She tugged at the hem of her apron with both hands with a look of deep worry.

"It's Monet. He became ill last night after you left. The doctor said his lungs were congested, and he had an upset stomach. He needs to stay in bed for a few weeks. I fear it might be the Spanish flu, even though that should be gone from here by now."

Alarmed, Oscar put aside his indecision and self-doubt. He'd seen healthy comrades die of the virus in a few days after contracting it. No telling what this would do to a man of Monet's age. "How can I help?"

Blanche let go of the hem of her apron and said in an agitated tone, "You must accept the position Monet offered you. Not only does he need help with his garden, but we also want you to live in the gardener's cottage. We must have someone available in case of an emergency."

"I don't understand. Monet didn't seem ill."

"He's been hiding his condition from all of us. Smoking has affected his lungs, and his drinking hasn't helped his digestion. Hopefully, that's all it is. I depend upon you to help us. Will you do that?" She sighed. "Just get us through this crisis, and we'll address the issues with Isabelle later. Will you, please?"

He must help. "I will. For as long as you need me."

Like so many times before in his life, the needs of others made decisions for him. He felt he had no choice but to agree. Monet and his family had helped him so many times. Working in the garden had saved his life. Besides, where was Isabelle? She couldn't expect him to put his life on hold, waiting to hear from her. Could she?

"Wonderful," Blanche said with a sigh of relief. Her mood lifted when she next spoke. "I'll get the gardener's cottage cleaned up today. You can move in tomorrow."

"*Merci. Merci beaucoup*," Oscar said as he set about planning his day.

The first thing he would do was finish the border along the *Grande Allée.* He wanted to show Monet his trust was well-founded. He needed Monet to be proud of his new head gardener and secure in knowing that he'd made the right decision.

On his way to the cold frames to get the flowers to plant, he asked one gardener, Armand, to bring the orange and yellow African marigold seedlings and the blue salvia starts from the greenhouse and finish the planting they'd started the day before. Oscar would plant the white impatiens himself to add shimmer to the pathway. Armand responded to his request as if someone had already told him about Oscar's new role in the garden. He was relieved that Armand didn't seem to resent his authority. Armand had worked there longer than anyone and was well respected by everyone.

"It's important that we complete the *Grande Allée* so *Monsieur* Monet can see it from his bedroom window. It may help him recover faster if he can see that the border is becoming ready to paint. It won't hurt to offer him a little motivation to hasten his recovery. Even something so small may mean a lot."

Armand nodded in agreement and went to get the plants.

The two of them spent the day finishing up the border and ensuring all was the way Monet liked. They even had time to remove dead and diseased leaves from the roses and remove any of the other canes in the trellises that were past their prime.

The work was completed, and Oscar prepared to head home when Blanche called out to him from the porch.

"Oscar, can you come here for a few minutes before you leave?" This time, she was smiling and looking much more like her usual self. "I'm pleased to report that Monet is feeling much better. The doctor visited this afternoon and said he was improving. It's early yet, but that's good news. There is no indication of the terrible flu."

"Wonderful. I hope Monet's up and around again soon." Oscar, relieved that he would recover, looked forward to continuing their time together. He couldn't imagine being here without Monet.

"I'm sure he will be," Blanche said with an air of confidence. "The doctor said I can help him come downstairs tomorrow. He looked out his window and was pleased to see how nice the *Grande Allée* border turned out. Your extra touches made him smile. He thinks you're becoming as picky as he is."

Oscar smiled at this compliment. "I'm afraid that's not possible."

He turned to leave when Blanche interrupted.

"The gardener's cottage will be ready for you to move in tomorrow afternoon if you like."

He looked down at his dirty hands and clothes. "If it's all the same to you, I'll move in on Saturday. I'd like to take the weekend to get a fresh start."

Blanche's face lit up. "Good. That'll give the girls extra time to make it nice for you. I'll have Sylvain bring the automobile by to pick up your things."

Oscar felt uncomfortable having Sylvain make a special trip just for him. "*Merci.* No need. I don't have that much to bring over. I'll bring them over on Saturday morning in the cart I use to carry the paintings. It'll only take one or two trips."

"That's fine. Let me know if you need help." Blanche seemed reluctant to let him go. "Monet would like to welcome you in person, but he doesn't want to expose you to his chest congestion. He says he doesn't want to weaken your lungs any further."

"I understand. Please let Monet know that I appreciate the thought." He wanted Blanche to relay how pleased he was with the opportunity to work and live in Monet's garden, but he wasn't sure how. "Please let him know that I'm thrilled at the way things worked out. No. Not that I'm happy he got ill. I can't thank you enough for supporting me in this position. It means more to me than I can say."

He looked down at his hands and then back at her face, hoping he had permission to leave.

Blanche smiled. "I'm thrilled you'll be here to help us. Your taking this position means a great deal to all of us. I'll let him know how excited you are about the promotion and the cottage. I'll also let him know how well you got on with Armand today. Run along home. We'll see you tomorrow."

It was strange that Blanche knew about Armand's response today. He must have told her that all was well with him taking over the manager's position. That was one supporter on his side.

Instead of going back to his boarding house, Oscar changed his mind and headed down the path to the gardener's cottage. The outside was painted pink with green trim, just like the main house. He opened the door and went inside to inspect where he would be living.

It was a small cottage but adequate for his needs. The front part had been divided into a living room with four large windows across the front. Behind the door on the left next to the fireplace was the bedroom. The kitchen lay behind the dining room swinging door on the right. The fireplace would keep the living and bedrooms warm, and the kitchen stove would heat the kitchen and dining room. Upstairs was an open attic for storage or to sleep children if he ever had any. They would be kept warm with the heat rising from below.

The rooms were cozy and clean, thanks to Blanche's assistants. It smelled musty from being unused for months or years. A good airing-out should take care of that. The cottage was decorated with comfortable living room furniture, a bed and dresser in the bedroom, and a small table and four chairs in the dining room. The kitchen with its wood-burning stove, sink, and cupboard had blue tiles on the main house walls. Like in the main house, the dining room with its yellow walls was open to the living room. The walls were cream in the living room and bedroom, and the ceiling was pale blue. A fresh coat of paint throughout made the cottage feel welcoming and helped with the musty smell.

He loved the place and smiled on his way back to the boarding house, where he told the landlady he would move out Saturday. As he raced upstairs to pack what little he had, he felt no regret leaving this dingy place for his cottage. He hadn't lived in a house since he'd left home for college. For the first time since he'd left the hospital, he had some direction to his life: a new job and a house to live in. Even a family, in a manner of speaking.

Oscar sailed through the next day with thoughts of the pending move uppermost in his mind. He kept looking at the cottage every time he went near it. There seemed to be a lot of activity in and around it. Blanche stopped by frequently, bringing bundles that he couldn't quite make out. She was smiling each time he saw her. Even the ladies working in the cottage seemed happy as they sang while they worked.

He finished his work and was on his way home to pack when Blanche stopped him.

"Monet has made his way downstairs and would like to see you in the studio/parlor. Do you have a few minutes to chat with him?"

"I'd love to see him if the doctor thinks it would be advisable." He was anxious to see how Monet was doing and to relay his appreciation for his elevated position.

"He permitted Monet to see a few friends this afternoon if he doesn't overdo it."

"*Magnifique,*" Oscar said with a broad smile and a light heart as he noted that she had included him in the friend category. "I'll be there as soon as I finish here."

He took a few minutes to brush the dirt off his clothes and shoes and wash his hands and face.

He had not been in the studio/parlor previously, so he looked around the room when he entered. Monet lay on the chaise longue so he could see out the large window overlooking his garden. He was resting with his back to the door and his head on a pillow. Monet had hung the walls of the room with his paintings that were painted over his long career. Oscar had heard they represented each stage of his life's work. A red and blue Persian rug covered much of the hardwood floor next to the window. A small writing desk and a settee completed that corner of the room.

Monet lifted his head from the pillow to greet Oscar when he announced himself with a discreet cough.

"*Bonjour, Monsieur* Monet."

"Come in, Oscar. Forgive me for not getting up."

He took a seat by the window so Monet could see him better.

"My strength is not quite what it should be. I wanted to thank you for accepting the head gardener position. I hope you'll enjoy living in the gardener's cottage. Your acceptance of this promotion means a great deal to Blanche and me."

"I assure you it means even more to me. I can't thank you enough for the faith and trust you have placed in me. The cottage is charming. I love it. It feels so warm and cozy. I'm excited to move in tomorrow."

"Let us know how we can help get you settled." Monet smiled and coughed.

"*Madame* Blanche and the ladies have done so much already. It's more than I expected."

Monet was quiet for a moment and then broached another subject. "I have one question to ask you before I must return to my bed. When we spoke the other day, you mentioned Philippe, my old Army friend, from my days in North Africa. You said his son was the one who taught you the trick about making combatants laugh at themselves during an argument. Can you tell me more about him? I've been thinking a lot about my friend since we spoke and thought maybe your friend could help me get in touch with his father."

"Would you like me to tell you a story about Philippe's son, Charles?" Oscar sat straighter in his seat and drew in a breath to prepare. He took a few moments to relax and begin. His chest tightened, and his throat was dry as he wasn't used to telling stories about his experiences in the Great War.

"That would be very nice," Monet answered with a smile.

I was talking to some friends in the trenches when the sergeant came up behind me and said, "Corporal Bonhomme, the captain wants to see you." After straightening my shoulders, I tried to tidy up my uniform. My shoes were hopeless, thanks to the thick mud of what had been the French wheat fields.

"Captain Monteil, you wanted to see me?"

"At ease, soldier. Your lieutenant is not returning to your unit as he died of his wounds this morning. We need to replace him. I have no officers under my command available for this assignment. You're the best man I have available to replace him. I'm giving you a field promotion to lieutenant. You'll take over the unit now and prepare for an attack at o-six-hundred tomorrow. Is that clear?"

The lieutenant's death shocked me, and my promotion overwhelmed me. "Oui, Monsieur. I understand, but I don't think I'm ready for this promotion."

The captain frowned and rose from his chair at my refusal. "You're ready if I say you're ready."

I stood straighter, pushed my shoulders back, and stuck out my chin. "The men respected and trusted the lieutenant. They won't like being led by an American who's new to this company."

"They'll trust anyone who promises to bring them back alive."

"I can't promise that. I can do my best. That's all."

"Then do your best and have the men ready to go over the top at o-six-hundred tomorrow. That's an order."

I rejoined the men in the trenches, where word about my promotion spread through the ranks like wildfire. Quite a few men were upset that I was being promoted over others of a higher rank and more time with the unit. Arguments started between those against an American taking command and those who supported me. Several fights broke out. That's when your friend's son, Charles, spoke up.

"Don't think of Oscar as replacing the lieutenant. Think of him as the 'Little Corporal Who Could.'"

He finished with "Choo-Choo" like the sound of the little engine that could. The men sniggered. That turned to laughter, which grew and grew as it spread down the line of men. Before long, the entire trench was howling. Even those who were about to come to blows stopped and were enjoying the joke.

From that moment on, I was Lieutenant Choo-Choo. The following day, I stood next to Charles in the trenches, preparing myself to climb the ladder and attack the enemy. It was a cold, foggy morning, and my mind was fuzzy from lack of sleep. I heard this murmur from the men down the line on either side of me. As the sound came closer, I could make out, "I think I can. I think I can," repeated as they prepared to move forward. The hour of o-six-hundred arrived, and I climbed the ladder to lead my troops over the top. When they saw me, they started chanting, "Choo-Choo, Choo-Choo, Choo-Choo" like a train building up steam as they followed me into battle. I did my best that morning, and most of the men lived through my first assault as their leader.

Several months after this, we engaged in the assault that nearly cost me my life. By that time, the men had changed our name from Company C to Company Choo-Choo. When we went over the top of the trenches that day, Charles was by my side as usual. The fighting was brutal since we were running straight into several machine-gun nests. We sprinted from bomb crater to crater across the field of battle at a terrible cost of lives. Charles and I became separated, then I jumped into an enormous hole. There, in a pool of mud and blood at the bottom, was Charles. He smiled when I jumped in and pushed a knapsack toward me. He said, "I filled this with hand grenades I collected from our fallen comrades. Please tell my wife I love her with all my heart. Now get out of here and deliver these to the Huns for me." Then he chuckled at his joke and died in my arms.

I had no time to mourn the loss of my friend. I took the knapsack, jumped out of the crater, and started running as fast as I could toward the enemy. At first I felt I was running to catch a train, then I was running in front of the train, and finally, I was the train. I started screaming, "Choo-Choo, Choo-Choo, Choo-Choo" and throwing hand grenades at the enemy position.

They didn't reach the gun emplacement but exploded above it, raining shrapnel down on the Huns. This must have caused the gunners to lose their aim because they kept missing me, mainly. At last, I was close enough to throw my remaining two grenades into the machine-gun nest, where they exploded and wiped them out. They shot me several times. I don't remember what happened after that until I woke up in the field hospital.

The men there still called me "Lieutenant Choo-Choo." I met Georges, or rather he met me, and you know the rest. So sorry I can't ask Charles about his father.

"Thanks for your story, Oscar. Please go now. I need my rest." Tears streamed down Monet's cheeks as he started coughing and waved for him to go.

It stunned Oscar to see Monet's tears. What had affected him so? Was it the death of his friend's son? Was it the sadness of the war? Oscar couldn't believe, at that moment, that his tears were for him.

Chapter 17 – Moving Day

Someone was banging on the solid old door to Oscar's bedroom, awakening him from a deep sleep with a jolt. He was unsure of what was going on.

"How did you get in here? Who are you? What do you want?"

Jean-Pierre's voice boomed back. "Wake up, sleepyhead. We're here to help you move."

"It's Jean-Pierre and Lily," Lily said. "Get up."

He'd expected no one to help him move, especially not these two. "I'll be right there. Give me a minute."

He got up, washed his face, and dressed in his clean work clothes. He checked the mirror to make sure he wouldn't frighten them with his appearance.

"Come in. I was up late last night packing and must have fallen dead asleep." He rubbed his eyes and stretched his head. "I guess I had accumulated more stuff than I'd thought. Why are you here?"

Lily, looking very chic in a pleated light-gray skirt and ice-blue top, kissed him on both cheeks. "To help you move, silly."

Jean-Pierre, dressed in white pants, plaid jacket, and skimmer hat, smiled and punched Oscar on the shoulder. "We thought you could use some help on your big day."

"That's very kind, but I'm fine with moving on my own. I don't have much to move. It won't take long." Why were they offering to help? He'd dressed for work, but they had dressed for a party. "I'm all packed except for a few small things."

"What about these two paintings tacked to the wall? Do you want to take them?" Lily crossed the room to scrutinize them. "This one's by Monet, isn't it? And this one looks like a drawing by Renoir." She looked at Oscar with a questioning glance. "I didn't know you were an art collector."

He blushed. "I'm not. These are portraits that Renoir gave me when Isabelle and I visited him."

"I thought I recognized Isabelle." Jean-Pierre moved to the wall. "I thought I recognized her," he said with a knowing smile.

Oscar felt more than a little flustered as he thought of that day in Renoir's studio with Isabelle. She'd looked so lovely posing for Renoir as they talked. "That's a sketch Renoir did of Isabelle the afternoon we arrived."

"Oh, yes," Lily said. "Now I recognize her, too."

She inched closer to get a better look at both pieces. They were both teasing Oscar about her leaving him so suddenly. He didn't mind a little humor at his expense. This seemed to be what brothers and sisters did.

Oscar sighed in relief. He thought they'd ask about the model Monet had painted.

Lily's face looked inquisitive as she asked, "Say, have you heard from Isabelle?"

Why did everyone keep asking him about Isabelle? He didn't like the attention her departure was receiving and the fact that he'd no answers to their questions. "No, not yet. I'm sure she must be busy with her father's illness."

Lily perked up at this response. "She hasn't written to you yet? That's odd."

"Hey, let's get started moving." He did his best to change the subject. "I'm eager to settle into the gardener's cottage."

Jean-Pierre and Lily looked at each other in amusement, then they smiled. "Let's go."

"We mustn't be late," she added.

Oscar frowned, seeing the look on her face. "Late. Late for what?"

He knew something was up with these two.

"Let's go." She grabbed a box. "I'll meet you in the automobile."

She then darted down the dark, old stairs with the worn carpet.

"Automobile? What automobile?" Oscar was frowning even more now. "I said I didn't need transportation."

He unpinned the two portraits from the wall and laid them on top of the box he was carrying.

Jean-Pierre called to Lily as he made his way down the stairs.

"You can't leave without me. I have the keys." He jangled the keys for her to hear them.

Oscar called from upstairs, "I have a few more things to bring before you drive off."

He felt comfortable and accepted by having people his own age welcoming him to his new home. He realized what taking this job and moving into the gardener's cottage would mean for his social life. Could this be the life he had always dreamed of?

He was glad to leave the musty smell and moldy walls before winter. It was affecting his fragile lungs. He took one last look around the room, remembering his first night here, the nights longing for Isabelle, and the lonely times sitting on his bed, writing to her with no response. It was past time to move on with his life and perhaps from Isabelle.

They left, and minutes later, the automobile pulled up next to Monet's house. The three carried boxes through the gate, into the garden, and down the *Grande Allée* to the gardener's cottage. Many guests chatted as they looked at the garden. Oscar didn't think much about it in his hurry to move into his new home. Monet's guests often came to admire Monet's garden but ignored him as he worked.

As he approached the cottage, he noticed streamers hanging from the eaves. Once inside, he looked up to see streamers of red, white, and blue crisscrossing the living room ceiling. The ladies who'd cleaned and painted his home were busy hanging them. They were also attaching paper lanterns to the windows.

"What's all this?" he asked his two friends.

Lily responded with a smile. "A party. *La pendaison de crémaillère.*"

"What? I'm confused?" Bewildered, he scratched his head.

"It's your housewarming party, silly," she said as she twirled around, holding two streamers. Then she tied them together. "We need to welcome you to your new home and family."

The ladies hanging the streamers sang while they worked. The sun streamed in through the windows, and Oscar sighed with pleasure. A party for him? What a treat.

"That's right," Jean-Pierre chimed in. "You're one of us now that you're living here."

"We've invited a few of the American artists who live nearby to make you feel more at home," Lily said as she started twirling again. "There are even a few lovely girls eager to meet you."

Oscar was surprised that anyone here knew of him. "Meet me? I've met no one in Giverny."

Lily spoke up as she finished spinning. "That's the point. You walk through the village early in the morning and late in the afternoon, and people are eager to learn more about you. Oh, I'm feeling dizzy." She fell into his arms. "Please take me outside for some fresh air."

He helped her to the bench on the lawn under the trees. "Are you all right?"

She sat up straight. "I'm fine. I just wanted to speak with you in private."

He was feeling overwhelmed by the morning events, and this latest episode with Lily didn't help clarify his thoughts. He sat down beside her on the wooden bench. "What did you want to talk about?"

"Isabelle. Have you not heard from her since she left?"

"No, not one word, or rather letter. Why? Have you?" His mind traveled back to see her walk off toward the ship. He felt then that he might never see her again. His heart was in his throat in anticipation of what she had to tell him.

Lily smoothed out her dress. "Yes, I've gotten several letters from her. She received your letters and feels that you're much more involved in the relationship than she is." She sighed. "There, I've said it. I'm glad I did. Someone has to let you know what's going on."

His chest tightened, and he struggled to catch his breath. "What's going on? What does that mean? I thought she loved me, too."

Lily shrugged. "You need to understand girls like Isabelle. They're in love with whomever they're with. Once you're no longer there, they'll love the next man they're with. She's seeing her father's junior assistant, who's helping take care of her father. He is young, handsome, and will be very successful as a doctor in Chicago. You are..."

"I'm just a lowly gardener who's trying to recover from his war wounds."

Lily looked sad. "I wouldn't put it that way, but yes. You're not able to give her the lifestyle she and her father want for her."

Oscar sank back on the bench, put his hands over his eyes, and sobbed. His body shook, and Lily moved closer to comfort him. She stroked his head while he cried Isabelle out of his system. At least, as much as he was able to.

"Now I'm the one who's dizzy." Oscar dried his eyes on his handkerchief and tried to pull himself together. "I don't understand. Doesn't she love me? There's nothing I won't do to make her happy. Even move to Chicago if she wants. Now you're telling me she's dropped me for some young doctor. What'll I do now?"

Lily took a deep breath and faced him. "I told you this because you're about to enter a new life. You have a new job, a new place to live, a new family, and some new friends. I don't want you to place your life on hold, waiting for Isabelle to return. Even if she does, it won't be the same."

"Do you mean that she may return?"

"Don't even hope that. It'll only impede you from enjoying your new life. Today, we've planned a party to welcome you into your new life. You need to join in the fun and enjoy meeting your new friends."

Her news tore a hole in his heart. How could he move on with his life with a piece missing from his heart? He'd just be going through the motions. "I'd rather run to the river and throw myself in."

Lily held his hand and kissed his cheek. "I know, but all that'll do is get you wet and cost you this marvelous job my grandfather awarded you. There're lots of people to meet, great food to eat, and some delicious wine to drink."

Oscar regained his composure and joked, "I think I'd better stick to water."

This time, Lily smiled. "That's better. I have a special friend for you to meet. Her name is Geneviève, and she owns the patisserie where you buy your breakfast and lunch. She's been watching you from the back room and would like to meet you. I can tell she's just what you need at this point."

He smiled at last. "Geneviève must be the girl with the curly blond hair I see standing next to the oven."

Lily smiled at his recovery. "Now we're making some progress. I'd like you to spend some time with her, but don't fall in love. I may have plans for you myself after you recover from Isabelle."

"Plans? What sort of plans?

"We'll see once you recover, if you ever do." Lily kissed him on the cheek again and ran off to the cottage.

Jean-Pierre strode down the path from the cottage and sat down next to him. "Did Lily give you the news?"

"About Isabelle?"

"No. That's old news. I mean about Geneviève."

Oscar felt anger rising in his chest. "Why is Isabelle old news? I just heard about her new love."

"I could've told you about her the day she left. She was out of your life when you told me she walked to the ship. Gone." Jean-Pierre snapped his fingers. "Out of sight, out of mind. You're better off without her. She's too much work. Now Geneviève is another story." He put his arm around Oscar's shoulders and leaned in to make his point. "She's a young widow. Very available. If you know what I mean."

Jean-Pierre looked at him and winked the way some men do when they have had too much to drink. It was a disgusting thing to say about a woman. If he wasn't Monet's son, he might be returning to the party with a black eye.

"*Non*. I don't know what you mean. I need to change my clothes for the party. Please don't refer to a young widow that way again."

Oscar shook his head at Jean-Pierre's behavior, escaped his grasp, got up, and walked toward his cottage. It was filling up with young people he didn't know. Ducking his head under the streamers, he slipped into his bedroom to change his clothes. The tan suit Monet had given him was his choice for today. After tying his new shoes, he braced himself for the visitors as he opened the bedroom door.

A cheer went up from the crowd when he stepped into the living room. He realized that Lily and Jean-Pierre had been on a mission to distract him and keep him out of the house until the party was ready. Blushing, he bowed to his guests.

Jean-Pierre handed him a drink of wine, not water. He drained the glass as Lily took him around the room, introducing him to the young artists who called Giverny home—some French, some from across Europe, and many from America. Oscar took a few minutes to exchange pleasantries with each person. Some seemed to know already he was from California and asked him about the 1916 earthquake.

"I was fighting here at the time and didn't experience it personally, but I've heard it was horrible." He paused to catch his breath. "The entire city burned to the ground. Many of my friends lost their homes. It was a sad time. I wish I could have been there to help."

It was a pleasant occasion where cider, wine, and conversations flowed freely. The food was plentiful and delicious. The guests were attractive and well-behaved. All were friendly and seemed pleased to meet him. Judging by the loud conversations in several languages and the nonstop laughter, everyone was having a grand time.

They seemed like a delightful group of artists wishing to follow in Monet's footsteps. A few were young locals working in the village and surrounding towns. Lily and Jean-Pierre introduced him to each guest, who briefly described where they were from and their Giverny activities. His team of gardeners was also here to celebrate his promotion.

When he'd made the rounds and met all the guests in the living room, Lily took him to the kitchen to meet a young woman. She had ringlets of blond hair trailing down to her shoulders. Her cheeks were pink, and her pale-blue eyes were bright and smiling. Her stomach and breasts bulged against her simple flowered dress, showing she was many months pregnant.

"When are you due?" Lily asked after introducing her to Oscar.

Oscar felt embarrassed to be part of this delicate conversation between two young women. He tried to withdraw, but Lily caught his arm and made him stay.

"In six months," Geneviève replied, with no hint of embarrassment or reluctance. "I got pregnant the last time Charles was home on leave, just before he returned to the front and…"

She turned away to dry her eyes.

"Did you lose your husband in the war?" Oscar asked the obvious question, hoping to move the subject away from the pregnancy talk.

"Yes, I believe you knew him. His name was Charles, Charles Beaumont. He was in your unit," she said, her intense blue eyes staring at his.

Oscar gasped. He couldn't believe the coincidence. "Charles was my best friend. He gave me my nickname, Lieutenant Choo-Choo."

He knew he shouldn't have mentioned that. Jean-Pierre was listening from nearby and began repeating, "Choo-Choo, Choo-Choo," over and over.

Lily and Geneviève laughed at his embarrassment.

"Charles was always teasing everyone, including me," Geneviève said. "He told me how well you took it. He was very fond of you."

"Charles mentioned he'd be a father. It thrilled him that you were pregnant. I miss his friendship and humor. As he lay dying, he asked me to tell you how much he loved you."

Geneviève wiped her eyes again. "I miss him every day. I hope you'll still visit my patisserie now that you live here."

"I will," he said. "I didn't know you were the owner. You look so young to be the owner of a business."

Geneviève looked offended. "You look young to be the head gardener at the most famous garden in France. I'm young to own my business, young to be a war widow, and young to be a mother. But I have no choice, so I'll make the most of the situation."

He smiled at her self-confidence. "I'm sure you will. I, too, had no choice but to take this position. You inspire me to do as well as you have."

Lily stepped between the two and interrupted their intense conversation. "Oscar, many of our guests would like a tour of the garden. Would you like to do the honors? You're in charge now."

Oscar drew himself up taller, strode into the living room, and announced, "Who would like to take a tour of the garden? Raise your hands."

When most everyone raised their hands, he smiled. "Then follow Jean-Pierre outside, and we'll get started."

With that, the crowd chanted in unison, "Choo-Choo, Choo-Choo," and out the door they trooped behind Jean-Pierre in single file as if they were train cars behind the engine. They grasped the person's waist in front of them and took a tour around his yard like a train.

Lily and Geneviève were the last guests to leave as they looked at each other, smiled, and followed along behind the others. Oscar, walking close behind, heard Geneviève whisper to Lily, "You're right. He's a fascinating man. I'm glad you introduced us."

He listened and watched as Lily chuckled and took Geneviève's arm as they went out the door together. He did not understand where this was heading.

Chapter 18 – Settling In

Oscar began his garden tour with a few brief comments to the guests in front of his cottage. He stood crossing and uncrossing his arms and took off his cap before addressing the crowd as he tried not to twist it into a knot. "I know most of you are eager to see Monet's garden and lily pond, but first, I'd like to explain a few things about what you'll see."

When he began, his voice quavered but then steadied as he spoke. "As many of you know, Monet has chosen to paint in many parts of France, Holland, Italy, London, and Norway. You may not know that he moved to Giverny nearly forty years ago to find local subjects to paint. His first subject was the Seine River, the surrounding villages, and even the grain stacks. As his garden grew and he created and expanded the lily pond, he focused on these subjects. Therefore, the flowers you see today are all selected by Monet and planted to create a subject for him to paint. Since it is early in the growing season, you will have to imagine what the garden will look like when it's in full bloom."

An artist with a French accent asked, "Do you mean that he planted the flowers to create a particular scene that he wanted to paint? How could he envision that in advance?"

Oscar looked up at the main house while the young woman asked her question. Monet watched from his bedroom window, which someone had opened for him to hear the tour introduction. Monet was smiling. The tour had started well. Oscar's self-confidence grew as he became more comfortable speaking to the group, using the speaking techniques he'd developed in addressing his men in the war. Answering questions from interested visitors helped him decide how to direct his tour.

"To answer your first question, that's what he had in mind. I can't answer your second question. That requires understanding the genius of Monet as a painter. Who knows?" He raised his hands and shrugged as the crowd chuckled. "That's beyond my expertise as head gardener. I'm just here to execute his wishes as best I can. Now let's take a stroll over to the *Grande Allée*. It's the section of the garden that he most often paints other than the lily pond."

The group followed him along the hedges and around the planting beds to the top of the *Grande Allée*. During the walk, three young women asked questions about his background and how he came to be working for Monet. Oscar told them of his work in San Francisco's Golden Gate Park and his studies at the University of California. As they reached their destination, he smiled and thanked them for their interest in his background. After waiting for stragglers to rejoin the group, he began his discussion again.

"You'll notice the *Grande Allée* has six arched metal trellises over the path. These support two roses each, one growing from each side." He grasped a trellis and pointed out how the roses join at the top. "These are trained to grow up either side of the arches from opposite ends, then they meet in the middle to form an overhead roof of pinks and whites. It's this floral roof that he uses to frame his paintings.

"We plant seasonal flowers, so we have fresh blooms throughout the season on each side to keep the pathway bordered with color throughout the growing season. As one variety dies, another comes into bloom."

The visitors took notice of the plantings and discussed these with each other.

"Yellow and gold nasturtiums carpet the ten-foot-wide pathway much of the year." Oscar picked up a branch of the flowers and handed it to several audience members to inspect. "Together, these three colorful elements—trellises with roses overhead, flowering borders on the sides, and the floral carpeted floor—create a tunnel of color that frames the main house as you look up toward it from lower in the garden."

He pointed out each element as he mentioned it, then moved his arms in a large arc to illustrate the all-encompassing tunnel effect.

A young artist with an American accent spoke up. "Are you saying that Monet designed this floral tunnel and then had it planted just so he could paint it?"

"Yes, he wanted to paint it, but he also wanted his friends and family to enjoy it."

The guests' faces showed amazement and pleasure at the creative design and execution of this creation.

"Now let's walk down the *Grande Allée*, through the rear garden gate, and up over the railroad tracks to the lily pond. Be careful not to trip on the nasturtiums or slip on your way up the hillside."

Oscar led the way through the gate at the bottom of the garden that led to the lily pond gate. Jean-Pierre remained on the garden side of the embankment to help the guests climb up the hill. Oscar could see him smiling as he helped the beautiful young ladies up the hill.

When all had assembled, he continued. "Ten years after Monet created the garden you just visited, he started this water garden. He designed this bridge based on the ones he found in his Japanese prints. Some of you locals know that the village government had a tough time agreeing with what he was trying to create. Getting permission to dam up the river and create the pond took years and the influence of a prominent man from Vétheuil, but I think you'll agree it was worth the effort."

He turned his head as his gaze swept over the length of the pond garden. The guests followed his lead and sighed as they took in the full view.

"Again, you can see that Monet designed the scenes around the pond so he could paint them." He pointed out some areas that Monet had repeatedly painted. "Look at the boat dock with the willows dipping their heads into the water, and you can envision how he would have painted it."

Oscar loved hearing the guests chatting and pointing out their favorite scenes as they enjoyed his tour. "At first, Monet planted the lilies to enjoy. Then one day, he realized the garden held the painting subjects he'd always been searching for. From that day forward, he has painted nowhere else. You'll notice some of the lilies have begun to bloom, but be aware that there are many more resting in the greenhouse to be brought out in warmer weather.

"Now cross the bridge and look at the scenes around the pond that he created to paint. Be careful not to join the lilies in the water that's still cold this time of year."

The guests chuckled at his little joke. He was enjoying himself far more than he'd expected.

Oscar relaxed on one of the green wooden benches as his guests toured the water garden. Geneviève joined him. She did not sit too close to him but just close enough to show her interest in what he had to say. He could feel her warmth and smell her scent. Her gentle conversational tone helped him relax and enjoy the warm rays of the afternoon sun and his new friends. He was at peace for the first time since Isabelle had left. He was torn between enjoying her company and feeling guilty for thinking of another when he was in love with Isabelle. Loneliness was driving his need for companionship.

The guests came up to him while he sat on the bench to ask questions about the garden's plantings and the pond. They seemed very interested in how Monet had created various scenes. He related what Isabelle had told him about the color wheel and how he'd designed his subject with a specific color palette in mind.

At last, it was nearing sunset. Oscar called an end to the tour and ushered the guests back across the bridge and up the *Grande Allée.*

He finished the tour of the garden with some last comments. "I hope you've enjoyed the tour today as much as I've enjoyed being your guide. We must do this again when it's warmer and the flowers are in full bloom. Thank you for coming."

He removed his cap and bowed his head. The guests cheered and then chanted, "Choo-Choo. Choo-Choo. We love you!"

Oscar looked up at the window to see Monet laughing.

The guests moved out the gate onto the street, where each man shook Oscar's hand and thanked him for the delightful party and tour, and each lady kissed his cheeks. They said farewell to Lily and Jean-Pierre, complimenting them on the party. All pledged to meet again soon.

Oscar hugged Lily and Jean-Pierre when the guests had gone and told them how much the party meant to him. He whispered to Lily, "Thanks for introducing me to Geneviève. She's an extraordinary person."

"Remember, don't fall in love with her," Lily said with a chuckle.

"I appreciate you making me feel welcome here. I'll never forget this housewarming."

With that, he headed to his new home in the cottage. He took off his jacket as he walked down the path and thought about this day and his new friend, Geneviève. The pressure of the day, speaking to a crowd of the people, and the afternoon sun had made him sweat. The evening breeze dried his shirt. He passed by the porch on his way to the cottage and stopped when he saw Blanche sitting there alone.

"*Madame* Blanche, please tell *Monsieur* Monet that the tour of the garden was a big hit with the guests. Leading the tour for the first time made me nervous, but the guests seemed not to notice. Most had only seen the garden from the railroad tracks or over the wall beside the house and enjoyed seeing it close up."

"I watched from here and could see that they enjoyed your tour. Did they understand what Monet has created in his garden?" she asked.

Oscar sat down on the steps and repeated some of the questions the guests had asked. "The mixture of colors that Monet has created with the flowers fascinated them. The beauty of the lily pond awed them. They kept asking me how he knew to create the scenes. I told them he studied how plants grew in the wild. They seemed to think the secret of the garden was in what Monet planted, rather than the emotional effect he created as an artist."

Blanche smiled and nodded. "I'm so glad you could give them the tour. You've spent weeks working on the garden with Monet. It's nice you could share what you've accomplished with others."

"Now I'm talked out and need the solitude of my new home. I don't remember ever talking this much in my life."

Blanche's acknowledgment of his efforts embarrassed him and gave him a warm feeling that spread throughout his body. She rose from her seat and took a bundle from the table next to her. "Oscar, please accept this housewarming gift."

He climbed the steps to receive the package wrapped in gold paper.

"It's a gift from Monet and me. I hope you like it."

"*Merci beaucoup.* You're always giving me such thoughtful presents. That's very kind of you."

He opened the package to find two frames. He thought of the presents from Renoir and Isabelle that he'd tacked to his bedroom wall. They would look beautiful in these frames. This was a wonderful gift from Blanche orchestrated by Monet.

Blanche smiled as he gazed at the gift. "We wanted you to frame Renoir's sketch and Monet's painting. The framer will mount them for you as part of our gift. Did Renoir say who Monet's model was? She must have been one of the young girls Renoir always surrounded himself with. He had a way of charming the ladies."

Oscar's heart raced at her comments. Did she know his secret? He hoped she didn't. Not yet.

"She's lovely," Blanche said as she cocked her head as if trying to remember. "I wonder where he painted her. It must have been when Renoir and Monet were painting together. Otherwise, Monet wouldn't have any reason to give it to him. I wonder if it was the last time they painted together in the south. It would be fun to learn more about that time they spent together. Monet didn't talk about that trip."

"I suppose that's true." Oscar stifled a yawn. "Sorry, but this day has exhausted me. I must go." He backed down the porch steps and headed toward the cottage. "Good night," he said as he was leaving. She had fallen for his diversionary yawn.

"Do you want anything to eat?" Blanche asked from the porch.

"*Merci. Non.* I have enough left over from the party to last me for several days."

He had avoided the discovery of his secret once again. He retreated to his cozy cottage and started unpacking his few boxes of personal items. In one box, he found his pen and a sheaf of paper. Taking it to the dining room table, he sat down and wrote a brief letter to Isabelle. When he turned up the oil lamp wick, the shadows of his loneliness and exhaustion retreated to the corners of the room.

He didn't want to accuse her of anything. However, because of what Lily had told him, he'd no longer pour his heart out to her in his writing. Perhaps if his letters were less emotional, she might, at last, respond to him. Perhaps she would at least tell him why she was ignoring his letters.

Dear Isabelle,

How are you? I hope you have received my letters by now and trust your father is recovering.

I've accepted the head gardener position and moved into the gardener's cottage today. Lily and Jean-Pierre threw a perfect housewarming party for me. They invited lots of young artists from the area. Some of them mentioned knowing you. I gave them a tour of the garden, my first. It went much better than the one I gave you when you came to dinner. But not as much fun as we had. I even told them about the color wheel as you explained it to me.

Geneviève, a young local girl I met, was the wife of my dear friend Charles from the Army. He is the fellow I mentioned who died in my arms during my last assault. It turns out that she owns the patisserie in Giverny, where I buy my breakfast and lunch. She's friendly and was very interested in the garden tour I led today. She and Lily are friends.

I'm excited about being the head gardener at the most famous garden in France. There's a great deal of work to do since there hasn't been a head gardener here since early in the war. Monet has been managing things by himself and has some things he wants me to put right. My schedule is busy with the planting, pruning, and plant replacement. As you can imagine, spring is a very hectic time in the garden.

I've been lonely since you left, but with the help of Lily and Jean-Pierre, I'm making friends and can't wait to conduct my next tour. Funny thing for me to say, but it's true.

I hope you're well and preparing for the Chicago spring that'll be upon you soon enough. Goodbye for now.

Love,

Oscar

He didn't mention what Lily had told him. He would let his tone and discussion subjects speak for him with no recrimination. He hoped she would see the change in his writing style and respond.

He put away the last of his things and laid the frames on the dresser with the portraits. It was funny beginning his collection of Impressionists with two of its best artists. Exhaustion and loneliness rushed back in as he blew out the light and crawled into bed. The sheets smelled so fresh. It was very dark in the garden, and the unfamiliar night sounds were disturbing. He would enjoy getting used to them.

Sunday was his day of rest. He took full advantage of it by staying in bed well past sunrise. He got up and started to make his bed when he realized he'd slept so soundly that he hadn't disturbed the sheets. Not like when he slept with Isabelle. He smiled at the memory of seeing her body in the firelight and tracing hearts on her breast as they cuddled in the morning. Then he frowned at remembering what Lily had told him about her.

He tried to put such thoughts out of his mind as he went to the kitchen and made breakfast from the party's leftovers—cheese and bread for the main course and lemon tart for dessert.

The birds singing in the garden interrupted his quiet morning. He opened the front door to hear their songs better and watch them searching for bugs in the yard. As he stepped out into the sun, he realized that, by some miracle, he'd come to a quiet and peaceful paradise. But could it last? Would it last?

Not today. Lily came strolling down the path and scared the birds away. She looked like spring, wearing a light-pink sweater over a floral skirt and a sun hat to ward off the spring sun and breeze.

"Oscar, do you want to go on a picnic?"

He had wanted to stay in the cottage and relax, but Lily was not one to take 'no' for an answer. "Where are we going?"

She cheered at his acceptance. "Just up the hill above the house. We can look out over the valley. It's a splendid view of the Seine and our tiny village."

"What can I bring?"

"Let's see what you have left over from the party. I can add to it from the kitchen if there's not enough."

"Help yourself. Who is going with us?"

As she headed for the kitchen, she said, "Jean-Pierre and Geneviève. It's her only day off, and she likes to spend it outside. I hope you don't mind."

"Fine. Let me get dressed." He looked at his garden clothes and then his tan suit. "I'll meet you by the back porch in half an hour."

Chapter 19 – The Picnic

Oscar packed the food Lily had selected, freshened up, and put on his tan suit. He chose his work shoes as they were walking up the hill through the fields. He rushed to the porch and was out of breath when he met the others by the steps.

As soon as he rounded the corner, there stood Geneviève in a white dress with a floral pattern. How could she keep it clean on a picnic? She had tucked her blond curls into a sun hat with a ribbon that matched the yellow wool sweater she carried.

Her soft blue eyes caught his gaze. "If you're wondering why I'm wearing a white dress to a picnic, it's the only nice one that fits over my budging tummy. This baby will be a big one like its father."

She laughed and did a twirl so he could get the full effect of the dress and baby bulge.

Surprised, he stammered, "You're beautiful. Bulge and all."

She blushed and smiled at his response.

Jean-Pierre had dressed in blue trousers and a gray jacket with a gray wool cap to match. "All right, you two. That's enough baby talk. Where's Lily?"

"I'm up here in the kitchen filling the picnic basket with necessities," she called to them from inside. "I love hearing about having babies. Please don't stop."

She emerged from the kitchen carrying a picnic basket and her sweater. "Are we ready for our trek?"

"My, you look lovely," Oscar said. "Let me carry the basket. I'll put the party leftovers in it."

"I've got the blankets." Jean-Pierre volunteered to carry the lighter load.

"I've got the mother and baby," Lily said as both women laughed, exited the garden gate, and started up the path through the field leading to the top of the hill. The area was filled with wildflowers amongst the short winter wheat stalks reaching up to the sun. The path was still wet and slippery from the winter rains and snow.

Jean-Pierre leaned closer to Oscar and whispered, "Let those two go on ahead. I want to talk to you in private."

Oscar nodded and slowed his pace to match Jean-Pierre's. This seemed like a strange request. He shifted the picnic basket from his left to his right hand to move closer to him. "What did you want to discuss?"

"I realize you're getting interested in Geneviève, so I thought it best to mention a few things. First, I'm sure you've heard that I was an ambulance driver during the war."

Oscar nodded again but was still unsure where this was going as he stepped across a mud puddle in the path.

"What you may not know is that I was on the battlefield the day Charles died."

Oscar paused so he could take in what he was hearing. "Then you were there when I got shot?"

"*Oui.* I was the first one to reach you. I didn't know if you were alive or dead. When we discovered you were alive, we loaded you on a stretcher and ran to the ambulance."

Oscar could feel the color draining from his face as he remembered fragments of that horrible trip to the hospital.

"But that's not what I wanted to talk about." Jean-Pierre leaned closer to him and whispered to be sure the women couldn't hear. "I saw Charles lying at the bottom of that crater before I found you. I went down to check for life. When I found none, I closed his eyes and moved on."

"Thank you for checking on Charles." Oscar felt his chest tighten. "I wish I could've done more for him."

"Me, too," Jean-Pierre said. "I've known Geneviève since we were childhood friends. I told her I saw him on the battlefield as soon as I returned. In those confusing times, families often didn't get notified of a death for months. As soon as I told her, she fell into a deep depression."

Oscar hadn't thought about the aftermath of Charles' death. He trudged on up the hill, thinking of his last encounter with Charles.

Jean-Pierre stopped to pick up a blanket he'd dropped. After brushing off the dirt and dead leaves, he continued. "We were all worried about her sanity. According to Lily, the day she found out she was pregnant, she recovered. Knowing a bit of Charles would live on in her child seemed to give her a reason to live."

Oscar stumbled over a rock and nearly dumped the basket. He was remembering how happy Charles had been about returning home to his wife. "Why are you telling me this?"

Jean-Pierre stopped and faced him with a stern look in his eyes. "I feel terrible about suggesting to you yesterday that Geneviève was a woman you could take advantage of. She's a wonderful woman and good friend and still too vulnerable for you or anyone to trifle with."

"*Non.* I would never do that. That's not who I am." He recoiled at Jean-Pierre's suggestion.

"I'm not accusing you. I want you to know that Geneviève's had a rough time, and you need to be careful with her." Jean-Pierre looked apologetic. "I'm sorry if I've given you the wrong idea about her."

"She's a lovely woman. I'll treat her with the utmost respect. I promise you." Oscar hoped this would end this conversation about his moral character.

"I'm glad that's settled. Now let's catch up with the ladies before they beat us to the top of the hill." Jean-Pierre started trotting up the hill.

Oscar picked up his pace and climbed as fast as possible, but he started gasping for air. He knew he was lagging, but it was hard for him to maintain a fast pace with his injured lungs. He had a lot to think about—a lot more than he'd wanted to consider on his day off. Today was a day for rest and a picnic on a hill surrounded by freshly planted wheat fields.

He arrived at the top well after the others. They chided him for being late. He caught his breath and responded to their teasing. "I knew you couldn't start without me. I have food and drinks."

Everyone laughed. Geneviève offered him a spot on the blanket next to her, which he accepted. Lily opened the basket and spread out the food as Jean-Pierre opened the wine.

Oscar settled himself on the blanket to chat with Geneviève, who said, "Turn around and look."

"Oh, *mon Dieu!* That's where we live. I can't believe it. It's even more beautiful from up here. There are the garden and the lily pond, and over there, that's my cottage." The fields were bright green after the long winter, the wheat stacks from last fall everywhere.

Lily nodded. "To your right, downriver, is where the Epte joins the Seine. You can see the village of Giverny, including the church where I was baptized. To your left, upriver, is the railroad to Paris. You see the wheat fields surrounding the village where Monet painted his series of wheat stack paintings."

"Lily, *merci beaucoup* for inviting me up today." Oscar continued to survey the scene below. "I've been so focused on the gardens and getting from the boarding house to work and back, I never took time to see how beautiful this valley is. I'm so lucky to live here."

"You're most welcome. Now, let's eat." Lily chuckled as she moved out of the way so they could enjoy their feast.

After pouring each one glass of wine, Jean-Pierre offered a toast. "Here's to our new head gardener and dear friend, Oscar. *Santé.*" Geneviève opted for the apple juice.

"Would you like me to fix you a plate, Master Gardener?" Geneviève asked with a smile.

"*S'il te plaît.* No onions."

"I'd never give you onions on a day like this," Geneviève said with a shy smile.

They dined on fine appetizers and a nice Bordeaux as they shared fun stories from their childhood and laughter at the trouble they got into.

Jean-Pierre sighed. "It's such a beautiful afternoon. I'm heading off to rediscover some of our childhood haunts. Would you care to join me?"

"I'll join you," Lily said.

"I'm too tired from the climb. Oscar, will you keep me company?" Geneviève asked.

"*Certainement!* This is such a quiet and lovely spot."

When the other two had walked off, Geneviève took his hand and placed it on her bulging belly. "I hope this doesn't offend you, but I feel it's appropriate since you were so close to Charles. There, did you feel the baby kick?"

His mouth fell open at Geneviève's request, and at the baby he felt stirring inside her. He hoped his face wasn't betraying his surprise by turning too red. "May I be so bold as to kiss the baby for Charles?"

"Please do. Charles would have loved that you did."

Oscar leaned over and kissed her belly. "I've never been so close to an unborn baby or a newborn. It's so exciting to be near the baby and so scary."

"I agree. I was panicked and delighted at the thought of being responsible for another human being."

He sat listening to her and gazed at the clouds and shadows that crawled across the valley.

"I can't think of such a thing. So let's not talk about it," he teased. "Tell me about your life growing up in this paradise."

"There's not much to tell. I had a wonderful childhood. My mother was the cook at Monet's house when he and his family first moved here. My father helped out in Monet's garden occasionally. That wasn't right away because Monet had his children work in the garden at first. They helped him water and plant those first few summers. At least, that's what I've been told as I wasn't born yet." She chuckled.

Oscar lay back on the blanket again as he listened to her and watched sunlight and shadows brush across her face and golden hair.

"When Monet became more successful, he started hiring people to help them in the house and the garden. That's when my father became his first head gardener. I've known Lily and Jean-Pierre since I played there as a child. We played together throughout the garden and even fished in the lily pond. They were always great to me. Jean-Pierre was older, so he was our protector and victim. We played terrible tricks on him, but he never complained."

"They've been so kind to me, too."

She smiled as she spoke of her memories of growing up. "We played up here and in all the fields below the house. In the summers, we spent a lot of time down on the Seine. The older boys borrowed Monet's studio boat that he used for painting and used it for a diving platform."

Oscar frowned and shook his head. "I can't imagine Monet liking that."

"He didn't, but we got away with it." Her eyes lowered. "Because we didn't tell Monet we borrowed his boat. I met Charles when I opened my patisserie. He was one of my first customers and became a regular. I'm not sure what he liked most, me or my pastries."

"Knowing Charles, I'd say he loved both." Oscar smiled. "I'm sure he found both very sweet."

"Oscar, you make me blush."

She reached over to mess his hair in fun.

"Don't stop. That feels so good."

"Charles used to love when I did that to him."

"The sun is so warm for this time of year, the wine and food were so filling, and the hike so tiring that I wish we could rest here forever," he said as he looked up at the blue sky and white clouds through the branches that were budding out in leaves.

"I know what you mean. Even though I love my business, sometimes it's good to get away from it and enjoy life outside of work."

"My new job is a dream come true, but I look forward to doing this again."

"If it involves climbing a hill, you can count the baby and me out for a while." Geneviève sighed. "The baby and I had better stick to easier walks for the next few weeks."

They both laughed at this and then fell silent as they listened to the birds vying for territory in the surrounding trees.

That's how they were when Lily and Jean-Pierre returned from their walk.

"Are we interrupting something?" Jean-Pierre asked with a sly smile.

"I'm just talking with the baby," Oscar said. "He or she has a lot to say."

"About what?" Jean-Pierre asked.

"About life," Geneviève responded.

Everyone burst into laughter. Even the baby kicked so hard, everyone saw it.

Lily spoke up. "Let's pack up and head back to the house before the baby decides to make an appearance. That is unless you want more to eat or drink."

"Not me," said Jean-Pierre.

"Count me out," Oscar added.

"The two of us couldn't eat another bite," Geneviève said with a chuckle.

On the way down the hill, Oscar held Geneviève's hand to assist if she slipped on the slippery path. When they reached the house, he couldn't let go. They watched as the late afternoon sun cast long shadows across the valley and highlighted the house and gardens in soft yellow light.

"Jean-Pierre and I are going in," Lily said. "Oscar, will you escort Geneviève home?"

His pulse quickened. "I'd love to if Geneviève doesn't mind."

"I doubt she minds," Jean-Pierre said as he gave Oscar a soft punch on his shoulder.

Geneviève just stood blushing and smiling as Lily kissed her on each cheek.

"Lily, thanks so much for inviting me." Oscar kissed her on both cheeks. "*Merci beaucoup* for everything. I mean everything," he added with a wink.

He took Geneviève's hand as he walked her toward her shop and her apartment above. They strolled while laughing and chatting about their day.

When they reached her house, he tried to let go of her hand, but she held tight.

"I had a wonderful time today," she said. "I haven't had this much fun since the last time Charles returned from the front." She smiled. "The baby and I needed this day."

"Me, too," Oscar replied. "I hope I can see you again soon."

"Just come by the patisserie anytime. We'll be here."

"Then I'll see you for breakfast."

He tried to leave, but Geneviève grabbed his arm and kissed him on each cheek and then a third one before she unlocked the shop entrance and disappeared inside.

Oscar stood in the doorway. He was finding it hard to leave and harder to believe what'd just happened. As he walked away, he couldn't wait for breakfast.

Just then, Lily's voice came into his head saying, "Don't fall in love with her."

Chapter 20 – Gustave Geffroy Visits

The restaurant was dimly lit. Round tables covered with white tablecloths lined the walls and down the middle of the room. Each table was set with more types of silverware and crystal than I could count. Standing in the red-velvet-draped doorway, I looked around the room at the well-dressed patrons dining, drinking, and conversing. I was out of place and outclassed in my soiled work clothes.

Isabelle was sitting with a man I didn't know at a table in the center of the room. My heart sank. She was dressed in a black sequined evening gown, drinking champagne, and holding hands with him. Shocked, I called out her name, and she turned to see me, then turned back to her companion. I kept calling out her name until my voice gave out. She didn't respond.

Walking from the shadows toward her table, I continued to implore her in a raspy whisper. "Isabelle, what are you doing here with this man? I thought you loved me. Isabelle, say something."

She stood up to leave and turned toward me. The bulge in her belly showed that she was pregnant.

"You're pregnant! Who's the father? Tell me. Do you still love me? Are you coming back to me?"

She walked away as my head dropped to my chest.

Oscar woke when the waiters were about to drag him out of the restaurant. What a strange dream—or rather, a nightmare he had.

He was dripping with sweat and had no idea what time it was when he got up and walked around the rooms in his cottage, frightened that she was with someone else and devastated at being abandoned by his love. It was too late or too early to be awake.

He sat down at his dining room table in the dark, shivering from his cold, his damp clothes, and his frustration at Isabelle in his dream. A dog howling in the distance and the wind whistling around the cottage attic made him even more afraid and lonely. The nightmare had been so vivid. Once back in bed, he rolled from side-to-side trying to go back to sleep.

He couldn't stop thinking of the nightmare. What did it mean? How could he mix up Geneviève's pregnancy with visions of Isabelle? He missed her more than he was willing to admit even to himself. She was his true love. She excited and challenged him more than anyone else had ever done.

Did she still love him? Had she ever loved him? Was she the right person for him? The thought of not being with her again ripped at his heart. She'd brought him back to life after years in battle and months in the hospital. What would happen to him without her? Would he shut the door on life again? He'd only known her for a few weeks. Was her love a product of his overactive imagination? Was it love or just lust?

He dressed and left the cottage earlier than usual. He needed a friend to talk with and something to eat, so he headed into the village. Was Geneviève the right person to ask for advice about this? He needed a woman's perspective, but would it be proper to discuss Isabelle with Geneviève? Was she that close of a friend? Was it too early in their relationship for such a discussion?

He stood shivering outside Geneviève's patisserie shop before it opened on this cold, damp Monday morning, trying to decide whether to ask for her advice. Someone was visible moving about in the kitchen. He knocked on the door and called out, "*Bonjour.* I've come for my breakfast. Is anyone here?"

Geneviève came out of the kitchen, wiping her floured hands on her apron. Her blond ringlets poked out from under her baker's hat.

"What are you doing here so early?" She caught a stray curl from her brow and tried to shove it under her hat as she opened the door. "Come in. You look tired."

He took off his cap and confessed, "I couldn't sleep. I had this nightmare that woke me early this morning. I kept thinking about it and couldn't get back to sleep."

"Do you want to tell me about it?"

"*Oui. Non. Oui.*"

"Sit here, and I'll get you some coffee as soon as I put some bread in the oven." She shook her head and smiled as she returned to the kitchen.

Oscar sank into the old wooden chair beside the door and looked about the shop. He'd been in here dozens of times but had never paid much attention to the decorations that must have taken her or someone a great deal of time and thought to put together.

There were three small, round tables and six chairs of assorted styles in the front window. Along the opposite wall sat a glass case in front of the entrance to the kitchen. The case held a variety of tempting pastries. Murals covering the side walls featured scenes of Paris, the *Tour Eiffel* on one, and Notre Dame. It made him feel that he was in Paris instead of Giverny. He smelled the fresh bread baking in the large brick oven. It reminded him of his mother's kitchen on baking day. He closed his eyes, and the smell carried him back thousands of miles and a dozen years.

When he smelled hot coffee, his head jerked up, and he opened his eyes. "I must have nodded off. Not enough sleep last night."

She put two cups of steaming hot coffee on the table in front of him and took a seat.

"Poor thing. Now I have a few minutes to talk before taking the bread out of the oven. What was your dream about?"

Oscar took a long sip of his coffee and told her his nightmare after explaining Isabelle's relationship. He began with their meeting on the train and finished as she left on the ship back to Chicago. He left out the intimate parts but was sure Geneviève got the gist of the affair.

Her expression turned from warm and welcoming to sympathetic. "Sounds to me like you've got a tiger by the tail. She must be a fascinating young woman. You say you haven't heard from her?"

He took off his cap and began twisting it in his hands. "No, I haven't heard from Isabelle. I hate to burden you with my problems, but I need a woman's advice on how to deal with this."

Geneviève looked perplexed. "It sounds like your nightmare is telling you something about your relationship with Isabelle. What do you suppose that could be?"

"That's what worries me. Lily says Isabelle has written her several letters. I just don't understand why I've received nothing. Perhaps she's angry with me."

Geneviève struggled to her feet and headed to the kitchen. Her pregnancy made her movements slow and deliberate. "Time to take the bread out of the oven. Be right back."

Oscar took a sip of his coffee and then assembled his thoughts before she returned. He wasn't sure it had been a good idea to tell Geneviève about Isabelle. However, it felt good to talk about her to a friend. But perhaps this new friend was not ready to hear this about his love life so soon after she'd lost her husband. Her confused expression told him to be careful about what he revealed.

Geneviève returned with two pastries on a plate. "Try one of these. They'll make you feel better."

Oscar took a bite of the soft, golden delicacy and got powdered sugar on his chin and shirt. It was delicious. "This tastes like food for the gods. What's it called?"

"Angel wings. It *is* food for the gods."

They both burst out laughing.

Her laughter helped lighten his mood and allowed him to relax as he told his story. "We were very close when she left. Even though we'd only known each other for a short time, I trusted her. Since I've heard nothing from her, I feel she's broken that trust. If I don't hear from her soon, I need to forget her and move on."

He had another bite of the angel wings.

She let him finish the first of the angel wings before asking, "Do you want my advice?"

"Yes, that's what I came here for."

Geneviève got up from her chair, checked the oven, and then returned to her seat. "First, I don't know Isabelle, and I've just met you. Therefore, my advice may not mean much. I can see you care for her a great deal, so give her more time to contact you. She may have an excellent reason for not responding to your letters right now."

"Like what?" he said with a trace of anger in his voice.

She shrugged. "I've no idea. Just give her more time. You owe her that much. In the meantime, get your own life and this new job in order. That way, you can take action when you hear from her."

"Her not writing confuses me. You're right about my needing to get my life in order. It's so disappointing that I haven't heard from her. I miss her."

"Since you mention being confused, I'm confused, too. You were flirting with me at the party and the picnic, and now I find you're still in love with Isabelle. Why were you trifling with me?"

Geneviève frowned and didn't wait for his answer as she went to the oven to take out some baguettes.

It dawned on him he'd hurt her in trying to ease his loneliness by flirting with her. He knew so little about treating women and was about to lose his new friend along with Isabelle. If only he'd listened closely to his mother's advice about how to respect women.

After a few minutes, she returned to the table and stood over him.

"I'm sorry, but I'm out of time to talk. I need to get ready to open the shop. I hope my advice helped." She crossed her arms and looked down at him. "I appreciate what you did for Charles, and I don't want to be rude. However, I don't have time for you to trifle with me. I have a business to run and a child on the way and can't play games with you. It'd be wonderful to be your friend, but that's all. Is that clear?"

Her response shocked him, but it didn't surprise him. He deserved this. "You're … you're right. I'm sorry to have disrespected you. That wasn't my intent. I like you and admire what you're doing. I need to sort out where I stand with Isabelle and get on with my life. *Merci* for the advice and the angel wings and coffee. I hope we can still be friends."

She looked relieved to have cleared the air between them and reached for a bag on the counter. "Here's your lunch. I'll see you soon. No charge for the food or advice."

"*Merci beaucoup.*"

Oscar got up to leave. She kissed him twice, once on each cheek, but not three times. He put on his cap and raised his collar to shield him from the chill, and lowered his head, ashamed of his behavior as he walked out the door.

Shuffling down the street to Monet's house as the sun was rising, he looked up in time to see the soft pink clouds heralding the sun and perhaps rain. Even this lovely scene couldn't take his thoughts away from the disappointed look on Geneviève's face. The sun peeked through the clouds. A rooster crowed to welcome the sun, and a cow bellowed to get milked. He felt like kicking himself down the street.

He had a good life here in Monet's paradise. It was time he appreciated it and stopped intertwining his love life with his friendships. It was time he accepted what fate had brought him. He decided he'd give Isabelle another chance and wait for her to make the next move. Geneviève would be just a friend. He wasn't strong enough to handle one intense relationship, and certainly not two at the same time. Besides, he still had to concentrate on finding his father.

As he rounded the house on the way to put his lunch in his cottage, Blanche called out to him.

"Splendid news! Gustave Geffroy is coming for lunch."

"Is Monet well enough for visitors?"

"He's always eager for a visit from Gustave. Monet wants you to have lunch with us and then give Gustave one of your 'excellent tours.'"

"My excellent tours?"

"That's what he said. Can we count on you?"

"Oui, Madame."

Oscar's spirits picked up. Blanche's positive attitude often had this effect on him. This would be a better day than he'd thought. He hadn't seen Monet in days. Meeting another of Monet's old friends would be interesting. Each of them had proven to be a character worth knowing and an essential member of the Impressionist community. His mind went to things he needed to do before showing the gardens to a visitor.

"*Merci*, I'll see you at noon. Now I must attend to some things before our guest arrives. I'm looking forward to seeing *Monsieur* Monet again. I hope this means that things will soon return to normal."

"He's eager to introduce you to his friend. You can begin the tour right after lunch."

Oscar rushed off to see that the gardeners had cleaned up a few critical areas while planting some tulip bulbs to come up in the spring.

"I can no longer smoke in the house because the smoke irritates my lungs, my eyes, and my children," Monet was saying to his guest as Oscar entered the dining room later. "Come sit by me, my boy. This is my dear friend and critic Gustave Geffroy. Gustave, this is my new head gardener and friend, Oscar Bonhomme."

Oscar was delighted to be called "friend" by Monet. He shook the soft white hand of the writer. Gustave shared Monet's intensity of appearance. He was of the same height as Monet but had a much shorter beard. His gaze, like Monet's, was penetrating as he greeted Oscar.

"I've heard so much about you from my old friend Georges Clémenceau."

"Good things, I hope," Oscar said with a grin. "Georges is a good man who's been very kind to me."

"Mostly good," Gustave said and chuckled. "I worked for him for many years. He has his moments."

Oscar smiled and sat down so no one would notice he hadn't remembered to change his work shoes. He observed Gustave as the two men spoke throughout lunch. Having never met an art critic, Oscar wanted to understand how one dealt with a master painter like Monet. Most critics weren't kind to Monet from what he'd heard and had often attacked him in his early years.

Meanwhile, as he watched, the two old men ate and talked about Monet's health concerns, the condition of friends like Renoir, and then circled back around to Monet's health. They focused on how this affected the status of the *Grandes Décorations*. Gustave had written letters to Monet encouraging him to complete his *Grandes Décorations*. He wasn't a critic that Oscar feared. He knew that if anyone attacked Monet, the entire family would suffer.

"I'm not sure I can finish these *Grandes Décorations*. My eyes are failing, and I can't seem to find the energy to continue painting," Monet said.

Gustave spent a few moments staring at him. "Clémenceau will not accept this. He says you're always complaining about something. He's worked for years to get you this museum, and he won't let you stop now. How far along are you with the series? Are you anywhere near done?"

"You'll see for yourself when you visit the studio. Take a tour of the gardens with Oscar, and I'll meet you in the studio in an hour. I need to take a brief rest first." Monet stood up and took his friend by the arm as he turned to Oscar. "Show him how you're preparing for the summer season. I'll meet you at the studio."

"*Monsieur* Geffroy, won't you please join me on a short tour of the gardens?"

Oscar led Gustave out the door, across the porch, and down the steps into the garden. Gustave joined him on what was the second time he'd lead a formal garden tour.

"I understand you've been on many of Monet's tours, so I must offer you something different to keep you interested."

Gustave chuckled. "Carry on. I'm eager to see something new."

"Let's start at the far side of the garden where we have our greenhouse and cold frames."

The two men walked across the garden as Oscar pointed to the location where he'd just planted the bulbs. "These will come up in the late spring and bring us a burst of color. That cheers Monet up. He loves color, as you know."

Gustave stopped several times to comment on the beauty of the design. Even though winter was coming to an end, he enjoyed the plantings' plan to see better without the flower blossoms.

Oscar explained as they stopped by the planting area. "This is the greenhouse where we keep our delicate flowers and water lilies over winter, so they don't freeze. We also use this area and the cold frames to propagate new plants from cuttings for the spring planting season. Have you visited here before?"

Gustave looked around the nursery and shook his head. "I've not been to this area before. It's interesting seeing behind the scenes. What do you do when it snows or rains heavily?"

Oscar pointed out the piles of peat mulch and hay behind the greenhouse.

"We pile this mulch on the new plants to keep them from freezing." He stooped to pick up a handful of each material and showed them to Gustave. "If we get too much rain and flood threatens, we must build a dike around this entire area to protect it from washing away. A flood gone unchecked could wipe out not only this season's plantings but the next season's, as well."

"Have you heard about the flooding in the mountains to the east in the Langres Plateau?"

"No, *Monsieur* Gustave. Where is that?"

"It's northeast of Dijon at the source of the Seine. This flooding, caused by the rapid spring thaw and heavy rains, might make its way to Paris and later arrive here."

"*Mon Dieu*! That means Giverny could be in danger. Are you sure the flood will come here?"

"No one knows. It's best to prepare for anything."

Gustave inspected the planting area and seemed to grasp the scope of the work required to manage the gardens. "This is quite an enormous responsibility for one so young. Not only do you need to care for and manage his garden, but you must also protect it and the house from harm. Monet must trust you."

"He doesn't have much choice." Oscar smiled as he dropped the mulch and hay. "All the senior gardeners died or suffered severe wounds in the war. Besides, I've been training for this position my entire life. From as a child working for my mother to my studies at university."

"Georges told me about your mother. She sounds like she was a remarkable woman. Sorry to learn of her passing."

"*Merci*." Oscar was reluctant to talk about his mother to Monet's friends after his conversations with Georges.

"I'm sure it doesn't leave you much time for leisure. I understand you haven't married?"

"That's correct." He remembered the morning's conversation with Geneviève and felt Isabelle's loss and his embarrassment at how he used Geneviève.

"I remember now. Georges told me you have a rather modern girl-friend from Chicago."

Oscar responded with a sigh. "It's more like 'had' these days. She returned to Chicago, and I haven't heard from her since."

"That reminds me of many an artist's relationship, only in reverse." Gustave smiled. "The young men had these lovely models whom they got pregnant. Then the artists left them to fend for themselves. Is that what happened to your mother? I understand your father was an Impressionist artist."

Oscar's breath rushed out of his lungs as he realized that Georges must have told Gustave more of his story than he'd realized. *"Oui,"* he said reluctantly. "Now I'm left trying to find my father."

"Why? What do you hope to gain from him?"

"Nothing. I would just like to know my father and learn if I have any half-brothers and sisters. I've lived my life with no family, and I'd like to see what having loved ones would be like." Oscar smiled at the thought of having a family to share his life with.

"You could also stand to inherit a lot of money if the artist were successful like Monet."

"Money is not important to me. I work to support myself. From what I've heard, inherited wealth is a curse." Oscar was offended at the accusation that he was seeking part of his father's wealth. "I've never given a thought to an inheritance."

"I see. You want family, not fortune. You must be a modern man. Perhaps that's why you've fallen for a modern woman. I hope you find the type of father you want and one that deserves such a fine man as you."

Oscar could feel his face turn red as he shook his head in denial and embarrassment. He never felt deserving of a kind and generous father, despite hoping to have one like that. The subject needed to be changed. He'd had enough of such speculation by a man he didn't know. "Yes, Isabelle's an artist and a modern woman. But at least I'm not pregnant."

Gustave doubled over with laughter. "You're right. I love your ability to laugh at your situation."

Oscar grinned at being the butt of his joke. "I suppose it's a sign of the times. Modern women are turning the tables on us men. Shall we get on to our next stop?"

Gustave looked around and followed Oscar through the garden

and over the tracks to the water lily pond. He grew serious and offered some advice. "You should be careful about getting too involved with these modern women. You have a great opportunity here with Monet. I'd hate for you to lose that."

Oscar opened his eyes wide and then the gate. He leaned on it as Gustave walked through. "I understand what you're saying, and I appreciate your advice. I suppose I should find a local girl who's not so modern."

They both chuckled as they moved on to the sluice that let water into the pond from the Epte River. Oscar took his time explaining its purpose. "This small gate allows us to regulate the water that enters the pond. The one at the far end of the pond regulates the water that leaves it. Too little water, and the pond becomes a swamp. Too much, and it becomes part of the river. Then the lilies and many other plants could wash away. It's our job to regulate these gates to maintain a constant balance."

Gustave knelt to study the sluice gate. He looked up at Oscar, then over at the Epte River and back at the pond. "I see, your job is to keep the two bodies of water in balance. How often do you check the gates?"

Oscar helped Gustave back to his feet. "*Oui,* I try to keep all things in balance. During normal times, I check the gates once a week. However, during times of heavy rain or drought, I regulate the gates daily or even more often if needed."

Gustave looked at Oscar and smiled at his observation about balance. Then he looked across the pond that Monet had spent the last quarter of his life designing, creating, and painting. "I've known Monet a long time, since the early years of his painting career. He spent much of his early career searching for a balance between what he wanted to paint and what the critics, like me, would accept. He also strived for a balance between his obsession with painting and his love of family."

"I can see that," Oscar said as he adjusted the gate so the pond would reach the level he wanted.

Gustave continued to offer his opinion about Monet and what drove him. "With Alice, Monet had a proper balance of love, family, and the freedom to paint. When she died, he fell into a deep depression that lasted for two years, during which he painted nothing. Now he depends on his stepdaughter, Blanche, to keep his life in balance. Without her, he couldn't or wouldn't have returned to painting."

Oscar thought about this for a moment. "*Madame* Blanche runs his house and his life as much as she can. I wouldn't be here without her insistence that he hire me. And Georges' introduction."

He smiled as he learned more about Monet from someone who knew him from his youth. It seemed that Gustave had learned more about him than he'd planned. But to what purpose? Why was he digging into his interest in finding his father? What was he trying to protect Monet from? Perhaps he was doing this at Monet's request.

"If you don't mind my saying, you might be better off finding a wife like Alice to share your life." Gustave offered his advice. "The flashy ones, like this Isabelle, might not be best for you."

After adjusting the sluice gates in the icy river water, Oscar stuck his hands in his pockets to dry them off and warm them. The more he thought about it, Monet had indeed made the correct decision to marry Alice rather than a woman like his mother. "I'm sure you're right. It's time for me to go to the studio so you can see what Monet has been up to."

Gustave smiled. "I'm sure it will be *magnifique!*"

The two men climbed the hill, crossed the tracks, and paused at the top to take in the view of the garden and house. Even heading out of winter, the garden had the power to delight and charm with a design that looked so orderly and charming in the pale winter light.

"It's a beautiful garden," Gustave said. "I can see why once he came here, he never wanted to leave. Do you feel the same way?"

"I'm beginning to. I love my cottage in the garden and the work that I do here. I feel so at peace here after the terrible war."

Oscar took Gustave's arm and helped him down the hill to the garden gate. They continued to chat about Monet until they reached the studio door. He was still suspicious of Gustave's motives, but he did enjoy spending time with him.

"Welcome to my studio, my old friend." Monet spread his arms to show off his new studio and his painting. He looked better after his rest and seemed to have more energy. "I trust you'll enjoy what I'll show you today. Oscar, please roll out the canvases as you did before. First the weeping willows, then the agapanthus, and then the others. We'll complete our tour of the *Grandes Décorations* with the evening over the pond."

Oscar rolled out the paintings in the order Monet had instructed. Gustave's comments were positive on each one. When he'd seen them all, he asked to see them in a circle around them as Monet would display them in the museum.

Monet gestured for Oscar to do as Gustave requested.

"This is a splendid way to crown your career. You can make no better ultimate career statement than this. I'm so proud to have met you when I did and to have watched your work develop into this." Gustave put his arm around the shoulders of his old friend.

"*Merci. Merci beaucoup*, my dear friend. I'm so relieved that you're pleased with this work." Monet lit a cigarette before continuing. "I was considering accepting the vacant seat with the Académie des Beaux-Arts if they offered it to me as a capstone to my career. Perhaps having the *Grandes Décorations* on display in my museum would be a better crowning achievement."

Monet offered Gustave a seat on the couch. The *Grandes Décorations* surrounded them and made Oscar feel as if he were beside the actual pond.

When he had settled in his seat, Gustave spoke up. "Georges and I discussed this at some length last week. We both agreed that your museum would be a far better tribute to your life's work. The Académie and its Salon denied you and your work so often that it hindered your career for years. They don't deserve to honor you now. They can't make up for a lifetime of their shoddy behavior by offering you a token position at the end of your life. You'd be the oldest artist ever offered a seat. That's the ultimate insult."

Monet coughed and coughed before regaining his breath enough to respond.

"These cigarettes will kill me." He snubbed it out and took a few minutes more to catch his breath enough to say, "You're right. They mistreated me from the beginning. Why should I accept their apology now? *Merci* for the two of you helping me make this decision. It's been weighing on my mind the entire time I've been ill. I'm glad that's decided. Now I must get back to my sick bed before Blanche catches me smoking."

Gustave and Monet rose from the couch and embraced. "*À bientôt,* my dear friend. Travel safely. I look forward to your next visit. Please give my best to Georges when you see him."

"*Certainement.* Georges will enjoy hearing that we had this discussion and that you've decided on this matter. I'll bring him with me on my next visit. Oscar, will you escort me to my car? It's getting dark, and I don't see so well at night anymore."

Oscar walked him out through the garden gate.

"My boy, I hope I wasn't too forward in discussing your mother and your love life today. Georges asked me to speak with you about this. He felt you could use some guidance from an older man who has seen it all and who has made many of the same mistakes with women."

They both chuckled at this admission.

"Georges is fond of you, you know. I hope you took this advice in the manner we meant it."

"By all means. I appreciate both of you looking out for Monet and me. I look forward to seeing you both soon." Oscar shook Gustave's hand of friendship and helped him into the vehicle behind his driver.

After Gustave had gone, Oscar retreated to his cottage to contemplate the day's conversation. Perhaps Geneviève should hear about what he'd learned ... then decided this wouldn't be a good idea. She'd been burdened enough with his problems. He opened his door, went in, and lit the lamp on his table. There, resting against it, was a letter with an American stamp posted from Chicago alongside a meat pie for his dinner.

Chapter 21 – Paul Durand-Ruel Visits

He yearned to tear open the envelope to see what Isabelle had to say after all this time. Then he realized that the letter would change his life no matter what she had to say. He decided not to face such a menacing event in haste. Some fortification was required before this grand opening. First he must eat, so he cut a slice of the meat pie still warm from Blanche's kitchen. His hesitation forced him to consume it a small bite at a time with a glass of Burgundy. After finishing a second—or a third—glass of wine, he opened the letter. Isabelle's long-overdue letter.

Dear Oscar,

I'm sorry that I haven't written to you earlier, but I've been so busy taking care of my father. I've so many exciting things to tell you, I don't know where to begin. First, Father is much better and is returning to his practice next week. His kind junior partner, Jerome, has been such a help to both of us during this entire time. I don't know what we would've done without him.

Second, I'm getting a small showing of my work at a local gallery. It's just a few of my paintings in a show with several other artists, but it's my FIRST show. I can't wait 'til it opens in June.

Speaking of art, the third thing is, the Art Institute of Chicago is sending me back to France to purchase a Monet for them. They want one of his latest paintings of the lily pond. It'll be my first business trip as an assistant art curator at the Institute. That's my new job. I started last week. Yes, Father and Jerome helped me get it, so I must prove myself worthy.

So sorry for the brief letter, but Jerome is here, and we need to take care of a few things at the office before Father returns. I can't wait to see you in a few weeks and tell you the rest of my excellent news. It'll be fun being with you again.

Hugs and kisses,

Isabelle

Oscar's heart ached as he read the letter three more times before opening the second bottle of wine. His head was swimming as he tried to sort out the meaning of the letter. She'd never come back to him. Her life had begun again in Chicago without him. He cursed himself for not leaving on the boat with her.

The last thing he remembered was cursing Isabelle and then sobbing at his loss of her love. He could barely get undressed before he crawled onto his bed and passed out. Morning came earlier than he'd hoped, and he read the letter once more before getting dressed and trudging off to breakfast, then work.

Standing outside Geneviève's shop, he was trying to see inside, but the windows were clouded with steam from baking. What was he doing here? She was a new friend that he had bothered too much already. She doesn't want to hear any more about Isabelle and me. It'd be best if I returned to my cottage and my work. He needed to forget about both her and Isabelle and focus on straightening out his life. He turned to leave just when the door opened, and Geneviève looked out at him, standing there in the cold.

"I saw someone standing in front of my window and thought it might be you. Come in."

She looked radiant with her pink cheeks and smiling blue eyes. Oscar couldn't leave after she'd caught him peeking in. He stepped into the shop from out of the chilly morning fog. "It's so nice and warm in here, and the smell of fresh-baked bread makes me ravenous. Do you mind if I crawl into the oven to get the chill off?"

They both laughed.

"Did you sleep well last night? I trust you're in a better mood today."

"So sorry about how I've treated you. It was wrong of me to take advantage of your kind nature." He hung his head in shame. "I promise I'll never do it again, and I won't flirt with you anymore."

"You're forgiven, but just this once." She started shaking her finger at him in mock anger. "From now on, we both expect you to be on your best behavior around us. Little Charlie didn't appreciate your behavior, either."

"I promise." He crossed his heart. "Little Charlie? I've never heard you use that name before."

Geneviève smiled at his question. "Charlie works as a nickname for Charles or Charlotte. Either way, I'm covered. He or she has a name: 'Charlie.'"

"It's so American. I love it." He took her hand. "And Charles would love it, too. Say, can I take you and Charlie to dinner Saturday night at the Hotel Baudy? I'd like to make up for my unacceptable behavior and to thank you for your friendship and excellent advice."

Geneviève considered his proposal for a few moments.

"It wouldn't be proper for me to visit a hotel with you. Most people in the village still consider me married until one year after Charles' death." She paused for a moment. "I suppose it might be acceptable for us to dine together if we invite someone else to be a chaperone."

"A chaperone would be fine. It'll be fun." He smiled and sat down at a table by the window. "I'm sure I can come up with someone from Monet's household."

"Would you like your usual?"

"I'll try two of those angel wings instead."

"Two. You must like the angel wings." Geneviève turned to go to the kitchen.

She wore a clean printed apron this morning instead of the old white one she wore most often. The ribbon around her baker's hat matched the apron print. He liked the improvement.

He called out to her in the kitchen, "I like your new outfit."

She called back, "We're trying to fluff up a bit. The other girls working for me have matching ones."

She returned a few minutes later. "Here's your coffee and angel wings. You mentioned my excellent advice. What part of my advice did you find worthy of a dinner invitation?"

"If you sit down, I'll tell you."

Geneviève looked at him askance, took the seat across from him at the table, and lowered herself into it. "I'm ready. I think."

He took a bite of angel wings and a gulp of coffee before he began. He rather liked the way one curl had made its way out from under her hat and hung in front of her left eye. "When I arrived home last night, I found a letter from Isabelle waiting for me."

Geneviève's smile faded, and she slid her chair back from the table. "That's wonderful. You got just what you've been waiting for. What did she have to say?"

"Not as much as I'd hoped." He clenched and unclenched his hands to help relieve the morning chill and the stress of telling her about the letter. "She is returning to Giverny in a few weeks. She'll contact me when she arrives."

"And, what else?"

"Not much. Isabelle's been busy and will tell me more when she arrives. Her art is being displayed at a gallery, and she has a job with the Art Institute of Chicago. She's coming to buy one of Monet's paintings for the Art Institute."

"That's all? She gave you no explanation of why she hadn't written to you earlier? Where is she going to stay?"

"That was all she said. I don't know when she's coming or where she's planning to stay. Most likely, she'll stay with her friends in Vernon. I don't even know if she still cares for me or not. I'm just pleased that she's returning. She also mentioned Jerome, her father's partner, several times." Relieved, he turned back to his breakfast.

"Are you pleased with this letter? It doesn't seem to have answered any of your important questions." She placed both of her palms on the table as if she was preparing to rise and leave.

He finished his coffee and one of the angel wings, fearing that he'd break down if he answered any more of her questions. "I'll take this one to go. Can I have my sandwich and my bill?"

"I don't understand you." Geneviève was cross with him. "You complained to me about how Isabelle has been ignoring you. Then she sends a letter with the briefest of explanations, and you immediately forgive her."

"I can't forgive her, but I still love her, and I don't know what else to do. She has me so confused. I'm bouncing from anger to forgiveness like the target in a game of boules."

Geneviève went to the kitchen, returned with his sandwich and the bill, and slammed them down onto the table. She mumbled, "Men!" Then she stomped off to the kitchen as fast as her condition would allow.

"Shall I pick you up here on Saturday night at about seven?" he called out but received no response.

He shook his head and trudged back to his cottage to begin this terrible day. He had angered her again, and he wasn't quite sure why. Perhaps she thought he was a fool, or she could be jealous. Either way, it was a terrible day.

As he walked past Monet's large studio, he noticed the light was on. It had been dark since Monet had taken ill. He stuck his head inside and called out, "Who's there?"

"Oscar, I'm glad you came in. I need help today."

"*Monsieur* Monet. Are you feeling well?"

Monet came out from behind one of his *Grandes Décorations* and smiled at him. "Much better. Can you spend some time away from the gardening to work in here?"

Oscar noticed the acrid smell of tobacco lingering in the air.

"I'm eager to help." He took a chance and said, "Does *Madame* Blanche know you're smoking in here?"

"That's none of her business, and you will not tell her. Right?" Monet snapped.

Oscar realized he had overstepped his bounds. "She'll find out, but not from me."

Monet stubbed out his cigarette without lighting another. He erupted into a coughing fit. When he'd caught his breath, he continued. "My oldest customer and benefactor, Paul Durand-Ruel, is coming in a few days for lunch. I must prepare paintings for him to purchase."

He sat down on the couch, his breath still coming in quick gasps.

Oscar stepped to the couch. "I'll ask *Madame* Blanche to come and help you.

Monet took a deep breath. "Don't! A glass of water will be fine. Blanche will smell the cigarette if she comes in now."

Oscar fetched the glass of water and then sat beside Monet. "I'll make sure the *Grandes Décorations* are in their proper order. I'll fetch any paintings you wish to offer him."

"You're a good boy, Oscar. That's what I need. I'll tell you which paintings to bring out to show Paul and which to hold back. He always wants the ones I hold back." He smiled as he sat back and sipped his water. "Geffroy enjoyed the unique tour you took him on yesterday. He found you to be a competent guide."

"I enjoyed meeting him. He gave me some friendly advice."

Monet gave a knowing smile. Oscar thought Gustave must have told him the nature of his advice.

"Did you know Paul supported me for years when I was first getting started? Without him, I wouldn't have been able to survive. He put food on my family's table and helped me to pay off my debts. Now I'm proud to help him by selling him paintings on consignment. He pays me when he sells them."

"Sounds like a wonderful supporter."

"*Oui*, an old and dear friend." He finished his water and rose to his feet. "He was the one who introduced my paintings to America. Dealing with Americans can be a nasty business, present company excluded, and he did it well. They are a tricky lot."

He winked at Oscar and laughed as he began searching for the paintings he wished to offer the Durand-Ruel Gallery.

As Oscar followed Monet into his storage area, he wondered what the wily old man knew about Isabelle's relationship and if he knew he'd received a letter from her. He was uncomfortable that his employer and his family knew so much about his love life.

Helping Monet select paintings for Paul Durand-Ruel proved much more complicated than it first sounded. That simple assistance request was followed by grueling hours of decision and indecision, then more hours of recriminations and revised judgments. Oscar's head hurt as he finally returned to his cottage and what he'd left of the meat pie from the previous evening.

Again he slept little. He lay awake, trying to understand what Isabelle meant to him. Geneviève had given her opinion of his relationship in her one-word pronouncement, "*Men!*"

He hoped for some additional advice as he entered the patisserie the following morning—no such luck. Geneviève was not there. The counter girl smiled at him when he entered and handed him two parcels containing his breakfast and one his lunch. He paid his bill and left without seeing Geneviève. Perhaps she was upset from the day before, and she chose to avoid him. Returning to his work in the garden, he tried to understand how he'd lost Isabelle to her new life in Chicago.

A few days later, Blanche invited him for lunch to meet Paul Durand-Ruel. He found him to be a very distinguished, elderly gentleman with gray hair and a thin gray mustache. His impeccable dress and manners seemed to be an ideal match for his wealthy art clients. According to Monet, his gallery was the first to specialize in selling

Impressionist paintings to clients in France, England, and America.

Blanche planned a short garden tour for Paul, much like his previous ones. Afterward, they would meet Monet in the large studio to examine the *Grandes Décorations* and the paintings that Monet had offered him. Oscar found Paul was sophisticated, charming, and approachable as they strolled down the *Grande Allée* to the lily pond.

"*Monsieur* Monet told me you're most interested in seeing the lily pond today," he said.

"I am and appreciate your taking the time to show it to me. I need to see the locations where Monet painted the *Grandes Décorations*. It'll give me a better understanding of the paintings I'm about to see and how to present them to my clients."

Oscar offered to take Paul's arm to help him up the hill, over the tracks, and down the other side to the lily pond.

"That's most kind of you, young man. I'm not as steady on my feet as I once was."

Oscar nodded to acknowledge Paul's comment. "The recent rain makes the climb slippery. When were you here last?"

Paul looked off in the distance as if remembering the last time he'd visited the pond. "It's been quite a while. Lately, I send my sons here to meet with Monet, but this visit is special."

He looked sad.

Oscar wanted to understand Paul's mood. "How so?"

"I'm afraid it'll be my last visit." He dabbed at his eyes with a handkerchief. "I'm getting on in years and not able to travel even short distances in comfort. Monet has been a great friend for over fifty years. Now we're both reaching the end of our careers. I wanted to see him one last time and judge for myself the *Grandes Décorations* that is the capstone of his career."

Oscar swelled with pride in Monet. "That's what everyone says when they see the *Grandes Décorations*. Let me show you where he's been painting since I've been here."

He took Paul first one place, then another where Monet painted.

"You can envision each scene and observe the patterns of light that Monet paints when he's here at a particular time of day."

Paul took time to experience each scene and then glanced around to take in the surroundings to add context to the pictures. "I can see what he was striving for with these scenes. Let's see the paintings that everyone seems to enjoy."

On the way down the hill and across the tracks, Paul spoke up. "I understand you know the daughter of an American client of mine."

Oscar couldn't believe how small the art community was. "*Oui*, she's Isabelle Brescher from Chicago. I've never met her father."

"You'd like Antoine," Paul assured him. "He's a very affable man who dotes on his only child. I understand he's recovering well after his heart attack."

"I heard that. Isabelle wrote to tell me she's returning to France soon. It'll be nice to have her back."

"I'm sure it will be. I doubt Isabelle stays long since she's engaged to marry her father's junior partner."

All the breath escaped Oscar's lungs. He slipped coming down the hillside and caught himself before he took Paul down with him. "I'm so sorry. I lost my footing. Are you hurt? You'd think I'd be more careful after climbing this hill several times every day."

Paul steadied himself and looked at Oscar's face. "I'm fine."

Oscar was embarrassed that he'd slipped but was more rattled by what Paul had said. She'd just written to say she was returning to him, and now he'd learned that she was engaged. He didn't understand why she hadn't told him.

"I saw her just last week in Paris. She arrived a few days before and was visiting some of her school friends. She's in the market for a Monet painting for the Art Institute of Chicago."

Oscar couldn't believe what Paul was saying. It was as if he was hearing him from a distance. He couldn't quite make out his words. How could she be in France and not contact him?

"How nice for her." It was all he could think to say.

"My friend Georges Clémenceau says you are here in search of your father. I understand he's an Impressionist painter. I've gotten to know all of them over the years. Can you tell me any more about him, and perhaps I can help you identify him?"

"*Non!* My mother wouldn't tell me anything else."

"Well, whoever he turns out to be, I'm sure he's proud of you if what Monet tells me is true."

"Why? What does Monet say about me?"

"He tells me you're a very decent fellow who can be trusted. That's wonderful because he needs a person he can trust as he gets along in years."

"I'm honored and humbled."

"You should be. You'd be fortunate to have a father like Monet, who took in a woman and her six children when he could barely feed his own two in addition to his ill wife. I couldn't think of doing such a thing as that, could you?"

Oscar thought for a few moments before responding. What a strange question. Was this some sort of test? What was Paul getting at? Was he trying to assess his character? "I certainly would do that if I loved the woman involved the way he loved Alice. I understand that she shaped his life for the better."

"That she did. You'd be fortunate to find a woman like Alice to help you shape your life. Is Isabelle such a woman?"

Oscar felt a weight was placed on his chest that crushed the breath out of him. "That doesn't seem to matter since you said she's marrying someone else."

"She hasn't married him yet. She's back in France. Perhaps you still have a chance to change her mind."

First Gustave and then Paul offer him advice on whom to marry. It sounds like someone is at work here. Monet, perhaps.

He couldn't listen to him anymore. Without saying another word, he escorted Paul to the studio, where they met Monet. He began moving the *Grandes Décorations* as Monet had instructed him on the previous showing.

Paul took time to scrutinize each one. He seemed to be trying to identify where Monet had painted each scene. Several times he inquired as to the time of day the painting had been created. Afterward, Monet asked Paul and Oscar to sit and enjoy a drink of *Calvados*. Monet fidgeted as he reached into his pocket for a cigarette and then brought out his empty hand. He was trying to quit smoking to keep from coughing and avoid Blanche's nagging.

"*Magnifique*, Monet." Paul clasped Monet's arm. "This is the best work you've done. You're moving Impressionism forward in a new direction. Buyers need to see these. You're capturing subtleties of light that no painter has ever even attempted."

Monet changed the subject away from himself. "Paul, did you know that young Oscar here is a collector of Impressionist paintings? He has a Renoir and a Monet so far."

"My, that's a great way to start." Paul looked at Monet with a sly smile. "Do you think he's ready to add to his collection? I have some of Pissarro's paintings at an excellent price."

"What do you think, Oscar?" Monet said with a chuckle.

"Not now. I'm hoping to pick up some damaged Monet paintings the next time he gets frustrated and attacks his canvases."

Paul erupted in laughter. "*Touché*, Monet. I think this young man could amass quite an art collection this way."

Monet grumped. "He knows better. Now let's get down to business. Oscar, please excuse us."

Oscar drained his glass and left them alone to conduct their business. He returned to his cottage and sat at his kitchen table until it turned dark outside. He reflected on what a fool he'd been, again. Would Geneviève forgive him this time? He'd been so lonely that he'd flirted with her after Jean-Pierre had warned him that she was not to be trifled with. Then, when he'd received a letter from Isabelle, he had been ready to forget about Geneviève and return to Isabelle.

Now he had learned that Isabelle had become engaged to someone else. Geneviève was angry with him for bouncing from one love interest to the next. He'd made a mess of his love affair and his friendship.

After opening and finishing a bottle of wine left behind from his party, Oscar realized that drinking was becoming a nasty habit. Somehow, he made it to his bedroom and fell asleep across his bed with his clothes on. In the morning, he tried to ignore his headache and made himself as presentable as possible before going to the patisserie to beg Geneviève to forgive his latest misbehavior. Forgiveness would be a hard sell this time.

He reached the patisserie long before it opened, hoping it was before the counter girl arrived. He knocked on the front window as he waved his white handkerchief as a gesture of surrender. Geneviève laughed as she opened the door.

"Are you giving up so easily? You're not much of a warrior for love. Come in and get warm."

"I'm brave and stupid. I'm also very sorry with how I've treated you. I read what I wanted to believe in Isabelle's letter when in fact, she came back to France to plan her wedding."

Geneviève listened to his news as her eyes opened wider. "Is she in France already? I assume she's not coming to marry you."

Oscar shook his head no.

"Who, then?"

He dropped into a chair at the table by the door. He buried his face in his hands and mumbled his answer. "Jerome, her father's junior partner in his medical practice."

He raised his eyes to see Geneviève looking down at him with concern.

"That makes sense. Jerome would be a good catch. She could retire and paint. Good for her."

"What are you saying?" he asked with a touch of anger in his voice. "What about our love? Is she just casting me aside?"

Geneviève shook her head in response. "Sorry to say, but I don't think you were in the picture to be dropped."

Oscar listened to her observation. He knew he wasn't angry with Geneviève or Isabelle but at himself for being a bigger fool than he'd first thought. "Then I've just been wasting my time with her?"

"*Non*. If you learned something about life and love, I'd say it was worth it. Wouldn't you?"

"I suppose you're right." He resigned himself to his fate. "It was an expensive lesson, though."

"Most good lessons are. Now, let me get your breakfast and lunch. How do you feel about more angel wings?"

"*Oui*, I need all the divine help I can get."

Geneviève made her way to the kitchen to fix his breakfast, humming a lullaby. Strange how she moved faster or slower depending upon her moods.

He began thinking about the lessons he'd learned from Isabelle. She'd brought him back into the world after his injuries that drove him to hide from people and life. He was hurt and frustrated that his loving her was not enough to bring her back to him. If only he could have gone with her to Chicago, all could have been different.

Geneviève returned from the kitchen with a steaming mug of coffee and cheeks flushed from the oven. She made such a lovely picture with her blond hair, blue eyes, and pink cheeks. The baby bulge made her even more attractive to him. He enjoyed being with her and talking about himself.

Now it was time to stop talking about himself and Isabelle. The baby was due soon, so it was time to discuss how he might help her through this troublesome time of having a baby without her husband. Through his trauma over Isabelle, he realized how important it was to have a friend like Geneviève. Now he needed to step up and be as good a friend to her.

So he plucked up his courage. "Are we still going to dinner Saturday night?"

"Well, about that. My mother would like to come along to meet you. Would that be acceptable to you?"

He took a few moments to sip his coffee and take a bite of his breakfast before responding. "Would your father like to come, as well?"

"He would, but he died a few years ago."

"Sorry, but I'm feeling the need to add someone else to my side of the table, so women won't outnumber me." They smiled at his joke. "Does she know Jean-Pierre?"

"They are old friends. Well, not friends exactly. She blamed him for getting us into trouble when we were young. She has forgiven him. I think he'd like to come along if you ask him."

"I'll ask him today. He might take some convincing."

"Tell him we can come back here for one of my mother's famous *tarte au citron.* He loved those when we were children."

"I'm sure that'll help."

Oscar finished his breakfast, took his lunch, and left. She caught his arm at the door and kissed him once on each cheek. No third kiss, but he felt he was back in her good graces once again. At least she was still his friend. Having a good friend was better than longing for a lost lover who'd left him for another man. Saturday would come soon enough. Now all he needed to do was convince Jean-Pierre to escort Geneviève's mother to dinner.

Chapter 22 – The Dinner

At last, Saturday arrived. Oscar had talked Jean-Pierre into coming along to support him with Geneviève's mother, Christine. The *tarte au citron* had helped persuade him. They learned that Christine was feeling ill and couldn't attend at the last minute, so Geneviève asked Lily to take her place. Oscar was relieved that her mother wouldn't be there to ask him questions about himself and disappointed that he wouldn't meet her and learn more about Geneviève.

They'd agreed to meet at the patisserie at six o'clock after Geneviève finished work. Oscar, Jean-Pierre, and Lily arrived a little late and rushed inside to escape the winter evening chill. They exchanged greetings as Oscar helped Geneviève into her shabby winter coat over an old black dress with a frayed collar. It was tight across her front. He thought she must be close to her due date.

Lily opened her black lamb's-wool coat with a fox-fur collar to show off her showy pink flapper dress with beaded mesh—at least, that's how she described it. Jean-Pierre opened his camel-hair topcoat to reveal his flashy, tan checked jacket and matching trousers. Oscar had no coat to wear over the gray wool suit that Monet had given him.

"Lily, we must go shopping after the baby is born and I regain my figure," Geneviève said. "I've got to get some new clothes. I've been so busy with the baby and the shop that my clothes have turned to rags, and I haven't had time to replace them."

Lily's face lit up. "I'd love to. We'll go on a trip to Paris and buy you some fashionable clothes. I love a good shopping trip. *Le Bon Marché* is my favorite department store. Don't you just love it there?"

Geneviève looked as though she'd enjoy the adventure. "I'm looking forward to it. I've never been shopping in Paris. I'd love to visit *Le Bon Marché*. I've heard so much about that department store."

"We must get a coat for Oscar, too," Lily added. "That is if he survives the winter dressed as he is."

They all laughed at this, even Oscar.

"Jean-Pierre and I'll go along to carry the packages," he volunteered. "Now we need to be going, or we'll be late for our reservation."

Jean-Pierre declared with authority, "Don't worry. You're with the Monets. Since Blanche made the reservation, we can arrive at any time."

As they walked along the street to the hotel, Oscar felt the party made an odd-looking group with a mix of clothing—two in fashion and two out. All three of Oscar's guests talked simultaneously, telling stories about their childhood days and the trouble they got into.

"Remember the time you girls went skinny dipping in the lily pond?" Jean-Pierre laughed as he told the story. Both Geneviève's and Lily's faces turned red.

Oscar felt guilty about thinking of Geneviève skinny dipping again when she was no longer pregnant. He couldn't help thinking about how beautiful she would look.

Lily punched Jean-Pierre on the shoulder. "You stole our clothes just as Monet was coming to paint the lilies. Lucky for us, he turned back toward the bridge at the last minute."

"I gave them back to you after he left," Jean-Pierre teased and bent over in laughter. "I was only trying to hide your clothes from him."

Lily faced him. "If so, why did you need to get our dresses wet in the pond before returning them to us?"

"I had to hide them somewhere," he protested and laughed again.

Then everyone laughed.

Oscar listened to learn more of the exploits of Monet's children and their friends. Their childhood memories made him feel closer to them. The four linked arms as they walked along as if they were still children. They might have skipped except for Geneviève's condition.

The Hotel Baudy was just a few blocks along the street from the patisserie, but the group took its time getting there. Geneviève had a story to tell about each of the shops they passed. This one was doing well. That one was just hanging on. This one's wife ran off with that one's husband. Her close friend, Cosette, owned the seamstress shop that tailored Oscar's suits. The light in her shop window was still on. Geneviève guessed that it was a late-arriving customer or a significant order that kept her in the shop past her usual closing hour.

"I have a seamstress story," Lily said. "According to what I was told, my *grand-mère*, Alice, and Camille, Monet's first wife, took turns wearing their one good dress on trips into Paris to get seamstress work. They did this to help feed the family when Monet's paintings were not selling."

"That's sad but true, Lily," Jean-Pierre added. "It was a hard time for the family. I remember going through one winter eating nothing but potatoes. Monet couldn't sell his paintings and wouldn't consider giving up or changing his style. Then we moved here, and our fortunes began to turn around. Most of the people here were kind and helpful."

On this cold, clear evening, Geneviève told Oscar about merchants in the village who had helped Monet, even if he didn't know them personally. It comforted him and helped him feel more like he was a member of the village, and the childhood stories made him feel closer to the family.

When the group arrived at the hotel and entered the glass front door, Oscar crossed the small lobby first. Patrons engaging in lively conversations crowded the restaurant. He introduced himself to the owner, Lucien Baudy, who smiled as he greeted him.

"I understand from *Madame* Blanche Monet that you're an American."

"*Oui*, I'm from San Francisco."

"We have many American guests in the hotel these days. I'm sure you can tell by their accents. We like Americans. They're good for business in our village."

Oscar realized that these patrons must be part of the American artist invasion that Monet complained about. The original art hung on the colorful walls of the restaurant was probably created by these artists. The kitchen, near the restaurant entryway, was small and vibrating with the merry-go-round of chef, sous chef, and dishwasher. Waiters were queueing up in the kitchen to pick up their orders. Cooking smells that escaped from the kitchen made his mouth water. With the evening's excitement, he had forgotten how hungry he was.

Lucien, a short, stout man with slick-backed, graying hair, bowed as he welcomed Oscar's party members. "*Bonsoir, Monsieur* Jean-Pierre, *Mademoiselle* Lily, and *Madame* Geneviève. It's my pleasure to welcome you this evening. Please follow me to our best table."

Lucien seated Oscar and the others at a large table in the front window to admire the street view. Blanche had told Oscar when she had made his reservation that the owners considered Monet and his family good for business. Monet drew the young artists to the village.

Lucien seated Lily and Jean-Pierre on one side of the table and Oscar and Geneviève on the other. "Please pay my respects to *Monsieur* Monet and *Madame* Blanche. I hope *Monsieur* Monet is feeling better soon. Have a wonderful dinner. Please call me if you have questions. *Merci* for dining with us this evening."

Oscar began reading the menu. "What do you recommend?"

Lily offered her expert opinion as a frequent patron of the restaurant. "It depends upon who's cooking. Angelina, Lucien's wife, is the real driving force behind the hotel and restaurant. When she's cooking, the food has subtle flavors and is prepared to perfection. When her assistant cooks, it's not as good." She smiled. "Lucky for us, I saw Angelina in the kitchen as we entered."

"In that case, what do you recommend?" Jean-Pierre asked. "I'm in the mood for the duck."

"There's duck confit in a honey sauce. It's one of Angelina's specialties," Lily pointed out.

Jean-Pierre smiled and rubbed his hands together. "What's your choice, Oscar?"

"I'm still deciding. Everything looks interesting." He looked at Geneviève. "What do you choose, *Madame*?"

Geneviève looked back at him and smiled. "Both the duck and lamb sound good to me, but not for little Charlie. I think I'll choose the salmon with Normandy sauce and the salad. Remember, don't order dessert because we have the *tarte au citron* at my shop. Mother made it before she realized she couldn't join us."

"How kind of her. Please thank her for me," Oscar said.

"I'll have the lamb with the salad. I don't eat lamb often," Lily piped up.

Jean-Pierre looked confused. "Who's Charlie?"

"That's the baby's name," Oscar said. "He or she is making decisions already."

Just then, Geneviève yelped in surprise. "Charlie heard that and kicked me. He or she doesn't enjoy being accused of interfering."

The entire table erupted in laughter.

Oscar made his choice.

"I'm having the *pâté de foie gras* and the Normandy salad." He winked at Geneviève. "If Charlie doesn't have any objections."

Everyone was sharing a bottle of Pinot Noir from Burgundy except for Geneviève and Charlie. Oscar thought it went well with the entrées the others chose. The table conversation turned to Monet's garden and what Oscar did there. Geneviève enjoyed hearing how he'd assumed her deceased father's role at the garden. Jean-Pierre focused his comments on the preparations for the spring weather.

"We've had a series of terrible springs in the past few years with heavy rains swelling the rivers and floods caused by rapid snowmelt in the mountains at the headwaters of the Seine. We need to make sure we're prepared this year." Jean-Pierre drank more wine and stared at Oscar. "There's been no one preparing for such disasters since Geneviève's father left us years ago. He was always well-prepared."

Geneviève nodded in agreement.

Oscar thought for a few moments before responding. "I discussed this with Gustave Geffroy on his recent visit. He expressed the same concerns. He told me about the flooding in the east that was moving down the Seine toward Paris and then here. I need to develop a plan to deal with whatever comes along. Thanks for reminding me."

The food arrived, and the conversation slowed for a few minutes. Oscar observed each of the parties to make sure they were enjoying the dinner. As the host, he felt responsible for their satisfaction. When he noticed that wine glasses were getting low, he offered them more to drink. "You all look like you're enjoying yourselves. More wine, anyone?"

"Everything is delicious. I'll have more wine." Jean-Pierre had finished his dinner before the others. "I've saved room for Christine's tarte. I want to do that justice."

Lily declined the offer of a drink.

Oscar poured the rest of the bottle into Jean-Pierre's glass and ordered another drink for him. "I've had too much wine these past few weeks. Please help me out."

"I'm always prepared to come to your aid. No matter my sacrifice." He laughed a little too much at his joke, but no one seemed to mind. He caught the waiter's eye when he finished the wine. "I'll have a cognac."

Lily looked askance at this indulgence.

After everyone had finished their meals and Jean-Pierre his cognac, the waiter cleared the table, and Lucien brought over the cheese tray and the dessert menu. Oscar stopped him before he could offer them more. "Geneviève's mother has made us one of her famous *tarte au citron.*"

"I can't compete with that. I wish Christine would make desserts for the restaurant. Our customers enjoy Geneviève's bread." Lucien patted his stomach. "They'd love Christine's desserts."

Geneviève spoke up. "You know she's retired, but I'll ask her to bring one for Angelina's birthday."

"My darling wife would love that. Shall I bring your bill?"

"I'll take the bill," Oscar said. Jean-Pierre tried to protest, but Oscar waved him away. "I said this dinner is my treat. I appreciate how each of you has welcomed me into your family and community. Your friendship has helped me recover from my injuries and get back on my feet again. This dinner is the least I can do to thank you."

He paid the bill and said *à bientôt* to Lucien and Angelina. The party left the warm and cozy restaurant to return to the patisserie. Geneviève unlocked the door and turned up the lamps before welcoming them into her shop. She had decorated one of her tables in the front window with a tablecloth, candles, and a vase of dried flowers.

Oscar smiled. "How charming."

"I felt we needed more **decorations** than my usual bare tables for this evening." Geneviève motioned for them to sit while she went to the kitchen to fetch her mother's famous dessert.

"Can I have a large piece?" Jean-Pierre asked.

Geneviève called out from the kitchen, "Some things never change. You always asked for the biggest piece of dessert."

They laughed, none so hard as Jean-Pierre, who was under the influence of his extra ration of wine and cognac.

When they'd finished their desserts, Oscar asked, "Can I take a piece to Monet and Blanche?"

Geneviève cut two large pieces, placed them on a plate, and covered them with a red and white checked napkin. "*Oui,* so long as Jean-Pierre doesn't carry it. I've never trusted him around girls or desserts."

Oscar chuckled. "I'll guard it with my life." Then he cleared his throat, feeling self-conscious. "I also want to thank each of you for helping me understand how to approach Isabelle." He coughed and continued his unrehearsed speech as soon as he'd caught his breath. "Each of you has listened to me complain of my difficulty coming to grips with her leaving me. Now that she may soon return, I thank you for helping me through this. I know that, no matter what comes next, I can depend upon you to help me. *Merci* for joining me tonight."

Jean-Pierre stood up and shook Oscar's hand, said *bonne nuit*, and staggered toward the door.

Lily jumped up to help him walk home. After giving Oscar and Geneviève a kiss on each cheek, she said as she raced after Jean-Pierre, "Remember, we're going shopping soon."

Geneviève called after her, "Not too soon, I hope."

Oscar smiled as he rose to say *bonne nuit* to Geneviève. "I guess it's time for me to leave, too. *Merci* for excusing my rude behavior, and I hope you enjoyed my 'apology' dinner. Please tell your mother how much we enjoyed her dessert."

Geneviève stepped closer. "I loved your 'apology' dinner and this entire evening. It was generous of you to treat us."

Oscar prepared to shake her hand, but she moved as close as she could, kissed him on each cheek, and then added one more for friendship. He felt his cheeks flush. "Friends?"

"Good friends. I'll see you soon." She smiled as she ushered him outside and closed the door.

Oscar watched through the window as she crossed the shop to the stairway leading to her second-floor apartment. He gripped the dessert plate in one hand and pulled his suit coat tighter around him with the other. Jean-Pierre and Lily were ahead of him on their way home, Lily holding Jean-Pierre up. Oscar would take the dessert to Monet and Blanche, but they were probably asleep, so he would deliver it in the morning.

He stared up at the starry night sky. The quiet evening enveloped him, and his nervousness at hosting his first dinner party faded away. Even the neighbor's howling dog was silent tonight. His dinner had been a success, and Geneviève had given him a third kiss. Friends. Good friends.

When he arrived at the cottage, he placed the dessert on his dining room table and got ready for bed. He sat on the edge, staring at Renoir's framed sketch of Isabelle on the wall above his dresser. He wondered where she was and when she might arrive.

He fell asleep thinking of the warm and wonderful evening he had shared with his friends and how much he'd learned. His friend Geneviève dominated his dreams.

In the morning, Oscar delivered the dessert just as Monet was finishing breakfast. Monet ate his piece of the tarte before Oscar left the dining room. He told Blanche how much they had enjoyed the dinner and thanked her for the reservation. Oscar returned to his cottage with two gardening magazines and a plant catalog that Monet had loaned him. He was planning an outing to a garden show and wanted Oscar to help choose what they should search for. Monet solicited his advice on what they should add to the garden design for the first time. Quite an honor.

Sitting in his chair by the fire, he was pleased with Monet's recognition of his expertise and studied the plant catalog, but he couldn't help thinking about the subject of disaster planning that Jean-Pierre had brought up. Since he had no understanding of preparing the garden for a disaster like flooding, he would ask Monet about past tragedies, like the flood of 1910, and what he needed to prepare for. Just then, a knock on his door startled him.

Who would visit him so early on a Sunday morning? He opened the door to find Isabelle standing there. She wore a tan coat open to reveal a fringed cream-colored dress with a matching hat and shoes, looking as lovely as ever. He gripped the door to steady himself and stood with his mouth open as she greeted him.

"Good morning, Oscar. I've returned." She waited a few moments for his response. "Aren't you going to say something?"

He mumbled something that she didn't seem to understand.

"What did you say? Aren't you going to invite me in?"

He felt his throat tighten and his knees grow weak as he gripped the door tighter. She looked annoyed. "Aren't you going to say anything?"

He stammered. "I can't believe you're here!"

Chapter 23 – Isabelle Returns

"Are you pregnant?" Oscar felt as if he were living his nightmare. He couldn't see that she was pregnant, but he knew she could be based on his nightmare and his fear from first sleeping with her. His heart sank at the idea that someone else had fathered her child. This was what he'd warned her about when they had talked at Jazzmatazz. His mind raced back to his painful childhood memories of growing up with no father.

She thrust her chin out.

"How did you know? That's not something I want to discuss on your front stoop." Isabelle's face grew red, her voice acquiring a defiant tone. "Now let me in, and we'll discuss it."

She pushed him aside, strode into his living room, and took over his couch, where she sat glaring at him.

Oscar closed the front door slowly and slid his chair away from the fireplace to face her. It took a few moments for him to sort out his thoughts after the shock of having her barge back into his life. His face felt hot, and his breathing was constrained. He had expected to see her, but not like this. He couldn't believe that she had shown up in his cottage early on Sunday morning, pregnant.

He needed time to think. "How's your father?"

"He's back at work and recovered, thanks to his partner, who has taken excellent care of both of us." She looked around the living room and shook her head with scorn at his humble home. "He's been eager to see his patients and return to normal."

Oscar tried to smile. "I've heard he's a very kind man, and I'm so happy for him and you. I'll bet he hated to see you leave again."

After they'd exhausted this surface level of conversation, he refocused on small, everyday things. Was his living room tidy enough for a visitor? Should a refreshment be offered? All that he had was water and tea. No coffee.

"Can I offer you something to drink? I have tea and water."

She turned up her nose at his offer. "What, no champagne? No, thank you."

He hated that she looked even more beautiful than ever. Pregnancy, even this early, put a glow in her cheeks that cosmetics couldn't equal. He felt his anger and composure slipping through his grasp. All he wanted to do was take her in his arms and kiss away his longing and loneliness. Feelings of passion impeded his reason like it had that Sunday by the lily pond when his mind battled his heart. His heart had won then, and it was winning now. He wanted her back in his life. Desperately.

"I know what you're thinking, Oscar Bonhomme." Isabelle's voice was full of recrimination. The tone of her voice added another brick to the wall building between them.

Oscar's anger was returning at her assumption that she could so easily read his thoughts. "Tell me. What am I thinking?"

"You're thinking back to the time when you warned me you didn't want to get me pregnant as someone did to your mother."

Seeing the anger in her face, he tried to defuse it by hiding his own.

"I haven't gotten that far." He lied because he was struggling to face the truth of the situation. "I'm still in ... in shock at seeing you here on my couch. I've imagined, dreamed, and longed for this moment so many times, and now you're here."

He hoped his words would loosen some of the bricks in the wall.

"Here I'm sitting on your couch, pregnant." She flung open her arms so he could see her bulging body that wasn't quite bulging yet, but the thought of having that body, her body, next to his caused his heart to race and his breath to come in short gasps. "Yes! The answer is yes. I'm pregnant. And what, pray tell, is your next question? I won't ask how you knew."

She sounded less angry but still looked disdainful at his reaction to her condition. She seemed to know that he was helpless, and she didn't care.

"Suppose you tell me." He couldn't help sounding condescending.

"The obvious question that all men ask in situations like this: 'Is it mine?'"

There it was, the ultimate question that would determine all future courses of discussion between them. After taking a few moments to consider his response, Oscar weighed options ranging from anger to love.

He chose love. "I'm hoping the baby's mine," he said with all sincerity.

She looked surprised by his response and took a moment to reply. "Yes, it's yours, my dear. However, there are complications."

"With the baby's health?"

"Not health complications. The baby's fine, as far as I can tell."

He sighed in relief. "What, then?"

She paused again. She appeared to be summoning the courage to tell Oscar something. "I'm not marrying you. I'm engaged to someone else."

Oscar had expected this news, but it still rocked him to his core. He felt his heart race faster and found it more difficult to breathe. The roar in his head was his mental picture of his life collapsing in flames.

"So I've heard." He caught his breath. "Did you think news like that wouldn't reach me even in this tiny, out-of-the-way village? Who's the lucky man?"

Isabelle looked relieved to have made that revelation without an argument. Her tone of voice softened, and she sounded more like the person he knew and still loved. One brick down.

"His name is Jerome Palmer. Doctor Jerome Palmer. He's my father's partner and a member of one of the wealthiest families in Chicago."

"So you're marrying money. Is that it?" He felt smug saying it. "I'm sorry that I'm not rich enough for you."

Then he realized he'd made a mistake with his tone. One brick back up.

"I suppose I deserve that." She rolled her eyes. "Yes, his family's rich. Rich enough to help me get an art gallery showing and influential enough to help me land a senior curator job at the Chicago Art Institute. Besides that, he's a kind, generous man."

"If he's the kind and generous man you claim, what are you doing here on my couch in my humble gardener's cottage without him?"

Isabelle paused as she prepared to answer this question.

"The reason is, Jerome doesn't want to raise another man's child. Plus, he doesn't want his family to know about my previous affairs. His family doesn't tolerate scandal." Tears welled up in her eyes as she continued. "He wants me to deliver the baby out of sight here in France and give it away before returning to him as a virtuous bride in white."

Something inside of him exploded. He was no longer in control of his tongue and lashed out in response. "Wow. That's a stretch!"

He knew he'd overstepped his bounds with that remark. Isabelle started crying. More bricks going up. He didn't know whether to take her in his arms or make her a cup of tea. He decided tea was the safer alternative and rushed off to the kitchen.

"I'll fetch us some tea."

As the water was boiling, he tried to understand what Isabelle still meant to him. He'd spent weeks painting the mental picture of their life together and didn't want to lose that image. But it was gone. She was marrying someone else. Now he could accept that fact and move on or continue to dwell in limbo between loving and hating her.

He needed to move forward and create a new picture of his life.

The baby—his baby—was to be the centerpiece of that picture. It would be difficult raising a child alone, but he had to salvage something of value from this investment of so much of his heart in his relationship with Isabelle.

He thought of the baby growing up, not knowing his father like what had happened to him. Sure, the child would have adoptive parents, but that wouldn't be the same. The father could be like Jerome and not want to raise another's man's child even if the mother did. He couldn't subject his child to such pain. But what could he do? Isabelle seemed determined to give the child away. He wished she would reconsider, but he couldn't see that happening. The love that had created this child seemed to have sailed to Chicago and not returned.

He decided to keep the baby and raise it on his own. That was his decision, and he would fight for it. Arriving at this new picture of his life helped him relax and deal with his anger toward Isabelle.

When he felt he'd given her enough time to dry her eyes, he returned with a cup of tea for each of them. He hated to see her cry. He would be helpless and lose all control. His love for her was more powerful than he'd realized before her arrival.

"I'm sorry if I've upset you. Have some tea. It'll make you feel better." He tried a softer approach to improve her mood. "You must have been through a lot. Please tell me about it."

Isabelle dried her eyes on her hanky and took several sips of tea.

"Thanks, I feel better." She gave him a faint smile. "I'll start from when I left you at the dock in Le Havre. My heart was breaking. I had every intention of being faithful to you and returning as soon as possible."

She sipped more tea and looked calmer as she took a deep breath.

Oscar couldn't help asking, "Were you ever planning to write to me?"

"Yes, silly, it's just that I fell ill as soon as the ship sailed. I was sick the entire journey. Looking back, I'm sure morning sickness played a role in how I felt, in addition to the seasickness. It was a rough crossing. I didn't realize it at the time. I just put it down to seasickness. It wasn't until I was on the train from New York to Chicago that I put it all together and realized I was pregnant because I was still sick. I knew being pregnant wasn't something I should write about in a letter. I wanted to share the wonderful news with you in person."

"Does your father know about the baby?"

Isabelle took a deep breath. "He was too ill to know anything other than that I was there with him. He depended on Jerome for everything. Jerome took care of my father and me for weeks after my return. I stayed at my father's bedside and thought of nothing else but helping him recover."

Tears rolled down her cheeks as she spoke of her father.

Oscar went limp as she related her love for the single parent who raised her. He wished she cared as much for him as she did for her father.

"As the weeks wore on, Jerome and I grew close. It was a very emotional time, and I needed someone to lean on. One evening, we went to dinner, and he asked me to marry him. It was a complete surprise to me."

Oscar leaned forward in his chair and was about to shout his objection until he remembered the decision he'd made in the kitchen. He softened his tone. "This may sound odd, but could you describe the restaurant to me?"

Her description didn't match the one in his nightmare. The only reality of the dream to come true was the pregnancy. "How could you say 'yes' if you still loved me?"

"I didn't. I told Jerome, 'No.' Then I confessed that I was pregnant." She looked as if she might cry again.

Oscar gripped his chair to keep control of his anger and disappointment.

"Jerome took my hand and told me he could accept that I was pregnant but that he could not raise another man's child."

Oscar sat back in his chair and let the realization sink in. Isabelle was trading him and their child for a life with Jerome and his money. He sat for some moments, thinking about her decision. He'd hoped she was more committed to him than that.

"Oscar, are you all right? Don't be angry. I'm sorry to tell you like this, but don't feel I'm rejecting you or our baby. It's important to do what's best for my father and me. He needs me to stay with him in Chicago. Do you understand?"

He lost control and jumped to his feet. "No, I don't understand! We were in love, or at least *I* was. Now, you're telling me you didn't love me."

Isabelle took his hands to calm him down. "That's not what I'm saying. I loved you. I still do. Jerome will be my husband, but he'll never mean as much to me as you do. You can still be my lover."

"And what about the baby? Our baby?" He yanked back his hand. "What do you suggest we do about the baby?"

Tears returned to Isabelle's eyes.

"She or he will be better off with someone else." She choked back sobs. "I'm not cut out to be a mother. I'm much too selfish."

"You are!"

Oscar stood up and went to the door and opened it to let in some fresh air and take action to calm himself down before he responded. He couldn't tell if the room had gotten warmer or if he was feeling hot because of his anger at the upsetting conversation. He left the door open to allow fresh, cool air to calm him down and returned to his chair.

"Let me get this straight. You're marrying Jerome, Mr. Moneybags. You want me to continue to be your lover. And we give the baby to some strange couple to raise. Is that what you have in mind, Isabelle?"

Before she could answer, there was a knock at the door, and Lily burst in.

She ran across the room to the couch and threw her arms around

Isabelle. "Isabelle! It's so wonderful to see you again. Let me look at you."

Lily stepped back to look at her. Her mouth dropped open. She looked at Oscar in surprise and then sank onto the couch beside Isabelle. "You look … you look pregnant. How did that happen?"

Looking surprised at the question, Isabelle snorted. "How did you know? I don't even feel pregnant yet. It happened in the usual way."

Lily chuckled. "Your breasts weren't that big when you left. Who's the father? Was this planned?"

"The father is standing right there." She pointed at Oscar. "We didn't plan it. Sometimes these things just happen."

Lily smiled. "When's the wedding?"

"In a few months, but I'm not marrying Oscar. I'm marrying Jerome."

Her words pushed Lily away, and she gave Oscar a look of disappointment. "Who is Jerome, and why are you marrying him? I thought you loved Oscar."

Isabelle gave Lily a defiant stare.

"Jerome is a doctor and my father's partner. Once we're married, Jerome will take over my father's medical practice. Then he plans to open his hospital." She straightened her dress over her stomach and breasts.

"How could you betray Oscar like this?" Lily shook her head in anger and disbelief. "Jerome must have a lot of money. Are you sure he can afford to fund a hospital? Besides, why would you even want that kind of life?"

"Jerome always gets what he sets his mind to," Isabelle said in defiance. "His family has lots of money. They're one of the richest families in Chicago. It would set me up for life, and I'd be able to do as I wish."

"That's just money and power. How about love? Do you love Oscar or not?" Lily's face turned red.

Oscar was uncomfortable with being the subject of their conversation, but he appreciated that Lily stood up for him. He wasn't sure how long he could listen to this.

"I love Oscar. We can still be with each other," Isabelle said with assurance to both. "Every year or even more often, I can come to France. We can be with each other then."

Lily looked cross. "If you expect Oscar to give up a chance for a normal life to wait for an occasional affair with you, you're even more selfish than I thought."

Isabelle's manner softened under Lily's inquisition. "Let's see how things go. I'll stay here until the baby is born, and then after someone adopts it, I'll return to Chicago and marry Jerome."

"You're what?" Lily looked shocked. "You're giving up your baby?"

Oscar jumped to his feet and went to the kitchen for more tea. He didn't want to hear any more of this without some fortification. He added brandy to his next cup of tea—or rather, some tea to his cup of brandy.

"Cup of tea, Lily?" he called from the kitchen. He needed time to think and to regain focus on his primary goal of keeping the baby.

Lily shouted, "*Non, merci.*"

The more he thought about the situation, the more he knew that raising the child on his own was far better than waiting for Isabelle to visit him.

When he returned, fortifying drink in hand, he found his two guests huddled on the couch in animated discussion. "What'd I miss? Have you worked out the plans for the rest of my life?"

"Isabelle's coming with me to stay in our house until she delivers," Lily responded. "It's not appropriate for her to live here with you if she's engaged to Jerome. In the meantime, we'll be looking for someone to adopt the baby. It'll be hard because so many women are in the same situation as our friend Geneviève. These women have lost husbands in the war and must work and take care of children by themselves."

"Wait a minute," Oscar interrupted. "As the father of this child, I have something to say about this. I intend to raise this child myself."

"Don't be silly, Oscar," Isabelle said. "You don't know a thing about babies. Besides, you've got your job to do. You can't do that and care for a baby at the same time. That's unrealistic and foolish."

Lily interrupted, "Let's not get into an argument over the baby. We have several months to figure this out. Oscar, I know your heart's in the right place, but you shouldn't take on something you can't hope to handle on your own."

Oscar drained his cup and spoke in a defensive tone. "I may be unrealistic about some things, as Isabelle says, but I'm realistic enough to know that there're plenty of women in this village who have no husbands, as you said. They need extra money to feed their families. It should be easy to find at least one of them who would want a job helping me raise my child. I'll not let some stranger adopt my baby."

Isabelle stood up and moved toward the door. "Lily, let's go. There's no reasoning with him. Can you help me move my things into the house?" She was retreating behind the wall they'd built.

Lily took Oscar's arm. "I'm sure we can work this out. Please come to lunch, so we can talk about it afterward."

"No, I have a lot to think about. *Merci* for taking Isabelle off my hands. I can't deal with her living here."

Lily turned back as she reached the door. "I almost forgot my reason for rushing over here. Matsukata from Japan, one of the major collectors of Monet's paintings, is coming tomorrow. Monet wants you to meet him and help present the *Grandes Décorations*. Are you available?"

"*Oui.* Tell Monet I'm honored to help him." He was trying to remember where he'd heard the name Matsukata before. "I'd better not come to lunch. I have a lot to take care of before the guest arrives." He hoped that focusing on the garden would take his mind off of Isabelle.

He spent the next few hours making sure the gardens were in the best condition for Monet's visitor. As he inspected each flower bed, he remembered Jean-Pierre's warning of flooding. He couldn't help thinking of the gardens' vulnerability to the raging rivers. He focused on imagining how the water could flood in and wash away the plants and perhaps damage the house. The more he studied this, the more he realized he needed to understand the Seine River valley's layout better. The best way to do this was to see it from above. That would require him to climb the hill across the road as he did for the picnic with Jean-Pierre, Lily, and Geneviève.

When he'd assured himself that the gardens were in good shape, he grabbed the walking stick he'd carved since his last climb and set out up the hill. This time, he'd walk at his own pace to appease his lungs. Besides, he had a lot to think about with Isabelle and the baby.

He arrived at the top, breathing easier than last time. Turning to look at the valley laid out at his feet, the beauty of the place he now called 'home' struck him again. The green fields of wheat were now growing in the spring sun, and the poplar and willow trees along the rivers were bursting with buds and young leaves. It was easy to see the fields and the contours of the land through which the three rivers flowed. It was also possible to judge where the water might overflow. The Seine, the Epte, and the Ru rivers joined near Monet's lily pond, making flooding a genuine possibility as there was little to impede the rivers' flow.

He could see there was no way to save the pond. He needed to safely move all the remaining lilies to the greenhouse with those waiting for the warmer weather. The rest of the plants around the pond might be lost in the ravages of the floodwaters. But he could save Monet's house, studios, greenhouse, and gardener's cottage if he and the other gardeners built a substantial barrier.

A wall of wooden posts, fence boards, and sandbags stacked against it could provide a substantial fortification for the existing stone walls that might hold back the water. They would need to fortify the existing walls around the property. If they could build these fortifications before it rained, they might save Monet's home and gardens. The construction must start as soon as the flooding was threatened. In the meantime, they needed to prepare by stockpiling the required supplies.

As he returned down the hill, he planned to measure the land that needed protecting and calculate the number of building materials he would need. He kept studying the landscape to make sure he considered anything that would cause his plan to fail. It would take all the gardeners at least a week to complete the work. They'd have to prepare for the project and then wait for a time he hoped would never come.

With his plan made and checked, his mind returned once again to Isabelle. Giverny was a great place to raise his baby. The child could enjoy growing up as Lily and Jean-Pierre did. He realized that caring for a little one was a tremendous responsibility that would take over his life. Was he prepared to give up much of his life to raise his child? Did he even want to try? Or was he offering to raise his son or daughter to make Isabelle regret her decision? Revenge was not a good reason to be a parent. But love was.

Chapter 24 – Japanese Collector Visits

Oscar had a fitful night of dreams that the three rivers had flooded the garden, and Monet's canvases were floating away. He rose early to continue working on his plans for protecting Monet's floral sanctuary. He reviewed his design, then walked to the patisserie for breakfast with Geneviève.

She needed to know about Isabelle and the baby—his baby. If anyone knew someone who could help him care for the child, it was her. The village houses were quiet, the two streets deserted. How would it look flooded? The shops would be filled with a foot or more of water. Merchandise ruined. Businesses closed and lives altered or lost. He wasn't confident the floodwaters would reach up to the street, but he knew that if they did, it could devastate the village for years.

He called out, "*Bonjour,* Geneviève," as he entered the patisserie.

She answered from the kitchen.

"*Bonjour*. Oscar, *merci* for the lovely dinner Saturday night. Charlie and I had a wonderful time." The oven door closed with a bang. "Angel wings coming up. Fresh from the oven."

These words were music to his ears.

She struggled out to the table and placed two cups of coffee and a plate of angel wings in front of him.

"How are you?" she asked as she lowered herself to her chair with great effort.

He took off his cap and reached for the coffee. Geneviève was flushed. "How are you? You look tired."

"I'm tired of waiting for Charlie to come. It's taking its time, just like its father." Geneviève gave a smile as she sipped her coffee and shifted in her chair.

Oscar summoned the courage to give her the news he had come to deliver. "Isabelle returned yesterday."

Geneviève smiled. "I know."

Her response confused him. "How did you know that?"

"Isabelle and Lily came by yesterday afternoon. Lily told her I'm pregnant." Geneviève shifted in the chair. "Isabelle asked if she could paint my portrait for her next showing in Chicago."

He was flabbergasted. "And you agreed?"

"Why wouldn't I?" she said with a chuckle. "She's charming. I liked her as soon as we met. We've several more modeling sessions planned for later this week."

He shook his head in disbelief. "I don't understand this. You two have nothing in common. What did you have to talk about?"

"We both have good taste in men." Her face lit up. "We talked about you and babies."

Oscar laughed at the absurdity of these two women meeting and talking about him. "What could you find to discuss about me?"

"She told me a lot about your likes and dislikes and some of your little secrets." Geneviève winked as she teased him.

He smiled and shook his head in disbelief.

"I'm in trouble now. Did Isabelle mention that I'm having a child?" He laughed and rephrased his question. "I mean that she's having my child."

"*Oui.*" Geneviève's expression turned cold but not reproachful. "She said you wanted to raise the baby on your own."

He took another sip of his steaming coffee and a bite of angel wings before he choked.

When he regained his breath, he said, "That's not true. I'd like to raise the child with her, but she's marrying someone else." He sat the coffee cup down and paused before he continued. "The truth is I'd rather raise the child on my own than let her give it to strangers."

Geneviève shifted in the chair again. "Sorry to be moving around so much, but no position is comfortable for me, neither sitting, standing, nor lying down. I admire what you're trying to do. I'm not sure you can do it, but I admire you for trying."

He reached across the table and took her hand. "I appreciate your saying that. I'd hate to think I'm unrealistic to consider this."

Geneviève smiled as she put her hand on top of his. "I'm not saying you can do this alone. She said that you realize you'll need help."

"I'll need lots of help. Do you know anyone that could help me with the child?" He released her hand and took another bite of the angel wings. "I'd be willing to pay."

"My mother and I might be able to help you." She looked away as she seemed to consider her offer to care for a second baby. "I've hired extra help to handle the shop for the first few months while I'm home with Charlie. The extra money from you would help me pay my staff and stay home longer than I'd planned. You'll need a wet nurse, too."

Oscar felt his face flushing, betraying his embarrassment. "I hadn't thought of that."

"Don't worry about it. I'm sure my breasts can feed two."

He took one long, admiring look at her ample breasts and then lowered his eyes to the angel wings. The heat in his body rose from his groin to his face and lit up his ears. He chastised himself for lusting after his friend.

She laughed at his discomfort.

Her offer to help relieved some of his anxiety. "*Très bien*. They won't both come at the same time."

Geneviève gave a playful moan. "I hope not. That would mean I'd be horribly late, or she'd be dangerously early. Or both. Let's not talk about that."

He smiled. "Geneviève, you've made me so happy. I can't thank you enough. How's Charlie behaving today?"

She smiled and placed her hands on either side of her belly to embrace her baby. "Charlie's fine. Very active in the kicking department, but otherwise sleeps like a baby."

Oscar reached across the table to retake her hand. "I'm so glad that you're my friend. I don't know what I'd do without you."

They sat at the table, enjoying their breakfast and each other's company. They chatted about babies, the weather, and Monet's guest arriving at noon. He felt relaxed and content in her company. No matter what happened, he could discuss it with her, and she'd help him find a solution. When he took his lunch and left for work, she gave him three kisses. It delighted him to have Geneviève as his good friend.

But there would be time enough for him to delve into the nature of their friendship later. He needed to speak with Monet about the needs of his guest. As he rounded the corner of the house, he spotted a light in the large studio. He checked to see if Monet was there.

"*Bonjour. Monsieur* Monet, are you in here?

"*Bonjour*, Oscar. Come in while I check on the *Grandes Décorations* that I'm showing to our guest. I'm also setting aside some paintings for him to choose from for his collection. He'll like these." Monet looked through more paintings he'd stacked against the wall of his studio. As he chose one, he would hand it to Oscar to set aside.

Monet's hand didn't hold a cigarette. Oscar was glad that today, Blanche was winning her battle against his smoking.

"Hang these canvases on the nails by the door, so my guest can inspect them."

Oscar hung the paintings as requested. He enjoyed seeing which ones he was choosing. This selection didn't tell him if the collector preferred a particular subject matter. The paintings' subjects ranged from the lily pond to the flowers in the garden to the Seine River at dawn.

Monet described his guest as he was selecting paintings. "Matsukata is a very sophisticated collector. He knows what he likes, and he can judge if it's some of my better work."

Matsukata must have impressed him with his excellent taste. As far as Oscar remembered, Monet's customers seldom impressed him with their taste in his paintings. Matsukata was an exception. He even made fun of some buyers for paying too much for what he considered his lesser works. This was done in private after the buyers had gone, of course.

Monet considered each painting again as they hung by the door. He rearranged the canvases into a sequence that seemed to make sense to him but not to Oscar.

Oscar interrupted the process with his burning question.

"*Monsieur* Monet. I hate to bother you with this, but I need your advice and approval on something important. Both Gustave and Jean-Pierre suggested that I prepare for the flooding of the Seine. They told me of flooding in the mountains to the east. I understand that such flooding happened before in 1910 and other years, and I'm concerned it will happen again. Perhaps I'm too cautious, but I'd like your advice on this."

"Oscar, it's wonderful that you're thinking ahead." Monet stopped to search his pockets for cigarettes and, finding none, focused again on him. "*Oui*, we've had severe floods in the past that threatened to destroy the garden and pond. I'd hate to see a repeat of those disasters. Do you have a proposal to keep us safe?"

"I've been thinking about it a lot these past several days and have developed a plan I'd like to discuss with you when you have the time."

He waved Oscar over to the couch where they could sit and talk. "My guest is not coming for several hours. Let's discuss it now."

Oscar was pleased to have Monet's full attention on this vital issue. "Yesterday, I went up to the top of the hill to view the valley and get a better idea about how the Seine could flood the valley. From what I can tell, there's no way to save the pond. It's too open to the

Seine and its tributaries. We can, however, save the lilies by moving them to the greenhouse."

Monet's eyes were piercing as he stared at Oscar. "That's sad, but it makes sense, my boy. What else can we do?"

Oscar sat up straighter to discuss the next part of his plan. "We need to fortify the walls surrounding the house and garden. The old stone walls will not hold back the water for very long. They will fall with the force of the water, or the water will wash over or under them."

Monet held up his hand to stop him. "I wish I'd never lowered the old wall along the road to let people see into the garden. Please continue."

Oscar leaned forward. "I propose fortifying the walls with wooden posts buried on the outside of the walls. Then we could build a heavy plank fence between them. The fence would support sandbags stacked against its base to keep the water out. Sandbags alone might wash away, but the fence could hold them in place and provide a barrier that the flood couldn't breach. This fence needs to completely surround the property on this side of the tracks."

Monet looked upset and concerned. "That's a massive project. How long will this take, and how much will it cost?"

Oscar tried to reduce his concern. "It'll take all of the gardeners at least a week. I don't know the cost until I calculate the amount of material we'll need."

Monet had a worried look as he leaned forward, shook Oscar's hand, and patted him on the shoulder. "Oscar, I can see that you have put a lot of thought into this. Proceed with estimating the materials required and work out the pricing. We can speak about it again when you're ready—*Merci* for all your hard work. We're fortunate that in the past, the Seine has taken a long time to reach here. It also takes a long time to return to its banks. Well done, my boy."

"I'll be back to you tomorrow with that information. Now I must prepare for your guest."

The two left the studio together. Each went separate ways to prepare for the lunch meeting. Monet climbed the porch stairs with difficulty and went into the kitchen to find Blanche, who was checking on the meal preparation. Oscar took his lunch that had now become his dinner to his cottage. He shouldn't have gotten lunch today, but he'd been so caught up in his conversation with Geneviève that he'd forgotten about his commitment to dining with Monet and his guest.

After he'd dressed for lunch and returned to the house, the guests had arrived. Monet introduced him as soon as he entered the drawing-room.

"Matsukata-san, I'd like you to meet my head gardener, Oscar Bonhomme. Oscar, this is Kojiro Matsukata and his lovely niece, Takeko Kuroki."

Oscar could tell by how Matsukata dressed in a well-tailored Western business suit and a shirt with wingtip collars and necktie that he was wealthy. Monet had described him as a "captain of industry" who was an avid collector of Impressionist art. His interest in Impressionism seemed to be in contrast with his conservative taste in expensive clothes.

Oscar bowed deeply, as his Japanese friends had taught him, in respect for Monet's guest. As he arose, he saw Takeko smiling at him from beside her uncle. His heart raced as he recognized her. "Takeko, is that you?"

Takeko smiled and answered. "Oscar, it's been a long time. I see you survived the war." She bowed to him.

Oscar wanted to throw his arms around his college girlfriend and embrace her but realized this wouldn't be proper and displease her uncle. He bowed again even deeper out of affection and respect.

"It is so nice to see you again." He smiled as he greeted Takeko, who wore a dark-blue silk kimono with a floral-print sash. "I remember the day of our graduation when you returned to Japan, and I traveled to France to join the fighting. It was such an exciting and sad day."

Takeko covered her smile with one hand. "Do you remember my uncle? You met him at the graduation ceremony."

"I do. I was thinking your uncle's name was familiar when *Monsieur* Monet said you were visiting. It's wonderful to see you again, sir."

Now that she mentioned it, Oscar remembered meeting Matsukata at their college graduation. He'd been such a pleasant man until Takeko had introduced Oscar to him as her boyfriend. He'd have been even more uncomfortable if he had known more about their intimate relationship. Both had known the affair couldn't continue past graduation, so they'd made the utmost use of their time together. Later, Isabelle had been the beneficiary of the lessons in lovemaking that Takeko had taught him.

Lily and Isabelle made quite an entrance in their short, fringed dresses with matching hairbands, Lily in yellow and Isabelle in red. Blanche spilled her drink when she saw them standing together, looking so inappropriately dressed for such a significant lunch.

Monet introduced the two young ladies to Matsukata and Takeko. Takeko smiled at her uncle's reaction. His eyes grew wide, and his mouth dropped open. He seemed accustomed to the latest Paris fashions at least, but not in an intimate setting like this. Oscar watched as Lily and Isabelle latched onto Takeko, pulled her to one side, and began asking her about Japan's clothing fashions.

Oscar overheard her explain to Lily and Isabelle, just before lunch, that her uncle was the son of a retired Japanese prime minister and a friend of the emperor. "He intends to take his vast art collection back to Japan and install it in his museum, the 'Art Pavilion of Pure Pleasure.' It'll be the first museum of Impressionist art in Japan."

Monet seated Matsukata on one side of him and Oscar on the other. Oscar listened as they began speaking of the Japanese woodblock prints that influenced the Impressionist movement. The images hanging on the walls of Monet's dining room represented many of the artists they discussed.

"Oscar is interested in Japanese prints. Atsuko gave him a book of woodblock prints when he visited her at Bing's."

Matsukata smiled as he turned to face Oscar. "Then you've met my niece Atsuko. She's the leading expert on Japanese prints in Europe. I'm seeing her soon and will tell her I had lunch with you."

Oscar was surprised that Matsukata mentioned Atsuko and that she was such a leading expert. "She was so very kind to teach me about the Japanese print artists after performing a tea ceremony for me. Please give her my best wishes."

Matsukata nodded. "I'll tell her. I'm glad she could help you."

When he turned back to Monet, they continued their conversation.

Oscar gave his full attention to Takeko, Lily, and Isabelle. Takeko mentioned that she and Oscar had been close friends in college.

Isabelle's face turned red, and she started laughing.

Lily looked shocked at Isabelle's response and whispered, "What are you laughing at?"

"Do you remember that I told you Oscar dated a Japanese girl in college who taught him so much about her ... ah ... culture?"

Lily snickered. "Oh, that culture! Is Takeko that girl?"

Takeko put her hand to her mouth and started laughing, too. She turned to Oscar. "What did you tell them?"

Oscar tried to hide his surprise and then embarrassment as he realized why the others were laughing. "It was not so much telling as showing."

He could feel his face flush as he realized that Isabelle had told Lily about his sexual exploits with a girl in college. Takeko was a good sport about their revelation, but Oscar felt like crawling under the table when he realized that Lily understood what he had said.

Blanche looked cross, signaling she disapproved of the behavior of the young ladies when she announced, "Dessert and tea will be served in the studio drawing-room."

As the guests rose to follow Monet, Oscar saw Blanche pull Lily aside and escort her to the corner of the room for what he suspected would be a reprimand. He moved closer to hear what they were saying.

"Young lady, I'm not sure what's going on between you and Isabelle, but it needs to stop this instant. It's making Oscar very uncomfortable. You seem to have gotten Takeko involved. Stop, now! Do you understand?"

"*Oui, Madame.* We were just teasing him, but we'll stop."

This should have put an end to it, but it didn't. Not for long.

When Oscar saw Blanche enter the sitting room, Monet's first studio decorated with paintings representing his entire career, she crossed to where Monet stood discussing his earlier works. "Matsukata-san, Monet told me you love French madeleines. I hope you enjoy the version we have prepared for you today."

Matsukata smiled as he took one from the silver serving tray she had picked up on her way into the room. "I'm sure they will be as wonderful as the excellent lunch. I very much enjoyed the serving of pike and baby eels. The eels in fish broth remind me of Udon noodles. After the madeleines and tea, I'll be ready for one of Monet's lengthy walks about the lily pond." He laughed as he took another madeleine.

Monet chuckled at Matsukata's joke and took a madeleine. "I'll take the long way around the pond just for you. Oscar will show you where Sylvain, our fisherman, catches the pike."

When everyone appeared to have finished their tea, Monet held up his hands. "If you wish to join us in the search for pike in the lily pond, please come along."

The guests continued chatting as they filed out of the room, across the porch, and down into the garden. As the group proceeded down the *Grande Allée,* Oscar watched Isabelle and Lily continue to chat and laugh with each other.

He waited for the others to file out of the room so he could speak with Takeko. "Are you returning to Paris tonight?"

"We are. Our ship leaves in a few days, and we must prepare for our journey back to Japan. I'd love to stay and visit with you longer, but our business here is complete, and we need to return home."

"I'm sorry that we don't have more time to spend with each other. When we parted after college, we were in such a rush to get on with our lives that we didn't take time to have a proper goodbye."

He felt sad to lose his friend again after all these years. They left the room and descended the porch stairs to follow the others to the lily pond.

"I know what you mean." Takeko stopped to look down the *Grande Allée* at the garden spread out before them. "I, too, wish that we had more time. But wait, there is one way. My uncle is interested in bringing a Western gardener to Japan to help design a garden on the grounds around his Impressionist art museum, much like Monet has done here. You'd be perfect for that position."

Oscar took a few moments to think about her suggestion. "That is an interesting opportunity. I could help with the Western garden techniques and learn more about Japanese gardening design. Let me think about this."

Takeko looked excited. "I'll suggest it to my uncle this afternoon. I'm sure the possibility will interest him. You'd be an excellent candidate with your degree in garden design, your work at the Golden Gate Park in San Francisco, and now Monet's garden. Let's catch up with the others. If this works out, we can spend days and nights getting reacquainted on the boat trip." Her smile was alluring and seemed to offer more than talking.

Oscar and Takeko hurried to reach the others. When they joined the group at the pond, Takeko took her uncle aside. In a few minutes, she returned to Oscar's side to tell him what her uncle had said.

"My uncle is interested in the idea, but first, he must discuss it with *Monsieur* Monet. He said it would be wrong not to seek his permission before discussing it with you."

Oscar nodded. "I agree and wouldn't think of accepting such an offer if Monet didn't agree."

"More good news. We're staying the night to conclude our business here. If *Monsieur* Monet agrees, you can speak with my uncle tonight."

"That's great. Let's not discuss any of this before I've spoken to your uncle and Monet. I don't want Isabelle knowing about my business, if you understand what I mean."

Takeko smiled. "I don't know what you mean. She seems to know so much about your business already. What's the harm if she knows this part? I assume you have a relationship with her."

Oscar shook his head at the realization that he'd caused his embarrassment. "I do. I mean, I did. I guess I don't know what I mean. She's told me some terrible news about her decision to return to Chicago. I'm not sure I understand it."

Takeko took a moment to consider what he was telling her. "She seems like such a wonderful person. I'm sure you could change her mind if you wanted to."

He sighed, and his shoulders dropped. "I don't think so and am not sure I want to change Isabelle's mind. Perhaps I just have to accept the decision."

"It's up to you. You could, or you could try to change it."

Oscar responded without thinking. "I'll consider changing her mind. I'm lost without her."

He couldn't believe the words coming out of his mouth. He realized how much he still loved Isabelle despite what was said and done to him. How could he be this deeply in love with someone who rejected him and their child?

Oscar and Takeko rejoined the group as it made its way back to the house, where they parted ways. Monet led Matsukata, Takeko, and Oscar into the large studio to see the *Grandes Décorations*. The others adjourned to the house. When Oscar had finished helping Monet with his presentation, he and Takeko returned to the others while Monet and Matsukata discussed business.

He found the others having wine and chatting in the studio drawing-room. He poured two glasses of wine and guided Takeko to a quiet corner to catch up on each other's lives and discuss the trip to Japan.

"I hope you join us in Japan," Takeko said with enthusiasm. "I'm sure you'd love it there. The job my uncle is offering would be such a boost to your career. I'm sure Monet won't mind your being gone for a year or two. Perhaps this will give you time to clarify your feelings for Isabelle."

"A year!" Oscar blurted out. "I'd no idea this would mean being gone for such a long time. There're obligations here that I must attend to. I hadn't considered the time this would take."

Takeko responded straightforwardly, "Yes, it'll take a month or more to travel there, and then the work itself will take at least a year to complete. Your return will take another month. I'd say it'll take you away for almost two years."

More food arrived, and the conversation slowed. Takeko started talking to Isabelle and Lily. Oscar took advantage of the lull, excused himself, and retired to his cottage. Neither Monet nor Matsukata tried to speak with him about the opportunity to work in Japan. He sat by the fireplace, thinking about leaving Giverny and the baby for months. How could he abandon his life here for two years?

A knock on his door interrupted his thoughts.

Chapter 25 – The Flood

Oscar heard someone knocking on his door again, only louder this time. He got up from his seat by the fire and walked to the door. "Who is it?"

"It's me, Takeko. Let me in; it's pouring out here."

He opened the door wide to let her in. After helping her take off the soaked outer kimono, he hung it on the chair in front of the fire as she sat on the couch.

"It must be pouring. It soaked your kimono." He threw more logs on the fire to help warm her. "Why are you here at this hour?"

Takeko frowned as she turned her back to the fire and faced him.

Her appearance concerned him. "What's wrong? You don't look happy to see me."

"I must give you some unpleasant news. My uncle and *Monsieur* Monet got into an argument when he told Monet about his interest in inviting you to Japan. My uncle said Monet seemed agreeable at first, but then he must have thought about it because his face grew redder and redder before he started shouting at my uncle."

Oscar backed away from Takeko. "What did Monet say?"

Takeko thought for a moment before answering him. "Monet shouted that my uncle was trying to take away a member of his family. He said he depended upon you to manage his garden, assist him with his painting, and save his home from the flood. Monet's angry and unreasonable reaction shocked my uncle."

Oscar started pacing the room. He could visualize all his progress toward becoming a part of Monet's family exploding in a fit of Mo-net's rage. "I didn't know that Monet would react that way. What am I going to do? How can I fix this? I can't leave here. I have too many obligations. Now I may lose it all if Monet no longer trusts me over this."

Takeko looked upset. "I'm sure Monet isn't angry with you. It's my uncle he's upset with. He's so angry that my uncle is leaving tonight. I may never see you again. Please forgive me for putting you into this position. I never meant to come between you and Monet. I feel terrible."

Tears streamed down her face.

Oscar took her hands and tried to comfort her. "It's not your fault. You were trying to help me and my career. Please don't blame yourself. Monet has a bad temper, and I've seen him like this before. I'm sure he'll have forgotten about it in the morning. He'll calm down. When are you leaving?"

"Now. I mean, as soon as I meet my uncle in our automobile. He's selected the paintings he wants to purchase, and he'll let *Monsieur* Durand-Ruel take care of the transaction and the transportation to our ship."

Oscar felt sad that he was losing his friend again. "I hate to see you leave so soon. I hope we can meet again."

Takeko smiled and began removing the rest of her clothing. "Will you at least give me a proper farewell?"

Oscar shook his head no. "I can't do that. It took me months to recover from the last time we parted. You deserted me once. I can't risk feeling that way again."

Takeko frowned and re-dressed. "What do you mean? We parted as friends after college."

He could feel his temper rising as his face flushed. "That's what I mean. We parted as friends. The two of us were lovers, and then your uncle showed up. You switched to our being just friends without me even knowing what had happened."

Takeko looked embarrassed. "I had to return to my life in Japan. You wouldn't have been comfortable there."

"I wouldn't fit in there then, but now I would?" His voice had developed a sharp edge. "Is that what you're telling me?"

"Now is different." She softened her voice to calm him down. "This time, my uncle would invite you to come with us. Can't you see how that's different?"

He realized it was different and felt calmer. "It devastated me when you rushed off to Japan without telling me why. I realize now that you were going your way, and I was going mine. We were both in such a hurry, we forgot to say 'Farewell' properly." It's just as well that I won't be traveling with you to Japan."

"I'm sorry I hurt you, Oscar. I didn't mean to. Come here so I can make it up to you."

"No!" He was forceful but no longer angry.

"Please. I feel so bad. Let me try to make up for what I did."

"I can't. It might hurt someone else."

Takeko smiled. "Who? Are you still in love with Isabelle?"

His anger returned. "Yes! No! I doubt it since I realized how self-centered she is. She wanted me as her lover but not her husband."

Takeko smiled as she paused for a few moments. "If not Isabelle, who is it? I can tell you're in love with someone. Is it Lily or Geneviève? Tell me."

There was a loud knock at the door. "Takeko-san, your uncle is impatient to be on our way. Please join us in the automobile now."

Takeko hurried to the fire, put on her outer kimono without hesitation, ran out, and then returned to give Oscar a passionate farewell kiss.

Oscar closed the door after watching her run through the rain toward the gate and fell asleep, thinking about the events of the day.

He awoke and rushed to meet Geneviève for breakfast. As he ran through the rain to the patisserie, he couldn't get Takeko and the events of the previous evening out of his mind. He'd lost an opportunity to sail to Japan and help design a Western garden at the museum, but he didn't much regret the loss. The trip excited him, but he had other priorities. He wondered if Monet would hold it against him for considering leaving. Did he need to convince Monet to trust him that Giverny was his home now and that this was his family? How could he persuade Monet that he couldn't or wouldn't leave them or his baby?

The rain was pelting down as he raced through the village. His thoughts of Takeko and the rain distracted him as he entered the patisserie.

"*Bonjour*," he called out as usual.

An unfamiliar voice responded. "Who's there?"

"It's me, Oscar."

An elderly woman with gray hair tied back in a bun and a long white apron came out of the kitchen. Something about her eyes reminded him of Geneviève.

She smiled as if greeting an old friend. "*Bonjour*, Oscar. I'm Christine, Geneviève's mother. She's taking the day off to meet with Isabelle."

He bit his lip. "Isabelle again. How's Geneviève doing? I know she's due any time now."

"Don't worry. Geneviève's fine, just a little tired. The baby will be here soon." Christine looked pleased and anxious at the same time. "She's told me so much about you. I'm sorry I missed dinner with you on Saturday. I hear you had a wonderful evening."

He smiled as he remembered their dinner. "We had a marvelous time. It's a shame you missed it. *Merci* for the delicious tarte. *Monsieur* Baudy asked after you."

"I bet he wanted me to make desserts for the restaurant?" She didn't pause for Oscar's response. "I understand you're looking for someone to help care for your child?"

He smiled at the thought of Christine helping him with the baby. From what Geneviève had told him, she'd be a loving grandmother.

"*Oui.* Geneviève mentioned that you may help me. I'd like to raise the child, but I can't do it alone." He took a seat at the table by the door.

Christine put her hand in her apron pocket and pulled out a yellow knit hat. "I made this for Charlie. I'm sure we can help you. It'll be difficult at first, but we can work it out. Where will the baby be living?"

"That's a beautiful hat. I'm sure little Charlie will love it. The baby will live with me in Monet's garden cottage."

Christine smiled as if remembering happier times. "I know it well. My husband and I lived there when I had Geneviève. We moved to our own place after she started school. I loved it there. It's a great place to raise a child. I'm glad you're taking responsibility for your child. Few fathers do. Would you like your usual breakfast and lunch today?" She turned toward the kitchen.

It surprised him that she knew what he liked for breakfast. "*Oui.*"

"I'll bring your breakfast right out." She chuckled at his reaction. "Geneviève told me what you like to eat."

She brought his breakfast, and the two chatted as he ate. She was a kind woman who agreed with his decision to raise the child on his own. With her on his side, he felt more confident that he could do it.

Oscar finished his breakfast and stood up. "I'd better be going to work now."

Christine went to the kitchen and came back with his lunch. "Mind the rain today. I've heard that the Seine in the east is overflowing its banks into the streets of Paris. I hope the flooding doesn't reach here. It was devastating last time. The flood almost wiped out the entire village."

Oscar took his lunch and frowned as he started toward the door. "That's what I've heard. My project for today is to construct a barrier to protect Monet's house and garden. By the look of things, I'd better hurry."

"Please be careful, Oscar. It would hurt Geneviève if any harm came to you." Christine smiled as he turned to leave.

"Give her my best. Let me know if I can help," Oscar called out as he went out into the rain and hurried through the water streaming down the street to the garden and the massive project. The village walls and houses were built on the road's edge, which made a channel that trapped the rainfall and created its own stream. The rain had soaked his clothes and jacket by the time he reached the garden.

He went to his cottage, changed into dry clothes, and pulled on a dry jacket and rubber boots to protect him from the rain while he measured the perimeter of Monet's property. He took a twine ball and tied it to each of the four corners of the walls surrounding the property. Some simple calculations supplied the fence measurements he would construct and the number of sandbags he needed to complete the barrier.

He wrote his measurements, calculations, and estimated costs on a paper presented to Monet during his lunch.

"*Monsieur* Monet, excuse me for interrupting your meal. I have a list of what we need for the fortification."

After handing the paper to Monet, he watched his face to judge his reaction to the estimates. He also wanted to see if Monet was still angry from the night before.

"Excellent work, Oscar. See Blanche for the funds you need. How long will this take to build?"

He sighed with relief that, as usual, his anger had passed, and he'd approved his request. "The other gardeners and I can finish in less than a week if we really hurry and the flood holds off."

"*Bien! Très bien.*" Monet returned to his meal.

Sylvain—full-time driver and part-time fisherman—drove Oscar to Vernon's supply store, where he negotiated to get the posts and boards delivered in the afternoon and the sand and the bags the next day. He started the gardeners digging the post holes as soon as he returned. There was no time to lose if he hoped to stay ahead of the flood. When the posts arrived, he and the gardeners started erecting them. They worked past dark and got over half of the posts erected. The rain-soaked earth made the digging easier than expected.

With only a few hours' sleep, Oscar climbed up the mountain to see if the rivers were flooding in the pre-dawn light. After climbing halfway up, he could see in the early morning that the water was flowing over the Seine's banks as the rain poured. It was hard to accept that the beautiful fields with neat rows of haystacks would be under water soon. The flood would devastate the farmers' lives by washing away the haystacks used to feed their animals. He estimated that water would reach the lily pond in five to six days. The barrier would need to be ready when that happened. Then the battle to hold back the flood would begin if the water's current grew swift enough to wash under the fence and stone walls.

He and the gardeners worked late into that night to erect all the posts and fill sandbags. Early the following morning, two of the men continued filling sandbags and stacking them near the posts. Oscar and four gardeners pounded fence boards into each post and piled sandbags against them to bridge the gap.

They worked all that day and the next four and finished just as the water began overtaking the lily pond. Oscar and the men stood on the railroad tracks, empty now of train traffic, watching as the waves washed against the hill below their feet. All they could do was to wait and see where they might need to shore up their barrier. He knew that losing the pond would devastate Monet, but that would be better than losing part of the garden or buildings.

He sent the men home to get dinner and rest. With his hands blistered and his breath coming in quick gasps, he had exhausted himself. But he couldn't go home yet. He had one last thing to check on.

It had been days since he'd seen or heard from Geneviève. He loaded up a cart full of sandbags and headed down the street to create a barrier around her front door. If too much water entered her shop, it might ruin her oven and put her out of business.

It took all his remaining strength to get the cart wheels to turn in the soft ground under the cart's weight loaded with sandbags. His lungs burned, and his hands throbbed as he gripped the handles of the cart. He gathered all his strength to give it one last push. The wheels turned and started rolling out of the mud and down to the street. After hours of pouring rain, the road had turned into a swift-running stream. He waded toward the patisserie with a renewed sense of urgency. The current flowed in this direction and helped lighten his load by pushing the cart as if it were a heavy barge.

The shop was dark when he arrived. After stacking the sandbags around the entrance, he turned to leave with his cart. Something made him turn back and peer into the shop. There, on the wet floor, was a white form, a body. He prayed it wasn't Geneviève. Perhaps she was with Isabelle again. It could be her mother.

He tried the door, but it was locked. He pounded on it with no answer. The body on the floor didn't move. Oscar kicked in the door and rushed to the person lying in the freezing water. He lifted the apron from the face, and it was what he feared the most. His breath caught in his throat. It was Geneviève lying unconscious. He felt her cheek. It was cold. Dread gripped his heart and squeezed with icy fingers. He put his ear to her chest to listen for breathing. There was a faint sound of breath.

He tried to revive her. Nothing worked. Panic crept in, but he beat it back. It took all his strength to lift her water-soaked body from the floor. His legs buckled from his fright, his exhaustion, and her weight, but he remained upright. He carried her to the cart. There was no time to rest as he stripped off his coat and covered her as much as possible. He used his rolled-up cap as a pillow for her head.

After securing the door with two sandbags, he headed the cart back up the street against the current toward Monet's house. He pushed it with all his remaining strength as rain and tears streamed down his face.

The ladies at the house could help Geneviève. They must. It was her only hope. There was no doctor in the village, and none could get here from Vernon in this flood. He pushed the cart as fast as his weary legs and burning lungs would allow. He tried to wake her by calling her name. She couldn't die. Not now.

"Don't leave me, Geneviève. Don't leave your baby. We all love you. I love you."

His lungs were in flames as he reached the house. He picked her up and shouted for help as he went through the gate and climbed the stairs to the porch. "Help! Geneviève has collapsed. Please help!"

Blanche rushed out of the dining room where the family was eating. "*Mon Dieu*! Oscar, what happened? Bring her in here. Ladies, clear the table and cover it with tablecloths. You men get out of here. Let us handle this."

No one appeared to be listening to Oscar as he tried to explain what had happened. "It's Geneviève. I found her lying on the floor of her shop. Unconscious. Please revive her."

"Oscar, be careful when placing her on the table. You mustn't injure the baby," Blanche said.

He stood, cradling her in his arms until the ladies had the table ready. The men scattered, and the women prepared the space. Oscar laid her down as gently as he could. The women removed her wet clothing and covered her with a blanket.

He leaned against the wall in complete exhaustion. "Is Geneviève going to be all right? Can you save the baby?"

Blanche pushed him out of the room as she and the others tried to revive Geneviève with warm towels.

She put her hand on his shoulder as he left. "You've done your part. We'll take it from here."

"Will Geneviève and the baby live?" he cried.

Blanche closed the door without answering.

Jean-Pierre took him by the arm and helped him into the studio drawing-room. "Here, drink this. You need some fortification after what you've been through."

Oscar sat down in a chair, exhausted, and took a long drink of brandy. "*Merci.* I can't drink too much. I need to get back out and check on the barrier."

Jean-Pierre looked disturbed at his statement. "For heaven's sake, why? You're soaked, exhausted, and covered in mud."

"The way the water is rising, I may need to stop a breach in the barrier." He drained his glass and struggled to his feet to leave.

"Wait!" Jean-Pierre said. "First, let me get you some food. I'm sure you haven't eaten today. Then I'll go with you. You might need me to rescue you if the water gets too deep. Remember? You can't swim."

Oscar looked at Monet. "Do you think Geneviève and the baby will survive?"

Monet took several moments to respond. "I've seen a lot of terrible things in my life—none like this. I can't imagine what will happen next. Geneviève is strong. If anyone can make it through this, she can."

Oscar was even more worried than before he'd asked the question and followed up with another. "And the baby? I'm not sure she could survive losing the baby."

Monet took a sip of brandy before responding. "Babies fight to stay alive. It could survive even if the mother doesn't."

Oscar sat, thinking about what was happening in the dining room. There was a lot of talking and the sound of people rushing about, but none were crying. He took that to be a reassuring sign.

He wolfed down the food without knowing what he ate. He couldn't remember the last time he'd eaten anything. With the food and drink warming his insides, he was ready to brave the storm, check on the fortifications, and then get back to the house to be with Geneviève.

While he ate, Monet spoke.

"I want to tell you how much I appreciate what you're doing." He smiled and leaned forward in his chair. "Not just the tremendous work you're doing to save us from the flood. Also, I'm happy you're not leaving us to go to Japan. Working on that project was a splendid opportunity and a great temptation for you. I apologize for getting so upset about it. We all think of you as part of our family, and we'd miss you."

Monet's words touched him. "It's an honor that you find that my work measures up to your high standards. I hope you understand that you are my family, and this is my home—*Merci beaucoup* for your trust. Now we've work to do. We must make sure the barrier is holding back the flood."

As Oscar and Jean-Pierre headed out the door, Monet came up and put his arms around their shoulders. "Be careful in this storm, my sons. We'll take care of things here. I have every confidence that the baby and mother will be fine."

Oscar felt a warm glow descending the stairs to the garden. He wasn't sure if it was the brandy, the food, or the love of Monet and his family. Now it was time to concentrate on the job at hand. He started on his tour of the property's perimeter with a lighter heart and a helpful, if inexperienced, companion. On the other side of the barrier, the floodwaters were still rising. It would be a long, dangerous night for him and Geneviève.

The two men walked along the wall with lanterns from the gate to the corner by the road, turned left, and continued along the property's side. All was as it should be, so far. When they neared the bottom of the garden before the hill, they noticed water covered their feet. In a few yards, the water was up to their ankles. Something was amiss.

Oscar worried as he looked at the water and then Jean-Pierre. "There's a major breach in the barrier. Let's skip going up to the tracks and hurry along the wall to find it."

Jean-Pierre looked frightened. "Are we in danger? What if the barrier collapses? Will we drown?"

"No! At least, I don't think so. You can always save me as you did on the battlefield. Right?"

Jean-Pierre chuckled. "At least I know how to swim."

The two crossed the back of the property and headed up the other side. The men were near Oscar's cottage when they saw it. The floodwaters had uprooted an enormous tree and slammed into the outside wooden fence they'd built. The tree had broken down the barrier, and the water had washed away many of the sandbags before it tore a gaping hole under the stone wall. A rush of water flooded through the breach, washing away more of the wall on either side.

Oscar assessed the situation and shouted to Jean-Pierre, "Stay here! I'll be right back."

He ran to the greenhouse where the extra fence boards, hammer, nails, and sandbags were stored. After loading the cart with what he needed, he grabbed a pruning ladder. It was challenging to move the cart back to the breach in the wet grass with the materials loaded. He forgot about his blistered hands and aching legs and pushed as if his life depended upon it. He made it across the garden and saw Jean-Pierre nervously pacing next to the wall.

Jean-Pierre looked relieved when he came into sight. "I'm glad you're back. What's the plan?"

Oscar was calm and deliberate as he gave instructions to his assistant. "Help me position this ladder on the left side of the breach."

"Why there?" Jean-Pierre looked nervous.

He had little time for questions. "It's so I can work with the flow of the water rather than fighting against it. We can't remove the tree, so I'll make it part of our barrier. Please do as I ask. We can talk later."

He started climbing the ladder with the hammer in his hands and nails in his pocket. "I'm going into the water on the other side, and I need to work fast. Stand on the right side of the breach. Hand me the boards as I call for them."

Jean-Pierre looked relieved to be following orders. *"Oui, patron."*

Oscar stood on top of the stone wall with his hand on the post. "I'll be back."

He jumped into the floodwaters that reached six feet up the barrier and disappeared under the black water for a few moments. When he resurfaced, he called for a fence board. "Hand me one end of the board, and you hold onto the other until I tell you to let go."

Jean-Pierre complied, and Oscar disappeared beneath the water again. He resurfaced long enough to call out to Jean-Pierre, "Let go of the other end now."

He felt the post shake as he nailed the board onto it. But it held firm. A few moments later, he surfaced again. "One plank up."

He took a deep breath and disappeared beneath the water once more with a second board in his hands. Moments later, the second post shook as he nailed the other end of the board into it.

He resurfaced and took long, deep breaths to revive his burning lungs. When he had caught his breath, he assigned Jean-Pierre another task. "Please pass me a sandbag. Keep them coming until I say 'Stop.'"

He took each sandbag underwater and stacked it against the fence board to keep the water from washing away the soil under the board and surrounding stone wall. He could see Jean-Pierre struggling to lift each wet sandbag and pass it to him.

"Stop. Now I need to add another fence board. This will be tricky since I must work around the tree. Hand me one end of the board."

As soon as Jean-Pierre handed it to him, he disappeared under the water again. He asked for more sandbags when he'd finished nailing that board to the posts and the tree. This time, he stacked them against both the board and the tree limb. They repeated the process until they'd rebuilt the fence with the tree held in place with sandbags and fence boards.

"Jean-Pierre, thanks to your help, we have the fence repaired, and the water slowed. I couldn't have done it without you. I'm sorry you ruined your clothes and shoes."

"We were so busy with the project that I didn't notice my shoes or that the water was slowing. We did it! Our work saved the house and the garden and even saved your cottage. You're a hero, and I'm an assistant hero."

Oscar chuckled as he gave Jean-Pierre one more task. "Please help me get the ladder onto my side of the wall so I can get out of this freezing, dirty water, *Monsieur* Assistant Hero."

His legs were so numb from the icy water that he had to force his feet to climb the ladder. Once on top, he pulled up the ladder, placed it on the other side of the wall, and climbed down to safety. As soon as his feet hit the solid, dry ground, his legs buckled, and he fell in a heap. Jean-Pierre helped him back to his feet and dragged him to the cottage.

"Let me get some dry clothes on and sit down for a minute before we go to check on Geneviève. I hope she's had the baby by now. Can you fix us some hot tea?"

Jean-Pierre went into the kitchen to fix the tea and a little brandy. Oscar put on dry clothes and started a fire. They sat together by the fire, sipping the steaming drink and chatting about their ordeal as they warmed themselves.

"Now I must go check on Geneviève," he said as he felt his fingers and toes once more.

"Why don't we wait an hour until it's daylight? That way, we won't disturb her in case she's sleeping."

Oscar leaned back on the couch as he contemplated sleeping for a few minutes. Sleep was something he'd enjoyed little of since the rains had started. "Excellent idea. I'll just rest here for a few minutes. I'll meet you at the house after sunrise. *Merci beaucoup* for all your help today. I couldn't have done it without you."

Jean-Pierre smiled as he rose to return to the house. "What are brothers for if not to help one another?"

Oscar chuckled as he reclined on the couch. He didn't stir until he felt someone shaking him awake.

Chapter 26 – Charlie's Birth

"Wake up, Oscar. Wake up."

Isabelle shook him 'til he opened his eyes.

"I heard you the first time. What time is it?"

"Noon. Now get up. You will be too late."

Oscar tried to clear his head from a deep sleep.

"I meant to sleep for an hour. I must have been more tired than I realized. What do you want? I need to get to the house and see Geneviève. How is she? Did she have the baby?" He remembered what she'd said. "Wait! What do you mean, too late?"

"Come quick. I'll take you to Geneviève. Just put your shoes on and come now." She was pulling him off the couch.

He slipped his shoes on, threw water on his face to wake up, and followed her out the door. He ran after her into the house and up to the bedroom above the second studio. Christine was crying as she passed him on his way into the gloomy room where Isabelle left him alone.

Geneviève was sleeping on the bed with the baby on her chest. Her curly hair framed her pale, tranquil face as she slept. The beauty of the peaceful scene of mother and child took his breath away. His spirits soared at seeing them in bed, safe and sound. He crept closer to her side. The baby cried out as he approached and fell back to sleep. Geneviève woke up.

Oscar whispered so as not to disturb the baby. "Charlie's adorable. Is Charlie a girl or a boy?"

"Her name is 'Charlotte.' She's doing just fine. She has Charles' eyes."

"And his mouth, by the sound of her."

Geneviève chuckled. "Don't make me laugh."

He smiled and reached out to touch Charlie. "*Mademoiselle* Charlotte, may I kiss your hand?"

Charlie opened her eyes and smiled.

Geneviève smiled with pride. "That's your answer. She likes you. Do you want to hold her?"

"I'm not sure I know how. I don't want to hurt Charlie."

Geneviève handed Charlie to him and instructed him on how to hold her and support her head.

"She's so small. Ah… Not that she is small by baby standards. Just smaller than I'm used to. I'm making a mess of this, aren't I? You know what I mean."

She chuckled. "I told you not to make me laugh. *Oui*, I know what you mean. Do you enjoy holding her?"

He grinned. "I love it. Charlie is so active. I bet she moves in her sleep. I could stare at her for hours. She has such lovely hair, and her dark eyes and pink cheeks make me want to kiss her and never stop. Maybe I can take care of her for you sometime, like when you're shopping for your new clothes in Paris with Lily."

Geneviève tried to sit up in bed but couldn't. "That's what I wanted to talk with you about. I need you to take care of her all the time."

Oscar's tone grew grave as his heart leaped to his throat. "What do you mean? Why do you need me to take care of her all the time? I don't understand."

"Oscar, I'm not well. I can't raise Charlie."

"I still don't understand. You … you look fine. A little pale perhaps, but fine. What are you saying?" Her declaration shocked him.

"Oscar, I'm dying." Tears ran down her cheeks.

His legs buckled, and he dropped to his knees beside her bed before he handed Charlie back. After taking her arm, he reached out and stroked her forehead. Her skin was icy to the touch. *"Mon Dieu!* What has happened to you?"

"After you carried me into the dining room, I started bleeding. At first, Isabelle told me I would lose Charlie. She delivered her but couldn't get the bleeding stopped. I must have injured myself when I fell."

"Why didn't they get a doctor?"

"They tried. All the roads and railroads are closed due to the flood. No doctor could get here. Isabelle trained as a nurse. She tried everything. Nothing worked. Charlie appears healthy. But I don't have the strength to carry on due to losing so much blood. I'm so glad you got here in time. There's so much to tell you."

The tears continued to roll down her cheeks.

Oscar buried his head in the bed covers and sobbed. His shoulders shook, and his breath came in gasps. How could a person so full of life one moment be at death's door the next? It made no sense.

"Oscar, stop. You're wasting what little time I have left. Besides, you're smothering Charlie." Geneviève dried his eyes with the sheet.

"I can't help it. I can't believe I'm losing you."

"Sorry, but you never had me. My heart always belonged to Charles. You know I almost didn't survive when I heard that Charles was killed. When I learned that I was pregnant, I rallied to bring Charles' child, our child, into the world. Now that work's done. I will join Charles. I need you to raise Charlie."

Oscar's lip quivered at the solemn responsibility being forced upon him. "You're the one who doubted that I could raise one child on my own. Now you want me to raise two. That's too much."

She looked tired but firm. "Who said you'd be raising both children alone?"

"I know. Your mother will help me. Who will breastfeed these babies? Not me." He smiled, trying to lighten the mood.

Geneviève's eyes grew brighter at his attempt at humor. "Not you. Isabelle."

"Isabelle? That's crazy. She wants no part of being a mother, and besides, she'll be in Chicago."

Geneviève's expression was firm. "She's already agreed to do it. Isabelle's staying here with the man she loves and who loves her instead of returning to Chicago and a man who just wants to use her."

"I don't understand. What about Isabelle's father and her life as a rich matron in Chicago society? Her Art Institute position? She has so many reasons to return home."

"She has all the reasons in the world except one."

Oscar looked confused. "What could that be?"

"You!"

"Me? Isabelle doesn't even like me at the moment."

"She's angry because you wouldn't go along with her plan to have both you and Jerome. You turned her down. Now she's staying here with you and the babies." She took a breath. "I'm not sure that she didn't make up the Jerome story to make you jealous."

"Really! Jealous? Me?" He took a long breath, which gave him time to think. "Of course I'm jealous. He's luring away my love. My friend. My life."

"*Oui*. She said she needs you to marry her for the right reason. Not because you feel you have to."

Oscar was stunned. Marry her? Why's she talking about marriage? "What reason would that be? What's the wrong reason?"

"She doesn't want you to be with her out of a sense of obligation because of the baby. She wants you to be with her because you love her and the baby. Does that make sense?"

He shook his head in disbelief. "I must take that up with her. I'll raise Charlie as you request."

Geneviève sighed. "It's good to have that settled. Since I'm running out of time and strength, you'll be my last visit."

Tears welled up in his eyes and ran down his face. He wanted to ask why, but he couldn't get the words out.

"I want to spend my last moments telling you about Charles and me, so you can tell Charlie about us when she's old enough. I want her to know her parents through these stories. Some people can tell her about other things, but you're the only one who knows and loves both Charles and me."

"I love you."

"I know you do, and I love you, too. I'll see him soon and look forward to telling him what a wonderful friend you've been to me. You saved Charlie's life. If not for you, we'd both have died in my shop where Jean-Pierre said you found me."

Oscar choked back tears long enough to tell how he'd found her lying in the floodwater on her floor. "I only wish I could've found you earlier. Maybe I could have saved your life, too."

"Stop! Don't do that to yourself or me. This happened, and no amount of wishing can change that. I want you to lie here beside us while I tell you my stories. I'm getting cold. You can keep me warm." Charlie woke up crying. "It sounds like she wants me to feed her. Can you put a pillow behind me so I can sit up and feed her?"

Oscar helped her sit up and put a pillow behind her back.

She uncovered her breast and helped Charlie nurse. He got into bed and cuddled with them. It was the most tender moment of his life. This was one story that he would tell Charlie when she was old enough.

"When Charles and I first met, he took me up the hill to where we picnicked with Jean-Pierre and Lily for our first date. We sat on the grass, staring out over the valley, and talked about growing up here. We talked about swimming in the rivers and playing in the fields. We had such a marvelous time that I fell in love with him that afternoon, and there was never anyone else for me. After visiting there so often, we came to think of it as our place. We loved it so much that we got married there."

"Wasn't it quite a hike for the wedding party?"

"Yes, but no one complained. After the wedding was over and our family and friends had gone, we sat there to watch the sunset and made love for our first time. Charlie was conceived there on our final visit before he returned to the front for the last time. I hope she'll love that story when she's old enough."

After a few moments, she dried her eyes and began another story.

He felt Geneviève getting colder and could hear her breath become more labored. In the next hour, she sighed and slipped away. Charlie fell asleep on her chest without knowing that the most significant moment in her young life had been happening right beneath her. She had become an orphan before she was one day old. Oscar kissed Geneviève goodbye. Once on each cheek and a third kiss on her icy lips.

He wrapped Charlie in a blanket the best he could and carried her downstairs to where the others were waiting. He handed her to Christine, mumbled something about checking the flood fortifications, and walked out the door.

Jean-Pierre called after him, "Wait, I'll come to help you."

He called back over his shoulder, "I'll find you if I need you."

He had said nothing about Geneviève's passing, and no one had asked. He assumed they could tell by the tears running down his cheeks. He stumbled to the front wall, turned around, and slid down into the mud. He covered his face and cried for Geneviève, Charlie, and Charles.

It was long before he noticed that the rain had stopped and the sun was warming him. He struggled to his feet and looked up at the sky to see if the clearing would endure or perhaps just clouds opening a short path for the sun to sneak through. The clouds were white, not gray. The blue sky lifted his spirits enough to help him begin his inspection tour.

He climbed the hill across the road from the house to assess the floodwater level. It was still covering the farmers' fields and Monet's pond. As expected, the haystacks had washed away. However, the Japanese bridge remained across what had been the lily pond, and it seemed to be holding. He'd heard it would take a long time for the floodwaters to recede. He was relieved to see that the water was no longer rising, and the current was not as swift as when it had slammed the tree into the wall.

He was about to start back down when he noticed where he was standing. It was Geneviève's favorite spot. With tears flowing down his cheeks, he fashioned a cross out of two sticks and stuck it into the ground. He fell to his knees and promised to raise Charlie the best he could and bring her back here often to visit the place that meant so much to her parents.

As he walked and slid down the hill, a double rainbow arched across the valley. He named them Charles and Geneviève. When he inspected the perimeter fortifications, he found no breaches in the barrier. Even the patch he'd built through the tree that had done so much destruction was still in place. Very little water was seeping in. He and Jean-Pierre had saved Monet's house and garden. He went to his cottage to get a drink to celebrate.

Isabelle was sitting on his couch waiting for him.

He was in no mood for visitors. "What are you doing here?"

"I think we need to talk," she whispered.

She wore a short dress that hugged her growing curves. Oscar shook his head to get lustful thoughts of her body out of his mind.

"That didn't turn out well the last time you were here."

It upset him that angry thoughts of her interrupted his quiet mourning. Even more distracting was his confusion over wanting her and wanting nothing to do with her at the same time.

"I sent a telegraph to Jerome today calling off our engagement. I'm staying here to be a mother to Charlie and our baby." Her jaw was set, and she looked determined in her decision.

Isabelle's announcement floored him. He couldn't understand this turn of events.

"I don't believe you. I thought it thrilled you to be marrying into the richest family in Chicago. You would own your hospital and work at the Art Institute. What happened?"

He didn't want to reveal what Geneviève had told him. If the Jerome story was a ruse to test his commitment to marrying her for her own sake, no need to argue about it. He wouldn't win.

Isabelle looked offended at his reaction. "After you turned down my offer, Geneviève and I talked as I painted her portrait. Then Lily got in on the conversation. They asked me why I would give up my child and the man who loved me for a loveless marriage of convenience. I didn't have a suitable answer. So I'm asking you to forgive me and take me back."

It upset him that she assumed he would forgive her this easily. "Forgiving you is one thing. Trusting you again is quite another. How do I know that you won't change your mind? You might try out motherhood and then flit off to Paris, Chicago, or Timbuktu."

"I'd be willing to marry you." She smiled. "Would that satisfy you?"

He was getting annoyed. "I haven't even asked you to marry me. I'm not sure I want to get involved with anyone as self-centered as you."

Tears came to her eyes.

"No matter what you think of me, we must raise two children together." She stood up and stomped to the door and threw it open. "Yes, I'm selfish, but I'm willing to change. Even if you don't trust or even like me, I know you still love me. I'll wait for your proposal. Now I need to help Blanche with the funeral plans."

Then she slammed the door, cutting off any further conversation.

Oscar headed to the kitchen for a glass of wine and returned with a bottle. Tomorrow would be another hard day. It would take the rest of today to sort out what had happened since yesterday. He'd saved the garden, saved a life, risked his own, received a baby, lost a friend, and gained a prospective wife if he wanted her. One glass of wine wouldn't be enough to unravel the events of the past.

Chapter 27 – A Dark Day

Oscar woke with a start from a nightmare of floodwaters rising and washing over his cottage. His hands were shaking as he tore open the floral curtains on his bedroom window. It was not raining, and the garden was not under water. It was just a nightmare. Still, he looked up at the sky to see if any more rain was on its way.

Tall gray clouds with black bottoms filled the dawn sky. He knew clouds like that could bring heavy rain. He couldn't handle more rain today, of all days. He dressed in his work clothes and wet boots and went out to make another inspection of the barrier holding back the flood.

As he slogged along the fortifications looking for significant problems, the sticky mud reminded him of the slop in the trenches, except that trench mud was much deeper and stained red with the blood of his comrades. He didn't find any breaks in his defensive line, but he saw a looming disaster when he climbed the hill and crossed the railroad tracks. He looked at where the pond once was and found that today the floodwaters were eating away at the bridge support, threatening to dislodge the Japanese bridge from its foundation.

He raced back down the path toward the greenhouse when his foot caught on a root. He fell and slid face-first to the bottom. The fall and slide sliced a gash in his left cheek and deep scratches to his forehead. He struggled to his feet and regained his balance, used the collar of his shirt to reduce the bleeding from his face, but he had nothing for the pain. Gritting his teeth, he realized he'd look a fright at the funeral. There was no time to wash his face or tend to his wounds. It was just like trench warfare. Never enough time to tend to injuries. He must rescue the Japanese bridge.

Blood continued to stream down his face as he ran to the greenhouse to find something to secure the bridge. After finding a large coil of thick rope, he carried it back up the hill, across the tracks, and down the other side. He was gasping for breath as he waded through the frigid water to reach the near end of the Japanese bridge.

After tying the rope to the bridge, he waded through chest-deep water with the coil of rope over his shoulder toward the other end. The rope was twice as heavy now that it was wet. He was busy cursing the heavy rope that cut into his shoulder when he stepped into the water that was over his head. A wave of terror washed through his mind since he couldn't swim. He spun around, reached under water, and grabbed a limb. He pulled himself out of the deeper water with the heavy rope holding him under. He clawed his way to shallow depths before the current tugging on the heavy rope could pull him under.

He tried again to cross the pond he couldn't see. This time, he worked his way along the bridge's underside hand-over-hand until his feet touched the solid ground on the other side of the pond. The cold water and heavy rope had sapped his strength, but resting was not an option. Not even for a minute to catch his breath.

The trees lining the opposite shore would hold the bridge's weight, provided the flood current didn't undercut their roots. He waded to them with all the remaining strength he could muster and tied the rope around one trunk after another. One or two trees might not hold the weight of the bridge, but six might.

Exhausted and cold, he waded back to the bridge and tied the end of the rope to the support beams. Now, even if the bridge broke free from its foundation, it would not float far away. After climbing onto the bridge, he sat down to catch his breath and warm his body. The gash in his face was too numb from the cold water to hurt. It just throbbed. After a few long minutes of rest, he mustered the strength to cross the water under the bridge and retrace his journey to the top of the hill, where he could stand beside the tracks to look for floodwater.

He looked across the flooded fields toward where the Seine had been and saw that the waters were still flowing fast, even though they had receded somewhat since last night. If the rain returned today, the water would rise, placing Monet's house in jeopardy once again. He hated seeing that fertile farmland had vanished underwater, but better the empty fields than Monet's garden.

Saving Monet's garden wasn't the only challenge he faced today. It wasn't even the most difficult one. Geneviève's funeral was due to start in the afternoon. Accepting the death of Charles on the battlefield had been hard enough. Accepting Geneviève's passing during childbirth was near impossible. It had taken him weeks lying in his hospital bed before he'd come to grips with the look in Charles' eyes as he lay dying in the bomb crater. Death was part of the war. Losing Geneviève to childbirth when he thought she should've had a successful delivery would take him much longer to overcome.

Just like when Charles had died, he had to continue the fight with no time to grieve. When Geneviève lay dying, he had to battle the floodwaters and couldn't take time to think about losing her. He hoped that as Charlie grew up, she'd remind him of the lives of her parents, not their deaths.

After inspecting the rest of the perimeter fortifications, he returned to his cottage, cleaned up, and got dressed in Monet's black suit that Blanche had given him for the funeral. He went to the house to see if he could help with the wake.

As soon as he entered the dining room, Isabelle took one look at him and grabbed his arm, and guided him into the kitchen. She wore a long black satin dress with a matching hat and veil. It bothered him to find her so enticing even though she was pregnant and attending a funeral. He couldn't control himself when he was with her.

She pointed at his cheek. "What happened to your face? You can't go to the funeral looking like that."

"I fell down the hill by the pond."

"You fell into the floodwater?"

"No, I waded in. Why?"

"Don't you know the nasty infections that filthy water can give you? Sit by the sink and let me clean you up."

He did as he was told. He didn't understand what Isabelle had in mind, but she had trained as a nurse, so he surrendered himself to her care.

"I'll clean the wound with alcohol and put a compress on it. You won't look great, but at least you won't scare Charlie or die of infection. Not today, anyway."

"Thanks. I know you were trained as a nurse, but where did you learn to dress wounds like that? That's a military dressing."

"I was a nurse in the hospitals at the front on weekends while I was attending the Sorbonne."

"You what? You never told me that."

"No time now. We must get into the parlor."

Monet's children and grandchildren, along with Geneviève's mother and friends, filled the large room with quiet and somber conversations. Monet's daughters had gathered in one corner around Christine. They were taking turns holding Charlie. She was part of the family since Geneviève had been their friend since childhood, and Christine had been their cook and part-time nanny. From what Oscar could see, Charlie entertained all of them with her lovely, peaceful appearance and occasional smiles.

Isabelle let go of his arm and gave him instructions. "Keep an eye on this group. When it's time, you need to line them up behind the bier carrying the casket. You'll join Christine and Charlie at the head of the procession from here to the church. Do you want to say 'goodbye' to Geneviève before we go?"

He nodded.

"Follow me."

He climbed the stairs to the bedroom where he'd last seen Geneviève. His chest grew tight as he remembered with each step their last time together. He'd not been with his mother when she died, so he didn't know what to expect when someone passed away. Geneviève had been telling him stories for Charlie, and then she stopped. The veil between life and death was so fragile. One minute she was there, and the next minute, the fabric of her life had dissolved and floated away.

Isabelle opened the door and ushered him into the room. Geneviève looked pale but peaceful, as if she were sleeping. He remembered the day they'd sat on the hilltop together. She'd been so excited about the baby and so full of life. Her smile had been infectious. He could still see her laughing at the Hotel Baudy and telling Lily how she longed for a new dress after Charlie was born.

"Doesn't she look nice in the floral dress? Lily bought it for her to wear to Paris after the baby was born. We didn't know that she'd need it for this. Lily wanted her to look sweet and natural, not cold and somber like some corpse in black."

Oscar didn't know how to respond. The tears blinded him. All he wanted was a few minutes alone with Geneviève one last time, but Isabelle continued to tell him things he didn't care to hear. Then he realized that she was telling him something that Charlie would want to know later.

"Christine brought the single strand of pearls that Geneviève wore on her wedding day. We thought she'd like to look her best for Charles. She had a habit of removing her wedding ring when she made pastries in her shop. Lily and I found it on the shelf beside the oven. We brought it for her to wear."

Oscar was choking back sobs and could barely speak. "I'm certain she'd love that you and Lily have made her look so lovely. I see you've found flowers for her hair. She'd have loved how thoughtful and kind you've been."

"We found them in the greenhouse. I'll leave now so you can have a few minutes alone with Geneviève before we have to go to the church."

Oscar nodded his appreciation as he walked to Geneviève and stood looking down at her peaceful face, then kissed her for the last time. Once on each cheek and a third time on the lips for Charlie. "Give my love to Charles when you see him. Tell him Choo-Choo misses him."

The tears continued to flow down his cheeks, and his throat closed so he could barely breathe. He bowed his head and stood beside her for a few minutes, remembering the fun times and conversations they'd had. He'd loved their breakfast talks that had helped him deal with the disappearance and return of Isabelle. They'd flirted with each other, but she'd known that Charles was the only man she would ever love. She'd been his close friend and confidant when he'd needed one the most. Charlie was her greatest gift. And his most significant responsibility. Every day of Charlie's life, she would remind him of her sweet mother and kind father. He knew he'd be a better person for having known them. Now they were both gone, and grief shredded his heart.

At last he could speak. "I promise to take care of Charlie to the best of my ability and tell her the stories you told me about her loving parents."

Then he dried his eyes on his handkerchief and descended to the gathering of friends and family.

Oscar looked around the room and then hurried outside to check on the funeral bier before the procession began. When he noticed the black shroud that would cover the casket, he ran through the garden to his cottage as fast as possible. After rushing into his bedroom, he tore the floral-patterned curtain from the window, tucked it under his arm, and returned to the bier as fast as his sore legs could carry him.

He didn't want to delay the start of the procession. His insistence on replacing the black shroud with the floral cloth shocked the four gardeners waiting to pull the bier. They started discussing his actions amongst themselves. One seemed to agree, and the other three didn't. It was easy to tell who agreed with Oscar and who didn't agree by how they were pointing their hands as they clutched their cigarettes. Armand, at odds with the others, crushed his out on the ground in disgust and walked to Oscar to light another.

Oscar felt the need to defend his decision to the men. "Black won't do for Geneviève. She was a woman of sunlight and flowers, not of sadness and despair."

All four shook their heads, followed him into the house, and went up the stairs to collect the casket. When they returned down the stairs, Oscar was ready to assume his mourners' leader duties. He crossed the room to be near Charlie, who had fallen asleep in Christine's arms. He reached out to stroke her cheek as she slept. Christine clutched his hand and looked up into his eyes with a sad smile. The light he'd noticed when they first met in the patisserie a few days earlier had disappeared. She looked older, frailer, and more exhausted than he remembered. Geneviève, the light of her life, was gone.

"Can I help you?" he asked.

She shook her head and gripped his hand tighter.

It was all he could do to keep from breaking down, but he couldn't. He had to remain strong for Christine and Charlie.

Blanche came to his rescue. "It's time to leave for the church."

He stepped away from Christine so as not to wake Charlie. "Please follow me out to the street for the procession. You'll need to line up behind Christine."

He took her arm and guided her and Charlie out to the street. "*Monsieur* Mayor and your friends, please follow me. *Monsieur* Monet, you and your sons are next. *Madame* Blanche, please have your sisters and grandchildren line up next. The house staff, and anyone else, are next."

He enjoyed how the floral print cloth looked draped over the bier instead of the traditional black. He felt that Lily and Isabelle would approve of his choice. He knew it would please Geneviève.

A cold mist that descended upon the procession contributed to the somber mood. The road was still wet from the flood. Mud marred the stone walls and buildings, showing the high-water mark. He worried that the mist would turn to rain before the service was over. He continued to hold Christine's arm and guide her as she carried Charlie at the procession's head. She seemed to be walking in a daze. He worried that if he let go of her for a moment, she might fall or drop Charlie.

By the time they arrived at the church, he could see that the mist had soaked those without umbrellas. His umbrella covered Christine and Charlie but not himself. The damp had penetrated his suit and chilled his chest, and that caused him to cough. The fact that he'd been far wetter and colder earlier in the day added to his congestion. The mist had not yet turned into rain. He might make it to bed without going back into the bone-chilling floodwater to rescue the garden again. He shivered with chills during the long viewing ceremony.

In front of the altar was the open casket where mourners approached to say farewell. When everyone had sat down, the priest began the funeral service for Geneviève, a member of his congregation since she was born. He spoke of her as a beautiful child who greeted everyone with a loving smile. Her patisserie served the community and brought love and good food to all.

In conclusion, he spoke of her family: Christine, her husband, who died fighting for France, and their infant daughter, born just before her mother passed away. As Oscar sat listening to the service, he looked around the twelfth-century church's whitewashed stone walls with its murals based on Biblical stories. He could imagine a young Geneviève attending with her parents and looking around the rows of wooden chairs to glimpse her friends, the Monet children. Today, those friends were, like him, somber mourners. They sat in the small, straight-backed chairs facing the altar. Several of these same friends had decorated the altar with flowers from their green-house. The flowers brought a lightness and color into an otherwise cold, drab day full of sorrow.

When the priest asked if anyone wished to say a few words about Geneviève, Oscar looked around to see if anyone would step forward. No one did, so he rose from his seat and lifted Charlie from Christine's arms. Walking to the church's front, all eyes in the church were on Charlie. Oscar, a stranger to most of them, didn't know what he would say. What they needed to hear.

"Ladies and gentlemen, Geneviève's friends and family, I'd like to introduce you to Charlotte. You'll come to know her as Charlie, the nickname her mother gave her. She's the child of our dear friend Geneviève and her husband, Charles, my army comrade. I'm one of the lucky few here who knew and loved both of Charlie's parents."

He coughed and tried to think of what to say next. At that moment, Charlie woke up and gave everyone in the church her best smile as she waved her hands in his face. The mourners smiled back at her.

"Geneviève blessed my friend Isabelle and me with the responsibility of raising Charlie. But, as the family and friends of Geneviève, we all share the responsibility of raising this beautiful baby girl. She'll be a part of our community, deserving of your kindness and love. The same kindness and love you showered on her mother. Please treat her as her mother treated you. I feel certain that you'll come to love her as much as I do. She's a wonderful child who can bring us together in our time of grief. *Merci beaucoup* for being here today and celebrating the life of our beloved Geneviève. After the graveside service, please join us at the Hotel Baudy to share some refreshments and memories of Geneviève."

Charlie fussed. He was unsure what to do, so he leaned forward and made a funny face at her. She smiled.

"Charlie is telling me I have spoken long enough, and she's ready to eat. We'll now adjourn to the gravesite."

Oscar returned to where he'd been sitting and tried to return Charlie to Christine.

Christine raised her hands and urged her back into his arms.

"Please keep her for now, Oscar. I'm worn out and need to rest and to grieve." She lowered her head as tears ran down her gray cheeks.

Isabelle took Charlie from his arms and gave Charlie a bottle. He helped Christine to her feet and escorted her to the church gravesite.

Lily handed a flower to each of the mourners as they approached the gravesite. The priest said a prayer, and then each person filed past and dropped a flower onto the casket.

After Jean-Pierre had dropped his flower, he took Christine's arm. "I'll take Christine home now, Oscar. She needs to rest. I'll join you later at the hotel."

Oscar kissed Christine on each cheek, then stood alone by the gravesite with a flower in his hand and a lump in his throat. He missed her smile already and was unwilling to drop his offering onto the casket because he felt that act would be an admission that his friend was dead. He wasn't ready to accept that finality.

Isabelle appeared next to him, slipped the flower from his fingers, blew a kiss to Geneviève's casket, and dropped it into the grave.

Oscar turned to her.

"Thank you for doing that. I miss Geneviève too much to let her go," he whispered.

They walked to the hotel together as Charlie finished her bottle and fell asleep.

As soon as Oscar entered the hotel lobby, an elderly couple approached him and Isabelle.

"I'm Philippe, and this is my wife, Mimi. We are, or rather we were, Charles' father and mother. You're holding our beautiful granddaughter."

They surprised Oscar. He hadn't thought about the other grandparents.

"I've heard so much about you from Geneviève and Charles," he said. "Charles spoke of you often. Our talks late at night in the trenches were about you, your wife, and Geneviève. He wanted us to meet. I was looking forward to visiting with you, and I'm so glad you're here."

Philippe smiled at him and then at Charlie.

"He spoke of your visit the last time he was home. He planned to bring you home to meet us, but he..." He broke off and turned his head away.

Isabelle handed Charlie to Mimi. "Charlie, this is your grandmother Mimi. Please give her your best smile."

Charlie awoke and obliged as Mimi took her in her arms, bent over her, and kissed her cheeks.

"I'm so glad to meet you. You're our first and only grandchild." She gave Charlie another kiss on her tiny outstretched fingers.

Philippe recovered his composure and turned back. "Oscar, I hear you saved *Monsieur* Monet's house and garden from the flood. We wanted to arrive in time to join the procession, but the river covered the road. We had to go the long way around. I hope we can return soon and get to know you better. I'd also like to meet *Monsieur* Monet. We were in the army together in North Africa, although I doubt if he'd remember me."

Oscar raised his head, caught Monet's eye, and motioned for him to come over. "*Monsieur* Monet, please come here for a moment. I've found the man you've been looking for."

Monet excused himself from the friends he was speaking with and walked toward Oscar. When he got next to him, he could see who Oscar was about to introduce him to.

"Philippe, *mon Dieu.* I've found you at last. *Mon cher ami.*" He grabbed Philippe, kissed him on both cheeks, and held him as each man cried. "I've been looking all over for you for years and to my surprise, you were living in the next town all this time." His face was awash with tears, as was Philippe's.

Oscar smiled and was about to finish the introduction when he felt a powerful grip on his arm. He turned to face the seamstress, Cosette, who had made so many alterations of Monet's suits for him.

"*Bonjour, Monsieur* Oscar. I have made some baby clothes for Charlie. I wrapped them and put them on the table over there."

He turned to look at the table she had pointed to and saw that packages covered it. "I don't understand. Why are there packages there?"

"They're gifts for the baby. You said that the community should show its love for Geneviève by supporting her daughter. We already thought of that." She smiled and walked away without another word.

He caught Isabelle's eye and nodded toward the table. He watched her smile as she turned and saw the gifts that friends and family had brought for Charlie.

As the wake ended, Oscar approached *Monsieur* Baudy. "*Merci beaucoup* for the lovely food and wine. How much do I owe you?"

"Nothing. We've been friends with Geneviève and her mother for years. We want to extend our appreciation to Charlie and you and Isabelle for taking on the responsibility of raising the child. I understand you'll have a child of your own soon. We look forward to welcoming him or her."

Oscar beamed with appreciation for the generous gift and the welcome for his child. "You're much too kind. We'll be back to dine with you often. Isabelle loves to dine here as much as Geneviève did. *Merci beaucoup.* I'm sure we'll see you soon. *À bientôt.*"

Oscar, Charlie, and Isabelle were the last ones to leave. Blanche and her sisters had gathered up the packages and taken them to the cottage, so Charlie could watch them being opened in the morning. The wet nurse Isabelle had hired had stopped by earlier in the evening to feed Charlie. She had given Isabelle several bottles of her milk that should hold Charlie until she returned to the cottage for the morning feeding.

Oscar struggled to get his legs to move at the end of this long, hard day. "Isabelle, can you stay with us tonight to help with Charlie?"

She looked upset. "Try and stop me. I'll be there. I'm moving in. We're in this together. I'll carry her back. You look tired."

He coughed, closed his eyes, and followed the two ladies back to his cottage. He said to himself loud enough for Isabelle to hear, "There goes my quiet solitude."

She laughed at him.

Oscar felt content as they strolled down the street to Monet's house and then through the garden to the cottage. It'd been a tough day, and there were many more challenges to come, but he was relieved to be facing them with someone he loved.

Love. He thought that was a strange word to associate with Isabelle, someone he was sure he couldn't tolerate just days earlier.

He opened the door for the two ladies, struck a light so they could see, and started a fire to warm them. "Our first night alone with Charlie. I hope all goes well."

Isabelle sat on the couch and smiled. "It won't, but we'll get through it. Together."

He worried. "Are you sure you won't leave me alone with Charlie in the middle of the night?"

Isabelle shook her head no. "I told you I'm here to stay."

"That's right, you proposed marriage to me. Now I remember." He grew somber. "The next time you propose, could you get down on one knee and offer me a ring?" There was a trace of a smile on his lips.

Isabelle's face flushed. He could see he had touched a nerve.

"I didn't propose. I said I'll marry you. Why are you making fun of me?"

He broke out in a broad smile. "Your face gets a beautiful shade of red when you're angry or embarrassed."

"I wasn't angry because I knew you were joking."

Both laughed, and Charlie smiled in her sleep.

Oscar went into the bedroom and came back to put a pillow and blanket on the couch. "I'll sleep here, and you can sleep in the bed with Charlie."

Isabelle smiled. "Are you afraid to sleep in a bed with two beautiful women?"

Oscar grinned. "It's been a fantasy of mine since I was a teenager, but this is not quite what I had in mind."

She chuckled. "You're not avoiding your responsibilities. Charlie needs both of us to take care of her. Before we go to bed, you must change her diaper."

"Then you'd better show me how. My army basic training didn't cover this."

She laid Charlie on the couch and explained the art of diaper-changing to Oscar. He was a quick study and had the basics down in no time. When Charlie was clean and dry, they headed off to bed, Isabelle on one side and he on the other, Charlie between them. Oscar bent over and kissed the baby goodnight.

Isabelle pouted. "Where's mine?"

He leaned across Charlie and kissed Isabelle for the first time since she'd left for Chicago. It wasn't the longest-lasting or most passionate kiss between them, but it was a start. They both smiled and held Charlie's hands as they all fell asleep.

Oscar coughed and coughed all night.

Chapter 28 – The Revelation

Oscar slipped out of bed, made a fire in the fireplace, and went to the kitchen to make a pot of coffee. Thankfully, Isabelle had insisted that he stock coffee in his kitchen when she moved in months earlier. He'd gotten up before sunrise to get a head start on the day of the big celebration. Charlie was being baptized. It was to be her big day, and he wanted everything to be perfect.

He returned to the fireplace with his cup of coffee and found Isabelle sitting on the couch wrapped in a blanket. He enjoyed seeing her hair, longer now that she had little time for her hairdresser in Paris, and her face creased from sleep. She was no longer the Parisian glamor girl he'd first met but more down-to-earth and alluring. Being pregnant gave her skin a pink glow that highlighted her auburn hair. He loved her more each day. He couldn't help it, even though he'd tried. God knows he'd tried.

He bent down to kiss her on the forehead. "What can I get you? Coffee?"

She sat looking at him for a few seconds, then a smile crept across her face. "No, my dear. I'd prefer you."

She opened her blanket to show him she had nothing on underneath and thrust her breasts forward. His heart's rapid beating caused a flash of heat in his chest that moved to his groin.

He stumbled backward and grabbed the mantel to keep from falling into the fireplace. "Me? Now? No!"

Isabelle's expression was lustful. "I haven't been with anyone since we left Lyon."

He raised his eyebrows. "You were engaged to Jerome. Do you mean to tell me he was not your lover?"

She shrugged. "Remember what I said? They don't like a scandal in that family. Now, how about a little attention from you? Haven't you forgiven me yet?"

"Not completely. I'll give your proposition some serious consideration." He smiled and backed away despite wanting to take her in his arms and smother her with passionate kisses. He wasn't sure how long he could keep putting her off. One of them would certainly give in soon to the mounting pent-up desires. "But I must let you know later. Now, do you want some coffee or not?"

He hoped his broad smile hid his desire for her as he changed the subject.

"How are we going to handle two babies while I'm working and you're painting?" he asked with concern in his voice.

Isabelle looked disappointed at his attempt at distraction and grabbed his cup of coffee for herself.

"Simple. We have the grannies to help. Christine and Mimi will take a day or two of each week. I've got it all figured out. I must work around the feeding schedule." She dismissed his concern with a wave of her free hand. "Now let's get back to the subject at hand. How about giving me some attention?"

He stepped back even further. "The wet nurse will be here soon for the morning feeding."

Isabelle placed her hands under her swelling breasts. "I'm not sure how long we will need her. Don't you think I could feed two with these?"

"At least two." He laughed. He longed to watch her nurse their child, or rather, children. He was still having difficulty getting used to having two babies in their lives.

They heard a soft knock at the door as the wet nurse stuck her head in. Isabelle pulled the blanket back around herself almost in time.

The wet nurse, Katherine, got a glance and blushed. "I'm sorry if I'm interrupting something. I can come back later."

Isabelle laughed. "We're just discussing breastfeeding."

Katherine came into the room and sighed. "My husband and I enjoyed discussing breastfeeding until our third baby came along. He hasn't mentioned it since. I miss those conversations. Here are several extra bottles of milk to get Charlie through the day. Since she'll be at Christine's tonight, I'll go there."

Isabelle chuckled as she stood up and led her to the bedroom, where Charlie was crying for her breakfast. "Sounds like Charlie's ready for you."

She turned to look at Oscar as she ran her tongue along her top lip. "I look forward to continuing our discussion later."

Oscar could feel his face flush as he hurried out to the safety of the *Grande Allée* to make sure it was ready for the celebration. The gardeners had set the venue up to be decorated. They had also cut back the nasturtiums so people could walk unimpeded. Their wives had decorated the dance floor and bandstand.

He couldn't remember the last time he'd danced. It must have been when he'd danced with Isabelle at Jazzmatazz. Dancing was unusual for christenings, but Isabelle was an unconventional mother, and she'd insisted. Perhaps they could dance together again. Due to her condition and his lack of skill, it would need to be a slow number. He longed for an excuse to hold her in his arms, but not too tightly.

His next stop was the greenhouse, where the gardeners' wives arranged bouquets of pink roses and white dame's rocket flowers for each table. "These are beautiful, ladies. The guests will love them."

"*Merci, Monsieur.*" The ladies smiled, and one of them explained. "We finished the garlands for the church, and they're being kept cool under the benches. See?" She unwrapped the cloth covering them. "We hope they meet with your approval. We'll take them over as soon as the church opens."

"*Merci beaucoup.* They're charming. I'm sure *Monsieur* Monet will like the colors you've chosen. I appreciate how you've pitched in to help with the celebration. Everyone is making the day special for Charlie and her grandparents."

He hoped Geneviève and Charles were smiling down on Charlie's special day. Oscar loved Charlie's portrait in her christening dress that Isabelle had painted. It was to be Christine's gift from Charlie and her new family.

He hummed a tune as he returned to the *Grande Allée.* He even tried a few dance steps on his way down to the bottom of the garden. Isabelle would say he needed more practice, but he laughed and danced on.

He and his men had constructed steps up the hill using the wood salvaged from the barrier. This was something they needed, now that Monet was getting older and more infirm. Oscar hoped that Monet would tell the men he appreciated the extra effort they'd made to improve things for him. He seldom thought to do this.

Oscar climbed the steps, crossed the tracks, and looked down at the pond that had been under the river water just a few months earlier. He was amazed at how quickly it had returned to its former glory. Most of the plants along the banks had recovered from being underwater, and many thrived from the rich soil left behind by the flood. He'd returned the lilies to the pond from their resting place in the greenhouse, and they bloomed in the warm sunshine. He and the gardeners had done what he'd thought impossible: They'd saved the plantings around the pond. Now it was ready for Monet's guests. This was the first time many of Monet's friends would visit the garden since the flood.

He strode across the Japanese bridge, pleased the raging water hadn't swept it away. Tying it to the trees had done the trick. But it had taken him weeks to get over the cold he'd caught from wading through the flood to secure it, not to mention the time he'd spent underwater patching the wall. Monet had thanked him for saving the bridge and the rest of the garden.

Oscar was proud of the work he and his men had done to save something that meant so much to Monet and his painting. With his head held higher and an extra spring in his step, he continued reviewing the garden's condition.

The gardeners had spent weeks removing mud from around the plants and replacing ones that had been lost or destroyed. Now the floral scene was ready for Monet to return to painting. His break from his brushes had lasted long enough. The restoration work had been more difficult and time-consuming than constructing the barrier.

Each night, Oscar had returned to his cottage, eaten dinner, played with Charlie, and fallen asleep with his two ladies. It had been backbreaking work but well worth it to see the smile on Monet's face when they'd finished. His ladies had put up with his work schedule and grumpy moods through the weeks that the restoration took. His persistent cough had told him he was pushing himself and his men too hard, but he'd done so to complete the work while the spring flowers were still in bloom.

He was looking forward to having time to recuperate before their baby arrived because, after its birth, there would be no rest.

He realized he was late to get changed for the christening. Isabelle and Charlie were waiting for him to return. He'd lost all track of time, and his ladies wouldn't be happy with him.

Oscar flew down the stairway into the garden and raced so fast up the cottage path that he lost his cap. When he stopped to look for it and catch his breath, he thought about how his life had changed in a few short weeks. One moment, he'd been alone and contemplating going to Japan. The next, Isabelle was back, and there was one baby to care for and another on the way.

Life was changing so fast that his emotions were having a hard time keeping pace. A warmth spread throughout his body as he thought of the family that surrounded and supported him. He'd longed for this kind of love all his life.

He entered the cottage to find Isabelle half-dressed for the celebration and doubled over in pain. She gritted her teeth and cried out. He stood transfixed, not knowing what to do.

"Get me a chair," she shouted. "I think I'm having a contraction."

He rushed to the kitchen and came back with a chair.

"Turn it around," she screamed. "I don't want to sit down. I want to hold on to it so I won't fall."

He could feel the blood draining from his face. He tried to hold the expectant mother so she wouldn't fall, but she pushed him away.

"Isabelle, what'll I do? I don't know how to help you."

She stopped gritting her teeth, and her jaw relaxed.

"The pain is subsiding. Please bring me a glass of water." She took several deep breaths. "I'm sorry I scared you. The pain is passing."

He ran for the water. "Are you having the baby now?"

"Not now, silly. Probably not even today. It's too early, but childbirth has its own calendar." She sat down on the couch and continued to breathe. "We can continue our plans for the celebration. I'll tell you when it's time for the baby."

"You scared me so much I couldn't think straight." He felt the blood returning to his face as he sat down next to her. "I'm sure you know about such things from your work as a nurse."

"Where I was working, no babies were being born."

"I'm sure some of your patients were in a similar amount of pain."

"Yes, many were. I trained as a nurse in Chicago, then came to France to volunteer to help with the war effort by working in the hospitals at the front. I was there long enough to decide that I'd seen enough of war and death for one lifetime."

He nodded. "I understand. I suppose that's why you studied painting. Tell me about the night Charlie was born."

She winced at another pang.

"The night when we were trying to save Geneviève and Charlie, there was such confusion that I had to take charge. I was the one who gave Geneviève the choice of saving her own life or Charlie's. She didn't hesitate to choose Charlie's life over her own." She took a deep breath.

Oscar sighed. "I feel much better knowing that you have medical training and can help if our children need it. There seems to be no one else in the village."

She smiled. "Yes, I studied painting because I wanted to celebrate life with art, expectant mothers, and babies. I still worked in the hospitals at the front on weekends to help. There were so many patients and so few nurses."

He clenched his fists, remembering his time in the hospital even though he had been unconscious much of the time. "Blanche said you met Georges at the front. You helped him find me. How did that happen? Why didn't you tell me?"

She looked surprised that he'd asked. "Yes, I did, in a way. I had wanted to tell you in my own time. But, yes, Prime Minister Georges Clémenceau sent a message to the army hospitals asking them to notify him if we admitted you as a patient. There were so many injured that the army didn't know where they took each soldier after various battles. You came to the hospital where I worked, and I told the administrator I'd found an American."

Oscar's mind raced back to the hospital. He couldn't believe she'd found him. "Do you mean that you were my nurse? I don't remember seeing you there."

"The doctor bandaged your eyes and gave you drugs, so I doubt you knew who anyone was. I treated you each weekend for a month or more. Then one day, I came to work, and you'd gone, just like that. No warning. No goodbye. I didn't know if you were alive or dead until I spotted you on the train from Paris that day."

He jumped back. "You what? You knew it was me, and you said nothing?"

He could feel his chest tighten and his cheeks pale.

Isabelle chuckled. "What was I going to say? I bathed you and tended your wounds. I knew you intimately, and then you left. Glad to see you're alive. Hello, my name is Isabelle. The truth is, I didn't want to add to your pain by reopening old wounds."

His chest relaxed, and his cheeks warmed. "I guess that would be a strange way to meet someone. Still, you could've told me later."

"When? While we were making love on the train? Would that have been a good time? When I was leaving for Chicago?" She shook her head. "No, I think now is the right time. Hello, my name's Isabelle. I've been in love with you since I first saw you lying helpless in that hospital bed. I've never stopped loving you. Now, shut up and kiss me."

The remainder of Oscar's anger melted away, and he did as he was told. He pulled her close and kissed her like he'd wanted to since she'd returned from Chicago. Then he jumped up.

Isabelle looked hurt and confused. "What are you doing? Don't you want to kiss me?"

"No. I mean, yes. I mean no. I want to kiss you but not now." He shook his head to clear it. "I'd better get dressed, or we'll be late for Charlie's christening. Where is she, anyway?"

"In bed. Look."

She took his hand as they tiptoed into the bedroom and stared down at Charlie. "She's adorable in that christening dress. I hope our baby will be half as lovely."

"Just wait and see." Isabelle winced from another slight pain.

"Are you going to make it through the ceremony?"

"I wouldn't miss it for the world."

Chapter 29 – The Celebration

Oscar wanted to resume kissing Isabelle, but he resisted, which took all the willpower he could muster. If they started down that path, Charlie would be late for her christening. Instead, he watched her finish dressing while doing the same. Giving in to lust, just a little, Oscar caressed her bottom as he buttoned the back of her dress. It was a struggle to maintain control as his hands warmed and wandered toward the front of her body as his heart pounded.

"Be careful, mister. You'll mess up my tulle dress." She smiled as she patted his cheek. "Did you notice the A-line silhouette that hides my baby bulge? I'll be glad to hold our baby in my arms and get it off my waistline."

Isabelle was fashion-conscious, even in the throes of giving birth.

"Of course I noticed your new dress. It's a lovely blush color that matches the pink roses the gardeners' wives are using to decorate the tables and the church." He smiled and thought of the afternoon that lay ahead of them. Celebrating with his lovely ladies thrilled him to his toes.

"Aren't you *Monsieur* Observant? What do you think of Charlie's christening dress? Your seamstress friend used white handmade lace with four tiny buttons at the back. Did you notice the delicate little lace that trims the neckline, cuffs, and hem?"

Oscar stuck out his chest with pride. "*Oui, Mademoiselle*. I've never seen such a lovely dress."

"Now, all we have to do is keep it clean 'til after the christening." She gave him a warning look. "Be careful. Don't let her near anything that stains. You know how she likes to put everything in her mouth."

Oscar picked up Charlie and moved toward the door. "That's enough fashion talk for today. I'm sure I'll read about it in the Paris newspapers tomorrow. Hurry!"

"Put this bib on Charlie. We don't want any drooling on the dress."

Oscar grabbed two bibs, one white and one pink, in case one wasn't enough. He couldn't help kissing Charlie's soft, pink cheeks. One kiss for each of her parents. "Charlie, you're so loved."

"And beautiful," Isabelle added.

"Yes, lovely, and late."

The three rushed, as fast as a pregnant woman can move, down the street where a crowd of well-wishers met them in front of the church. It looked like the entire town was there, plus Monet's family and friends. Many of Isabelle's artist friends were also in attendance. Georges Clémenceau, Paul Durand-Ruel, Gustave Geffroy, and others had come from Paris. Oscar knew Monet's guests were visiting to see the garden restoration, but he hadn't expected so many to attend the christening. He jiggled Charlie to keep her happy.

He spotted his employer. "*Monsieur* Monet, it is wonderful to see so many of your friends here to celebrate your garden's recovery."

Monet smiled, leaned close, and made funny faces to make Charlie smile.

"*Oui*, my son. They're also here to support you. I've told them about the incredible job you did saving my house and garden. They want to thank you for that and for taking it upon yourself to raise your friends' child." He placed his arm around Oscar's shoulder as he leaned close to whisper in his ear. "They also wanted to feast their eyes on your enchanting friend, Isabelle."

"*Monsieur*, it's kind of them, but I didn't do this alone. The other men worked night and day in this effort. It'll make it hard to work with the men if I'm given all the credit."

Monet released his hold on him and gave him a piercing stare.

"*Merci* for mentioning this. But fear not, I thanked them and gave each of them a bonus for their work."

Oscar had never known his boss to be so generous. He took a deep breath to calm his nerves and summon his courage. "There's one thing in what you said that upsets me."

Monet looked quizzical. "What's that? Are you worried about your bonus?"

"*Non. Non.* Not at all. You called Isabelle my 'friend.' Since we're having a child together, I think we should get married. Our child deserves to have two parents. Don't you agree?"

Monet sputtered and coughed before he responded. "*Oui.* You should do something about that as soon as you can. We've been hoping that she'd marry you now that she's back from Chicago."

Oscar was thinking about how he could ask her to marry him when the priest summoned them inside for the christening. As the guests were finding their seats, he took Charlie on a brief tour of the sanctuary. They visited the altar and touched the roses on the garland. Her little hand came away with a few petals that went into her mouth but were quickly retrieved. He held her up so she could see all the people gathered for her christening. She giggled as he raised and lowered her in front of the crowd. The guests smiled, and some waved to her. When everyone was in their seats, he took her to meet the priest.

She was awake and quiet throughout the service until it came time for the water. She didn't like her head getting wet and was not hesitant in telling everyone how she felt. Oscar rocked her in his arms, and she soon quieted down.

After the service, when the baby's head and most of the guests' eyes had dried, Charlie's godparents, Jean-Pierre and Lily, took turns holding her. The crowd was getting onto their feet to leave when Oscar took Isabelle's hand and dropped to one knee. The guests fell back into their seats to witness this unanticipated part of the event.

Monet stood to address the crowd. "Pardon, *Mesdames* and *Monsieurs*, but we seem to have an additional component of our ceremony today. Oscar seems to finally have summoned the courage to take a decisive action. Oscar, is that so?"

Oscar said, with a red face and a constricted throat, "*Oui!*"

"Isabelle, are you interested in hearing what Oscar has to say to you today?"

Isabelle beamed with joy and nearly shouted her reply, "I most certainly am."

"Oscar, you can carry on. Just don't take too much time. Our lunch awaits."

With that, the entire congregation erupted in laughter, especially the speaker.

"Isabelle, mother of Charlie and our child, love of my life, and my *raison d'être*, will you marry me?"

Isabelle's expression turned from surprise to laughter to tears in an instant. She looked into Oscar's eyes. "You're my wounded war hero, my lover, and the kindest, most loving man I've ever known. Of course I'll marry you, silly. Let's do it right now?"

He was shocked. He'd had little hope that she'd accept his proposal and no idea that she would want to do it now. How stunningly impromptu and utterly practical of her. His mind was a mess of amazement and exhilaration.

Oscar struggled as he took his mother's ring off the chain around his neck and placed it on Isabelle's finger, a perfect fit. The crowd reacted with glee. The priest gasped and shook his head as he started rearranging the participants into a proper wedding party configuration. Lily and Jean-Pierre transformed from the godparents into the best man and maid of honor. Monet laughed with gusto as Isabelle led him to the back of the church. Blanche had tried to quiet him but failed as others in the church started giggling at first and then joined in with full-throated laughter. The laughing continued until the organist played the wedding march.

Oscar had the dazed look of a startled deer as he stood next to his best man. "Where did the organist come from?"

Jean-Pierre turned and smiled. "You know Isabelle. Nothing is impossible if she wants it enough. She got you to propose to her, didn't she?"

Oscar shook his head in disbelief. His overstimulated body was damp with sweat.

Isabelle started down the aisle on Monet's arm. Oscar had never seen her look so lovely. She was right about the dress hiding the fact that she was so pregnant. She had converted the dress she was wearing into a bridal gown by adding a full-length lace veil that matched her outfit. The same type of lace that adorned Charlie's dress. The guests smiled, heads turned as she passed, and the ladies whispered to each other. Where had the veil come from? Who attends a christening with a spare veil? Did you see those flowers she's carrying? Where did they come from?

When Monet, who filled in for the father of the bride, presented Isabelle's hand to Oscar, he whispered in Oscar's ear, "The veil reminds me of our shimmering flowers, don't you think?"

The wedding was coming together too fast for him to keep up. He felt like he was playing a role in a play that someone had written and rehearsed without his knowing. Since the action was moving in the direction he wanted to go, he ceased trying to understand how he got here and continued playing his part. An important thing was that his baby's parents married, saving it from the shame he'd endured growing up. But the most important thing was that the woman he adored agreed to become his wife.

The ceremony was plodding along until Isabelle winced with another contraction.

"Can we speed this up?" Oscar asked the priest.

Still, it seemed to drag on forever. Oscar could tell Isabelle was in pain by her tight grip on his hand, but her face radiated calm throughout the ceremony. She was much stronger than he had thought.

The priest hurried through the ceremony and finally said, "You may kiss the bride."

Oscar kissed Isabelle, gripped her arm, rushed down the aisle and out of the church into the sunlight.

"Thank you, my darling husband. I feel much better outside. Let's greet our guests and then get to the reception. We don't have much time."

He did his best to not look as worried as he felt. He greeted Monet's friends and family first. "Lily, can you help me get Isabelle to the reception? I'm afraid the baby may arrive before we get there."

Lily whispered to Jean-Pierre, who disappeared behind the church. He returned moments later, driving his automobile decorated in the same pink and white flowers as the church.

Oscar shook his head in disbelief as he whispered to Isabelle, "Ask for an arm, and Jean-Pierre brings a chariot."

They laughed as they climbed into the back seat, and off they went down the road to Monet's house. "Will you take my name, Isabelle? We haven't had time to talk about it."

She smiled and grimaced at the exact moment. "Isabelle Bonhomme. I think I like it. It'll look wonderful in my paintings, don't you think?"

He kissed her as the vehicle slowed to a stop in front of the house. Jean-Pierre helped Isabelle out of the back and offered to help Oscar carry her to the cottage.

Isabelle looked determined. "Don't make such a fuss. I'm feeling much better now. You owe me a dance. Did you forget that?"

"I've been looking forward to it all day. I want to hold you close and never let you go, *Madame* Bonhomme."

"You won't be able to hold me that close with the baby squirming to get born. There'll be time to hold me close afterward."

They laughed on their way to the head table with its pink and white floral decorations. "I love how the ladies decorated the church, the automobile, and now the tables. You must thank them for me."

"I thanked them early this morning. The ladies did a wonderful job. We can thank them together when they arrive with their husbands."

The guests arrived in small groups and found their place cards on the tables. Monet, Blanche, Jean-Pierre, and Lily joined Oscar and Isabelle at the head table. Christine and Charlie were nearby. Blanche's sisters, seated together at one table down front, were engaged in a lively discussion. Oscar could hear that the topics were Isabelle's dress, veil, and condition, but he no longer cared what they thought. She was his wife now, and that's all that mattered.

Monet stood waiting for the guests to quiet down before offering a toast to the couple. "Please raise your glass to Oscar and Isabelle. They've brought so much joy to our lives. I'm honored to welcome them into our family."

This comment set the sisters' tongues to wagging again. Oscar could almost hear them chortle, "What did he mean by 'Welcome to the family'? What is the old devil up to now?"

"Now I'll tell you why I was laughing in the church before the wedding." He waited as the guests got quiet and then launched into his explanation. "Isabelle approached me some time ago to hold Charlie's christening, followed by her wedding to Oscar."

The sisters were all atwitter. Heads were bobbing, and fingers and tongues were wagging. Oscar turned pale in shock at this surprise announcement. This was the play that he was part of without knowing it.

"Yes, ladies, this was a surprise wedding." Monet nodded toward the sisters. "Oscar wanted to marry Isabelle before their baby arrived but was reluctant to ask her. I asked Isabelle if he'd asked her to marry him. And her answer was…"

Isabelle shouted out to the crowd, "No. Not yet."

The guests looked confused, and the tables were buzzing with questions.

"Shouldn't you wait for him to ask you before you plan the wedding? I asked. And her answer was…"

Isabelle shouted again, "No. You must have faith that he will."

The crowd laughed at this exchange.

"I could only say, '*Oui*,' at this point. Blanche and Lily helped make all the arrangements, except no one thought to tell the priest. That's why I was laughing. We were at the christening with a wedding getting ready to begin, but the groom and the priest hadn't a clue about what was about to happen. Without warning, Oscar dropped to one knee and proposed and shocked the priest, who started arranging participants. Oscar performed his part with grace and style, even if he didn't know what his part was." He raised his hands to the crowd and asked, "Don't you all agree?"

The guests instantly considered the question, then laughed as they rose to cheer the couple. Oscar felt most were cheering Isabelle for orchestrating the best surprise wedding they'd ever heard of. He smiled and shook his head before he stood up, pulled her to her feet, and kissed her the way he'd wanted to in the church.

He only stopped kissing her when Monet tapped him on the shoulder to say, "It's my turn to kiss the bride."

With Monet's announcement, Lily grabbed Oscar's arm, spun him around, and kissed him deeply on his lips for longer than was proper. "Someone should kiss the groom. Any takers, ladies?"

Isabelle shot a narrow-eyed glance at Lily and then laughed.

Blanche took one look at this scene, turned to motion to the band on the stage behind them, and announced, "It's time for the bride and groom to enjoy their first dance."

Oscar took his wife out of Monet's arms and led her to the dance floor. The first dance was a slow one that suited him and his pregnant wife. When the dance had finished, Isabelle collapsed into his arms with a shriek.

"Now it's time," she cried between clenched teeth.

On cue, Oscar lifted and carried her through the tables of guests to the cottage. He could see Blanche and the sisters, who seemed to know what to do, follow close behind. He laid her on their bed, and Blanche ushered him out of the room and the cottage.

He wandered back to the party to get a drink and await the outcome of the following hours of labor. His mind was consumed by the day's events, and he didn't see Monet approaching from behind until he tapped him on the shoulder.

"Grab your drink and follow me." He staggered as he walked toward his large studio.

Chapter 30 – *Fin et Début*

Oscar's mind was focused on Isabelle and the baby being born, and he wasn't interested in distractions from Monet. He thought to himself, "When the boss calls, I need to answer."

He downed the glass of wine in his hand and reached for another. As he followed Monet through the garden, he realized this could be a difficult night for several reasons. Luckily, the wine was beginning to have the desired effect, and his heart rate slowed to normal.

He entered the studio to find Monet placing a painting onto his easel.

"I want you to see the finishing touches I've made to the painting you carried to Renoir."

"I don't understand why you're working on it now." His tone was colder than he'd meant it to be. "Renoir gave it to me."

Monet frowned at his objection. "I had Isabelle retrieve it for me. The model left before I could finish it."

"Why finish it now?"

"I wanted you to have a completed painting from me." He smiled and looked like he was seeking Oscar's approval. "I never could get her smile just right until I saw yours. They are the same, you know. Do you like it?"

"*Oui, Monsieur*. It looks just like her."

Monet's eyes widened. "It does indeed."

"You've made quite an improvement. I love it." Oscar stood back to take in the full effect of the changes. "Lovely. Very nice. You captured her warmth and charm exactly as I remember her."

Monet looked even more inquisitive. "What do you mean that it looks just like her?"

The intensity of his piercing gaze nearly burned Oscar's eyes like the mustard gas at the front.

Oscar fumbled for a response.

"Oh, ah, nothing. I mean, that is how my mother looked as long as I can remember, and she never changed. At least not in my mind." His mind was racing. "My thoughts are somewhere else, as you can imagine."

"I realize that, my son. That's the reason I called you in here. I thought we could have some time to talk and take your mind off Isabelle until she delivers." Monet patted his arm. "Now sit down here on the couch. Would you like another glass of wine?"

Oscar drained his class and weaved as he joined Monet on the couch. "I'd love a glass of *Calvados* if you have some."

Monet smiled broadly, rose from the couch, and went to the sideboard. He brought back a dusty bottle and two glasses. "This is a bottle I've been saving for such occasions. I trust you'll like it."

Oscar took his glass and admired the amber color of the liquid fire. "I've grown to like *Calvados* since you gave me my first taste the day I started working here."

Monet poured himself some and studied the color of the liquid in his glass, as well. "It's an acquired taste. This bottle is old. It's the last bottle from the case that the Tatin sisters gave me when I married Alice. I've been saving it for a memorable occasion like this."

Oscar raised his eyebrows. "I'm honored to be drinking it. When did you do this painting in the south?"

"I think it was in 1888. I was painting the cliffs of *Étretat* then. I went down south to paint with Renoir. *Oui*, it must have been in '88. Why do you ask?"

Oscar tried to act nonchalant. "No reason. I was born in Antibes in 1889 and was just curious."

"I thought you said you were from Lyon?"

"My mother was from Lyon, but she moved south to work in the luxurious gardens along the sea."

"Is that where she met your father?" Monet tilted his head to one side and stared into Oscar's eyes.

Oscar cleared his throat and tried to avoid Monet's gaze. "I don't know about my father. My mother wouldn't talk about him."

He left out the fact that his mother had told him his father was a painter.

"I see." Monet closed his eyes as if contemplating something. "You just said the painting looks like your mother?"

Oscar's hands shook as he took another sip from his glass. "*Oui*! It looks like her, although younger. Can you tell me more about the model in the painting?"

"She was a lovely young woman who was so much fun to be with. I remember Renoir trying to get her into his bed, but she laughed at him in her special teasing way. That's why I sent the painting to him." Monet smiled as if remembering those times. "He was always such a ladies' man and always on the hunt for a new conquest."

Oscar probed for more of the story behind the painting. "Your letter to Renoir seemed to hint you had bested him in some contest."

Monet blushed. "It wasn't a contest, at least not on my part. He didn't know it, but I fell in love with the model. She wasn't a model, mind you. She was a brilliant and self-confident woman who posed for me for the adventure of it. I admired her independence and inner strength and tried to capture that on the canvas. She was an accomplished garden designer who learned from her father and grandfather, who designed the *Parc de la Tête d'Or* in Lyon. I was painting in the garden along the cliffs above the sea when she gardened there. I asked if she would pose for me, and she agreed so long as it wouldn't interfere with her work."

Oscar could feel his chest tighten and his face burn. "She was a gardener like my mother. What was the model's name?"

"I only knew her first name. I remember because it was the same name as Charlie's grandmother, Christine. She never told me her last name."

Oscar stood up but was unsteady on his feet. He drew a deep breath to fortify himself.

"Her name was Christine Bonhomme. Bonhomme, the same last name as mine." He swayed back and forth and then collapsed on the couch.

Monet smiled and began saying something several times, but couldn't get it out, so he sat in silence.

"*Monsieur*. Tell me more about my mother. I have a right to know."

Monet's eyes opened wide in response to Oscar's direct question. His voice wavered. "You are my son! I noticed the resemblance that first day but dared not hope that I was right."

Oscar watched Monet as he began perspiring. "Please tell me about you and my mother!"

Monet looked anxious as he drained his glass and poured each of them another.

"I loved her. I returned to Antibes after having a tremendous fight with Alice. Alice never trusted models. She'd seen what happened with me and my first wife, Camille. Many of my friends got their models pregnant and then had to marry them. That's why Alice forbade me to paint with models. I was only allowed to paint our children. When I returned from the south and told her about painting your mother, she told me to go back and get her out of my life or to stay away."

"Did you end the affair with my mother, then?" he snapped.

"I couldn't make that decision and was struggling with what to do when your mother decided for me. I awoke one morning to find she had gone."

"Just like that? Didn't you try to find her?" He felt better about Monet confirming that his mother had left him. Not the other way around.

"I looked everywhere for her. I even took the train to Lyon and visited the *Parc*." Monet's voice was still shaking. "Since I didn't know her last name, I had little hope of finding her." He took a deep breath. "I gave up looking after several weeks and returned to Alice."

Oscar shook his head in sadness. "My poor pregnant mother had to fend for herself?"

Monet's eyes squinted as he shook his head in dissatisfaction. "I would never have given up if I'd known she was pregnant. How could I know? She never told me even after you were born."

"She didn't contact you, but she contacted Georges."

"Georges?"

"*Oui.* Georges Clémenceau." Oscar frowned. "They met at a gardening conference in San Francisco where he attended the League of Nations and became friends. When she was dying and couldn't contact me in the French army, she asked Georges to find me on the battlefields."

"I know. Georges told me as soon as he returned." Monet's skin turned as gray as the fabric of the couch he sat on.

Oscar felt compassion for Monet, who was trying so hard to tell him about what happened. "Georges found me in a field hospital, thanks to Isabelle."

"Isabelle?"

"*Oui.* It turns out that she was a nurse and took care of me when I first came to the hospital. Once Georges established contact, he arranged for me to come to work for you when I was released."

Monet sniffed and wiped his nose on his handkerchief. "That's correct. When he told me about her, we devised a plan that would enable me to meet you and assess your character. Many of my friends were approached by young people claiming to be their bastard children. I didn't want that to happen to me, so I was conscientious and had you checked out. What can I do to make it up to you?"

"What do you mean that you had me checked out?" Oscar was fuming at being accused of being someone of low character.

Monet took a drink and began his story. "You already know that

Georges met your mother in California. What you don't know is that he spent time meeting her friends and judging her character. He wanted to confirm his opinion of her."

"What did he find out?" Oscar was even angrier at this revelation.

"He learned she was a flirt and a person held in the highest esteem by all who knew her, including her friends in the gardening world and academia. He even met her Japanese friends, who vouched for her honesty and kindness."

"Who else did you find to check me out?"

"Renoir gave me a full report after he met you. He thought you were every bit a gentleman and a credit to your parents." Monet chuckled at his joke.

Oscar was feeling less angry. "Who else?"

"Gustave, Paul, Atsuko, and Matsukata."

"Matsukata? How does he fit into this?" Oscar grew more curious.

"Atsuko told Matsukata that you were a very decent and curious young man. His brother knew your mother in San Francisco and spoke very highly of her. Besides, his niece had an affair with you in college, so he asked her about you. I got him to offer you a position in Japan to see if you would leave me or not."

"Do you mean I wasn't being offered that position?"

"*Non*, the offer was genuine. Matsukata wanted you to come, and so did Takeko. You must understand. If I admit you to our family, it's a great gift to let you access my fortune. Besides, I love you like a son and don't want you to be hurt or disappointed. So I did a great deal of research to keep that from happening. Do you understand?"

Oscar was about to say, "You can't expect me to understand such actions," when the door burst open.

Lily shouted, "Oscar, come quick. The baby is coming."

Oscar looked at Monet. "I need to go."

He wanted to stay and finish the conversation with his father, but he was compelled to see his wife and child. He was being torn between two loves and responsibilities.

"The urgency of the present takes priority over the regrets of the past," Monet said in a voice full of sadness and joy.

As Oscar was leaving, he turned round to see Monet do something he hadn't done in months. He lit a cigarette and slumped back on the couch.

Oscar, frightened into sobriety, bolted across the lawn and into his cottage to see his baby.

Lily ran up to him and threw her arms around his neck. "It's a boy. You have a son."

"*Mon Dieu!* How's Isabelle?"

Blanche came out of the bedroom. "Mother and child are both doing fine. Go greet them, but don't stay too long. She needs rest. It was a very rough delivery. He's such a big boy."

Oscar entered the bedroom and slid a chair next to the bed as Isabelle opened her eyes. She pulled back the blanket so he could see his son.

"He's adorable. How are you doing? I hear you had a long night bringing this big boy into the world."

"Let's just say you missed the opportunity we discussed this morning." Isabelle gave him a faint smile. "The way I feel now, you'll miss it for some time to come."

He kissed her hand. "*Madame* Bonhomme, I waited this long and will wait forever for your love."

"He looks a lot like you, especially around the eyes. All three generations of men have the Monet eyes."

"Do you think so? Speaking of three generations with the same eyes, I talked with Monet just now."

Isabelle looked concerned. "About what?"

He lowered his eyes. "About my mother."

"Oh, no. Not now, of all times."

He raised his eyes and frowned. "I didn't want to get into this discussion with him now, but it slipped out when he started talking about my mother's portrait he'd just finished."

"He asked me to bring it to the studio so he could do some finish work." She looked worried. "How was I to know what he had in mind?"

"Once he showed me what he had done to it, I began asking questions about the model, and it just slipped out."

"How? What do you mean?"

He could feel his face heating as anger rose in his chest. "I asked him about the contest he was having with Renoir, which he denied. Then he told me she'd left him in the middle of the night."

"Why?"

"Because she was pregnant with me, I suspect, and Monet needed to return to marry Alice."

Isabelle's face turned red as she grew angry, too. "Weren't you furious with him for abandoning her?"

"Yes, until I realized that it was she who left him and never told him why she was leaving or where she was going. He never knew she was pregnant. He tried to find her but didn't even know her last name. The strange thing is that he has known I was his son since I came to work for him. He's had his friends meet me and check me out."

"What in heaven's name for?"

"To make certain I was worthy of being acknowledged as his son and join his family."

She calmed down with that news. "I suppose you could forgive Monet for testing your character."

"He asked what he could do to make it up to me, but then Lily came in with the news that this big boy was arriving before I could respond." He stroked the baby's cheek. "What's his name? We never decided."

Isabelle thought a moment. "The name we discussed may no longer be appropriate."

Oscar shook his head as well, contemplating the name she had suggested weeks ago. "Let me think about that. I'd better leave so you can rest."

"Here, take your son and introduce him to Monet and the family. You should forgive him since he's not the only one to blame in this."

"I know. I'll take the baby with me for a few minutes, so I can show him off." He bent over the bed and kissed Isabelle long and hard before picking up his son wrapped in his blanket. "I won't keep him long."

Oscar took the child from his mother and gazed at his pink cheeks. At a loss for words, he stood staring at the baby with tears of joy streaming down his smiling face.

He left the room and ran into Jean-Pierre and Georges standing next to the fireplace. Each took turns looking at the new baby and smiling. When Monet approached, Oscar handed him the baby.

"Meet your new grandson."

Monet smiled at him and held his grandson up for all to see. "Please welcome my grandson to our family. Oscar and Isabelle need our help and support to raise their two babies. I'm Oscar's father. He's the result of an affair I had after Camille died and before I married my dear Alice."

The noisy gathering grew deathly still as Monet drew his shoulders back and thrust out his chest in pride. "I won't go into details now, but I want you to welcome Oscar as your brother and Isabelle as your sister-in-law. You now have a niece and nephew who deserve all the love and support you can give them as members of this family. Now I must return this boy to his parents, and we must leave so they can get some much-needed rest."

Oscar took his son back and watched as the crowd began to file out.

"Before you go, I'd like to add to what Monet said. I came here searching for my father and found him and all of you, my family. The more I know you, the more I feel blessed to be a part of this family. You've been so kind and accepting of me. I hope that you share that love and kindness with Isabelle and our children. *Merci beaucoup* for being so loving."

The family, including Monet, Blanche, Lily, Jean-Pierre, Berthe, and Germain, clapped and cheered at Oscar's statement.

"I have just one more thing to add. My son's name is Claude Oscar Bonhomme. À bientôt, mes amies."

ABOUT THE AUTHOR

Joe Byrd's BS in Journalism and MA in Communications degrees inspired him to become a pioneer in electronic publishing. As a McGraw-Hill editor, he developed one of the first computer publishing systems. In the rapidly developing PC software industry, he co-authored one of his two books using PC desktop publishing software, the first for a major publishing house. He developed the first technical support website in the software industry. He published magazines, wrote research reports, and produced conferences in the US and Europe for the digital photography industry in his fifty-year career. He launched one of the first digital photography dot-com companies. This is his first novel.

When you finish reading this book, please leave an honest review on Amazon. It will help others decide whether this book is for them and provide valuable feedback to the author.